I0662232

Sangre Matriarca

The Story of Women Who Persisted

Maribel Rubio

Sangre Matriarca

© 2017

All rights reserved. No part of this book may
be reproduced in any form without permission
in writing from the author. Reviewers may
quote brief passages in reviews.

Published 2017

ISBN 978-0-9978394-7-0

DISCLAIMER

No part of this publication may be reproduced
or transmitted in any form or by any means,
mechanical or electronic, including
photocopying or recording, or by any
information storage and retrieval system, or
transmitted by email without permission in
writing from the author.

Dedication

This book is dedicated to my ancestors, especially the women.

I want to celebrate their strength and resilience –

Thank you for your stories.

Preface

The idea of writing a book once seemed like a far-off dream, but I always knew that one day I would write it. At first, I thought I would write only about my father, but the project evolved into something much deeper—something bigger. Something I could no longer ignore.

I wanted to document my family's history in a way no one else in our family had done. I wanted to be able to tell these stories to my son, and to the generations that will come after him. I didn't want to forget the details. I wanted to acknowledge the sacrifices of my foremothers—to honor their hard work, their values, and the better futures they carved out for their children. I wanted to connect the dots between their acts of courage and my own privilege. I wanted to make sure their legacy wouldn't die with them. I wanted to immortalize them... for me. I wanted to know where I came from, and who I came from. I wanted to recognize them because they are all part of my story.

To exhume my family's buried past, I tried to remember the stories I had heard growing up about my grandparents. Then I started asking questions. As many as I could. I believed that every answer might unlock a new path to follow. But asking questions is not easy when trauma lies beneath the surface. Some stories were simply too painful to tell. Some were met with silence, or deflection. Others, I was told outright, were better left buried. But I kept asking.

Along the way, I learned things I could never have imagined. Stories of great resilience and hidden heartbreak. Truths that might have remained secrets if I hadn't asked.

Something unexpected happened during this journey: my questions sparked a ripple effect. Conversations spread through our family. Relatives began asking their own questions, and together we started to piece together our shared history. We examined old photographs, traced family resemblances, uncovered inherited traits, and brought our ancestors closer to us. They became real again. Not distant names or mythical figures—but dreamers, survivors, people who had once wanted the same things we still want today: peace, opportunity, education, dignity.

When you're the child of immigrants, especially the first born on new soil, you often feel like you're living in two places at once. Most of my immediate ancestors were born in Mexico. For their own reasons, they left. They did what many Latin Americans have done for generations: they moved north, seeking better opportunities. I happened to be born in the United States. They saw that as a privilege—and it is.

It's a privilege because I didn't have to make the same wrenching choices they did. I didn't have to leave home. But I've also experienced racism, systemic inequality, and the pain of being treated as a second-class citizen in the only country I've ever called home. Even so, I know how fortunate I am. I didn't always recognize my privilege. But I do now. And that awareness shaped this book.

While I know I wrote this book for myself, I also wrote it for others—especially those who identify as bicultural. Our ancestors may have migrated voluntarily or by force. Some crossed man-made borders. Others were here before borders existed. But no matter how we got here, we carry with us the weight of history and the hope of a future. This book is for them—for the dreamers, the displaced, the brave, the silent, the women and children who bore the brunt of patriarchal systems, and the men who suffered silently beside them.

This is the story of my family. Thank you for taking the time to get to know us.

Foreword

Right before I published *Sangre Matriarca*, I was overcome with doubt. I asked myself whether I had the right to tell my family's stories—my foremothers' lives, and some of their secrets. Sharing our stories is necessary if we want to preserve our people, our ways, and our history in a world where Black and Brown voices are so often erased. I believed then, as I do now, that my family's story is also my story—and that I was right to share it. But believing something and living it out are two very different things.

One night, during the writing process, I had a dream. In the dream, everyone knew that Mamá Chuy had passed, but we were also expecting her return—twenty-five years after she'd gone. It was as if she had journeyed through the spiritual world, gathering wisdom, and had now come back to share it with us. On the day of her return, I walked into the woods, where a small wooden cabin stood. That's where she would be greeting us.

A long line of people stretched out from the cabin—miles long. It was a breathtaking scene: the tiny house nestled among trees, Mother Nature embracing it on all sides, the sky glowing with a clear light, and a golden sunset casting shadows from the mountains in the distance.

As each person reached the door, Mamá Chuy embraced them. That warm, firm, soul-wrapping hug only she could give—the kind of hug where it felt like your spirit was being braided together with hers. People wept, kissed her, told her how much they missed her, how they longed to hear about her spiritual travels. One by one, they entered the house that somehow swallowed them all, no matter how small it appeared from the outside. And then it was my turn.

I stepped forward, expecting the same welcome. But she didn't say a word. No hug. No kiss. Not even a smile. She just looked at me, eyes locked on mine, silently. Then she stepped aside, opened the door, and motioned for me to go in—with only her eyes.

Even though I was dreaming, I felt a lump in my throat. In real life, I was crying in my sleep. I woke up believing her silence was a message. That she disapproved. That I had crossed a line by trying to share what had been so private, so sacred. I stopped writing. I found every excuse not to continue.

Weeks later, I flew to Chihuahua to meet one of my aunts and her daughter. Together, we planned to travel by bus to Santiago Papasquiaro, in Atotonilco, Durango—where Mamá Chuy had been born and raised before moving to Ciudad Juárez. I stopped in El Paso first to spend time with my mom. During a visit to one of my aunts, I asked if I could see Mamá Chuy's old trunk, hoping to find inspiration.

My mother's oldest sister brought it out and left me alone in the room.

Inside were mostly dresses, skirts, and blouses she had sewn herself. I don't think she ever bought clothes; she was an incredible seamstress. I found her purse, just as she had left it before being hospitalized all those years ago. A few pairs of shoes. Photos. Trinkets. I don't remember her ever wearing flat shoes, not even the smallest heels. I ran my hands over her dresses, traced her handwriting on scraps of paper, and cried.

Looking at those dresses, I wondered if I truly looked like her. I knew I had her face, but I began thinking of my body—my strong arms, wide hips, solid frame. I was only twelve when she died, still a skinny brown girl, not yet a woman. On impulse, I undressed and chose the dress I remembered her wearing most.

A flicker of doubt crossed my mind: Is this crazy? Is it disrespectful? Creepy?

But something louder and deeper said, Do it. As if an angel and a devil on my shoulders were whispering in perfect unison. So I did.

I stepped into the dress, pulled it up, turned toward the full-length mirror that covered the wall in my aunt's room, and zipped it up. It fit perfectly. Not just like it was made for me—but as if my body had been made for it. I gasped. Covered my mouth. Tears poured freely. I stood there, frozen in awe.

Then I tried another dress. And another. Each one fit the same way: perfectly. Of course they did. They had been tailored by her, for her.

I sat on the floor, staring at them. Does this mean something? I wondered. I felt foolish. But then I put the first dress back on.

From the corner of my eye, I spotted a single shoe—light brown leather, three-inch heel, strap across the top. I took off my socks, picked it up, and closed my eyes as I slid my foot in. It fit like it had been waiting for me. I put on the other shoe, stood up, tied my hair into a bun.

And when I looked into the mirror again, it was no longer me looking back—but Mamá Chuy.

I walked into the kitchen, where my mom and two of her sisters were sitting, deep in conversation. As soon as they saw me, they stopped mid-sentence. Their hands flew to their mouths. All three of them began to sob.

It was at that moment that everything became clear. That overwhelming feeling of love wrapped itself around me—tingling, electric, alive. I took it as a sign. A blessing. A confirmation.

She was in me—in my heartbeat, in my breath, in my blood. Her matriarchal strength pulsed through my veins.

After that, I traveled to Durango. I walked the same streets she walked as a child and young woman. I paid homage to her life, to her memory, to her spirit. I stood where she stood. I prayed. I listened. I remembered.

And when I returned from that trip, I had the same dream again.

This time, as I approached her door, she was smiling. Her eyes twinkled. She reached out, pulled me into her arms, and held me with the warmth and strength I had yearned for. Still, she said nothing. She didn't have to. She embraced me, and then—gently, lovingly—she welcomed me into her cabin.

That was her answer.

That moment is why this book exists. It's why it's called Sangre Matriarca and why the cover features a photo of her as a young woman... and one of me, wearing her dress and shoes, recreating her image.

She is me.
And I am her.

Part I

Beginnings: The Maternal Side

Chapter I

María de Jesús, or as everyone called her, Chuy, was born on New Year's Day in the year of 1934 in Atotonilco. It was a very small town with fewer than 200 inhabitants in the municipality of Santiago Papasquiaro, located in the Mexican state of Durango. This town was, as the saying goes, a *pueblo chico, infierno grande*. She was the fourth of seven children of Jose Carmen, a baker by trade, and Nasaria, a housewife.

Chuy lost her mother when she was seven years old. She died while giving birth to her seventh child, at the age of 33. Nasaria's death was somewhat ironic as it occurred on Mother's Day. In Mexico, Mother's Day is always celebrated on May 10th regardless of what day of the week it is.

The loss of her mother was a huge blow to Chuy. As the oldest sibling still in the household, she automatically became in charge of the younger children, including the newborn. The oldest three children had already gotten married and left the house to start their own families, despite their young ages of 17, 16, and 15. Although they would've liked to help, they had struggles of their own. Each had moved to the neighboring town of Los Herrera, which was not necessarily around the corner. Few people in the area had motor vehicles at that time, and 261 kilometers was a long way from home when they had to ride in a buggy pulled by a mule or a horse. They could hitch a ride with someone who had a truck and was going back to their hometown to visit family or do business once or twice a month, but that wasn't frequent enough to really help.

It was soon decided that Chuy had to leave school after completing third grade to take care of her three younger siblings. Her mourning increased with the absence of education. In a short time, she had lost what she loved the most: her mother, her limited freedom, and the opportunity to go to school.

She was a very smart child and she loved school. She loved learning and exploring everything she could get her young hands on. In the town of Atotonilco, not many children went to school after sixth grade. As a matter of fact, they were lucky if they finished sixth grade. Literacy levels were low or very basic. But Chuy wanted to be different; she wanted to know everything there was to know about every topic. Her curiosity and insatiable thirst for knowledge led her to fantasize about all the things she could do in life. She didn't know much about the world or opportunities that might have been available to her, but she knew she wanted more. Despite Chuy's small world, she had a great imagination. She loved learning so much that she never complained about the nearly five kilometers she had to walk one way. Chuy sometimes even walked barefoot across town and would trek out of the way to cross the river that separated the school from where her family's house was located. Along the way, Chuy would think of all the things that an education would afford her when she grew up. She would fantasize about being a respected lady in the town. Her imagination would take her to places she would wish she could visit, places she had seen in some of the books she had access to in school, and she would keep her mind focused on those fantasies so as not to feel the elements and the harsh conditions of the land.

She always had shoes in the winter, but she was still very cold. Regardless of physical hindrances, Chuy enthusiastically attended every day of class. To help with the cold, she would imagine herself walking somewhere warm, with a beach maybe, to distract herself. The pictures of tropical sands she'd seen in books seemed glorious. She wished one day to see the ocean, but until that day, she would travel there in her mind.

Walking through frosted fields her body would shiver and her tiny fingers were almost frozen and unmoveable, but her soul was warm and happy. In her mind, she could always sense the breeze of the ocean, cool on her skin with the radiance of the hot sun rays beating against her face and warming her cheeks. When she least expected it, she was at school, always on time. The same routine would work going back home. During the hotter days in the summer, her imagination would take her to cooler places, mostly she would remember the winter days and that would help her keep going forward. Her education was worth the inconveniences of the weather.

All of this ended the day fate snatched her mother from her and turned her juvenile life into a whirlwind of things that didn't make sense. From then on, her childhood was over, her freedom was gone, and her education was halted. There was nothing she could do about her new circumstances. Chuy's father worked long hours at a small bakery that was the only supplier of baked goods in Atotonilco. The shop owner had decided to expand his business by "exporting" to neighboring towns, so her father found himself working even longer hours. This helped him in a sense, by providing a bit more income to support his family, but there was no one to take care of the young children, especially the newborn. In her mother's absence, Chuy looked after them, bathed them, cooked for them, sent them to school, and tried with all her might to nurture the new baby, José Inés.

Being a child herself, she didn't have the skills or knowledge to take care of an infant. Some of the women who lived close by would stop in and give her a little help whenever they could. Some would take leftover food for them to eat, give them used clothes their children had outgrown, and give her advice on newborn babies. The whole community felt a sense of responsibility. In small towns, many people embrace the mentality that it takes a village to raise a child. However, Atotonilco was still a very small and underprivileged town, and even with all the help, it still wasn't enough. Everyone felt sorry for the baby, and they felt sorry for the children. They all wished Carmen didn't have to wait an entire year of mourning to be able to get married again. It was obvious that he needed to have proper help with his small children. Unfortunately, customs were strong, and he had to follow the conventional social etiquette. Chuy's father couldn't just start dating or courting anyone, even if it was for the good of his family. Traditions were meant to be followed, despite everything. Many felt that ignoring traditions would certainly bring the end of civilization as they knew it, and they couldn't allow that to happen.

Things at home were very difficult for Chuy. She carried a heavy heart because she missed her mother terribly and taking care of the house and the children was debilitating. She also missed her older siblings. They seldom visited, but when they did Chuy would take a break and rest or she would remember how to be a child again by going outside to play a little. She would allow herself to remember going to school and reading whatever she could get her hands on. Most of the time, however, she was too tired, and would simply fall asleep whenever a break from household duties became available. It broke everyone's heart, but there was nothing to be done. It wasn't like they could take the children to live with them. They were as impoverished as everyone else was.

Less than a month after his wife passed away, Carmen made one of the most difficult decisions a father must make: he sent the baby to live with his late wife's sister. There, he could be taken care of properly and Chuy would be relieved of that huge responsibility. However painful it was to be separated from her baby brother; Chuy understood. This decision brought immense reprieve to her tender little mind and allowed her more time to rest properly and to concentrate on the other two children. Because of this, they grew up very close to one another. They all suffered the same losses and only had each other for comfort.

Chuy's father was eventually remarried to a woman named Altagracia. She was younger than Carmen by at least ten years, had never married before, and had no children of her own. As was expected, she took care of the household and the children, although the baby José didn't return to live with them until much later. Altagracia taught Chuy how to crochet, knit, and sew. Naively, Chuy had high hopes of returning to school. She did not mind that she had already lost an entire year and would have to go back to the same grade; she had already made peace with it. All she wanted was some normalcy. If she went back to learning and being a child, she would be fine with whatever came her way.

Fates shifted once again when more children came shortly after the wedding. The increased duties forever ended Chuy's hopes of going back to school. She never did return. Nothing had changed for her, even though she had a stepmother who would take the role of the mother of the family. She stayed at home helping with chores and taking care of her siblings. Chuy worried that her father had forgotten about her mother and was now forming another family with his new wife. He was still working long hours and had no time for her. With a new wife and more children, he had to work harder, sometimes even on weekends. The shop had been successful in the expansion of the business and had to hire a full-time driver delivering goods to other towns.

Chuy took solace in her needlework to maintain her sanity in a world where she felt completely isolated. Her loneliness was diminished only by her vivid imagination as time went by. She owned two dolls that, for years, would keep her company. These dolls helped her improve her skills as a young seamstress; she spent countless hours making dresses for them. They were small so she didn't need much material. The workmanship had to be precise since the stitching was on such a miniscule scale. She would take old socks that were not useful anymore and she would make one long cut and stretch the material out. Then she would place the doll on top of the sock and cut out little pieces that she would later stitch together to make tiny clothes. Sewing helped her salvage part of the childhood that still remained, and it gave her a useful skill that she would possess until the day that she died.

Chapter II

Within a few years, Chuy found herself married with a daughter while still a child herself. Her new husband was named Alfredo, and he was almost as young as she was, only three years older. It had been a very short courtship and they had only exchanged words a few times and for a handful of minutes each time. In Atotonilco, she could not allow herself to be seen talking to a man she didn't know at her young age. Public exchanges meant risking her reputation as a responsible young lady and potentially ruining the possibility of getting a good husband. Chuy and Alfredo lived on opposite sides of town, and he had first noticed her a month prior at the general store. He wondered how it was possible that he hadn't seen her before.

Alfredo liked her from the first time he saw her. She wore simple, modest, yet beautiful dresses that she had made herself by hand in an artisan manner. She had light skin, dark long wavy hair, piercing olive green eyes, and an evident poise in her demeanor. There was a somber look in her eyes, even when she smiled, as if life had dealt her a bad deck of cards.

Chuy thought of her mother often. She desperately missed her and longed to see her or hear her sweet loving voice, even if only in her dreams. Chuy never dreamt though, if she did, she could never remember them even for a second. She was usually exhausted throughout the day and was content when she went to bed, thankful for the short rest she was about to enjoy. When she did rest during the day, she would thank God for allowing her a little bit of relief.

Chuy was often so distracted that she had to repeatedly encounter Alfredo as she shopped at the same location before she eventually took notice of him. He had previously asked about her to some of the older families and was told she was the little girl who had taken care of her family a few years back when her mother died. He knew the story very well. Gossip spread swiftly in small towns and everyone knew everyone's business. If they didn't, they made it up to keep things interesting. Most of the time, things that were talked about were rumors mixed with sprinkles of truth; there was not much to do in Atotonilco but visit with neighbors and gossip.

For many weeks, Alfredo didn't have the opportunity to meet Chuy in person as she had only left the house when she needed to buy supplies for her dressmaking or to run errands for her stepmother. Altagracia had already given birth to three of the six children she would have and Chuy's responsibilities in the family home had grown accordingly. She never had an idle moment.

One afternoon, he chose to act. Alfredo waited for Chuy's father outside the bakery for hours to have a serious conversation.

"Buenas tardes, Don Carmen. Can I please talk to you for a minute?" Alfredo announced as he

23

intercepted Carmen. The young man immediately took off his hat as a sign of respect.

"Buenas tardes. Alfredo, right?" answered Don Carmen, trying to remember Alfredo's family.

"I would like to talk to you about your daughter, María de Jesús," said Alfredo abruptly. It was clear he was uncomfortable; he was nervously rolling the side of his hat between his clenched hands.

"You want my permission to visit her at home? Maybe take her out?"

"No sir. With all due respect, I would like to ask you for her hand," Alfredo replied, his voice breaking with anxiety.

"Oh! Have you talked to her about this? Does she know of your intentions?"

"No sir. I thought I'd talk to you first, as a token of respect."

"Alright then Alfredo, let me think about it for a day or two and I'll talk to Chuy and see what she thinks. She must agree to it, you know? That's an important requirement" Don Carmen answered with a smile to break the tension.

Alfredo returned his smile and nodded.

The two men shook hands and said goodbye.

Don Carmen knew how much Chuy had suffered and how hard she had worked, he just wanted her to be happy. He wondered if marrying would help ease the weight on her shoulders and give her a good life. She would be fine once she started having children of her own. She already had a few years of experience in running a household. Marriage would free her from the servitude-like life she had inherited. Despite never complaining and always carrying out her duties to the best of her abilities and with great pride, he knew she wasn't living a joyful life. Her stepmother was not sweet and tender the way her mother had been. Sometimes Altagracia acted as if she resented her or was jealous of the way her father respected and loved her. Altagracia had taught Chuy many things and she was grateful, but she was not her mother, and she was reminded of that fact often.

After a brief conversation between Chuy and her father, it was decided.

Chuy and Alfredo married two months after their engagement became official and went to live in a very small and modest house he had built himself with the help of his father and his cousins. The newlyweds' new home consisted of one large room which served as a bedroom, kitchen, and dining room. In the corner, they had one small firewood heater. The toilet was an outhouse some 75 meters behind the house. Although it was a nuisance to go out in the middle of the night, especially in the winter, the outhouse was necessary since they did not have running water or sewage.

Chuy was so proud of her home and especially of her husband for being such a hard worker and provider. Her only complaint as a new wife was that Alfredo occasionally drank too much. This detail did not occupy her thoughts much though, instead she focused on her new role. The house completely belonged to the young couple, and she was officially the lady of the house. This pleased her, and soon she turned their humble abode into a lovely home. The first things she made were curtains for the windows to add a touch of hominess. She was an expert at turning a plain house into a home with her creations. She was very proud of it. By this point in her life, curtains and tablecloths were child's play. They were so easy to make that she was done in no time. Her husband was pleasantly surprised to see the house look completely different only a few days after moving in. All she had to do was take measurements, lay the cloth down on the table, match the measurements and cut. She also had hand-made sheets and a quilt for the bed. It didn't bother her that the house was smaller than most. Her home was her castle, and she was the queen.

Chuy realized she was pregnant a few months after they got married. The pregnancy was not a difficult one and she radiated with beauty. She looked healthier and happier than ever. Her skin glowed, her hair shined, and the look in her eyes was piercing. It was as if the infinite potential of life in her womb made her beautiful. Throughout her pregnancy, Chuy was relaxed and well-rested. Her husband couldn't be happier, and he let her know by bringing her little gifts after work. If she had a craving in the middle of the night, it pleased him to satiate it immediately. He spoiled her with attention, love, and giving her the little gifts he knew she liked.

Chuy knew he would be a wonderful and loving father, so she didn't mind the daily drinking she still observed. Although he could be the sweetest man on the planet, at times the drinking became excessive, and he would become controlling and possessive. At other times, he did his best to show her his love by the way he would touch and kiss her belly, the way he would tell her constantly how beautiful she was, and the way he would sing to her.

His songs would pour out of his heart, he would smile at her, and his eyes would shine bright imagining the possibilities of their future child. Most men want boys, especially their firstborn. But he was different, he wished for a daughter; a little girl that would look exactly like her mother. He knew that having a boy would be amazing and would make his own father very happy, but this was his child, and he wanted a miniature version of his beautiful wife running around the house with her naked little toes. He could already see her small and delicate feet that he would tickle with soft kisses from his hairless face. He could hear her laugh hysterically while putting her tiny chubby hands on his face to make the tickles stop.

Chuy's morning sickness lasted only a few weeks. The entire pregnancy went on like a breeze, with very little discomfort. She was as healthy and strong as could be and so was the child growing inside of her. She marked her seventeenth birthday and then, only two months later, she gave birth to a gorgeous little girl who she named Daría. She was a perfectly beautiful combination of Chuy and her husband.

Daría had a full head of dark hair, beautiful grey eyes which had the potential of turning green or hazel. Her skin was soft and velvety caramel. Chuy saw the similarities between her new daughter and her husband. He had dark skin and a captivating smile, a strong jaw, almond-shaped eyes with thick eyebrows, but no facial hair. Alfredo was a beautiful man with a quick temper. Despite his occasional flare-ups, he made Chuy feel like she was the most important woman on the planet. Her and baby Daría were his entire world and he made sure to tell her this every day. They were very happy. It felt like a fairytale out of a storybook. She couldn't believe so much bliss was possible. Chuy had the suspicion that she was finally going to be happy.

When Daría was only two months old, she developed a very high fever. She had been a little fussy one day, but Chuy thought it was probably the heat. That summer had been unusually hot. The state of Durango is diverse in climate. Part of the state is covered by grasslands, shrub lands, and even small forests, but the area in Atotonilco has a hot and dry desert climate with very little rain. The heat didn't help the baby's fever. Chuy fanned her naked little body and would place potato peels dipped in white vinegar on her fragile forehead to try to lower the temperature. She knew of a little boy in town who had seizures because of an uncontrollable fever. His mother had been told to put him in a bucket of iced water as a last resort to try to help him, but she had been too late. Everyone in town said his little brain had fried like an egg on a pan.

One of Chuy's neighbors had told her that she should breastfeed Daría more than usual to prevent dehydration, but the baby wouldn't latch onto her breast. She grew desperate and didn't know what to do. She didn't want her baby's brain to cook inside her small skull, and the idea of seizures scared her to death. Despite Chuy's efforts, Daría wouldn't stop crying and her body was on fire. After a seemingly endless day and night of caring for their baby alone, Chuy saw Alfredo coming up the path to their home. It was early morning and the smell of alcohol was strong. He'd gone to the bar after work the previous night, ignoring the severity of their baby's illness and his wife's desperation.

Chuy ran to the door to ask him for assistance now that the situation was clearly an emergency. She didn't want to move the feverish baby and she didn't want to take her out of the house in her delicate condition. Even if she had wanted to transport her daughter, the doctor's house was almost 4 kilometers from their own house and there was no one to take them to the clinic.

Sobering up in an instant, Alfredo finally understood the grave circumstances. He squeezed his wife's arm and then took off running towards the doctor's house. He was soon exhausted, with blisters on his feet, his temples throbbing, and his lungs burning. He had to stop every few minutes to catch his breath and he thought his head was going to explode. It took him a while to get to the doctor's home. When he arrived, he had to lean against the wall to catch his breath and answer the doctor's questions.

After a brief exchange, they packed up the doctor's supplies and headed to the infant. Both Alfredo and the doctor knew a very high fever in an infant could be fatal. They wasted no time as they took off on foot deciding to take a shortcut through some private property. They had no time to lose.

Chuy had started getting nervous thinking Alfredo had not found the doctor, or that maybe the doctor had been in some other town on an emergency call. If that was the case, that would take hours to find him and get him to her house to make her baby girl better. It broke her heart to hear her crying incessantly and not be able to do anything to comfort her. She gave her a cold bath and it appeared that it was helping her reduce the fever but as soon as she took her out of the bucket the fever would go up again. The water in the bucket was warm after the baby was taken out but her shivering didn't stop.

When the doctor rushed in through the front door, he went directly to the baby. The concerned parents held each other in their arms watching every movement the doctor made, paying attention to everything he did and said. There were tears in their eyes as they stood helplessly in the background.

The doctor's diagnosis of the baby's illness was an acute respiratory infection which required antibiotics to make her healthy again. Unfortunately, he had run out of medication the previous week and was waiting for the next shipment to come in. The delivery truck had been delayed after the river overflowed its banks, taking out the road. There was no other access to the town. The doctor usually had a surplus of medication and tended to order in advance, but these shipments were sometimes delayed. The timing wasn't good. He gave Daría something to lower her temperature and maintain it at a safe level, but the antibiotics would be key to her recovery.

The doctor gave Chuy instructions on how to care for her child and how to administer the fever reducer. He promised to come back as soon as he received the antibiotics. Alfredo offered to walk the doctor back home.

"Amor, I'm going to walk the doctor back to his house. I can't let him walk by himself after helping us with Dari," Alfredo said, rubbing his temple.

"Please don't stay out too long, I need you here."

"I'll be back soon, but I'm going to stop by the bar on my way back. I'm looking for Antonio and I'm sure he'll be there. Besides, I need the hair of the dog, you know? I feel like shit."

"Be careful, please," pleaded Chuy, feeling completely spent.

Alfredo went to the bassinet and kissed his daughter softly on the forehead and his wife on the cheek.

After escorting the doctor home, Alfredo made his way to the bar. He didn't find his cousin Antonio but stayed for a bit to see if he'd show up. He was usually there at that time. While he waited, Alfredo took the painkillers the doctor gave him for his headache and ordered a drink.

Two hours passed and his headache had not gone away. Alfredo had only downed a handful of whiskeys, his favorite drink, but he felt drunker than usual. His alcohol tolerance had increased after years of heavy drinking, but fatigue from the evening's events and the painkillers he took amplified his incoherent state.

He suddenly felt a hand on his shoulder and saw his neighbor sitting at the table next to him. Alfredo hadn't noticed him sitting so closely.

"*Vecino*, how's everything at home? Your wife came over last night to ask if I'd seen you. The baby was sick, I guess. How did you find her?" the neighbor asked with concern.

"The doctor came to see her this morning. We're waiting for antibiotics, she's going to be okay," Alfredo responded with a slurred voice. He was having a hard time keeping his eyes open.

"In the morning? Why didn't the doctor come last night? Chuy was very worried; I'd never seen her like that before. She had this look of panic on her face. And what a face! Man, your wife is very beautiful."

Alfredo got up from his chair immediately and fell to the floor. The man tried to help him up but he swatted his hands away and got on his feet with great effort.

"What did you say about my wife, you piece of shit?" Alfredo questioned, spitting in the man's face.

"Calm down man, I meant no disrespect. It's a compliment, your wife is a beautiful woman," reasoned the neighbor, surprised at Alfredo's response.

"I'm sorry man. It's just not respectable to talk about someone's wife, you know? I have this headache..." Alfredo's apology trailed off while he held his head in his hands.

The moment was interrupted when Alfredo heard someone else two tables out shout, "Yeah! His wife is a hot piece of ass!"

Everyone in the bar laughed except for the neighbor who had to hold Alfredo back as he lunged at the vile man who had dared to insult his wife in his presence. He could not allow him to get away with it. It took more than a few men to hold Alfredo, which prompted the bartender to tell them to dump him outside. The bartender was not going to have another fight in the bar and see it destroyed in minutes, as it had in the past. The disrespectful man who had provoked Alfredo kept laughing mockingly as Alfredo got thrown out.

With no way back into the bar, Alfredo rushed to Antonio's house. The insult had sent him in a tailspin, his head throbbed, and his ego was extremely bruised. How could he protect his family when he couldn't even defend their honor at the bar? He forgot about the baby, he forgot he'd promised his wife he would come home soon. He was needed at home, but his fragile masculinity demanded respect.

He knocked on the door loudly and incessantly.

"*Primo!* What's going on? What the hell are you doing? Can you please knock like a normal human? The girls are sleeping."

"Antonio," he said in a slurred voice "I need you to come with me to the bar, bring your gun!"

"What are you talking about, man? You're fucking drunk, come inside."

"Okay fine, you don't have to come with me. Just let me borrow your gun. I'm gonna teach this motherfucker a lesson! He's gonna learn he cannot disrespect me like that, no one talks about my wife like that. Go on, get your gun."

"Listen brother, I love you and you know I'd fight with you by your side any day. But you're drunk, man. You can't win a fight like this, not in a million years. Go home and be with your family. We'll talk about it tomorrow," advised Antonio, trying to calm his cousin down.

"I will not be laughed at by the entire town," Alfredo screamed and went directly to the place where he knew his cousin hid the gun, away from his children.

Antonio followed him with concern, he saw him turn around with the gun in his hand. He tried to talk to him in a calm manner so Alfredo would listen. The more Antonio talked, the angrier Alfredo felt. He felt humiliated by the men at the bar, he was laughed at, and now betrayed by his cousin and best friend.

"I'll go out there myself and kill that son of a bitch if it's the last thing I do."

Antonio knew he'd have to do something drastic if he wanted to save Alfredo from himself. Antonio lunged at him and went straight for the gun. Alfredo wouldn't budge, he was committed to punishing the man who had disgraced him in the worst manner possible. Alfredo, in his drunken state, felt that he had to punish him. How could he ever face anyone again if he didn't? He would stop being a man if he didn't stand up for his wife and that was worse than prison or even death.

They struggled for a few seconds before there was a loud bang. They looked at each other straight in the eye with panic. They fell to the ground, Alfredo was lying on top of Antonio, there was a pool of blood under their bodies.

Antonio's wife Margarita was at the entrance of the kitchen, completely in shock, her hand on her mouth. She was holding their small daughters back, she yelled at them to go back to bed, and they did as they were told. Margarita ran to the seemingly lifeless bodies in her kitchen, she rolled Alfredo to his back so she could see her husband. Antonio's torso was drenched in blood, Alfredo's blood. He got up and grabbed Alfredo's hand, the gun fell from it. Antonio placed Alfredo' head on his lap, blood coming out of his mouth. He tried to say something but was interrupted by a slight cough and more blood.

"You're a fucking fool, *hijo de perra!*"

"Brother..." whispered Alfredo, muffled by the gurgling noise of the blood.

****

Chuy woke with the sunrise to the sound of her neighbors screaming her name repeatedly. The neighbor's voice became clearer and clearer. As soon as she was fully alert, Chuy put the baby on the bed and ran outside. Behind the man yelling out for her was a big cloud of dust coming from an old farm pickup truck that belonged to her husband's cousin, Antonio. It was coming faster than usual, lifting the dust and forming a large brown cloud. Her heart sank to the floor and she ran outside to see what had happened. Antonio jumped out of the bed of the truck before the driver had the chance to come to a complete stop and almost fell to the ground. Carefully he gained his balance and asked the driver and the man in the passenger seat to help him bring Alfredo in the house.

When Antonio turned around to look at Chuy, she knew something terrible had just happened to her husband. Antonio's hands and clothes were drenched in blood; some of it had splattered on his face. Before he had an opportunity to say a word, Chuy fell on the ground with one hand covering her mouth and the other one on her chest. No sound came out of her, it was as if her voice had been paralyzed by the immense sorrow she felt. She couldn't react because of the shock. It wasn't until she saw Alfredo's body being dragged out of the truck that she made one long and loud painful shrieking wail that was heard in the entire neighborhood. Women were very familiar with this sound of extreme grief; many of them had lost children at a very young age, most of them before the age of five. Childhood mortality was a common thing in those parts of the country due to poverty. She didn't know if she should run back inside the house to see her child or stay by her husband's side.

She ran to hold the lifeless body of her beloved.

Alfredo was laid on the kitchen table. Chuy helped his mother and sister clean his body to get him ready and presentable for the viewing that evening. The next morning his body would be transferred to the funeral. After her husband's body was tended to, Chuy started making herself a black dress for her mourning. She sat on the floor and concentrated on her design and her work. She laid out the black cloth on the floor, slowly smoothing it out like she used to caress her husband's hair at night right before falling asleep. She treated the cloth with the utmost respect, closing her eyes while running her soft white hands on it. And almost still with her eyes closed, she would run the sharp metal scissors through it with precision. She knew exactly what she was doing, like walking a path she'd taken a million times with her eyes closed; following her skill, her instinct, her heart. She knew her measurements by heart, so she was already ahead of the game. After the cloth was cut, she started pinning pieces together and forming a pile.

The last time she felt this much pain was when her mother had died. She wished so much for her mother to be with her now; to comfort her, to give her advice, or even just to hold her. Chuy piled the pinned pieces together and moved over to the corner of the house where Alfredo had set up her sewing. She sat down in front of the black, foot pedal Singer model 221 that her husband had given her as a wedding present. It was the most beautiful thing she had ever owned. She wept with happiness when she first saw it. She hummed a lullaby as she pushed the pedal with her foot, as if she was rocking Daría's bassinet. She worked as fast as the non-electric Singer would allow her to. When all the large pieces were sewn together, she tried it on. It was perfect. She took the unfinished dress and sat on the bed next to her sleeping baby and finished the job by hand. In a matter of a few hours, she was appropriately dressed for full mourning.

Women from the town came in to bring food and help her take care of the baby in case she felt paralyzed with grief. Two days passed in a blur of guests and grief before Alfredo was laid to his eternal resting place in the town cemetery next to his brother, who had died as a child a decade prior.

Chuy was deeply depressed, but having to care for her child, whose delicate health was not yet out of the woods, kept her going. Daría's fever had been kept under control, but the baby coughed every day, and she would cry in pain when she did. Her lungs were on fire, that's how the doctor described it, as the infection was taking over.

When the shipment with the medication came in, the doctor showed up at the house immediately to care for the baby. She was so frail because of her young age. The infection hadn't been treated for almost a week and he worried about her. He gave her a shot that day and another one at the same time for the next two days. She had looked a lot better for a while and the doctor was optimistic as he hoped for the best.

On the fourth day, Daría was having a difficult time breathing and the fever returned. She was pale and didn't seem to have any energy, even to cry. It was early in the morning and there was no one to take Chuy to the doctor's office so she grabbed her baby, bundled her up in a blanket and walked as fast as she could to the clinic. The streets were deserted as everyone had gone to work before sunrise to beat the scorching heat of the sun.

When Chuy and her suffering baby arrived, the doctor said there was nothing more he could do. Although the infection appeared to be getting better, there was some liquid in her lungs that had resulted in pneumonia. With a heavy heart, he told her to prepare for the worst. She had thought that the worst had already happened the day that Alfredo had died by the hands of his own pride and senseless machismo. She wondered briefly if people had the slightest idea of the consequences of their negligent macho actions. She was so alone when she needed her husband more than ever.

The baby succumbed to her inevitable fate that evening. The doctor told her respiratory infections, like pneumonia, were by far the largest single cause of mortality in children under five who live in small towns. Malnutrition and indoor air pollution were major contributing factors, especially during colder days when families try to warm their houses by burning fires indoors. Vaccinations can save a life if there is access to them, unfortunately, the access was almost always in the cities. Daría was buried next to her father only a week after his death.

Chuy was devastated. Her life was turned upside down just when she'd thought she would finally be happy. She had defied the odds and found a loving husband who had treated her with respect. He had cared for her in a way which no one had before in her life. They had been so happy during the birth of their baby girl. Back then, Chuy had felt her fates shift for the better; she had thought that nothing in the world could go wrong.

Views were mixed when it came to Chuy's luck. She had heard neighbors murmuring that tragedy never strikes in singles and they knew that something else as big as Alfredo's death would come, it was just a matter of time. As far as she was concerned, tragedy kept coming to knock on her door since the day her mother had died while bringing life into this world. She soon learned that there was more heartache to come.

It could have been that pain and grief had clouded Alfredo's mother's mind, but she refused to let Chuy stay in the house her son had built for them.

At this low point, Chuy felt abandoned by God. It was as if her entire life was a complete failure, and no one was on her side. Her siblings hadn't even had the opportunity to come see her since Alfredo's accident. They were busy with their own lives and trying to make a living and survive. They all had children as well and their growing families were their priority.

Chuy was given a week to gather her belongings and vacate the house. She didn't want to go back home, back to the same life she had painfully endured for the first half of her existence, but she didn't know what choice she had.

Alfredo

Chapter III

Chuy hadn't eaten anything for two days after burying her family, she was in a state of deep misery. Food that the neighbors had brought for her had gone uneaten and spoiled in the same spot where they were dropped off. One woman had tried to stay to keep her company and feed her, but she was politely asked to leave. All Chuy wanted was to be alone with her broken heart, with her pain, with her failed life and her failed future. She was alone again; maybe that was her fate, loneliness. Although she was physically and emotionally exhausted, she could not sleep.

The doctor came to check up on her on the third day and he was concerned for her health. He had heard from some of the people that she was like a shell. They all feared she was going mad. He gave her some vitamins and forced her to eat a little bit of chicken soup his wife had made especially for her. He then gave her a sedative to calm her anxiety which eventually also put her to sleep. The doctor left after administering the sedative. He knew she needed time and he wanted to give her privacy to mourn and wail if she needed to. She needed rest, she needed nourishment, and she needed love. For the first time in her life, she wondered if not living anymore would be the best option for her, to be reunited with all the people that loved her and meant everything to her. As much as she had loved life, living was painful, and she was bone-weary and didn't think she could go on.

The next morning when she awoke, she prepared a hot herbal bath with a medley of leaves consisting of rosemary, parsley, and mint hoping it would make her feel better. She had never taken an herbal bath, she hadn't had time before to even think about it, but her soul was calling for it and the house smelled so good. She got in the tub in a depleted manner, sighing with grief and a knot in her throat that seemed impossible to expel.

She wanted her mother, she longed to feel her strong arms around her holding her tight, rocking her like a baby and singing sweet lullabies softly in her ear as she cried all of her pain out. While she sat in the bathtub, trying to relax, she contemplated what her future would look like if she survived these new tragedies. Her mind was racing, trying to imagine what would happen next, how the following chapter in her life would start and when that would be. She felt more and more relaxed as she sat there, the hot water felt good on her skin, the smell of rosemary relaxed her, the parsley seemed to heal her bruised heart, and the mint made her skin tingle in a pleasant manner. She felt tired and her eyes heavy, so she decided to get out and lay in bed for a bit. Her ebony curls were up in a bun to keep them dry. She put a robe on and laid down in the bed she had shared with her handsome and sensitive husband and their daughter. She didn't even have time to think about her anguish, immediately she fell sound asleep and did not wake up again until the next morning.

That next day she woke up much later than usual. The sedative had helped ease her distress, the bath had helped clear her mind, and the chicken soup had swept her away in a whirlwind of mixed emotions about life and death. That morning she was in better spirits; the rest had done miracles on both her body and her mind. She had dreamt of her mother sitting next to her on the bed. One of her hands was caressing her face and the other running its fingers through her silky black hair. She looked straight into her eyes and softly said, "My sweet daughter, you must go. Go now! Save yourself! Breathe a different air. Go wherever you want to go but you can't stay here. It will kill you."

When she got up, she prepared coffee on the wooden stove as she thought about what her next move would be. She had heard people in the past talk about leaving town temporarily, to find work in a city up north towards the border. They would do it seasonally when there wasn't much work to do at home. After the harvest, the wives would take care of whatever work was needed and they would go and try to make money to last them through the winter. She finished her coffee and without a second thought or a slight doubt in her mind she packed the few things she owned in a small suitcase and headed to the bus terminal. Her mother was right, she had to leave Atotonilco if she wanted to survive. No, she might *survive* in Atotonilco, but what she wanted was to live, to thrive, and to be happy. The small town was nothing but pain to her, where she had lost the three most important people in her life. If she stayed, their memories would haunt her forever and she would never recover. She had to walk several kilometers to purchase her bus fare, but she didn't mind. She didn't know where to go, she had never been outside of her own neighborhood, but she knew she couldn't stay.

When she reached the bus station, the attendant asked where she was going. She stood quietly for a second and lowered her eyes to the counter. She had no idea. He asked again in a somewhat frustrated voice because there was a line behind her and he wanted to keep it moving. She didn't know what to say so she said,

"North. I want to go to the border. To one of the cities on the border."

There were a few options of border towns, she was told, after a sigh of obvious annoyance. She didn't care about the people behind her, she also didn't care that the attendant was annoyed with her. She asked him what her options were. From west to east: she could go to Nogales in Sonora, Ciudad Juárez or Ojinaga in Chihuahua, Piedras Negras in Coahuila, Laredo in Nuevo León, or Reynosa in Tamaulipas. She didn't care where she ended up, if it was far from her hometown, the town that had broken her heart so many times and on so many levels. She asked the attendant if he had to leave right now, where he would go.

By this time, he knew there was no way out of this, either he helped her choose a destination or he wouldn't get rid of her and the people in line were starting to get impatient. He told her in a much calmer voice that Ojinaga was the closest one, if distance and travel time mattered to her. She told him that sounded perfect, and he asked if she wanted two tickets.

"Only one, please," she answered shyly.

"Very well. When would you like to return?" he asked without looking at her.

"It's going to be one way only," she answered with determination.

"Oh, are you leaving us for good then, *mi'ja*?" asked the man, no longer annoyed.

"I am."

"Good for you! You go and never look back, you hear? You'll be glad you did, I promise," he smiled at her, and his eyes sparked a bit.

She gave him a bereaved half-smile and asked how much the ticket was and what time it was leaving. The bus for Ojinaga wouldn't leave for another week. There was only one scheduled bus with that destination, and it had left the day before. He saw a bit of distress in her eyes and said, "Listen mi'ja, if you really don't care where you end up, there's a bus leaving for Ciudad Juárez tonight. It is a bit farther up north, but I've heard wonderful things about that place. God knows I've wanted to leave myself for a while now, but how do I go and leave my wife and my children? I'm a father of four and my wife is expecting. They need me here. I wouldn't be able to live with myself knowing that they are here alone. At least here I can do things for them and make sure they're safe. But you, you are determined, from what I can see and you will be just fine. Trust in yourself and your gut, have faith, and I promise you that God will guide you. Don't ever doubt your decision whatever you do and, if your plan is to prosper, please don't ever come back here."

He was talking to her with a very compassionate tone in his voice without making eye contact. He was preparing the ticket that would take her to a foreign land from her miniscule universe.

"It will be twenty-three pesos, mi'ja," he said, looking directly at her.

She searched her coin purse and produced a few coins and handed them to the attendant through a little hole in the glass that separated them. She bought the passage without giving the decision a second thought.

"Muchas gracias, for the ticket and the advice. I truly appreciate it."

"Vaya con Dios mi'ja, and remember... do yourself a favor and don't you dare ever look back, but most importantly, always trust your gut," the attendant said as the next person in line was getting ready for his transaction.

"Thank you so very kindly," Chuy answered, grasping her ticket.

He smiled at her and nodded his head in a sympathizing manner of approval.

Although she had felt a bit of panic when she took the ticket, she knew she was doing the right thing for herself. There was nothing for her in that town anymore. Her entire life there had ended; she had to start a new one in a place where she didn't know anyone, and no one knew her. Possibilities could only really be endless in a place with opportunity, and that was not anywhere in Durango, not even in the city. She felt proud of herself. She knew her mother would be proud of her, too. Chuy felt it in her heart that if Alfredo could see her right now from wherever he was, he would be proud as well.

She had a few hours to kill before the bus departed, so she went to the store and bought herself some snacks for the road. She picked a handful of fragrant guavas, a bag of green grapes, the only *mamey* she could find, and a bag of salted pumpkin seeds. She walked back to the bus station and sat outside waiting for the bus to arrive to take her to this Ciudad Juárez that would be her new home and where she would give life a new chance. She alternately sighed weakly or sobbed silently while sitting on that bench. She wasn't hungry, but she knew that if she wanted to overcome her life's tragedies, she would have to take care of herself.

Chuy suddenly wondered how that was done. Up until this point she had only taken care of others.

She took the *mamey* out of the bag. This was Alfredo's favorite fruit. She looked at it for a few seconds and felt the softness of it in her hand. She could tell it was ripe and probably very sweet because it wasn't hard; they tend to soften slightly when they're ready to eat. It was a large one, nearly round, with a short but thick stem at the end. She took a knife out of her bag, the only item she had packed in case she needed it for her own safety. She wasn't sure how the world outside her small town would treat her.

Chuy used her weapon to cut through the brown peel from point to point and through the soft flesh until she reached the large seed inside. She opened it and held one half in each hand while some of the juice dripped to the ground. She put the half containing the seed down next to her and removed the brown, scruffy peel from the other half. She took a moment to smell and enjoy its fragrance, the inside flesh was dark salmon color, and she knew it was going to be of excellent quality. She took a bite out of it and with her eyes closed tasting a sweet flavor she had been anticipating since she first stuck the knife in. She inhaled its strong and pleasant aroma and smiled briefly.

She couldn't stop thinking about Alfredo and how much he loved *mamey*. He had loved its rich flavor so much that she had used it in her cooking on many occasions. The *mamey* is so versatile that she had made milk shakes for breakfast, had canned jams, made *mamey* flan for dessert, and even glazed a spiced chicken with it. He had loved every variation and loved her for her imagination in incorporating his favorite fruit in different dishes, drinks, and desserts.

Once she had finished half of it, she picked up the other half and removed the seed the same way she removed the pit from avocados, cupping the fruit with her left hand and slightly jabbing the seed with the knife, then twisting it to loosen it from the flesh and out it came. She took a big bite out of that half after having removed the skin and saying as a prayer, "this one's for you, my love."

She smiled at the sunset as she waited for the arrival of the bus. The afternoon had cooled down some, but she could still feel some beads of sweat form on her upper lip and at the tip of her nose. Chuy used one of Alfredo's handkerchiefs she had brought with her to wipe the sweat off. She picked up her small suitcase and placed it on her lap, hoping to feel more secure on the bench and in her decision to leave everything behind. Only then had she realized she had not told anyone about her plan to leave. She didn't care much about that detail, but she made a mental note of it, nonetheless. The way news traveled in that town; she wouldn't be surprised if people were already talking about her. Chuy was tired. She let out a deep sigh and put her head back, resting it against the wall. She fell asleep immediately and didn't wake up until the bus driver was shaking her to ask her if she was going to board the bus or not. She got up immediately and gave the driver her ticket and suitcase. Chuy was the last one to board and find a seat.

Her humble suitcase was stashed at the bottom of the bus with all the other luggage although she could've easily taken it with her in the cabin. Her cloth bag was small and wouldn't have taken up too much space. She suddenly became nervous not having it close to her; those were the only belongings she had now, everything else was left behind. All she had now was a clean slate to work from.

Chuy sat on a seat all the way at the back of the bus, the only seat left open. It was uncomfortable but she didn't mind it too much, she was just glad the bus hadn't left without her. As soon as the bus took off, she fell asleep again. Chuy had been sleep-deprived for several days and now it was catching up to her.

Chapter IV

When Chuy arrived in Ciudad Juárez, after a rough and bumpy 16-hour bus ride, she was ready for food and a hot bath. Her heart was heavy, but she knew she needed to find a job immediately. This city would provide her with independence and a better future. Just the idea of a fresh start gave her relief. Chuy told herself that no matter how bad things could get in this new place, it wouldn't be as heartbreaking as the traumatic experiences she'd had back in her hometown. She was done with the small town and the hell she'd endured there. Everything she held so dear to her heart had been violently taken from her *en un abrir y cerrar de ojos*.

She had finished all the fruit and the rest of the snacks during the bus ride. It should have taken a lot less time to traverse the route, but the driver kept stopping in small towns that were not scheduled so he could use the restroom. He repeatedly apologized to the passengers for the delays and tried to make up time whenever he could. It was evident to everyone aboard the bus that he was not feeling well. They could see the pain in his face, and he sweated profusely. At first, people were annoyed by the constant stopping, but after a while they just felt sorry for the poor man and relaxed. Some passengers went to sleep, some gossiped, others imagined what their lives could be like once they reached their destination. The bus was full, as if every citizen of Durango's small towns had decided to flee and look for a better life at the same time. They wondered if a brighter future awaited at the border. Some people got off in Chihuahua, new passengers boarded to join the Juárez bound route, and some planned to continue their trip to other cities.

Once Chuy had reached the city that would be her new home, she got off the bus and waited for her luggage to be returned to her. Most people had stuffed their belongings in a cardboard box and tied it shut with a thin twine. She had her things wrapped in a bed sheet which made it much easier for her to transport with her. All she had to do was throw it over her shoulders and carry it on her back. At this point in her life, Chuy recognized that she didn't have much. The man unloading the bus handed her bundle to her and when she reached for it, he held tight to it and smiled.

"You're here alone, *chula*?"

She also held tight to the bundle and pulled slightly with both hands. He scared her. She didn't feel safe.

"How rude! Cat got your tongue?" he insisted.

He laughed knowing he had made her uncomfortable. He winked at her and then let go of the bundle. He had managed to reach his goal in record time, inflating his masculinity by intimidating a young woman.

"Goodbye, princess. You should smile; you'd look prettier if you did."

Chuy knew she wasn't being rude; she simply wanted her luggage back like every other passenger. No, a cat hadn't gotten her tongue and she hated it when someone told her to smile. She wasn't there for his entertainment, and she had absolutely nothing to smile about. He didn't know her. How dare he? He was the rude one! She took a deep breath and tried to concentrate on her mission. She needed to find a place to eat, a place to stay the night, and a place to work.

She stepped outside of the terminal and was confronted with busy streets, people walking in every direction, and honking cars. During that time, Ciudad Juárez had a population of approximately 150,000 inhabitants: a sea of people for a young girl from a very small town. She took another deep breath and told herself she would not be intimidated. Chuy was very cautious with every step she took. Her entire life was in a bundle wrapped tightly within the bed sheet. She couldn't lose everything she had left from her previous life, so she held onto it for dear life.

Chuy had never seen so many people in one place at the same time. Even the yearly town fair in Santiago Papasquiaro didn't have this many people walking around. A rush of anxiety enveloped her. She stopped and leaned against a wall for a few seconds to steady her heartbeat, collect her thoughts, and focus on her mission. She refused to be paralyzed with fear and ruin her future; she had to move forward, there was no choice. She was determined to change the fate that had been handed to her the day she was born. The thought of ever leaving her hometown had never previously crossed her mind. Now she was being forced to use the strength she had been developing since her mother had died to forge a new path for herself.

Once Chuy felt better, she went to cross the street. Crossing the street in Santiago without looking for cars was perfectly normal. There was no need, she had only seen a handful of cars in her life, and they belonged to the wealthier families in town. Her idea of wealth took on a whole new meaning in the city. It appeared as if everyone had a car. She was completely disoriented when a driver honked and cursed at her through his car window. He barely slowed his vehicle as he almost ran her over. She apologized in a murmur as if talking only to herself and ran to the other side of the street.

Mixed emotions surged; she was thankful she hadn't been hit by the car and at the same time a part of her was disappointed she hadn't died. Despite her efforts to move on amongst the living, she still wanted to be with her daughter and husband. Chuy briefly imagined herself lying in the middle of the road. She could envision the broken bones, blood everywhere, no one stopping to see her or render help; everyone minding their own business. She had heard that city people were callous, self-centered and sometimes just plain mean. She hadn't believed this, she always thought people were good, but for a second that thought fueled her fear. Once she was safe on the opposite curb, she reassured herself that people weren't heartless, people really cared. She had to believe it if she was going to survive in this new place.

Chuy's stomach growled. She didn't have to spend much time looking for a place to eat, there were plenty of restaurants and shops everywhere she looked. Two or three on every block. She went inside the first restaurant she saw. She hadn't grown up with many food choices, so she wasn't picky. Chuy was thankful for everything that came her way.

She ordered potato and bean tacos from the lady at the counter. The employee looked at Chuy and slightly laughed.

"What kind of meat do you want, *chamaca*? Do you eat meat?"

"Yes, I do ma'am" she answered shyly.

"Well, do you want meat in your tacos or not?"

"Yes please," she replied without making eye contact.

"Well, what kind? Asada, barbacoa, pollo, tripitas, al pastor, lengua, cabeza, cachete, morcilla. Choose one. Or choose three, you can combine the tacos."

She was overwhelmed; she had never had many choices. She was used to beans and rice with a tortilla or two.

"I'm not sure. What's good?"

"Everything; they're tacos! Tacos are delicious no matter what you put in them," answered the attendant, laughing.

"One asada and one barbacoa, please," she blurted out as if making a tough decision.

"You want them with everything?"

"Yes, thank you. Pardon me, what do you mean by everything?"

She realized she disliked the overwhelming feeling of so many choices and wondered what else she needed to know just to order tacos.

"Have you ever had tacos before? Onions, cilantro, and salsa. Where are you from?" the attendant asked with a mixture of annoyance and curiosity.

"Oh, I'm so sorry! Yes, please, with everything; thank you. I just got here from Santiago Papasquiaro."

"Ha! Fresh off the boat, eh?"

"Actually, I came in a bus," she said confused.

"Yes, of course. I should've known. Anyway, sit down wherever you'd like mi'ja, I'll bring them to you when they're ready," the attendant told her with empathy.

Chuy went to sit at a table by the corner and waited for her food. When the tacos were ready, the attendant took the plate and a cold Coca Cola to her table and sat down with her.

"Eat *nena*, you look like you're famished!" inspecting her as if she was a rare species.

Without saying a word, she grabbed the plate, thanked her and slowly ate the best tacos she had ever had in her entire life. She gave thanks to God after she was finished.

"What are you doing in Juárez, child?" the attendant asked her to lean forward on the table as if to catch every word.

Chuy knew there would be many more questions. She didn't want this woman to intrude on her grief. All she wanted was to eat in peace and find a place to rest. She thanked the woman for her generosity and for the food, avoiding the question.

She asked the attendant if they were hiring or if she knew of a place that needed a *muchacha* for help. She didn't care where or what she had to do if it was a decent job.

"Not here, but if you go to Doña Licha's *fonda*, they've been hiring there since yesterday. You can't miss it, it's only a block away. Here in this corner, turn right and you can see it from there. It's a blue building with yellow letters that say "Doña Licha".

"Thank you very much, I'll head there now," Chuy answered while handing out money to pay for her meal. The woman put her hand on the money and gently pushed it back towards Chuy, shaking her head.

"No *muchacha*, save it. You'll need it later. The tacos are on me. Welcome to Ciudad Juárez," she answered sweetly as she got up from the table.

"Thank you so very much, for the food and the job prospect," replied Chuy, placing her hand on her chest and bowing her head slightly.

"Buena suerte, *chamaca*. If you need anything, let me know. If Doña Licha is not hiring anymore, you come back, alright? I'll try to see if I can find out who else is hiring. I work every day, even on the weekend. Maybe you can even spend the night at Doña Licha's, she should have a vacant room. She'll probably like you with that face and those fierce looking eyebrows, they suit you; they're very nice. You're a real looker!" The woman sounded like a maternal figure as she assessed Chuy.

Chuy thought of this encounter as proof that people really were good. She felt hope in her heart and was grateful for that. Grief was not the only thing she wanted to feel anymore. She realized that she'd only been complimented a few times in her life about her appearance. Alfredo really knew how to make her feel loved and appreciated and now she missed him terribly. A knot creeped up her throat, she felt sadness and hope at the same time then thought about the potential job waiting for her. There was no time to lose.

She needed that job more than anything at this point. The small savings she and her husband had been able to put away would only last her a week, at best. She needed that money for a room and food. She knew she had to budget, maybe she'd skip a meal or two a day until she could find a job. This strategy would help her stretch it as much as she could, if it came to that.

She left the restaurant and followed the directions she had been given. This time, paying attention to traffic and looking both ways before crossing the street. She was a fast learner. She didn't get this far just to lie dead on the road after being hit by a car. She turned the corner and saw a bright royal blue building with big yellow letters that read "Fonda Doña Licha". The place was a restaurant and bar with a boarding house in the back. She walked into the brightest building she'd ever seen. Back home all houses were made from adobe, and the businesses she had seen were all the same color, the color of earth. A couple of wealthy farming families had painted their houses white to make them stand out from the rest. The rest of the town couldn't afford it and didn't really care about trivialities. They had a house to live in and that's all that mattered.

When she walked into Doña Licha's, she noticed a woman sitting behind a counter reading the newspaper. The place was empty except for a couple of men having lunch while wearing hard hats that had been white at some point and overalls. She approached the counter and didn't say a word, she did not want to interrupt. The woman saw her, but pretended she hadn't and continued reading the newspaper. After a couple of minutes, she put the newspaper down and looked at Chuy saying:

"Can you believe this *Carretera Panamericana* deal is actually happening? And the government is backing it! Men and their "sports," they're stupid if you ask me! Let them race those cars at that speed. Just let them... they're going to kill themselves and other innocent people, that's what's going to happen," she tapped the counter violently with one finger.

"Mark my words! They can't even drive properly in the streets around here at a slow speed and they want to go faster. They're stupid, I tell you! Anyway, I'm blabbering now, what can I do for you, *chula*?"

"Hi, good morning. My name is María de Jesús and I'm looking for work. I moved from Durango, and I was told to come here because you might have an opening. I'm hoping to talk to whoever is in charge and offer my services," Chuy answered confidently.

"What can you do? Do you have any type of experience?" the employee asked her, looking at her from head to toe.

"I haven't done much, really. But I can learn things fast and I really want to work. I can cook, I can clean, I can sew, and I can learn."

"Where did you say you're from?"

"I'm from Santiago Papasquiaro. In the state of Durango. I just got here today."

"Ah, the great state of Durango! I know the area; my husband's parents were from there. Thankfully they moved here when he was just a boy, so he grew up in the city. I've been there once, kind of depressing, really. Didn't feel like going again. I hope you didn't bring any scorpions with you, I'm terrified of those ugly things," said the woman, joking. "So, what brings you to Juárez?"

"I'm starting over," Chuy confessed.

"What happened to you, sweetheart? I can see sadness in your eyes." The woman clearly wanted details.

"Can you please tell me if you or someone could give me a job?"

Chuy learned fast that people from the city liked to ask the type of questions no one would have even dared to ask back home. Her family and neighbors all treasured their privacy.

"Thatbad, huh? Okay, I get it. None of my business. Anyway, we *are* hiring. Doña Licha needs someone to help with the restaurant. The girl that works nights had to go back to her hometown to take care of her parents. In Coahuila, if I'm not mistaken. They're older, you know? And well, her sisters told her it was her duty. I don't know why they can't look after them, they live right there. She's the only unmarried one in the family and she's out here and they've convinced her, or better yet, guilted her into thinking it's her responsibility. I'm not sure if the boss lady already has someone in mind though. If you do get the job, you'll probably have to start right away. Would you be able to start immediately?"

"Yes, I am available now if I'm needed," Chuy answered enthusiastically.

"Oh, you know what? Doña Licha will need someone else too. In case she already had someone else. I forgot that Teresa, one of the girls that works nights, eloped with some *pela'o* and he didn't let her come back to work after one week of being married. Before they got married, he told her he was okay with it and then he immediately changed his mind. He said a decent married woman shouldn't be waiting tables at a restaurant. He knows that a lot of men come in here and there's a lot of temptation. He

65

said he should know because he had met her here! She's a good girl, that Teresa. Poor thing, now she's just at home taking care of her husband and the house."

Chuy did not like to hear things about other people. She always thought gossip was venomous, especially about people she didn't know. It made her extremely uncomfortable, so she refrained from commenting on anything that didn't have to do with the job.

"And where can I find Doña Licha?" she asked impatiently.

"She worked last night herself because we are short-handed. You know Teresa, the girl I told you about? She won't be coming in until four. You can come back and talk to her then."

"Can I wait here?"

"For seven hours? Yeah, I mean, if you'd like to. She'll be impressed. People around here don't like to wait, and they expect everything just when they want it. Hiring you may be perfect. I figure if she hires you then I won't have to pick up extra shifts when she gets tired of working Teresa's shifts. I am tired, you know. You're a good-looking girl, you have that to your advantage," she finally concluded.

"That's the second time I heard that today. I'm not sure how to respond. As for waiting, I really don't have anywhere to be, and I really need the job. I'll just wait for her."

"Well, it's true. And just so you know, pretty girls get better tips. I don't get much in tips because I'm old, but you can make good tips. Sometimes they'll be better than your own salary, like on the weekends. Doña Licha likes to have good looking girls working for her, it brings in more clients."

Chuy started to wonder what kind of place Doña Licha was really running. Back in her town she had heard rumors of places in the city where men went and spent a lot of money on women and alcohol. They would neglect their families by not sending back enough money, or sometimes they had no money to send at all. She was hoping this wasn't a bad place; it didn't look like one, but still she wondered.

The old waitress noticed the concern in her eyes.

"Oh, don't you worry *chula*, I know what you're thinking. This is a decent restaurant. When the kitchen closes at night, we're still open and it's more like a bar. Sometimes we have some live music from local people, trios, bands, and sometimes we bring in mariachis. When the party gets good, we move the tables to the side to make room to dance. It's a lot of fun to see people enjoying themselves. On the weekends, we get a lot of American soldiers. They like cold Mexican *cervezas*, good Mexican food that they can't get in *el otro lado*, no matter how many Mexican restaurants they have, and a pretty

67

mamacita to chat or dance with. Don't worry it's a decent place and you'll have a decent job here," the old woman assured her.

Chuy thanked her. She felt relieved. She couldn't imagine herself working at a place that was not decent. She wondered if she would, if she was forced to, if she was starving and there was nothing else. She was certain she was put on this earth to survive, and then to thrive. Nothing was going to stop her. She thought that the worst that could ever happen to her had already happened, and whatever came next, she would happily live it. No matter what that was.

"Here, let me give you a menu so you can study it while you wait for Doña Licha. I think she'll like you. God, I need some time off and you might just be my ticket out," she said, pinching Chuy's cheek and smiling.

"You really are very pretty, and I love your eyebrows. They really are something."

Chuy was, in fact, a beautiful young woman. She had white soft skin, piercing olive green eyes, very well-defined full lips and dark shiny curls just above her shoulders. She had a very solemn look that made her look mysterious and attractive to people. They wanted to know why a girl so young could look so serious. They wanted to know more about her. There was something in her that made them trust her. For some reason people would immediately open up to her. Her black dress made her skin look whiter, even mourning looked good on her.

She was determined to get that job; she had to. Most of her first day in the city had been spent at this place and she knew she didn't have much time. Getting hired by Doña Licha would give her peace of mind, food on the table, and a roof over her head, if she was lucky. She prayed while she waited.

After all the pain and suffering she had experienced, it was time to get a lucky break. She had never really felt control of her own life. Her fate and her life had always been controlled by others, by her circumstances, and by tragedies. She'd had very few choices of her own and choosing to leave her hometown gave her strength and confidence. She was afraid this opportunity would change the course of her fate.

She sat down at a corner table in the restaurant and studied the menu. She learned the regular prices as well as the specials. She learned about the refreshments and alcoholic drinks offered. She memorized the names of the bands that played at night during bar hours and what days of the week they played. She felt that luck was finally on her side and, this time, she would not lose.

When Doña Licha showed up for her night shift that evening, the old waitress informed her someone was waiting to talk to her. She filled her in on what it was about. Chuy was exhausted from her long trip and had fallen asleep on the table, using her bundle as a makeshift pillow to rest her head. Her back hurt and her neck was stiff. She had only wanted to rest and find some relief from her pain but had inevitably fallen asleep.

When Doña Licha approached her, the old waitress had already told her everything she knew about Chuy. Without saying a word, Doña Licha pulled out a chair and sat down at the table where she saw the young woman sleeping. She cleared her throat loudly, making enough noise to wake her up. Startled, Chuy woke up and stood in a flash, fixing her dress and touching her hair.

"Please, take a seat child. My name is Licha, I own this restaurant. Lorena told me you were waiting for me. Are you looking for a job?" Doña Licha asked.

"Yes ma'am, I am."

"Did you just get here today?"

"Yes ma'am, from Durango. That's where I'm from."

"Is there anyone with you?"

"No ma'am, I'm here alone," Chuy answered, trying not to give too much information if she could avoid it.

"That's a bit dangerous, if you ask me. I hope you had safe travels though and I'm glad you're here," Doña Licha said matter of fact, but showing concern.

"Yes ma'am, I do think it is. But I also think that sometimes staying someplace may be even more dangerous than taking a potentially dangerous trip to escape it."

"You're very right, child. I apologize. I don't presume to know your story and I have been lucky to not have to feel like leaving. You must be tired," she answered apologetically.

"I needed change in my life, God knows I tried my best. Now I am going to try my best here," Chuy said proudly.

"How old are you, child?"

"Eighteen."

"Do you have family here, or friends? A place to stay."

"No ma'am. Once I secure a job, I'll look for a place to stay. That was third on my list."

"I see, what was the first?"

"Find somewhere to eat. The place I stopped at told me maybe I could find a job here, so I came straight after breakfast."

"Well, it looks like you have your priorities in place. I like that, very responsible of you. You don't really look eighteen. I mean you look young, but the look in your eyes makes you look wise beyond your years. There's also a mysteriousness about you which makes you interesting, even at first glance. Anyway, you're not going anywhere at this hour, it's getting late, and you don't know the city. How about you have dinner here with me? I'll introduce you to the staff, and then I'll show you to one of the vacant rooms at the back of the restaurant. You can stay here tonight; this is a *fonda* after all. If you find another place tomorrow then you can go if you want to, if not, you can stay here. I can deduct room and board from your pay and that will give you a roof over your head and sustenance. You can make additional money in tips. The friendlier you are with customers, the better tips you'll get. People like to talk, share information about their days, you don't have to be interested in their stories but if you pretend to be, you'll always get better tips. We'll talk more about it tomorrow when you've rested."

Doña Licha was a great human being, Chuy liked her immediately. She was a self-made woman and against all odds. She had a difficult childhood and an abusive marriage along with a long list of unfortunate events throughout her life. But she was strong and succeeded in whatever she set her mind to. She owned a few rooms to rent directly behind the restaurant. She was trusted by her employees and the community, and she liked to help people whenever she could. She was a kind of maternal figure to people; some saw her as a fairy Godmother and Chuy was no exception. She had a gift of recognizing needs in people, as she was no stranger to unfortunate circumstances, which had made her very empathetic towards the plight of others. One of her life's personal missions was to help women and encourage others to do the same, passionately lifting them up. She was an example, she did not judge, and she hated gossip.

"You said you could deduct room and board from my pay, does that mean I have the job?" Chuy asked incredulously.

"Of course, you do sweetheart. I know you'll do just great; I can see you are a strong girl and will accomplish anything you want in life. I'll help you any way that I can. Besides, Lorena told me you probably already know the menu, specials, drinks, and everything there is to know about the job. Now, go to the kitchen and ask Sergio to make us some dinner, he's our cook. You must be hungry. Come find me when you're done. I'm going to get your room ready while our dinner is being prepared. I have plenty of time before I start my shift. We can talk a little more while we eat."

"Oh, thank you so much, I am so grateful for you and your kindness. I will not let you down, I will work very hard. I promise."

"I know you will, child."

This had indeed been a very lucky day. She could feel the wheels of her fortune turning and changing to her favor with every passing minute and she finally had hope in her heart.

Sergio was a middle-aged man with kind eyes. He was one of Doña Licha's accomplices in making people feel better; her with her words and kindness and him with his cooking. He hardly ever said anything, but when he did, it touched people. When people went into Doña Licha's, they left their troubles outside and entered a safe place where they ate, had a good time, drank, and danced. Sergio inspired trust; his voice was soft and caring. Chuy felt it in the way he talked to her, his demeanor reminded her of her father. She missed him so much. She remembered the little silly jokes he used to tell her late at night after a long day at work.

He'd sit her on his lap and ask how her day had been. He always wanted to know how she was. She would recount her day: how the kids behaved and what they'd eaten for dinner. Eventually, he would stop her in the middle of the sentence, "I asked about you and your day. Tell me, how's my girl?" He would hold her tight and stroke her hair softly and kiss her head a thousand times. She never doubted how much he loved her; he was a great father. She had a great longing to feel his strong arms around her like when she was younger. Her eyes filled with tears and a knot in her throat would make it difficult for her to say anything.

Doña Licha had finally come back, and they sat down for dinner. Chuy, still with the knot in her throat, found it difficult to swallow the chicken soup Sergio had prepared for her. Doña Licha didn't say a word, she knew her new employee needed to grieve. She wanted to give her privacy and a feeling of safety.

"No crying while eating *mi'ja*, that's the rule," Sergio instructed from the doorway.

"You want your tears to dilute the flavor? Come on, that's sacrilegious. Now, wipe those pretty green eyes of yours and savor your meal the way God intended. You should always enjoy your food, it's sacred, and it's good for your soul. Remember, *Dios aprieta pero no ahorca*. Have faith, you will be just fine," Sergio finished, serving spoon in one hand and the other on his hip.

"Gracias Sergio, this soup is the best," Doña Licha answered so Chuy didn't have to.

"It is, isn't it?" answered Sergio looking at Chuy only "On a serious note though, Doña Licha es *un pan de Dios*, I'm glad you found us. She's amazing and you are going to love it here."

He entered the dining area from the back of the kitchen, serving spoon still in hand, and sat next to her. He patted her softly on the back. He didn't know her yet, but he could see great pain in her eyes. More pain, suffering, and a sense of longing than he'd seen in a while from someone so young. He was aware of her need for human connection.

"Good company and a good meal always lift the spirit," Doña Licha said after finishing her dinner.

Sergio sat there with them for a while since it was a slow day. He talked about his wife and children. He talked about the business, what to expect at night during bar hours, especially when there was a live band playing. Doña Licha listened to him, smiling, not taking her eyes away from Chuy.

"You'll be just fine here Chuyita, Doña Licha has a big heart, like a big fancy hotel where a lot of people come and stay when they feel lost. That's just who she is. Welcome to Juárez, I know you'll like it here," declared Sergio as he got up from the table and winked at Doña Licha.

Chuy smiled to herself, that's what her family back home called her, Chuyita, and she felt a warm welcome. She suddenly knew she would be able to build a new life here and she really liked the employees. She felt safe and away from the place where everything had hurt her.

"Oh, stop it! You're making her have high expectations of me, I don't like it. Maybe you should go make more soup and stop talking so much about me. I am your boss, you know?" Doña Licha told Sergio jokingly.

After the chat and dinner, she went with Doña Licha to her new room. It was nicely fixed especially for her. The restaurant and the rooms were separated only by a small alley that could be accessed via the restaurant by a door in the back of the kitchen. She showed her how to get to it and gave her a key and a tour of the place.

"Don't feel rushed to start working, you hear? You need to rest. Take a bath and sleep if you need to. Tomorrow is a new day. You're in good hands here, you're safe, and you are welcome," Doña Licha gave her a tight warm hug and walked out, giving her some privacy.

Chuy locked the door behind her and placed her bundle on the bed. There was a steaming cup of hot chamomile tea on the nightstand by the bed which was meant to help her sleep better. She looked around and found herself in a small yet very cozy room, very simple. She walked to the bathroom and was amazed at the sight of a prepared hot bath; Doña Licha really was a very caring person. She could see a little bit of steam coming out of the water and couldn't wait to get in. She brought her tea with her and sipped on it slowly before taking her clothes off. She got in the tub gently, allowing her body to acclimate to the heat. This would help her relax, she thought.

Laying in that bath felt so good that for a second, she feared all this was too good to be true and she suddenly started sobbing. Everything had happened so fast and so hard that she realized she hadn't really had any time to think or to cry. She knew she was still mourning. Her circumstances and the gravity of the series of events had left her in shock. Even so, she was still trying to find a solution, thinking on how to put an end to the misery that always followed her like a little black rain cloud hovering over her head. She didn't know what would happen in the future, but she knew that things were going to change. She kept telling herself that she was fine, that things were going to be fine, everything was up to her maker now; *uno propone y Dios dispone.*

She cried hard for a long while, until she felt the water getting cold. She hadn't realized time had passed until she saw goose bumps on her body, she was trembling. She finished the tea and got out. Two fluffy clean towels were waiting for her. Her heart and soul were warm and full of gratitude at the opportunities these good people had afforded her with. She felt very fortunate and thanked God for it. There were always prayers before going to sleep, but she was so spent that she fell asleep as soon as she got in bed. It was a deep, hard, and dreamless slumber.

The next day she didn't wake up until almost midday, she had never slept for almost fourteen hours before. If she was lucky, she'd get a good five hours. In this house, however, one didn't wake up to the cock-a-doodle-doo of roosters, mooing of cows, chirping of birds, or barking of dogs all in unison in the great symphony of a farm life. There were also no children needing to be fed or bathed and dressed for school, no husband to send off to work with coffee and lunch, no daughter to nurse, and no stepmother to be a maid to.

There were no people to please, anyone to care for, no one depended on her and that was a great feeling. She felt liberated and let out a great sigh of relief followed by immediate guilt.

She asked God for forgiveness for feeling selfish and she prayed for the eternal rest of her lost loved ones. She thought of her beautiful little angel. She thought of her eyes, how she'd look at her and smiled with her perfectly shaped red lips as if she was wearing rouge. Her skin was white like her own and there was always a pink hue on her chubby little cheeks, she looked like a perfectly beautiful porcelain doll. She could hear her laughter in an echo. Daría's father had been handsome, Chuy was beautiful, and the baby had looked exactly like her. She looked like an angel.

Chuy was not a thin woman, she had never been, but she was also not big. She was a bit plump or appeared to be. She had full cheeks and a round full beautiful face. The shape of her perfectly arched eyebrows added fire to the look in her eyes. She was captivating. Her lips were full and naturally red. Her perpetual somber demeanor made her appear older than she was, and certain people felt intimidated by her seriousness and strength. Her reserved character gave her a sense of mysteriousness that made her interesting in the eyes of those that didn't know her very well. She had a certain presence that was felt by all, and people naturally gravitated towards her. Life in a small town, however, had made her a bit insecure and unaware of these strong characteristics she possessed, and it would take her a long time to discover them and to unleash the spirit within her.

Once she started working, she realized Lorena was right, her beauty had led her to good tips. On her first day in the restaurant, Chuy worked as if she'd been a part of the staff for a while. She knew the menu, prices, and specials. She was also good at engaging with her clients, although still a bit shy and very reserved. At the end of her first day of work, she sent a telegram to her father to let him know she had arrived in good health. She also told him the good news about her job and her little apartment.

Chuy's salary went mostly towards her room and board which was all she really needed. Even so, her tips were also put to good use. On her first day off she wandered around the city and found a fabric store. She made a big purchase consisting of different types of cloth, lace, buttons, and zippers to make herself some new dresses. This gave her something to do on her days off for the first few months in her new home. Previously Chuy hadn't had the want or need to explore the city in depth and thought there would always be time in the future; after all, she was there to stay.

Chapter V

After six months of living and working at Doña Licha's, Chuy had started to come out of her shell. She was more confident. She could look at people without the need to avoid eye contact. Doña Licha mentioned once that she had a little bit of glow in her eyes, as if her hope in life had increased. It was true, she felt hope and the possibility of happiness. She still had not shared much about herself, she was a private person and retained a bit of reservation and mystery. This newly acquired confidence piqued a bit of curiosity in her and she finally decided to venture out.

Up until this moment, Chuy had only explored a couple of blocks around the restaurant, and she was ready to see more of the city. In preparation for her outing, she wore her favorite dress from the few she had just made, and she'd even bought herself a new pair of shoes. The pumps had slight heels that made her look a bit taller and she walked the streets of downtown with confidence.

Once out in the city, she realized that just like her, other people also did what they could to survive. She noticed young children with clown faces standing in the corner of streets breathing fire for spectators in exchange for a few coins. There were cars and buses everywhere, a couple of horses, and people walking.

The town square was visible on her path, so she decided to head towards it. She bought a candied apple while trying to take everything in. Without a care in the world, Chuy sat on a bench next to a gazebo and enjoyed the mariachi band playing to a crowd of people. She was so content that she sat there for a while after she had finished the apple. From her seat she could smell roasted peanuts in the air coming from one side of the square and freshly made cotton candy from the other. She took out a sketchpad she had in her purse and started drawing dresses that she would sew herself, each inspired by the women she saw strolling in the plaza.

Eventually, Chuy got up when she spotted a photography studio. Like a curious child, she decided to go see it. She couldn't remember the last time she had her picture taken. Chuy felt a hand on hers as she reached for the door handle. She let go immediately, shyly turned around and saw a handsome young man in a military uniform.

"Oh! Pardon me. Please, after you, *señorita,*" the handsome man broke the silence.

Once inside the studio, he introduced himself as Victor and started a conversation with Chuy. It turned out he was originally from Chicago and had moved to El Paso right across the border when he joined the military. Victor lived in the barracks at Fort Bliss military base and although he wasn't allowed to go to Mexico, he loved eating in Juárez and strolling through the city on his days off. He had only worn his uniform across the border this particular day because he was going to have his portrait taken to send to his mother. He concealed his uniform under a long coat and didn't wear his cap to avoid getting in trouble.

Chuy listened attentively but said very little. She would answer only questions he would ask her: her name was María de Jesús but her friends called her Chuy. She was from Durango and had moved to Juárez a few months back. She lived and worked at Doña Licha's restaurant not too far from the studio. She was 18 years old.

When the attendant at the front desk winked and smiled at Chuy as she called her in to take her portrait she said,

"I absolutely love your dress. The color really makes your eyes pop!"

"Oh, thank you!" Chuy answered, blushing.

She said this in the shyest manner, and she knew it. She was still shocked every time someone complimented her in the slightest way about anything at all. It felt good deep down inside, but somehow, it would still make her feel self-conscious. Victor heard the compliment towards her and smiled; he agreed with the statement and thought the way she had blushed made her even more beautiful than before.

When the portrait session was over, she was told her portraits would be ready for pick-up in exactly one week. She said she would return then and turned to Victor to say goodbye.

"It was a pleasure, Victor. I hope you have a very nice day."

He got up from his seat and shook her hand slightly then gently raised her hand to his lips and kissed it. She nervously clutched her purse with her left hand, the kiss made her feel strange.

"The pleasure was all mine, Chuy," he answered with a nervous smile. "Would you like to wait ten minutes for me to have my portrait taken and then maybe we can go have dinner together? That was my next stop, and I know a great place."

"Oh, I don't know," she hesitated.

"Have dinner with me, Chuy. Please. It would do me a great honor." Victor insisted.

The photographer was waiting for him and coughed to remind Victor that he was next.

"Sir, we have two other people after you. The sooner we get yours done, the sooner we can get the rest of the clients."

"Oh, absolutely! I apologize. I am just waiting for this beautiful lady to agree to have dinner with me.

Once she says yes, I will be right in," he said with an innocent, yet mischievous look on his face.

Victor smiled at the people waiting their turns. He threw in an extra wink to all who were watching before returning his gaze to Chuy. She mentally noted that Victor was very handsome and charismatic.

"Please. It's just dinner. Come on, what do you say?" he begged her, exaggerating a pout and placing his hands together as if praying.

She looked straight into his eyes and felt her face flush.

"I will have dinner with you if you are out in ten minutes, if not, I'll be gone when you come out," she threatened with a smile.

"Perfect! Come on *compadre*, let's get this done. We can't have Chuy waiting for us, we're hungry," celebrated Victor.

She sat back down and kept looking at her hands, suddenly noticing that they were sweaty. No one had ever asked her out to dinner before. She didn't know how to talk to a man. The only man she'd ever talked to was Alfredo and yet they hadn't really had a conversation until they were already engaged. She realized this was how people in the city lived and if she was to be a city girl, she would have to adapt to the new culture. Victor seemed like a nice guy, so she gave herself permission to relax.

He came out in less than ten minutes looking at the clock on the wall and then at her, smiling.

"Your wish is my command, my lady. I couldn't risk being in there another minute and potentially losing my dinner date. I do hope I come out nicely in the portrait. Either way, I'm sure my mother will like it, you know how mothers are. Or I can always come back next week and retake it."

She smiled sheepishly.

He put his arm out softly for her to put hers through it and walked out together into the city. He took her to his favorite downtown restaurant. He did most of the talking, not because he was a talker, but because she wasn't. She usually stayed quiet when she wasn't fully comfortable. He was still a stranger, and she was out of her comfort zone so she left her guard up.

No one had paid so much attention or shown so much interest in her. No one had been interested in what she had to say. He was different. He wanted to know about her; too much, she thought. He noticed she was very shy from the beginning, so he was grateful for whatever she was willing to share and he didn't push for more. "When you want to catch a butterfly, you don't go chasing after it; you let it come to you," he thought.

After dinner, he offered to walk her home, but she refused. She wanted to walk back alone and think. He did not insist. He always prided himself in being a perfect gentleman and respected her wishes without question.

"Can we then agree to pick up our portraits next week at the same time? Then we can have dinner again and maybe we can go to the theater and watch a picture." Victor offered.

She had never been to the cinema before, and that invitation piqued her interest. She agreed to a second date. When they walked out of the restaurant, he said goodbye kissing her hand once again and then smiled.

"Until next week then, same time as today" he reminded her.

She smiled back at him.

"Until then. Thank you for dinner Victor, I enjoyed your company," she answered.

"Please, don't mention it; it was my pleasure. Next time you'll have to do a bit more talking. Deal?"

She told him she would and walked away. Her face and ears were burning as she crossed the square on her way back to Doña Licha's. She didn't remember ever feeling that way, not even with Alfredo. She had never really been courted. Everything was so different in the city. She wasn't used to it, but she could certainly try. She thought for a second that what she had just experienced would have been completely inappropriate in

Santiago and would more than likely never have happened. She would be the talk of the town for simply having dinner with a man she'd just met. She was expected to be in mourning for at least another six months.

People were expected to mourn for a year after a loved one had died. But it was also frowned upon to stop mourning exactly after one year. Women were scrutinized and some would mourn for longer so they could prove their faithfulness as a virtue. Otherwise, it would make them seem impatient to get on with their lives. They were expected to be miserable, praying nightly rosaries for the poor souls in purgatory. Reputations were important in small towns, sometimes, it was the only thing people had.

Sergio noticed something different about her when she walked in the restaurant that evening. She went straight to her room through the back door and didn't say a word to anyone, but she had a smile on her face. He asked if she'd like him to prepare her something to eat to try to get her to spill the beans about her afternoon, but it didn't work.

"No Sergio, thank you. I already had dinner. I'm tired so I'm going to take a bath and then go to bed." she replied.

She didn't go back to the restaurant the next day until her shift was about to start. By then Sergio had already moved on to other gossip and forgotten about Chuy's seemingly eventful evening.

Seven days to the date, she went back to the photography studio as she had agreed. She was there a little early and to her surprise, Victor was already waiting for her outside the studio.

"I was impatient, so I got here an hour early. That gave me the opportunity to pick up our portraits. Here's yours, it's my treat, please accept it as a way of thanking you for keeping me company last week."

"Oh no, please. Let me pay you for it," she answered, embarrassed.

"Absolutely not! I am a gentleman, Chuy. Please allow me this pleasure."

"I'll allow it if you allow me to pay for dinner," she said playfully.

"No, ma'am."

"The picture shows at the theater then," she negotiated.

"The popcorn!" he offered.

"Done!"

They both laughed as they walked towards the square. They sat on the same bench she'd used before and looked at the portraits. Later, they strolled through the city with her arm in his. He was a gentleman indeed, but not the kind of "gentleman" she had been used to. She was not used to talking.

She had felt that men always talked but never listened when a woman had something to say. Women were never taken seriously, their opinions never counted, and they only existed to be wives and mothers. Her whole life she had been very reserved and did not really talk unless she had something important to say. Even then, she would second-guess herself. This is not how Victor made her feel. When they were together, she felt the exact opposite: valued.

Victor was different, not only would he ask her about herself, he seemed genuinely interested in everything she said. Paying meticulous attention to her words and her body language, as if what she had to say was the most important thing he'd ever heard. These gestures made her feel appreciated; she wasn't used to the experience of someone paying so much attention to her words. It was surreal; he truly wanted to know her, her essence, her mind, and anything else she was willing to share. The only thing he had asked of her was to spend time with him, she enjoyed that, and he enjoyed learning about her. She felt respected and independent. She liked it and she liked him. She learned to trust him almost immediately.

She let him walk her home after the show, walking slowly while discussing the movie. He joked with her, and she laughed so much her stomach hurt. She realized she had never laughed so hard that she felt physical pain in her abdomen. It was a good kind of pain though; she could get used to more of it. When they turned the corner where they could see Doña Licha's, she stopped and told him she would walk home from there.

"Are you sure? You don't have a crazy jealous and possessive husband waiting at home for you, do you? Or a father sitting on the porch with a shotgun waiting for the bastard that tries to court his beautiful daughter before seeking his approval?" he asked while playfully waving a finger.

"No, but we'll talk about some of that next time," she said with a serious tone.

"So, there is another 'later' then? Yes! Thank you, Jesús!" he exclaimed.

"You're welcome," she joked back.

"Thank you, Jesús? Oh, I see what you did there... María de Jesús! That is hilarious. That is probably the first joke you've said since I met you."

She smiled at him. He kissed her hand and closed his eyes when his lips touched her skin.

"I really like you, Chuy."

"Next week, same place? We can meet at the square," she asked.

"I must go away for work for a while, but I can meet you here in three weeks. Twenty-one days exactly. In the square. I'll wait for you there, same time as today."

"I'll be looking forward to it then," she answered flirtatiously.

"I can't wait," he winked at her.

"Until then, Victor," she said softly with a subtle smile.

"Until then, Chuy."

She walked away with a smile on her lips and a sigh in her heart.

Three weeks went by slowly for Chuy. She had become fond of Victor in the short time she'd known him and couldn't wait to see him again. At work, people could see the difference in her, but she refused to share details about her new relationship. She always thought people should keep their personal lives to themselves. She knew very well how gossip started, and she did not like gossip.

Chuy's discrete nature had always frustrated everyone at Doña Licha's, she was very vague when she was asked anything. They even speculated that she might have a dark and dirty secret and that's why she had escaped from her hometown. Then she sometimes seemed as if she was daydreaming, she would smile to herself during her chores in the restaurant and they knew that something was up.

"Why are you so happy, Chuy?" they would ask, relentlessly.

"What is wrong with being happy? I am happy because I have a place of my own, a job, and I'm alive. I enjoy my life. What's wrong with that?"

She would answer with a smile on her face and that would add to the mystery. She knew she was torturing them by not giving in, but she didn't care. It really wasn't any of their business. Besides, she didn't want to tell them anything until she was sure what was going on with Victor. She would voluntarily share if things developed with him, and she hoped that they would.

By the time the three weeks went by, Chuy had finished making a new dress for the occasion. She wore it beautifully. She headed to the square at the time they had agreed to meet. There was Victor, waiting for her. He looked so handsome. He was wearing a suit and tie and a matching hat with a bouquet of flowers in his arms. He got up and started walking in her direction when he saw her. He had a big smile on his face.

They embraced nervously and then he gave her the flowers and kissed her cheek. There was so much tenderness between them. They were obviously smitten with each other. Those three weeks had made them think of one another much more than they had anticipated.

They sat on the same bench as before where she told him she needed to talk to him about herself before any more time went by. He looked nervous, he didn't know what to expect, but made no assumptions. The possibilities made him feel uneasy and she saw it in his eyes.

"It's okay Victor. I would just like to share a little bit about myself. I feel like I am being unfair to you. Last time I saw you, I learned a great deal about you and I didn't say much about my life. You shared some personal stories with me, and you still don't know anything about me. I'd like to change that today."

"Thank you, Chuy. I would really like that. There are things that I have been able to learn about you without one word. Sometimes I can read a person's eyes, their mannerisms, the way they speak and the way they carry themselves. But I would love to hear anything you would like to share. Also, I want you to know that I haven't been able to stop thinking about you. These three weeks were torturous, and I really looked forward to today. I couldn't even sleep at night just thinking about seeing you again. I feel like I'm falling in love with you."

"Oh!" she answered surprised.

"Please, forgive me if I'm being too forward or if I am making you uncomfortable. That was not my intention. I do feel a very strong connection with you. I'll stop if you want me to."

"Let me tell you a little about my life first. You may not like what I have to say, maybe you will, I don't know, but I owe you this much," Chuy interrupted.

"Oh no, you don't owe me anything," he assured her.

They sat in the plaza chatting for hours. She talked about her life, and he listened intently to her as if his life depended on it. There were no interruptions. His admiration and respect for her grew with every sentence, with every confession, with every detail of her life. Every anecdote she shared made him like her even more. He wanted to know everything, he was fascinated and completely lovestruck.

She told him everything she thought was important for him to know. It was crucial for him to know that she was a widow and had lost a child. She hoped he would understand why she had been so reserved with him, so pensive, so sad. She was healing from great pain and her wounds were still fresh. There was fear and doubt in her mind, and they were difficult to shake off.

She wasn't sure how he would take the information she'd give him. He was different from everyone she'd met before, but he was still a man. Men weren't so kind to women who had already been married. Widows were automatically men-repellent. It was as if the dead husband received all their respect and she lived in his shadow forever. Divorced women were usually blamed for the end of the relationship, even in case of abuse and adultery by the husband. Women never won, they were never right, and they never had sympathy, even from other women.

She started at the beginning of her story, with her mother's death. She talked about her crushed childhood dreams of an education. She described her sudden transformation from child to caretaker. She shared memories of the summers and scorching sun-filled days of working in the field with her brother, Rito. She explained how hard they had to work to help her father feed the family. She told him about her father's new wife and their new children who were favored over her and her siblings. She lamented how they sometimes went to bed hungry because her stepmother would only make enough food for herself, her husband, and their own children. And, finally, she told him about Alfredo and their very short-lived marriage and the sudden and premature death of her child which served as a catalyst in her life that would lead her to escape and end up in Juárez.

Chuy talked for hours without interruption. Victor listened intently with tears in his eyes while tightly holding her hand.

"Oh, my sweet Chuy. You've had such a difficult life. Listening to your life has made me appreciate the life I have had. Thank you so much for sharing, you have no idea how much it means to me. But I must say, even before I knew your story, I could see sadness in your eyes."

"I don't know how else to live, this is all I have known. This has been my normal and to tell you the truth, I didn't know people could have different lives with different outcomes. I guess we're all a bit more sheltered in small towns and we think that's the life everyone has. Maybe we just take it because we don't know what else to do or how to change things."

"What would you think if I asked you to be my girlfriend, Chuy? I'll do my best to complement the new life you've chosen for yourself. I truly admire how you've changed the course of your own life by taking matters into your hands. I respect you and I would be honored to have someone as yourself as my partner. We can't erase the past. I can't replace your losses. I can't make any of that go away, but I can be a support to you. I can love you and I can give you my attention and devotion. We can be great together."

"I'm still mourning for my family, Victor. I need to heal myself before I can think of any of that. There's not much I can do right now other than wait. *No hay mal que dure cien años, ni cuerpo que lo resista.*"

"I understand. I also want you to know that I love you, especially now that I know more about you. I want to be with you and if you accept, I would like to make you my wife one day, if you will have me. I talked to my parents about you; I told them how beautiful you are, inside and out. Sharing your life experiences with me has solidified my resolve. My mother can't wait to meet you and I know she will absolutely love you. I want you to know that I am willing to wait if you need me to."

She felt so fortunate, and she thanked God for hearing her pleas and answering her prayers. He gave her so much more than she asked for or expected. She was happy. She was full of hope and love. This man, who was still getting to know her, was wonderful. He loved her. But she was still very tender and wanted to wait.

He kissed her lips and held her tight. When it was time for dinner, they walked together around the square stopping at different restaurants until they decided what to have for dinner. When they finally found a place, they talked some more. He explained what he did for work and talked about his life. His parents were Mexican who had immigrated to the United States before he was born. His mother had been a doctor in Mexico but couldn't practice medicine in the United States. There was a language barrier and none of her credentials or experience as a professional were accepted as valid. So she stayed at home as a mother, wife, and homemaker.

His father had always worked in the fields and the *Bracero Program* gave him an opportunity to find a job in the US. It was officially known as the Mexican Farm Labor Agreement, which had been implemented in mid-1942. All his father's skills consisted in working with his hands. He could do woodwork, construction, asphalt, but most of his experience was in the fields. He would tell Victor that no matter how poor they were in the United States, they were better off than in Mexico. His mother had different opinions about the matter. She missed working so much that she would get depressed staying at home all day. She felt she lost her identity by staying home. She lost her career and the feeling of respect and admiration her patients and coworkers felt for her. She was known as a smart, capable, and invaluable person. In the United States, she was a nobody. She didn't know the culture or the language. Society wasn't interested in anything that had to do with her past.

Victor felt he had the privilege and good fortune of having been born in the United States. His most valuable accomplishment, in his opinion, was being a proud member of the US military. He was an only child who had been completely loved by his parents and he felt it. They were very supportive of him, especially when it came to obtaining an education.

"A pen and a notebook are lighter than a shovel or a pickaxe," his father would tell him, "and better on your body and mind than the physical and emotional toil of picking fruit in the fields."

Victor had listened to his parents' advice. He was aware of the sacrifices they had made to ensure he had a bright future in their new country. He respected his parents above anything and vowed to make sure their sacrifices were not in vain. He was already a sergeant in the US Army and planned on making a lifelong career in the military.

After dinner, Chuy let him walk her all the way home.

"Good night, my sweet Chuy. I'll pick you up next week here at home. I'll plan something fun for us to do. Thank you for trusting me and sharing your story, it means the world to me. I feel honored."

She smiled at him and thanked him for being so patient. He kissed her hand and she walked in the restaurant with the flowers in her arms.

Lorena and Sergio had been waiting for Chuy to come in so they could ask all about her day. She noticed the excitement and anticipation on their faces. Before they could get a word out, she said "Not now, please" and raised her hand as if telling them to stop.

"We'll chat tomorrow."

They both looked at each other, shrugged their shoulders and went back to work.

The following day, Chuy finally told everyone about Victor during breakfast. Doña Licha had already heard rumors from Lorena and Sergio, but ignored everything that didn't come directly from the source.

"*Ay mija*! An American soldier? He sounds like heaven; you may have hit the jackpot with the gringo. Do you know that?" Doña Licha blurted out enthusiastically.

"What does that mean, Doña Licha? I feel very lucky to have met him, he's like nothing I've ever experienced. I don't care that he's American, I care that he's kind, and refreshing, and cares about me," Chuy replied defensively.

"You have no idea how many girls would kill to hook up with an American soldier," added Lorena.

"Maybe, but I am not most girls. That's a very shallow way of thinking, if you ask me," Chuy retorted.

"Don't you get it? If you end up marrying him, you'll go live on the other side; you'll become a gringa yourself. With your white skin and green eyes, you'll fit right in. You both win, of course, look at you, you're a doll!" Lorena concluded.

"I don't care about that. I just want to be happy; you know? I want to be treated right. I want to catch a break. I'm tired," Chuy replied.

"I don't know if you're trying to be corny or you're just naïve. Take advantage of the opportunity, Chuy!"

Doña Licha and Sergio looked at each other, then at Lorena and Chuy. Doña Licha noticed that the conversation was not going the way it was initially intended. Chuy was beginning to look uncomfortable with Lorena's shallow comments.

"Alright everyone," announced Doña Licha, getting up from the table. "Today is going to be a long and busy day, so we better start getting ready."

Everyone got up, following Doña Licha's lead, and went to tend to their individual duties. Doña Licha touched Chuy's elbow and asked her to stay for a second.

"Chuy don't pay attention to Lorena. You have a heart of gold, and we all know you're not like that. I know you would never trade your integrity for a secure life with anyone, no matter how comfortable or tempting it is. That's what I love about you, child; your heart is pure and it's all love. All we want is to see you happy, Chuy."

"Thank you so much for saying that" answered Chuy, giving Doña Licha a warm hug.

She was happy. She had never felt so productive, so free, so independent. This new life showed her everything she had never even imagined, and she liked it. For the first time in her life, she had the time, freedom, and autonomy to realize she could do great things, and she felt very proud of that.

For the next few months, Chuy and Victor saw each other on the same days every week; their days off always coincided. He'd pick her up at Doña

Licha's at the same time every day he could. They would walk to the square and then sit and chat on the same bench that Chuy now almost felt belonged to her. After a while, they would stroll around and try different restaurants and later they would go to the theater when a new movie was released. When the state fair came to town, they had the time of their lives. Their growing respect and admiration towards one another inevitably turned into love and affection. People would smile at them in the street because they looked very happy together. Their happiness was impossible to ignore even at a glance.

Victor had been unusually quiet one day. In the evening when he was walking her back home, she noticed him less affectionate and distant, as if he had not been paying attention to her. She had had to repeat herself on several occasions.

"What is it, Victor? You've been distracted today, is everything okay?" she asked, trying not to assume the worst.

"Oh sweetheart, I am so sorry! I guess I have been a bit distracted. I have some work things that are bothering me, and I was waiting to share with you until the end of the day. I didn't want it to affect our time together, but I guess I failed at that. I am so sorry" he answered, kissing her on the cheek.

She nodded and waited for him to continue.

"I know you're still mourning the death of your dear husband and daughter. I don't want to overstep any boundaries. They're shipping me away at work on a three-month assignment. I also just found out that once this mission is completed and I come back home, I'll be stationed in another base. I will not be living in El Paso anymore. I'll have to move out of Fort Bliss." Victor held her hands in his as he gave her this information.

"When do you leave?" she asked surprised, feeling her heart plummet to the pit of her stomach.

"Tomorrow. I wanted to tell you earlier but didn't know how to start and it never felt like the right time to talk about it. I just wanted us to have a pleasant time. Can you forgive me?"

"I just wish we would have had time to talk about it during the day instead of just dropping the news at the last minute. Right before you leave for such a long time. We could've had time to talk about what happens next. If there is a *next*, obviously. I don't want to assume anything," she was hurt and defensive.

He saw a hint of anxiety in her eyes, so he grabbed both hands in his and kissed them. He regretted having caused so much uncertainty in her mind, even if for a short time.

"I'll be gone for three months starting tomorrow. We can write to each other every week or even every day if you want to. We can talk about anything. We can talk about our days, our love, our thoughts, our fears. We can talk about our future together and plan whatever we want; anything at all. When I get back, hopefully you'll feel ready to be with me, in a serious and more permanent way. If I can have your hand, as my wife, you'll automatically be able to enter the country with legal status. We'll move to our new home, and we'll start a new life together."

"Do you know where you will go when you come back?"

"Springfield Illinois, it's in the north of the country, very close to Canada. Listen, I love you Chuy, please say you'll marry me. Say you'll be my wife and you'll come with me. I can't imagine leaving without you and not seeing you again. The last few months have been the best and the next three will be very difficult. But I can deal with it knowing that we will be together when I get back."

"I love you too, Victor. And I can't imagine not seeing you again, you have helped me see life in a new color. Just when I thought I would never love again, you show up in my life. I want to be with you. There is nothing holding me back in Juárez, or in Durango. I will marry you," she said, smiling enthusiastically.

There were tears of joy running down their faces as they embraced each other. He kissed her lips holding her face in his hands, then kissed her hands. He dried her tears with his lips and they both smiled. The future seemed bright for both; they were full of hope. They agreed to write to each other every opportunity they had until they met again. He promised the next time he saw her, he would put a ring on her finger and they would take off as husband and wife.

From that point on, Chuy was happier than she had been most of her life. At times, she would pinch herself to make sure she wasn't dreaming and then she would laugh at herself. But it was reality, this was happening to her.

She received four letters from Victor every week. She kept them in a box organized by dates and would re-read them when she missed him most. She wrote to him every day. They would say how much they missed each other, about the love they felt for each other, trivial things that happened during the day, and the life they were going to have together. Three months was not a long time, but to them, it felt like an eternity. They were both impatient to be together.

Chapter VI

She kept improving her work at Doña Licha's. After mastering her restaurant duties during weekdays, she got moved to the night shift. She would go to work in time for an early dinner and stay late into the night until the bar closed. Different skills were needed for her new shift, but she was good with people. Little by little, she became more sociable and was better with the customers, which led to even better tips. Working at the bar was more lucrative because her guests became more generous after they had consumed several drinks.

One evening while working the bar, a group of police officers came in after their shift. They knew the ambiance at Doña Licha's was great, always helping people have a good time. The officers needed a place to celebrate the promotion of one in their group, so they decided to check it out. Chuy had just started her shift when they arrived. They sat in her area, moving a few tables around so everyone could be together. Although they were rowdy, they were also polite with her and mostly kept to themselves, except for one man. He was quiet and very handsome. He had asked for her name when she brought their drink orders.

"My name is Corporal Contreras. You can call me Manuel. I actually just got promoted, so we're here celebrating my first day as a Corporal."

"Very nice to meet you, Manuel. Congratulations on your promotion, your first drink is on the house for a job well done. If you need anything else, please let me know."

He nodded and smiled in appreciation.

"Enjoy your time at Doña Licha's. I'll leave you to your celebration, I'll come check on you guys to make sure you're all taken care of. If you need anything at all, please let me know. My name is María de Jesús, but you can call me Chuy," she offered with a polite smile.

"You're very kind, Chuy. We're fine for now, but I promise I'll keep an eye on you in case I need anything else," he gave her a flirtatious wink.

The celebration didn't last all night. They decided to check out another place someone had recommended, and possibly to a third one. When Chuy went to clean the table, she noticed that the man she had spoken with had left a very generous tip, almost as much as they had spent on their entire tab.

The following night the new Corporal showed up again. He was alone. He stood by the table looking around until he saw her. He walked up to her, took off his hat, and smiled.

"Señorita María de Jesús, so nice to see you again. Would you please allow me to buy you a drink?" Manuel asked.

"Oh, thank you. That's very kind of you, but I am working, and I don't drink," she answered dryly.

"If I am not mistaken, you can drink if a patron buys it for you. Am I correct?"

"You are correct Manuel, but I don't drink. I appreciate the offer though."

"I guess I'll have to have my drink alone then," he concluded with a juvenile pout as he sat down at the table of his choice.

When she came back with his drink, she could tell that he was determined to at least have a conversation with her and would not easily give up. Chuy braced herself.

"So, tell me, what's a girl like you doing working in a place like this; full of alcohol and men?"

"I am working. What is wrong with that? And what do you mean by a girl like me?" she was offended "You don't know me."

"Well, you don't drink. A girl that doesn't drink."

"I don't have to drink to work in a place where I take drinks to people. I am making a living. Men and women come in and I take their order and if they want to drink alcohol, I bring it to them. What's wrong with that?" She had a tone of defensiveness.

"If you won't drink with me here, then allow me to take you to dinner. You do eat, don't you?" he asked sarcastically.

"I just started my shift so I can't go anywhere."

"How about dinner on your day off? I respect a woman who works hard to earn a living. I wouldn't want to disturb your routine."

"I am not off until Sunday, but I am already spoken for. I am engaged to be married soon; in case you're wondering. I'll save you the time you're starting to waste," she now had fire in her eyes.

"Oh! Well, what a lucky fellow, and congratulations to you. However, you're still not married, and I don't see the harm in having dinner with a friend, do you? We can go celebrate your engagement!" he insisted.

"I just met you, so we are acquaintances, not friends. Now, can I bring you anything else?"

"We can deal with all those issues at once if you go to dinner with me, get to know me, and we become friends. It's an easy fix."

"Corporal Contreras, I have already stated my situation and my decision. If you need anything else from the bar or the kitchen, I will send Lorena to take your orders. Now, if you excuse me, I have other tables to attend," she turned around and walked away.

"I won't give up easy Chuy. I just want you to know that." He paid his check to Lorena without even taking a sip from his drink and left.

She hadn't seen Manuel for over a week, and she was glad. He had been too direct, and his insisting manner annoyed her at best. At worst, she felt she was not in control when he was around her and she did not like that. Hadn't she made it clear immediately she was not interested? She thought he had been disrespectful in the way he had talked to her as if he was determined to get his way no matter what. There were absolutely no subtleties in his tone. She could tell he was a man who was used to getting what he wanted, who enjoyed dispatching orders and being obeyed.

With every passing day, the number of letters from her beloved kept piling up and so was commitment towards him. She was more impatient than ever after comparing Victor to Manuel. She wanted to see him again, to see his face and feel his hands in hers and his lips on her lips. Victor was always respectful, he never interrupted her, and she loved him for that. She appreciated his gentle ways with her, especially after having experienced Manuel's aggressive demeanor. She didn't think writing to Victor about corporal Contreras was a good idea. There was no point. Chuy felt confident she had put him in his place, and she didn't want to upset Victor or for him to worry about a thing. She would tell him after he came back for her and they were far away.

The following week, corporal Contreras came back with a couple of men. They were all in uniform. She noticed he had a single white rose with him, but she avoided him completely. He approached her and asked if he could talk to her alone, handing her the rose. They moved towards the bar so he could talk.

"María de Jesús, please allow me to apologize for the way I behaved last week with you. Accept my most sincere apology and this white rose as a token of my regret for what I did. I was wrong. I came on too strong and was disrespectful for not taking your choice into account when presented to me."

"Thank you corporal. I hope there are no misunderstandings about my decisions, I do appreciate the sentiment."

"Call me Manuel, please. I am not a selfish, perverted man as I appeared to be that day. I am a gentleman. I know it's not an excuse, but I had an awful day at work. Crime never rests, you know?" he offered.

"I am sorry to hear that."

"Clean slate, please?"

She looked at him with distrust.

"That's fine. Will you be ordering anything today?"

"Don't worry about it, Chuy. We'll order with Lorena. The last thing I want is to make you feel uncomfortable."

"It's fine, this is my job, and it will be my pleasure, really."

Corporal Contreras was not used to rejection, and she had hurt his ego. He was a handsome man, his strong voice compelled people to obey, not only his workforce subordinates, but people in general. He looked as if he could be ruthless and at the same time a misunderstood gentleman. His charisma afforded him certain privileges; he didn't have to be forceful when he wanted something. People tended to follow him like a bee to honey. He used that to his advantage to manipulate them.

After they made peace, he started frequenting the bar at night after his shift at work. After a couple of weeks, she thought he wasn't that bad. Her only bad experience with him had been with his rude aggressiveness towards her. But he apologized and treated her with respect after that. He was polite and a great tipper.

He began sharing about his marriage once he felt her guard had slowly gone down. He told her stories of his failing marriage, of his unhappiness with his wife, of his longing for true love. He talked to her with such apparent sincerity. He portrayed himself as a broken man and she felt as if her company helped lift his spirits.

Two weeks before Victor was to arrive, his letters stopped coming. He had mentioned in one of his previous letters that he was assigned to a special mission that was to last two weeks. He was still officially scheduled to return on the same date. He regretted that this mission prevented him from having any communication with anyone, including her, but that she should not worry. Everything would still go on as originally planned. This saddened Chuy greatly, but she understood the responsibilities and implications of his job. This did not deter her from continuing to write to him. From her point of view, nothing had changed. He would still receive her letters all at once when the mission was over.

Manuel kept visiting Doña Licha's with the intention of seeing Chuy. One night while having some drinks after work, he appeared to be uneasy or distressed. He didn't seem to be quite himself, maybe because he was drinking too much. He asked her to sit with him to chat during one of her breaks. She listened to him talk disrespectfully about his wife and it made her very uncomfortable. She let him vent his frustrations without interruption; that's what bars were for. He told her he was done with his wife, that he was leaving her, and that he couldn't live in that house anymore. He declared that his life was unbearable, and he was greatly unhappy.

Not feeling confident in matters of the heart, she felt inadequately prepared to provide him with any type of advice. The only help she could offer was to listen. He insisted that she was a good friend and thanked her for her kindness by being so attentive to him. He described how at ease he felt in her presence, and he liked her because she was a fine woman.

Then he abruptly grabbed her hands and told her in a drunken stupor that he was in love with her and that he had to make her his. She immediately got up from the chair and yanked her hands away from him.

"I certainly hope I have not given you the wrong impression for being a good friend to you, corporal. I will repeat what I said the first time we met, I am engaged to be married. I am in love with someone else. He is a very special man and we both deserve your respect." Chuy was appalled at his advances.

"And where is this gallant man you're so in love with?" he said mockingly standing up with his arms extended out and looking around the restaurant for her fiancé.

"How come I've never seen him around here before? Are you telling me this tale just so I will leave you alone? Or, if he does exist, how can he be so in love with you and not be here with his woman? Letting her work in a place where any man could propose indecencies to her? He must be a fool!" he laughed hysterically at his own observations.

Manuel then grabbed her arms and pulled her violently towards him and forcefully kissed her on the mouth. She could feel the unyielding smell of alcohol and cigarette smoke on his breath. His arms were strong. They were around her body holding her hard against him. She tried to get away from him but could not break free. When he finally let go of her, she slapped him across his face with all her might. He stumbled backwards and landed on the chair he was sitting on earlier. She was furious and terrified all at once. Her retaliation had left a hand mark burning red on his left cheek. He tried to get back up again but couldn't find his balance. He touched his face with his hand and felt heat coming from the spot where she had struck him. He laughed sarcastically. No one had ever hit him before, especially a woman.

Sergio saw everything and hurried to Chuy's aid. Everything happened so fast that when he got there Manuel was already on his feet once more, stumbling. The people at the other tables just watched, not daring to intercede. Sergio grabbed him by the arm and dragged him towards the door to kick him out.

As he was being thrown out, he yelled at her laughing, "I like you Chuy, and this only makes me want you even more!"

Chuy did not know what to do or how she had ended up slapping him. She had never laid hands on anyone before. Up to this point in her life, she had thought of herself as peaceful and rational. Suddenly, she had mixed feelings about what she had experienced and what she had done. She knew she needed to protect herself and her reputation, but it was still a form of violence. Chuy didn't recognize that what he had done to her was a violent act. She noticed Manuel's subtle and yet offensive cologne on her dress; she must've gotten it on her when he held her close against him. A thin layer of his aftershave mixed with a hint of musky sweat lingered on the hand she had used to defend her honor.

Although her coworkers tried to calm her down and make her feel better, the altercation made for a very long shift. She could not wait to go home, take her clothes off, get into a hot bath, and scrub any hint of him off her body.

The next day, a police officer named Juan Carlos showed up looking for Chuy. He had attended Manuel's promotion celebration at the bar. It was Chuy's day off and she had gone out. Don Sergio told Juan Carlos he could find her in the town's square in a very reluctant manner and asked what his intentions were towards her. He promised he was there to wave a white flag of peace from Manuel and assured him she would be safe.

On her days off, Chuy would go to the square and walk around the plaza where she and Victor would spend time. Sometimes she would catch a picture show at the cinema. She hated going by herself, but it reminded her of him so she would do it to satisfy her heart's longing. It helped her remind herself that soon they would be together again, and that time passes, no matter what.

She was sitting on the usual bench in the square when the private saw her. He had been very kind and respectful towards her in the past, so she didn't feel threatened when he approached the bench. She was careful though, because she knew he was Manuel's friend.

"Good day, Chuy. May I please sit?" the private asked politely.

"What do you want? If you're here to talk on behalf of your friend, I am not interested in the least. Do yourself a favor and just leave now."

"Please Chuy, let me talk to you for a minute. I promise you once I've said what I came here to say, I will leave you alone and will not bother you again."

She had her arms crossed and did not look at him.

"Make it quick, I would like to enjoy the rest of the afternoon and not think about unpleasant things caused by your friend Manuel," she said in a stern voice.

"Look, Chuy, he came to my house last night, he was drunk and very upset. I couldn't let him leave; he could've hurt himself in the condition he was in. He told me what happened to you; please believe me when I say this to you, that's not who he is. I don't know what has gotten into him. I seriously have never seen him like that, I honestly am worried about him."

"I don't care, none of this has anything to do with me."

"Well, you're right and you're wrong. See, he *is* in love with you and he's hurting because you don't reciprocate his feelings. He's also very unhappy at home and he's left his wife. He feels torn because now he can't see his children as often as he did before."

"I still don't see how any of this has anything to do with me. I have nothing to do with his unhappiness, his wife, his children, or his inability to accept rejection. I am not an object that he can take because he wants to possess it. He was a child when he threw a tantrum when he realized he couldn't have me. He is not my responsibility," she stood her ground.

"No, I totally agree with you. He's just hurting, and a broken heart makes people do certain things they wouldn't otherwise do. He really is a gentleman, if you give him a chance to get to know him..."

She stopped him right there.

"Don't talk to me about broken hearts. You know nothing of other people's difficult lives. I have my share of experiences and I have never had the urge to act in any inappropriate way because of it or even use it as an excuse. I am not interested in talking about Manuel anymore. No, he is not a gentleman. Gentlemen don't do what he's done. I cannot believe how he treated me, like a piece of property he can grab whenever he feels like it," her face flushed.

"I know. I understand that and so does he. Look, he was drunk and hurting. That's all I can say. Alcohol and pain mixed... look, he loves you. Give him a chance to at least talk to you so he can apologize properly. He feels terrible."

"Absolutely not! He's done enough. I gave him a second chance after the way he acted the day I met him. I don't want this to become a pattern."

"Okay, fine. Then, let's you and I talk about something else. We're friends, right? Tell me, who is this fine fellow you're engaged to? How come we never see him around?"

She sighed at the thought of Victor, thinking how different he was from Manuel. Victor was a real gentleman.

"We are not friends, private. I don't know you. But I don't want to discuss Manuel anymore."

"I promise," the private said, raising his right hand, then sitting down next to her.

"His name is Victor. He's a soldier in El Paso. He is very respectful, and he is a true gentleman. He makes me feel amazing. We are planning to get married as soon as he gets back from his special mission next week. He's coming to get me so we can get married and then move to Illinois where he is being reassigned. I can't wait to get out of here and never see your friend Manuel again."

"Whoa! I hear the excitement in your voice. You *should* be very excited about all this. I could see the change in your look when you started talking about him. That's great Chuy, I just hope he keeps his word," he said with a shrug.

"What do you mean? Why wouldn't he? You don't know him!" she snapped.

"Look, in the field I work in, we see a lot of American soldiers come to this side and they build grand castles in the sky for young inexperienced girls such as yourself and then they never come back for them," he said, shaking his head.

"We write to each other every day; I have all his letters. Of course he loves me! We are going to get married soon. Why would you think he would lie to me? That would be extremely cruel. You don't know him; he is not like that."

"Letters don't mean much to me. Why don't I see a ring on your finger?"

"I don't think that is any of your business. You, Private, don't know anything about him. And you sound just like Manuel."

"No ring and just a bunch of letters; seems awfully convenient is all I'm saying."

"There is nothing convenient about being separated due to his work, not seeing each other, the demands his job places on him. He has no reason to lie to me. You don't know what you are talking about and you're upsetting me. I'd like to be left alone now, please."

"Men don't need a reason to lie, Chuy. Don't be so naïve. Sometimes it's just the thrill of the chase, that's all."

"Well, he'll be here for me next week. We're meeting here on Sunday at 2 in the afternoon like we did every week before he left. I can't wait to leave with him, so I don't have to listen to your nonsense or Manuel's disrespect of me and Victor."

"I sure hope you're right; it would make me incredibly sad to see you suffer because of him."

She had nothing else to say so she left, and he stayed on the bench. She didn't want what Juan Carlos said to bother her, but she couldn't help it. He had already succeeded in planting a tremendous seed of doubt in her mind and she couldn't shake off the anxiety she started to feel. She wished she hadn't given him the time of day or so much information.

Once she was out of sight, the private laughed sarcastically, stretching his arms and legs while sitting on the bench where Victor and Chuy spent so much time together. He thought how easy it was to manipulate some women.

Chapter VII

Chuy hurried home and went straight to her room. She prayed to God for Victor's safe return; she knew that he would not be capable of the horrific behavior the private had talked about. What was wrong with him? She was emotionally taxed and decided to take out the box of letters from under her bed. She read them all from the first to the very last one. It made her feel better and his words reassured her of his love and devotion to her.

The night before the rendezvous with Victor she couldn't sleep, she kept tossing and turning in bed. When she finally went to sleep, she dreamed about him. She got up earlier that morning knowing that he'd been early every single time they met so she was planning on going to the square early enough to walk around.

She went to the square and sat on their bench by the gazebo. Her lips were dry, her palms sweaty. There was a knot of anxiety in her stomach, she was nervous with the anticipation of seeing him again. She missed him so much, especially in the previous two weeks when his correspondence had stopped.

She tried to imagine how her new life would be by his side, how different it would be to be married to him from her marriage to Alfredo. She wondered how Illinois looked and if it was much different from where she was now. She thought of the opportunities she would have; would she learn the language and assimilate into the new culture easily? Obviously, that was to be seen, but it was certain that whatever came her way, she was ready for it, especially with Victor by her side.

Meanwhile, two blocks from the international border bridge, private Juan Carlos and his patrol partner who went by "*La Perra*" had been driving around, back and forth along the border, for two hours. They were patrolling along the road that led to the bridge towards the square where Victor would walk to meet with Chuy. It wasn't a long stretch driving a vehicle, but it would take someone about an hour by foot. They started patrolling the street with enough time to make sure they could intercept the person they were looking for. Special attention was needed, since they did not know how he looked.

Far off in the distance, on the Mexican side of the bridge, they spotted a handsome young man walking alone. They had seen many people crossing, but they were either families or groups. This was the first lone male that matched the characteristics they were looking for. They followed him for a couple of blocks, maintaining their distance so as to not arouse any suspicion, but close enough to keep an eye on him.

After the third block, they turned on their siren, driving slowly next to him. *La Perra*, from the passenger side, lowered his window and politely asked him to stop walking. When he did, they parked the car in front of him and got out. Victor didn't know what to think and suspected they were possibly confusing him with someone else.

"Good afternoon gentlemen, is everything alright?" Victor asked with confusion.

"Why don't you tell us? As far as we are aware, American soldiers are not allowed to cross over the border. What are you looking for here?" questioned Juan Carlos.

"I am not in uniform, officer, it's my day off. Today I am a civilian and it is perfectly permissible for me to be here. I am here only for a short period, I have come to pick up my fiancé and I'll be gone before you know it," he answered happily.

"Oh, how romantic! You're not going anywhere, gringo. Get in the car!" commanded *La Perra*.

"Am I being arrested, officer? How did you know I am a soldier from the other side?"

"We know everything around this area and no, you're not being arrested. We are just so kind that we might just give you a ride to find your lady. It would be fun to be little cupids today, it's a slow day and we're bored" said Juan Carlos and both officers laughed sarcastically.

Victor reluctantly complied and got in the back seat of the car. He did not want to cause any trouble on this special day. He thought that nothing could ruin this day; he had been looking forward to it for weeks. Victor tried to focus on how he would finally get to hold his love in his arms again and it would be the beginning of a wonderful and happy life with her. This was obviously a mistake and if he was delayed, he could always go to Doña Licha's and explain what had happened.

"Or maybe not," said *La Perra*, and both laughed again as they made an abrupt turn.

Private Juan Carlos drove away with Victor in the opposite direction from where Chuy was waiting for him. Victor again tried to ask questions to find out what was going on, but to no avail. He told them that his fiancé was waiting for him and that she would be distressed thinking something had happened to him. He asked them to please put themselves in his shoes. He was certain they were trying to pass their time and have a little fun with him. He tried to talk some sense into them, maybe make them empathize, but they just laughed at him.

They stopped the car right on the outskirts of the city and parked in a vacant lot. Everything was deserted; no one was around. The officers violently dragged Victor out of the car and started beating him. They took turns punching him and kicking him while he was on the ground. At one point, Victor tried to get up and defend himself, but *La Perra* grabbed him from behind and held his arms while Juan Carlos took turns hitting him with his fist and his baton. When Victor was unable to stand on his own from the pain, *La Perra* let him go and he fell on his knees. He felt suffocating kicks on his stomach and his back. All he could do was cover his head with his arms as he crouched to a fetal position to try to minimize the blows.

Once they thought he had had enough, they grabbed him and slowly helped him back to the car as if they cared for his well- being. They asked him smugly to watch his head when getting in and shielded it with their own hands so he wouldn't get hurt. They drove slowly and told him the smooth ride back home was for his own good, that they cared so much about him that they were doing him a favor. Victor still did not know what had happened or why he had been abused by these corrupt cops. All he could think about was getting to the square and looking for Chuy. His face was bloody, one of his eyes was swollen shut, his clothes torn and dusty with patches of caked blood. He had a difficult time breathing and every time he took a breath, he felt stabbing pains on his sides. Struggling to speak, he asked to please be dropped off at the downtown square and he would leave soon after and promised to never come back. They laughed at him and asked him to forget about his fiancé.

"All women are the same, compadre. The sooner you realize that, the sooner your life will make better sense," said Juan Carlos.

"Please officer, I beg you. She's waiting for me!" Victor had started to cry.

"Listen, you idiot! She's not waiting for you. She got tired of waiting for you and she married my boss while you were gone. I'm telling you man; women are the devil. How do you think we heard about you and when you were coming? She told him everything and she was afraid you'd get violent with her for betraying you. He loves her, so he sent us to protect his bride. They're enjoying their honeymoon right now actually, as we speak," explained Juan Carlos.

"You're lying!" cried Victor, bloody spittle staining the back of the seat.

"Listen Victor, do yourself a favor and go back to gringoland where you came from and never come back, brother. Go to Illinois and make your life over there, maybe find a nice little *güerita* and have a lot of little *gringuitos*. Man! God bless the great American Dream... right, Perra?"

"Stop the car! Let me out. I'll walk there myself! I know she's waiting for me."

Victor tried to open the door, but it was locked. He wanted to jump out of the moving car and run to Chuy.

Juan Carlos stopped the car abruptly, which slammed Victor right into the back of the driver's seat, hurting him even more.

"Listen man, it's over alright? She belongs to someone else now. She didn't love you enough to wait. She's now a married woman and you should just walk away and let her be happy. If you love her, just let her go."

They arrived at the border and stopped the car to drop him off by right by the pedestrian walkway at the bridge. The officers helped him out of the car with care, and tried to fix his clothes, they patted him down to get rid of the dust. Juan Carlos took out a handkerchief from his pocket and gently cleaned Victor's blood off his face. Victor snatched it from him and tried to clean himself as best he could. He turned around and was visibly struggling to walk back to the other side. The struggle was both physical and emotional. After he had walked a few steps, *La Perra* yelled at him "if we see around here again, you won't survive the next go round *gringuito*. You better watch your back."

Victor walked towards the bridge, defeated, in pain, with a bruised body and a broken heart. He stopped halfway back, right in the middle of the bridge, pulled out a small red velvet box out of his pocket and looked at the ring inside it. He came so close to putting it on the finger of the woman he loved. He leaned towards the railing and extended his arm with the ring between his fingers. He was holding it so tight his fingers turned white at the tips. He closed his eyes, with tears rolling down his cheeks, he let out a pained groan and as he released his breath, he released the ring. The ring fell right in the middle of the Rio Grande, and he walked back to El Paso never to return.

Back in the square, Chuy impatiently waited for Victor on their bench, completely unaware that he would never come. It was a warm day, and she could feel droplets of sweat forming on her upper lip. Her hair was up in a bun to help with the heat. The sun was harsh. She got up to see if she could spot him and, on her way back, she purchased an *agua fresca* from one of the vendors. She stood under a tree fanning herself in relief, there was no sign of Victor.

She decided to take off her white gloves, which had added a touch of elegance to her outfit. They paired perfectly with the new dress she had made for their reunion. It was a beautiful navy-blue skirt with a white top that had matching blue polka dots. Her hands had initially started sweating because of her nerves and excitement at the idea of seeing her handsome sweet man. She could already smell his fresh cologne. Later in the day her hands were sweating because it was a hot day. Eventually she was sweating because of both the heat and her growing anxiety. Despite her concern, she was determined to wait for him the entire day if it was necessary.

Chuy waited for Victor for two hours after he didn't show up at the time they'd agreed to meet. She paced through the plaza slowly, running all possible scenarios in her mind, trying to remember his exact words. He had asked her to meet him at their usual spot. But what if he had told her to meet him at the restaurant? She was positive that everyone would have told him where she was if that was the case; everyone in the restaurant knew exactly what was happening that day.

What if something happened to him on his way? What if something had gone wrong at work during this secret mission and he was hurt somewhere, unable to get to her and unable to communicate with her? What if he had changed his mind or his heart? What if the private had been right? No, he couldn't be. She knew Victor and he was not that type of man. He loved her, she knew it like her name was María de Jesús. Those had been his words after all: he adored her and couldn't wait to marry her. It hadn't been an encrypted message potentially left for interpretation. They had both been explicit and completely honest about their feelings.

She was growing more afraid that something bad had happened to him at work. She tried to calm down. Chuy sat back on the bench and thought some more, trying to objectively assess the situation. She had to be patient and she had to believe in him. If something had happened to him, surely, he would let her know in due time why he couldn't show up for their meeting. She thought she would receive a letter or a telegram letting her know what prevented him from getting to her. He would give her new instructions for the new date of their reunion when it was possible. She remembered his words explaining his last mission was secret and he wouldn't be able to communicate with her, maybe the mission got extended and he was still working. Maybe he was not able to get a message out to her to let her know.

She decided to go back home and rest. The sun and the heat mixed with her emotional state had drained her energy almost entirely. She walked home with a heavy heart, praying to God for his safety. She had to be right, she had to trust her instincts. The private could not be more wrong on his assessment of Victor's character when he had never even met him. She told herself she would soon learn the reason for his delay, and they would go on with their plans as if nothing had happened. She would then remember this day as nothing but a bad dream.

Corporal Contreras had been watching her from the corner of the square at a vacant shoeshine stand since she had initially gotten to her bench. He pretended to read the newspaper while keeping an eye on her. When he saw her walking away, he felt an urge to approach her, but he didn't want to raise any suspicion. He could not afford to be found out, so he let her go and thought of maybe going over to the bar later that evening. Once she was out of his sight and around the corner, he folded the newspaper and thought that now that the wheels were in motion, he could work hard at making her fall for him. She would be in a vulnerable stage, feeling betrayed, abandoned, and forgotten. This worked to his advantage because now he would be there to console her.

Before he got up, he saw Juan Carlos and *La Perra* approach him slowly in the patrol car. They had been looking for him around the square where they were sure he would be. Both men were hoping to report the events that had just taken place with Victor. Juan Carlos was excited to recount what they had done step by step in meticulous detail; he was proud of his work. *La Perra* didn't say a word.

They were interrupted before they could begin.

"I don't need any details, private! The less I know about what happened, the better. Just tell me it was done," Corporal Contreras announced.

"Yes boss, it was done. You should've seen him! I'm positive he will never show his face around this place... or what's left of it," answered Juan Carlos laughing sadistically.

"Well, how can you be certain?"

"He believed every word we fed him."

"How do you *know*, private?" the corporal asked impatiently, raising his voice.

"You can see those types of things in a man's eyes, boss. Breaking a man's body doesn't do much, but when you break his soul, when you break his spirit, now that's something that will give you results. Only then can you do whatever you want with them. Let's just say that his spirit was shattered, and he mirrored that through the look in his eyes. They were like broken windows."

"Trust us boss, he's not coming back," *La Perra* added.

"Good" said the corporal. "Here's a little something for your troubles. You can split it between the two of you," Manuel answered satisfied.

The corporal felt assured. He knew that Juan Carlos liked to show off and most of the time talked too much, but *La Perra* was different. He was a man of action and didn't talk much. When he did talk, however, he did not play around. Overall, he was a very trustworthy sidekick.

"Christmas came early this year! Vámonos *Perra*, let's find ourselves some little ladies to spend this on," rejoiced Juan Carlos.

"Alright you two, now stay away from Doña Licha's. I don't want Chuy to see you, especially drunk. I can't afford to have you acting like idiots and possibly talk about what happened today. Everything must be perfect; I don't want her to suspect anything."

"You got it, boss!" said Juan Carlos firmly patting *La Perra* on the arm as they left. Once he was left alone, the corporal made a plan and decided to wait a couple of days before showing himself at the restaurant. After a few minutes, he went home to his wife and children.

Two days after the incident, Manuel went to have a late lunch at Doña Licha's before Chuy's shift started. He knew he would find her there. She was strong and would not let the disappearance of her fiancé interfere with her work. Without Victor, she did not have anywhere else to go and he knew she'd stay there in case he came to find her later.

Manuel was happy to know that the only obstacle that stood between Chuy and himself had been removed like a pest. He would make Chuy love him, even if it was the last thing he did. He sat in his regular spot and ordered dinner and a cold beer from Lorena without saying anything else. Lorena was typically a little bit of gossip, but even she knew that this was a painful and serious issue. With Victor missing, she tried her best to keep her mouth shut around Chuy to not hurt her. But not spilling the gossip around Manuel was beginning to feel like a challenge. She knew that Manuel was smitten with Chuy and would probably want to know that her fiancé never showed up. She had to fight her urge to tell him everything she knew about it, but she was going to be a good friend and keep the juicy information all to herself. She figured he would find out soon enough, and then she'd be free to give her two cents about it all.

When Chuy started her shift, she was absentminded and did not notice Manuel sitting in his usual spot. Doña Licha had given her two days off to try to get some rest and sort through her feelings and get her mind right. She was an emotional wreck when she got back home that day. No matter how much she tried to be positively objective, she couldn't help some of the bad thoughts that somehow wiggled themselves in. She had hoped to have heard from Victor by that time and not knowing what happened to him was killing her. She could not concentrate and had already gotten a few orders wrong, which never happened before; even when she had been a brand-new employee.

Manuel signaled to get her attention. When she didn't notice him, he got up from his chair when she walked by his table. She was so distraught that she had completely forgotten the way he had treated her the last time they saw each other. He gently held her hand and pulled her softly towards one of the chairs at his table and asked her to take a seat.

"Oh, Chuy! What a surprise, oh am I happy to see you here! I thought for sure that by now you would be gone," Manuel remarked, feigning concern.

"What are you doing here, Manuel?"

"Well, I stayed away like you asked me to, but I was sure you wouldn't be here anymore so I didn't see any harm in coming for dinner. The beers here are the coldest in town and the food is the best, you know this. You live here, don't you? I also couldn't stop thinking about you and I wanted to sit at my table. That's the only way I could think of to send you good vibes and good luck with my thoughts, even if it does sound silly," he said in a most sincere way.

She seemed as if she had not heard a single word, he had said to her.

"Please Chuy, talk to me. What's going on? You don't seem right. Is everything okay?" he asked with a concerned tone, still pretending complete ignorance.

"Victor did not show up when he was supposed to, when we had agreed to meet after his secret mission trip for work," she answered in a matter-of-fact way.

"What? That bastard! How could he?" He looked genuinely surprised and disgusted by the news.

"I am worried about him, Manuel. Please do not talk about him that way. Something must have happened. I know him and this is very unusual of him," she answered, defending her love.

"Well, you're right. I shouldn't speculate about cowardice on his part without knowing him. I hope he is safe. One never knows what happens in secret missions with the military. I mean, literally anything can happen."

"Last time I saw you, if I recall correctly, you said cruel things about him. What happened? Why are you here now hoping Victor is well?"

"Listen, Chuy. I know I was terrible. I was drunk and green with envy and jealousy to think of you in another man's arms. It was a bad combination of alcohol and weakness in human emotions. I regret everything about that evening because I care about you, and my behavior was very uncouth. I honestly hope he's fine and that you'll hear from him soon. I hate to see you this way."

"Do you really mean that?" questioned Chuy, wondering about his motives.

"Absolutely! Of course, I do, sweetheart. I care about you so much that I would rather see you with someone else if that makes you happy, than the possibility of me being with you."

"Thank you, Manuel. If this is true, this means so much to me. For a while I believed you were a jerk without any regard for anyone's feelings but your own."

"Come on Chuy. I recognize that at times I can be a little annoying and maybe come off as rude and arrogant most of the time, but I don't wish ill on anyone. As a matter of fact, I wish I could help you, I really do."

"That's very sweet of you but I don't think there is anything anyone can do to help me at this point. I don't even know what he did for work exactly. I never asked him, and he never told me. If there was only one way for me to know that I could possibly call them and ask them about him. I don't know what to do. He stopped writing when he went on his last mission because it was so secret. I still wrote to him though; I sent them to the only address I had from before but they were returned a month later. There was a note on the envelope saying he had been moved and the new address was classified. I still have those letters, you know? I was going to wait for him to get here so I could give them to him in person. Oh Manuel! What if something terrible happened to him in this mission of his? What if he got hurt or worse?"

She let out a deep sigh and started sobbing uncontrollably. Manuel got closer to her and held her tight. His shirt was wet with her tears and her hands were grabbing his shirt tightly, making pronounced wrinkles on his chest.

"Shhh, there, there. Everything is going to be fine; I promise. Don't you worry about a thing. I am positive he'll show up soon and will have a perfectly good explanation for everything that happened. His mission probably just got delayed. It happens all the time, you just never know."

"You really think so?" she asked with a hint of hope in her eyes.

"Of course, I do. He would be an idiot to have stood you up otherwise. Who would do that to a pretty little lady like yourself? I know I never would. You're amazing, Chuy."

She only heard the parts that had to do with Victor being delayed and that he would more than likely contact her soon. She wanted to believe that everything would be okay. Everything else he said escaped her, she was not interested.

The restaurant traffic started to pick up with time and she knew she had to get back to work; she had to get herself together. She told Manuel she had to get back to work. As she was getting up, Lorena walked by her and petted her on the shoulder.

"You stay there a little bit longer, doll. I got this for now. You've been having a bad day," Lorena whispered empathically.

Manuel told her she should listen to Lorena. He took out a handkerchief from his shirt pocket and dried her tears. He told her she could keep it. She felt comforted by him for the first time, and it felt good to hear him say things would turn out the way they are supposed to. It seemed that he had a good heart after all.

"Listen, Chuy. I know you're still at work and I just wish we could leave here and spend the afternoon together and chat so you can vent and feel better, but I also don't want to get you in trouble. So, I'll get the check and head out. But if you want and feel comfortable enough, let me take you out to coffee one of these days and we can just talk. I promise this is just a friendly invitation."

She felt like she had nothing to lose and could really use a friend outside of work. She accepted his invitation on the condition that it would be simply as friends; he agreed.

When Manuel finally left and she got back to work, she felt a bit better although her eyes were swollen, and anyone could tell she had been crying for hours and had hardly slept in a couple of days.

Chuy decided to do something different that night. Instead of working in the bar, she washed the dishes in the kitchen. This gave her time to think and assess her situation. As she performed her new duties that shift, she felt better for about an hour. Her spirits were lifted, and she became optimistic. She knew that no matter what, based on her life experiences, that no matter what happened, everything would work out. *Dios aprieta pero no ahorca*, she would repeat to herself.

Chuy had forgotten to eat during the previous two days. Sergio asked her when she had last eaten, and she couldn't remember. He shook his head and left to cook something special just for her. Sergio, Lorena, and Doña Licha would take turns subtly making sure she was comfortable. They would sometimes resort to coercion or force to try to get her to eat something small, when she insisted, she was not hungry. *Las penas con pan son menos, chamaca*. And so, she would eat.

Chuy stood by the sink and looked at the pile of dishes she still had to wash. For a slow night, there were still mountains of dirty pans, silverware, plates, and glasses. Based on the remaining stacks she almost wondered if any dishes had been washed at all. Maybe that was just a day in the life of a dishwasher. She wouldn't know, she'd never really been to the kitchen to work. That experience gave her some perspective on what it takes to do the different chores in the restaurant. She was able to appreciate the people that worked behind the scenes that no one ever sees, but made the restaurant run smoothly. Chuy had a new appreciation for the dishwasher. She couldn't imagine how the kitchen looked on the weekend when the place was packed.

Through her fatigue and heartbreak, she started with the larger pots to make the chaos look less crowded. One dish at a time she slowly rinsed food off them and then started scrubbing. The kitchen looked better simply by clearing some things. After an hour, it appeared as if half of the entire kitchen had already been cleaned out.

There was always a very meticulous way Chuy liked to do things. Always doing things right the first time was her mantra. *El flojo trabaja doble,* she would say. It was known that if things were not done right the first time, they would have to be done a second time. Chuy knew it was better to do them right and it saved time.

She moved some of the smaller items to the sink to start rinsing them before the scrub. The water was hot and soapy and felt good on her hands. The detergent's smell was also pleasant; it had been the same her mother used back home. She picked up a pile of plates and put them on one side. Her stomach had been growling for a while without her noticing.

The first few plates had beans and mole sauce still smeared on it. Everything on that plate reminded her of her mother's chicken mole. She remembered it being so good it was to die for, not too spicy and not too sweet; the sauce had the perfect thickness. A side of beans and rice would pair up perfectly. Simply reminiscing about that meal made her mouth water. She hadn't eaten chicken mole that tasted that good for at least a decade. There had been no delicious food after her father had remarried.

Chuy came out of her reverie and began rinsing the plates with her hands, feeling the beans and sauce with her fingers. Her stomach made a loud noise, and she felt a sharp pain at the pit of her gut. Her throat immediately formed a knot. She closed her eyes and tried taking deep breaths while her hands were still in the hot water. She remembered what it meant to not eat, longing to taste something, anything, and not being able to. She thought of her younger siblings, the ones her own mother had given birth to, and she could hear them crying in the middle of the night because they hadn't eaten. They would sleep in the same bed huddled up together and they could hear a symphony of growling stomachs. Chuy, having been the oldest in the house, was given the unofficial role of house servant, or at least that is how it felt to her. With a growing family, there were times where there was not enough food for everyone, and Chuy and her siblings were the ones to go without. However, there always seemed to be enough food for her stepmother and her stepmother's children. Chuy's father never found out about the neglect his children were being subjected to.

Chuy and her siblings would eat if there were leftovers after dinner. Only then would they be able to get something in their bellies. Their meals usually consisted of beans and hard corn tortillas.

Her stepmother and the children would eat chicken and beef when it was available, the rest of the kids would get gristle and fat with some broth. Sometimes they would get a piece of hard bread. At times, Chuy would give her own food to her siblings, so they had enough energy to learn something in school. When there was no food for days, it was impossible to sleep, and when sleep did come, so did the dreams.

Her nights of slumber were nothing short of feasts where there was an unlimited supply of food. The smell of the mole was so melancholic that she got emotionally transported back to Santiago. She could see a younger version of herself washing the dishes after dinner and hearing her stomach rumble. She saw herself licking the remnants of beans that were left on the plate after her stepmother had finished dinner with her kids. She remembered looking through the pantry for something to eat, anything. She felt weak after not eating for a couple days other than the occasional lick of beans off a plate or grim leftovers. She had looked in every corner of the house for food and was lucky enough to find a box full of vegetables.

Her stepmother had hidden them so well that she'd forgotten all about them and they had spoiled! Chuy was able to salvage some of the vegetables by cutting out the spoiled pieces and keeping the rest. She washed them making sure the mold was all gone and that afternoon, she and her siblings had vegetable soup for dinner. She hid it under the bed, and they ate it cold, she couldn't risk her stepmother finding out. Her stepmother never said a word about the missing vegetables, Chuy always wondered if she even remembered she had hidden them there. Chuy never forgot that day.

She had been experiencing a strange feeling in her stomach while washing dishes in the restaurant. It was a combination of hunger and anxiety triggered by the painful memories that had scarred her. Chuy had tried to repress the heartbreak from her youth, but everything comes back to the surface no matter how deep one tries to bury the problems.

The restaurant kitchen started spinning and she couldn't catch her breath. Soon she was on the floor hyperventilating and sobbing uncontrollably yet trying to not make any noise and raise any worry. She allowed herself time to embrace the feelings and the thoughts. She counted to ten and then back to one. She forced deep breaths into her lungs and reminded herself that she was in a new place. She was safe, that she would not go hungry again, ever. She had a choice, and that choice gave her power. The anxiety lasted for a few minutes before starting to subside. To Chuy, it felt like hours. She knew at some point she had to eat something and take care of herself. She vowed to never again allow her circumstances to dictate her mental or emotional state. She got up, confidently wiped her face, and asked Sergio for something to eat while she finished cleaning the kitchen.

"That's my girl" was all he said to her.

That evening Chuy went to bed with a full stomach and a busy mind. All the crying had liberated her soul from stagnation. For days she forced herself to remember her past pains, no matter how difficult it was. She methodically worked through them crying, embracing her anxiety, and then letting them go. All of her baggage was being left behind. This healing was the only way she could ever have a happy, or at least a peaceful, future with or without Victor. Everything in life had a purpose and her past had served its own.

Chapter VIII

Victor's mysterious disappearance worried and distracted Chuy. As much as she tried not to think about him, she couldn't help it. It was impossible to avoid, especially on her days off when she had all the time, without distractions, to think. She knew she had to do something. She couldn't continue feeling like she was in purgatory, that place between heavenly bliss and the hell of the unknown. She wanted to use her energy to concentrate on doing something more with her life, for herself and herself alone. It could be done, she thought.

She had just mourned the tragic loss of her husband, the devastating loss of her child, and now she would deal with the loss of Victor. If she never saw him again, she would deal with that, but she chose not to spend more of her life living for others. Ultimately, the main reason she had left Durango was to be her own person. Still being employed at the restaurant on days and on some busy nights at the bar was a blessing and Doña Licha was a godsend.

To fill her days further, Chuy decided to start taking clients who needed seamstress work. She could work on her days off. The years of sewing for her dolls as a child, and the practice of making her own clothes had given her great experience. Her dresses looked professionally made. She loved doing a good job and her meticulous attention to detail and love of her art helped her produce amazing work. *El flojo trabaja doble*, was her sacred mantra. She was going to use her vivid imagination with great diligence to create beautiful work that everyone would love.

Manuel kept visiting her periodically to "check on her and see if she had received news from Victor." The feelings of antagonism Chuy felt towards him started to diminish and she started to believe that he could be a good friend after all. He had been so supportive of her after Victor disappeared, something she had never thought he'd be capable of. She even felt guilty for misjudging him and his intentions. She thought maybe she had been too tough with him.

She forgave his arrogance, telling herself that he most likely felt pressured to be a "real man" in front of his subordinates. That's the way men in power are, after all. He had to let everyone know he was to be respected, he had a new position and added responsibilities to his duties. His behavior was excused with the mentality that boys will be boys, and just like that all of that was in the past.

A couple of months had passed with no word from Victor. By this time, Chuy started to think that she would never see him again, but never lost hope that maybe one day she would know the truth. *La esperanza es lo último que muere,* she would tell herself in times of desperation.

Manuel showed up on one of her days off and convinced her to get out of her room and have a little bit of fun. She had been working nonstop for weeks. She agreed to take a break and clear her head and loosen up a bit. He offered to take her to a show with a live band that played great *danzón,* Cuban music made popular in Mexico. She immediately agreed. There was no damage in having a little bit of fun.

The night was undoubtedly very pleasant, just what she needed. They sang and danced the night away, music made even her internal organs happy with its rhythm. She had a great time with him. There was some newfound affection towards him. She felt he respected her, he gave her the space she needed, and he was helping her not think about Victor so much. She had never had alcohol before that night. There were more stories than she could talk about violent, drunk men losing their lives all because of alcohol and not wanting to "lose face" in front of others. Chuy had witnessed alcohol cause so many problems.

Manuel had a certain quality to him that allowed him to have his way all the time. He was able to convince Chuy that alcohol could be consumed in a responsible manner, and he promised to take care of her. She tried one drink and her face felt flushed. In no time, she started to feel more relaxed, allowing herself to let loose. She had never felt that way before, as if nothing that had happened to her mattered. Only the present and the future mattered now, and she knew her future would be bright. She had another drink. She was ready to leave her past pain behind. It was time, she thought. She would not wait for Victor and allow him to hold her back anymore. If he ever showed up then they could work things out, but she wasn't going to sit around waiting for him.

She had one more drink and they joined the dancers, the lovers, and the free spirits. Manuel kissed her on the dance floor and this time, she didn't stop him.

The next morning when she woke up, she found Manuel sitting on her bed, next to her. He had been watching her sleep and stroking her hair. She couldn't remember much from the previous night. The pain she felt pounding in her head prevented her from asking him too many questions. She didn't want to be rude in her disoriented state, so she stayed silent. He handed her a glass of water and a couple of aspirins. He looked at her with a smile on his face.

"Take these please, they will make you feel better and make your headache go away." Manuel was talking gently, almost whispering.

"I hope you don't mind, but I've prepared a hot bath for you. It's ready for you; here let me help you. You'll feel like new afterwards."

"Thank you" was all she could say and taking his hand, she got out of bed. She was wearing his undershirt and she felt vulnerable and uncomfortable.

She took the pills with the water he gave her and massaged her temples softly. She had never felt that way before. Until this moment, the worst she had ever felt was after crying for two full days when her baby perished. This was much worse, in the physical sense.

"I ordered breakfast from the restaurant. I asked Sergio to wait a bit to start it, I hope it will be ready by the time you are done with your bath. You'll need to eat something, even if you don't feel like it. I promise it will make you feel better. I'm starving but I'll wait for you so we can eat together, okay? I'll be outside smoking a cigarette while you bathe, and then I'll bring breakfast as soon as it's ready. I'll make sure to knock first."

"Thank you," she whispered.

Chuy did not fully understand what was happening. She didn't remember much after the kisses they shared on the dance floor the night before. She remembered his strong arms embracing her and his hands caressing her curls. His eyes on her revealed a sort of admiration, obsession, love maybe. They sparkled when he was with her now. This new look of his was different from the one he had when he first tried to force a kiss on her months prior.

She did not love him. In fact, she had just learned to tolerate him. She needed to think about what had just happened. She submerged in her bathtub completely and felt a sense of relief although she was still hungry and tired. The desire to go back to her bed convinced her to work on her sewing at another time.

The bath was a blur and eventually she got out. She carefully dried herself and put some fresh clothes on. Manuel had been right, that bath was just what she needed. She thought about him, and wondered how old he was. He had to be at least twenty years older than she was. He'd been married a long time and had older children, maybe almost her age. She smiled thinking of the soft kiss from the night before and then laughed thinking what her town-home people would think of her if they found out. There would be so much gossip for a while. Thank goodness she had left that place behind.

There was a knock on the door and immediately after he walked in carrying a tray with food. The knock was not so much for permission to come in, but an announcement that he was entering. He had a bouquet of red roses under his arm, a half-smoked cigarette in his lips, and a smirk of triumph. She ignored that he entered her home like he now owned the place. She watched as he carried everything to the other side of the room where he placed the tray and flowers on the small table in the corner. She was too tired and ill to think about his mindset right now. All she needed was food and more rest. On the tray, Manuel brought coffee, fried eggs, potatoes, beans, and some warm tortillas. Nothing seemed or felt right, and they ate in awkward silence.

When they were done with breakfast, he got up and put all the empty dishes on the tray, kissed her on the forehead and headed towards the door while taking out a cigarette out of the pack with his free hand.

"Get some rest, kid. You need it. Tomorrow you will feel new. Maybe put the flowers in some fresh water so they last longer."

He winked at her as he turned to go. She realized at that moment that she was not interested in whatever game Manuel was trying to play. She thanked him for the breakfast and the bath as he left. She left the flowers where he had placed them, laid back in bed and fell asleep.

When she woke up later that afternoon she felt as if she had not felt in a very long time; relaxed. She had never felt so rested and, despite the strange developments with Manuel, there was not a trace of worry in her mind. She kept thinking of her plan to be independent and it was as if a weight had lifted. From now on she would continue to work hard, create, learn, make money, and most importantly she would get over Victor. She prayed for his safety, for his well- being, and for his happiness wherever he was; then took a deep breath and released him. By letting him go in this manner, his absence would no longer weigh down on her heart. She was free.

Chapter IX

Nine months later, in March, Juan Manuel was born; shortly after Chuy had turned twenty. She had reluctantly stopped working at Doña Licha's as soon as Manuel found out that she was pregnant. He stated his opinions very strongly and he never wavered. There was no way he was going to allow for the mother of his child to work, not in an environment where alcohol and men were involved.

Manuel rented a small house close to the US border on the other side of town and they moved in when she was three months pregnant. She missed working, but she especially missed the people, they had always been so sweet to her and helped her in whatever way they could. She felt indebted to Doña Licha for having helped her so much when she first arrived in the city. She was like a mother figure to Chuy from the beginning.

Manuel had a very complex schedule consisting of a rotation of long shifts between days and nights, so she was often alone with the baby. She had continued her work as a seamstress from home and the only time she went out was to purchase material for the orders she had. She had bought more than enough material to last her a few months, this would allow her to work uninterrupted while the baby was still an infant. When the baby was a few months old and she felt safe taking him out, she loved to go downtown. She would visit her favorite store and return home with bags filled with buttons, zippers, thread, and cloth, and the baby strapped to her chest with a shawl. The trip downtown would take her almost two hours via bus since she had to transfer three times, but she enjoyed getting out of the house.

The neighborhood they lived in was not completely developed yet and there were almost no neighbors. They lived a quiet life, and she was grateful for the silence. Juan Manuel was a good baby who almost never cried, so her time off work allowed her creativity to be unleashed. She sketched the many ideas she had on the graph paper notebooks she had purchased while still living at Doña Licha's. Most of these sketches would end up as actual dresses that she had designed for herself, her clients, and the new baby. This new career made her feel more useful than ever and somewhat independent.

For weeks she had gone to the fabric store with Juan Manuel without any issues. She would catch the bus a few blocks from their house on one of the main roads. Manuel's three older unmarried sisters lived alone in a house on the way to the bus stop. Chuy had not met them yet because according to Manuel, they were almost never home and were very busy. She told him she had been thinking about dropping by to introduce herself and the baby, but he was against it. He promised he would soon plan a dinner where introductions could be made. She didn't think much of it.

One day on her way to the bus stop, Chuy saw the three sisters sitting on the porch of their house. She thought that if she had more time, she would stop by to meet them, but since she was running late, she did not want to risk missing the bus. She could hear the sisters yelling something and looking towards her as she was approaching.

She walked towards their porch and, with a smile on her face, she waved at them and said, "*Buenas tardes.*"

One of the sisters got up from her chair and threw a rock at her, missing her by a few inches.

A second one got up and yelled "*zorra, mujerzuela, eres una prostituta!*" Shortly after, the third one yelled "*roba maridos!*" also throwing a rock. She knew she wasn't a slut, a bad woman or a prostitute and she also wasn't a husband snatcher. He wasn't with his wife when they moved in, at least that's what he had told her.

Chuy covered the baby with her arms to protect him from harm and started to run to get away. As she went by, she could hear the sisters yelling at her, they were all obscenities. She wished the earth would swallow her, baby and all.

She did not feel safe until she was inside the bus. It was shortly before rush hour so there were plenty of empty seats available. Once in her seat, she frantically inspected the baby to make sure he had not been harmed. She covered her face with her headscarf and cried while holding her child close and rocking him to ease his fussiness. Nothing could make her understand what had just happened. Is it possible that the sisters were confusing her with someone else? Why were they yelling those terrible things and throwing rocks at her? She hadn't done anything to them. She knew she had done nothing wrong; not to them or anyone else.

On the way back home later that afternoon, Chuy got off the bus a few blocks away from her usual stop and took a different route back to the house. She did not want to have another dangerous encounter with Manuel's sisters.

During dinner she told Manuel what his sisters had done to her and his son and demanded an explanation. They did not know her; how could they be so callous? They weren't even interested in Juan Manuel; he had their blood running through his veins!

"Listen Chuy, I had been married to my wife for a long time. They all love her, and they probably think that they must pick sides. You know how women are, nothing but drama. It's possible they feel loyalty only to their friend, my ex-wife, and accepting you into the family probably feels like they'd be betraying her. After all, she was part of their family for almost twenty years," he said without an apology.

"You're really going to sit there and defend them? I don't care if they don't like me, *no soy monedita de oro*, they don't have to accept me, they don't have to talk to me, and they also don't have to be interested in meeting their nephew, your son! But they also had no right to yell those terrible things at me, they don't know me, Manuel. They threw rocks at us. They could've hurt your son! If you don't care about my well-being that is one thing, but they could've hurt your son! Do you understand that?"

"Calm down, *mujer;* nothing happened. You and the baby are fine. I promise I will talk to them and put them in their place. They can't be behaving that way," he said without interrupting his dinner.

"I'm telling you, either you put a stop to it and keep us safe or I swear I will leave and take my child to a safe place where those crazy women can't hurt us," she threatened.

He slammed both palms on the table and got up with a look on his face that made her body feel cold all over.

"He is my son, and you will not take him anywhere," he bellowed. "I will put those three bitches in their place, and they will not ever act that way towards you again and I also don't want to *ever* hear you say that again. Understood?" His voice shook with anger.

"Thank you, Manuel. I just want him safe, I will not lose another child," she replied in a submissive tone.

He wiped his mouth and walked towards her. Kneeling in front of her he softly took her face in his hands and tried to convince her he would keep them both safe.

"I love you both more than anything else in this world. They will not bother you again. I give you my word."

Manuel was the youngest of five and his older siblings had always spoiled him. He grew up believing that no matter what he did, he would always be right in the eyes of his family members. Unfortunately, this time, no one approved of his relationship with Chuy. They firmly believed that marriage was forever. They felt he should not have left his wife, whom he had been married to for twenty years and had several children with. They saw Chuy as an evil temptress that seduced him by casting a love spell on him. They could not understand the hold they believed she had on him, and for this, they never forgave her. They did not know Chuy, but they knew they hated her. She and her child would never be accepted as part of the family.

The sisters stopped blatantly antagonizing Chuy after Manuel talked to them, but they would still sit on the porch and stare her down when she walked in front of their house on her way to the bus stop. Sometimes they would start walking in the same direction as her and follow right behind her, making her feel very nervous. They used different intimidation methods, but Chuy wasn't scared. She knew Manuel wouldn't let anyone hurt them. The bus stop became her sanctuary. She would leave her house just with enough time to make it. She would reach the stop just as the bus was arriving to pick up its passengers and with no time to spare. Chuy would get on the bus and the sisters would stand there staring at her, sometimes they would point and laugh. Only after the bus had taken off would they walk back to their house. They may not have yelled at her or thrown rocks, but the harassment continued, nonetheless. They enjoyed bullying her.

The toxic environment started to wear on Chuy. She even had a difficult time concentrating on her seamstress work. Every little noise she heard outside her house made her nervous and she was starting to lose sleep at night. She would wake at all hours to check on Juan Manuel. While she worked, she would stop and look inside his bassinet to make sure he was safe. Those evil sisters lived too close, and she knew they hated her and her son; she could not convince herself they were safe. She had talked to Manuel about it again, but he assured her they would not hurt her or the baby. That didn't ease her mind though. She knew he thought she was overreacting. It always felt like he was equating her fear to irrationalities. She lived in constant anxiety, especially when Manuel worked the night shift and she was alone in the dark house.

The last straw for her came when she was making breakfast one early morning. She had moved the baby's bassinet to one of the windows next to the kitchen. She liked for the baby to get some morning sun. She heard a loud noise that startled her and immediately ran to the baby. The window was broken, there was a large rock lying in the middle of the living room, and shards of glass inside the bassinet. Someone had physically tried to harm them. There was glass everywhere and the baby had gotten scared and was crying inconsolably. She thought the baby had gotten hurt and, for the first time in her life, she was filled with rage. She immediately grabbed him and inspected him thoroughly, removed all his clothes, and bathed him. When she was done, she put some fresh clothes on and wrapped him tight in a light blanket. He was left on the bed while she cleaned up the shards. The exhausted baby fell asleep right after the bath.

While he slept, Chuy returned to the site of the assault. She picked up the rock and noticed a rubber band around it holding a piece of paper. It was a note that read, "Manuel's real wife is pregnant with their fifth legitimate child." She didn't care about the note or what it said. All Chuy cared about was her son's safety and the fact that the rock could've hurt him. She was done worrying about Manuel and his drama.

She packed a few of her things and all the baby's clothes and went out to catch the bus. She had all of her savings with her; she was leaving and had decided not to look back. All this was much more than she could tolerate. She just wanted to be happy and safe, and she knew she wouldn't have either if she stayed with Manuel.

When she got to Doña Licha's, everyone was surprised to see her there, but happy to be able to hug her and finally meet the baby boy. Lorena brought her something to eat and while they all had breakfast together, she told them why she had left. Doña Licha mentioned her old room had not been rented out yet and she could stay as long as she needed to, pinching Juan Manuel's chubby little cheeks. Chuy had barely touched her breakfast; she was still in shock.

"Come on child, eat! Always remember, *las penas con pan son menos,*" barked Doña Licha.

Lorena laughed.

"What are you laughing at, Lorena? What the hell is so funny?" asked Doña Licha, confused.

"Well, maybe that's why we all keep gaining weight! Because we try to drown our sorrows in all that mole sauce." Lorena answered, covering her mouth playfully.

Chuy was happy to be back surrounded with familiar faces where she could feel safe. She knew these people loved her and they would never hurt her.

Chapter X

Two weeks after being back at Doña Licha's, Chuy decided to go out on a walk with the baby. She needed to think about what she was going to do next. She hadn't heard from Manuel since the last time she saw him at home but knew that there was no hiding from him.

He knew Doña Licha's was the only place she would go, she had no one else. Chuy thought that maybe he had decided to go back to his wife since she was having his baby and was relieved. She had gone out before, but the baby had stayed home with either Lorena or Doña Licha. Everyone at the restaurant would talk to baby Juan Manuel as if he understood the conversation. He was told stories and current events and was even asked questions. The baby would move his little arms and legs with excitement at the bonding interactions.

Today she was taking the baby on a stroll in the square. She wanted to talk to her baby about the importance of that place, show him her favorite bench, the gazebo, and the street vendors that she'd gotten familiar with. Then suddenly, she felt the hairs behind her neck stand up. Something was wrong, she could sense it. It was a feeling of being watched or followed. She turned to look at the street and saw a patrol car driving slowly right behind her. She did not recognize the officers in the vehicle but felt very anxious.

"Good afternoon, officers," she said with a steady voice.

"Good afternoon, madam," the officer on the passenger seat replied.

They sped up and stopped the car right in front of her. Startled and her heart in her throat, she thought she was going to panic. It took all the energy in her body to stay calm. Both officers got out of the car and walked towards her. One grabbed the baby trying to snatch him from her arms. She tried to cling on to him as much as possible, but the officer was forceful, and she didn't want Juan Manuel to get hurt.

"Let him go please, you don't want him to get hurt, do you?"

She let go of her grip. The other officer grabbed her arm and pulled her towards the vehicle.

"Let's go, get in the car," he demanded in a low voice.

"What have I done, officer? You have the wrong person! Let me and my child go!" Chuy begged.

The two men laughed.

"We have the right person, alright. Of that, we are certain," said the officer with the baby in his arms.

"Am I being arrested?" she asked frantically.

"You'd keep your mouth shut if you knew what's good for you," the driver answered.

Chuy sat in the back seat of the patrol car trying not to panic. She would feel better if she had the baby in her arms. The officer in the passenger seat was playing with him; there was baby talk from both officers, and Juan Manuel laughing innocently playing with the man's mustache.

"Please don't hurt him!" she pleaded.

They completely ignored her, refusing to answer any of her questions. She didn't know what she had been picked up for. It didn't seem like an arrest, they hadn't handcuffed her, they hadn't read her any rights, and she hadn't done anything wrong. She knew some of the particulars of what an arrest looks like because Manuel had shared some stories with her.

After what seemed like a very long drive, they arrived at a police station. They hadn't taken her downtown, where she thought they would, but to a station on the outskirts of the city. Without turning the engine off, the driver got out of the car and opened the door for her and asked her to get out.

"What about my son?" she asked him, with panic in her eyes.

"I said, get out of the car," the officer yelled, grabbing her arm and dragging her out. His fingers were digging deep into the soft flesh of her slightly plump arms.

"My son, give me my son back!! Where are you taking him? What will happen to him? My son needs me, give me back my son!" She tried to remove her grip from the officer, but his fingers kept digging in deeper. He held her arms tight with both of his hands and threatened to handcuff her if she continued resisting.

"Listen, your son will be fine, I give you my word. Now, you need to calm down and cooperate. Don't make a scene, please," the officer carrying the baby told her in almost a whisper. There was a hint of compassion in his gaze.

"Tell me why I'm being arrested! Did Manuel pay you to do this?" she demanded an explanation.

"I can't talk about that with you, I shouldn't even be speaking a single word to you. Just be patient, everything will turn out fine," he replied, fixing his gaze towards the floor.

"Please, help me!" Chuy pleaded.

"I'm sorry ma'am, I really am. I promise your baby boy will be safe." He got the baby close enough for her to kiss his tender brown face before taking him away as the other officer pulled her arm and shoved her inside the building.

When they walked inside, he took her directly to the back of the building. There, he let her go and opened a metal door then asked her to walk inside. She refused to move, holding her head high and looking directly into his eyes. He sighed and shoved her in, though she did not resist. The place was musty and humid; she could not take the terrible smell and gagged while her stomach turned. There were cockroaches on the ceiling, crawling in the cracks on the walls and corners. She tried not to panic and to maintain her composure, her pride, and her dignity. She didn't care what happened to her anymore, her only concern was Juan Manuel's safety. The officer walked her inside the cell and locked it on the outside at once. He avoided looking her in the eyes and as he was leaving, he murmured, "I'm sorry" before leaving her alone with her thoughts and fears in that filthy place.

No one had asked her for name, they hadn't recorded her arrival with the officer at the front desk, yet they knew exactly who she was. The officer had promised her the baby would be perfectly safe. Everything seemed so implausible. She contemplated everything that happened that day, and like a punch in the gut, she knew. There was only one thing she could have done to end up in a place like that. Would Manuel really be capable of doing something so low to the mother of his own child? Her confusion was gone, she knew exactly what had happened and the crime she had committed. She sat on the bunk and tried to collect her thoughts. A whirlwind of emotions overtook her.

She felt an immense need to cry, to sob, and to scream, but her body would not respond; she was completely numb.

She inspected the cell and although there was very little light coming from the skylight, she was able to see a toilet on the other side of the room. There was a bucket of water next to the bed. Chuy inspected the bed for cockroaches, and it appeared to be clean, with semi-fresh sheets and one blanket. She was still in shock, her mind racing, her vivid imagination along with a million questions were running through her mind. She didn't know what else to do but pray and as soon as she did, she was able to cry. The Virgin Mary and the Santo Niño de Atocha were her favorite to pray to.

"Oh, dear virgin Mary, mother of God, please do not forsake me. Please afford serenity in my heart so that my mind can think." She prayed furiously.

She prayed the rosary three times in a row just as her mother had taught her when she was a child. She didn't have her rosary or any beads, so she counted the prayers with her fingers. Prayer always helped her clear her mind and feel less anxious when she couldn't control her circumstances or situation. She needed to think and act, she was going to get her baby boy back if it was the last thing she did.

After finishing the rosary, Chuy realized she hadn't eaten anything, and her stomach was growling incessantly. She did not know how long she had been in that cell, but she could see it was dark outside by looking through the skylight. Her mind recalled her plan earlier that day. She was going to stop at one of her favorite restaurants to eat with her baby boy. All of that had been ruined by those two officers. With the way things were going, she assumed there would be no dinner that night. She was spent and her knees hurt. She remembered when she was a little girl learning to pray the rosary, complaining to her mother that she was in pain, she asked if she could sit or stand instead.

"The fact that we are kneeling even though it hurts must be very pleasing to Our Lady, the virgin" her mother had told her in a soft voice while stroking her hair softly.

"Why?" she asked.

"We are showing our devotion to the most holy, my daughter, and not running away for comfort when we feel pain. Even if we cringe in agony during the entire rosary, imagine the pain our Lord endured on the cross for our sins. A little bit of pain on our part is nothing compared to his sacrifice for the forgiveness of our sins," her mother explained.

Chuy never questioned again, and with great pride she would always pray the rosary on her knees, convinced that kneeling showed God that she was a faithful, submissive, and a faithful servant. She got up slowly and sat on the bed for a few minutes, made the sign of the cross with her eyes closed, and tried to get some rest.

The next morning when she woke up, there was some light illuminating the cell through the skylight. She didn't want to use the toilet so she held her bladder as long as she could. She promptly realized there was no telling how long her nightmare would last so, she changed her mind. She sat where the toilet seat was supposed to be. Holding on to the wall with one hand and her knee with the other, she prevented herself from falling in the toilet. She waited in that manner for a few minutes until she felt she was dry enough; there was no tissue in the cell. She then washed her hands and face with the water in the bucket and heard her stomach growling again and that sound of hunger was difficult to ignore. She had not been that hungry since she was a young girl in Durango.

There was a sound at the other end of the hallway, the main door to the corridor had opened and she could hear steps getting closer. An officer who she hadn't seen before stopped in front of her cell door with a tray of food. She tried to talk to him, ask him if he knew why she had been arrested, if she'd get to talk to a judge or a lawyer, if he knew when they would let her go. He looked at her in an apathetic way and did not respond. He gave her the tray of food through a slot in the cell bars, gave her a sarcastic smile, and said "I hope you enjoy your meal madam."

She was desperate. What she had in hunger, she lacked in appetite. Her only emotional escape was to cry and pray so that's exactly what she did.

"Dear Virgin Mary, I turn to you for protection. Oh, holy Mother of God, please listen to my prayer and help me in my hour of need. Save me from danger and protect my baby boy. I humbly beg of you to intercede for me before Christ, your beloved son, and our Heavenly Father in heaven. Oh, most merciful mother, please do not forsake me. You, that are so close to the Holy Spirit, bring peace into my heart so that I can forgive. Do not allow my spirit to become hard and full of hate. Oh, Holy Mother, I welcome you into my heart just like the beloved disciples welcomed you into their homes, for you are the mother of all the living. I place all my hope in you and the Holy Spirit...

...Mary, that never was it known that anyone who fled to your protection, implored your help, or sought your intercession was left unaided. Inspired with this confidence, I fly to you, O Virgin of virgins, my Mother; to you do I come; before you I stand, sinful and sorrowful. Oh, Mother of the Word Incarnate, despise not my petitions but in your mercy hear and answer me. Amen."

Chuy prayed and cried with desperation for hours. She had never been apart from Juan Manuel and his absence was more than she could bear. Not being close to her son reminded her of the loss of her most cherished baby girl and the pain in her heart was insufferable.

She approached the breakfast tray, the food cold and unappetizing; there were a few flies hovering around it. She took a cold and hard biscuit but took a bite out of it anyway. She had no appetite but was aware she had to maintain her strength. She had been nursing, so she knew she needed to be healthy in order to produce milk. The thought of Juan Manuel and being reunited with him is what kept her going.

She wondered how long it had been since the officer had brought her breakfast when she heard the door open and recognized the footsteps. With a loud sigh and not a single word he swapped the seemingly untouched breakfast tray with lunch.

"You've got to eat something you know? I can't have you get sick on me. I don't know you and I don't really care about what you do or what happens to you here. If something does happen to you, I might get in trouble, and I can't have that. So, make sure you eat your lunch. I don't want to have to resort to force".

There was no reply from the cell. He walked away.

Chuy took the tray with her to the bed and tried to eat some of it. She didn't know what it was exactly, but it looked like oatmeal mixed with rice, soggy and sticky. She gagged as she took the first bite but forced herself to swallow. She couldn't eat any more so with tears in her eyes, she returned the tray back to where she picked it up. Exhaustion from all the crying had set in and laying down on the bed to rest, she immediately fell asleep. She dreamt of her babies Daría and Juan Manuel playing together on the floor back at Doña Licha's. The three of them were blissfully happy and she could not remember a painful time in her life. That is all she had wanted, peace, happiness, and the safety of her babies. In her dream, she felt like nothing could touch her and dropping to her knees, she thanked the Virgin Mary for answering her prayers and promised to never leave her children.

Several hours had gone by when she woke up with a clammy face. The cell was damp, and the air was stale, she felt suffocated. Thinking about the dream, once more she dropped to her knees and prayed with the most faith a human being can possibly have.

"Oh, dear Virgin Mother, if anyone can understand my broken heart it is you. You who saw your only son suffering on the cross, I beg of you, take pity on my poor soul. Help me get back to my child for he needs me and I need to be with him. I will die of sorrow if I don't ever see him again. I will do anything to never lose him again, anything. Oh, Holy One, I am now certain of the reason I am here and I give you my word that if I am reunited with my boy, I will never try to leave again. I will never place myself or my child in danger. In the name of Jesús Christ, Amen."

In desperation, Chuy had just given herself a life sentence with a man she despised in the hopes that she would be with her son again. She was willing to sacrifice her entire life for Juan Manuel, *y que sea lo que Dios quiera*.

That evening, a new officer showed up with a dinner tray. As if instructed to give her the silent treatment, he was gone in a matter of seconds after swapping the old tray for a new one. He didn't even look at her; she was invisible in that place. This time, with her heart full of hope, she ate everything that was given to her and tried not to pay attention to the awfulness of the food. She walked around the cell for a few minutes; she didn't want to go to bed on a full stomach. As she paced, she did the only thing that made her feel better; she prayed.

That night as soon as she went to bed, she had disturbing dreams about Manuel and his sisters. In one of the dreams, Manuel harassed his sisters, yet they took revenge on Chuy. They barged into her house and two of them dragged her out of the house while the third one took the sleeping baby from his bassinet. They threw her in a dark and foul-smelling room then she realized she was locked inside an outhouse back in her hometown. The room was dark, but some light came in from between the boards that made up the room. She could hear the buzzing of flies flying around her and, if she tried very hard, she could see cockroaches running up and down the walls. Chuy started to panic. There was a rat by her feet trying to climb up her leg. She could feel its tiny legs on her shin and the tail dragging behind it. She shook her legs and waved her arms in the air and started screaming.

She woke up from her nightmare and saw a real rat eating the remnants of food that she'd left on her dinner tray. She moved to the corner of the bed against the wall and hugged her legs to her while keeping an eye on the rat. It was probably daybreak as the skylight no longer appeared pitch black. Frantic, she could not go back to sleep knowing there was a rat in her cell, so again she prayed.

Chuy could not imagine herself being stuck inside the cell for much longer.

The sun came out and its rays eventually lit up the room through the skylight. She was startled by a loud noise from the corridor door and realized she had dozed off. Chuy frantically looked for the rat, to no avail.

When the officer from the previous morning appeared at her cell, he found her standing on top of the bed looking around the room in panic.

"You haven't been in here that long to have lost your mind. What on God's earth are you doing? Come, get down from there. You're going home," he said in a monotone voice.

"What? I'm going home?" she answered incredulously.

"Would you rather stay in this place? If that's what you'd like just let me know, we can make arrangements," he said with a snide chuckle.

"No, please! Get me out of here, I need to see my son!" she cried.

"Well let's go then," the officer said as he opened the cell door.

Chuy didn't know how or why she was being let go, but she wasn't going to argue against it. He gently held her arm with his strong hand as he led her through the corridor and out the door to the main office. Being in a shadowy cell for almost 48 hours made her eyes sensitive to light and it took her a few minutes to adjust to this room full of sunlight.

There in the waiting area were the officers who had picked her up from the street two days before. She looked at them with disdain but did not say a single word; she did not want to jeopardize her release.

"Good morning, ma'am," the officer with the mustache said with a timid smile on his face. "I hope your stay wasn't too terrible."

She looked him straight in the eye and besides raising her eyebrow, she did not say anything. The officer who drove the patrol car grabbed her arm and she submissively allowed herself to be led.

"You know, I'm trying to be as polite as possible to you and I receive no answer, that's pretty rude on your part, don't you think?" said the driver.

Still, she kept quiet. The officer led her outside through the front door where she had previously entered without being booked. She was positive what these people had done to her was illegal. Outside the building was their patrol car and she was asked to get inside. The officer with a mustache placed his hand on her head and helped her get in.

"Watch your head please... thank you."

It was a long and uncomfortable ride in silence, neither one of the officers dared to say a word. She could see the familiar downtown area from the window as they drove by, but she wasn't completely sure where they were taking her. Chuy assumed they were going to drop her off at home, but she wasn't confident just yet. Almost an hour after they picked her up, they turned into the street where her house was located.

They parked their car by the front door, opened her door and walked on either side of her up her front steps. The driving officer knocked on her front door as she stood bracing for what would happen next.

Manuel answered the door and made exaggerated gestures of thankfulness. One of the officers handed him her purse as she walked in. She heard him say, "thank you for bringing her home, gentlemen" before closing the door behind him. She stood in the middle of the room, not moving, not saying a single word. He took her arm gently and led her to the kitchen table, pulling out a chair for her to sit on.

"Come in, sweetheart. Oh, you must be starving! Here, sit down, I made a delicious breakfast for you. I'm sure you haven't gotten much nutrition in that terrible place the last couple of days. I'm sorry, love. Here, I fried some eggs with potatoes and beans. Your favorite! Let me heat up some tortillas. Do you want coffee? Here it is. Be careful though, it's hot so make sure you don't burn yourself; the water was boiling not one minute ago."

Chuy could not believe what was happening in front of her eyes.

"Look, I need to go to work, but I won't leave until you have eaten your breakfast. I *know* you haven't been eating well. Remember you need to be strong for Juanito, he needs you. A child always needs his mother. He's fine, no need to worry about him at all. He's such a good boy, you know? But he definitely missed you. He's all bathed and clean in his bassinet so make sure to not disturb him, it took me almost a whole hour to get him to fall asleep. He'd been awake since three in the morning, that little rascal!

Anyway, I'm going to fix a bath for you to clean yourself up and relax a little because... jeez, you came home stinky! I'll make the water extra hot, so

178

the temperature is just perfect when you get in. How's breakfast? Good, no? I didn't even need help making it.

You know that lady that lives a couple of blocks from here? Her name is María, she is going to come over in a bit and stay here with you to take care of Juanito while you rest. Just for today, you need to sleep and recuperate, you need to feel better."

Chuy ate her food slowly. She had a knot in her throat trying with all her strength to hold her tears back. She had just finished all the food on her plate as well as the coffee when she heard a knock on the door.

"I'll get it darling; you get yourself ready for your bath... oh look! It's María at the door, thank goodness. Come, come to the door so I can introduce you."

Chuy approached the door with a visible lack of enthusiasm. Manuel made the introductions and as María settled in and started cleaning the kitchen, Manuel gave Chuy a long tight hug and whispered in her ear.

"If you ever pull that shit again and try to leave, I swear to everything that is holy to you, you will never see your son again. I hope you now understand that I have influences and I will always win. Chuy, I always get what I want and there is nothing anyone can do about it." His entire demeanor changed from a husband pretending to be concerned to a manipulative patriarch.

She stared at him with emotionless eyes and, without saying a word, turned around and went to take her bath.

"Love, I have to go, I'm a little late for work but I promise I'll be back for dinner. Make sure you get some good rest, you need it."

Turning to the guest, he said "Thank you for coming over and helping my wife out, María; I truly appreciate it."

Through a haze, Chuy made her way to the bathroom. The hot bath was just what she needed. While soaking, she realized she was not surprised to find out that her suspicions had been right. Everything had been illegally orchestrated by Manuel for her "crime" of having left him. The first thing she thought about was packing up her stuff and getting on a bus somewhere. She didn't care where she ended up.

She could go anywhere, far away from this man who would go so far as to incarcerate the mother of his own child to get his way. He was just like a stubborn child who refuses to lose. Then she remembered the pact she had made with the Virgin Mary the night before, and all her hope vanished. The only thing she'd ever had was her word, and she had just given it to the Holy Mother of Jesús. Chuy felt she had to keep her promise. She believed the virgin had kept her side of the bargain by granting her freedom and now it was her turn to keep hers. How ironic, she thought; that she had finally come out of that terrible cell only to walk right into a new form of imprisonment.

Chuy and Juan Manuel

Chapter XI

It took a few weeks before Chuy said a single word to Manuel; she was in a deep state of depression. Ironically, the only thing that kept her going was also the only thing that kept her prisoner in this life sentence with Manuel, their child. She was extremely unhappy.

The first actual conversation between the two occurred one night over dinner. He got home after work with a bouquet of flowers. He kissed her on the cheek and put the flowers in a vase with water. They sat down to eat together, which was uncommon due to his erratic work schedule. They sat in silence at opposite ends of the table. Halfway through dinner he moved to the chair next to her and held her hand.

"Look sweetheart. On the day you left, I came home that night from work and didn't find you here. I saw the broken window and the rock on the floor, glass shards in my son's bassinet, and the two of you missing. I was going crazy thinking something had happened to you two. Then I saw the note attached to the rock and recognized the handwriting. That was perpetrated by one of my sisters... don't worry, if they didn't get the message before, they get it now. They will never hurt you again."

She had stopped eating and was staring at nothingness, completely avoiding his gaze.

"About the note, I don't know what to say. One day I went home to see my children, as you know I try to do as often as I can. I want to spend as much time with them as their mother allows me. You know how much I love my children, Chuy. Shortly after I got there, one of my sisters came to pick them up. Apparently, she had promised them they would go watch a show at the cinema and I didn't have the heart to ask them to stay with me. They were just so excited. Their mother asked me to join her for coffee and I said yes. It was getting late, and she started making dinner as we talked about the kids. We had dinner together and one thing led to another. We ended up sleeping together, but I swear it meant nothing to me. Chuy, you have to believe me!"

She finally turned to look at him and, without a single emotion on her face, she spoke to him for the first time since being held in a cell.

"Manuel, I don't care. I don't care about you and her, I don't care about her new pregnancy, I don't care about your sisters. If your entire family feels the same way about me, I also don't care. I don't care about being with you, I don't care what you do with your life, I don't care if you tell the truth or lie because I can never trust you either way, so it doesn't matter. I don't care about anything except my son and his safety. That's all I care about, and if you'll excuse me, I've lost my appetite and I need to feed the baby," she concluded and left the table.

After he finished his dinner, Manuel got up from the table, grabbed his hat, and headed towards the door.

"Don't wait up for me, I'll be home late. I don't want you to worry about me; so, I want you to know I'll be at the bar with some friends from work."

"I don't think you understood what I said to you before... I don't care what you do, Manuel," she said in a flat voice from the bedroom doorway.

"Okay then, see you later, Chuy. I love you," Manuel blurted out as he left.

She wondered if he even listened to what she said, or if he even cared. It appeared that the only thing he cared about was getting his way no matter what.

Chuy woke up early the next morning. She fed the baby and cleaned up the kitchen from the night before then made herself a cup of coffee. She was about to give Juanito a bath when there was a knock on the door. Cautiously, she approached it with hesitation.

"Who is it?" she asked, keeping one hand on the door and the other on the knob.

She didn't know what to think anymore and the idea of someone she wasn't expecting outside her house made her extremely anxious.

"My name is Celso. I'm Manuel's father. Can I please come in? I would like to talk to you. I promise I will not take much of your time," the man on the other side of the door asked.

"I'm sorry, Manuel is not here. You should come another time when he's home," she did not want to talk to anyone from that family.

"I'm not looking for my son; it is you I want to talk to."

"What do you want from me?" she asked without opening the door.

"I just want to talk to you; I believe I might be able to help you."

"Help me with what, Don Celso? I don't need your help or anyone else's, I can take care of myself," Chuy answered defensively.

"Please, I am not here to harm you. Think of your son."

That's all she could think of, her son. With trepidation, she slowly opened the door and saw a handsome older man. He was very well dressed. He had on a three-piece suit and a hat. She could see the resemblance and understood where Manuel had gotten his good looks. He did not walk inside the house without her permission.

"Good morning, María de Jesús. Can I please come in?" Don Celso asked.

"I'm sorry, yes. Please come in, sit down. I just made some coffee; would you like a cup?"

"You're very kind but I won't stay long. What I came here to say will only take me a couple of minutes." He paced, looking around the place. She knew he was judging the way they lived.

The baby had been fussy all morning and because of the unexpected visit, the bath he was about to take would have to wait. Chuy went to the bassinet and picked up her naked son and wrapped him up in a sheet and took him with her to the kitchen where his grandfather was.

"Oh! He looks so much like Manuel."

"Yes, he does. This is your grandson Juan Manuel, Señor Celso. Would you like to hold him?"

"Oh God no, thank you. I wouldn't know what to do with him. Please sit down, María, would you? I'd like to discuss something with you of great importance," Don Celso said with gravity.

Chuy sat down with the baby in her arms so she could give this man her undivided attention.

"Listen, María de Jesús; I don't believe my son knows what he wants. He's always been very stubborn and at times obsessive. I think this thing he has with you is a passing thing, you know... he's bored from his married life, and he probably thought he'd go out looking for some fun to relieve him of his daily routines and burdens. I must admit, you seem very young and are very beautiful; I can see why he picked you and as a man myself, I don't blame him. But let's be honest. He is still married; they have children together. You already know his wife is pregnant again, don't you? I heard one of my daughters came to tell you in the most unconventional and violent manner. That action, of course, I do not condone. I gave her a piece of my mind about that. Decent people don't behave that way; I am ashamed of what happened. Anyway, I know you don't have much and now with your child it will be much more difficult for you both when Manuel decides he no longer wants to be with you. We all know he will eventually return to his wife as is his duty. I would like to help you and my grandson. Tell me how much money you need, or want, and I will bring it to you immediately. You can leave my son and go away, far away where he will not be able to find you." Chuy felt he had a look of false concern in his face.

"Señor Celso, if you really want to help and do me a favor, please get away from me and my child and get the hell out of my house!" she demanded.

"I beg your pardon?" answered Don Celso incredulously.

"I know you heard me. Get your arrogant and condescending self out of my house!"

"You don't know what you're doing, Chuy. You are going to suffer greatly if you stay. Do you know why he is not here now? He was at his home last night, with his wife and children where he spent the night. He might even still be there right now."

"You don't know me. You also don't have to pay me to leave your son. I tried to leave him and something terrible happened to me. I don't care what he does. As a matter of fact, why don't you stay and wait for him? I am not keeping him here by force. To tell you the truth, he'd do me a great service if he'd pick up his things and leave. I agree, it would be better if he would go back to his wife and his family. I wish he would, believe me I do... but he won't."

"This is not a game María; the offer is still on the table. Don't make a mistake, I can give you enough money to give your son a good life."

"I don't need anything from you. You can't buy me. How about I do you a favor? You can take your son with you free of charge any day. My son and I don't need or want your money. I'd rather live on the streets than take help from your family."

She learned where Manuel got his personality; that family trait was obvious. She got up and walked to the door and waited for Don Celso to leave.

"Thank you for stopping by to meet your grandson and to warn me about your son. I appreciate the concern, I really do. But I have a lot of things to do. You have yourself an excellent day."

He picked up his hat and walked to the door.

"This offer is only good until the end of the week. If I don't hear from you again, I will assume it has been rejected and I will not make another offer. Please, just think about it."

"Don't waste your time waiting please, or your breath. I reject your offer as of now. Goodbye!"

She closed the door behind her leaving Manuel's father outside. Chuy felt as calm as she'd ever been before. She was proud of herself for how she'd defended her character; she could not be paid off to risk her life trying to leave again. Without another thought she went to prepare the bath for Juanito.

Chapter XII

Rosa María, named after Manuel's grandmother, was born in March of 1956. Only ten months after Manuel's wife had given birth to their son Francisco and a month before Juan Manuel's second birthday.

After Francisco had been born, Manuel finally decided to separate from his wife for good. They had not lived together before he got involved with Chuy, but he would stay the night from time to time giving her hope that he would soon return to them and stay. That reunion never happened.

Manuel's family thought his infatuation with Chuy would be short-lived. They were certain it was a simple romantic adventure. A sort of precocious mid-life crisis compelled him to go out and sow the wild oats he had not been able to sow in his youth. He had been married to his wife since they were both very young and naïve. Although he loved his children with her dearly, there was nothing that could stop him once he had made up his decision about something. They knew him and that's how he was.

The arrival of Rosa María, his second child with Chuy, worried his family but they still had not lost hope. They were certain that at any time his passionate obsession with her would end and he would return home to his wife and children. However, that did not happen. When Rosa María was ten months old, Chuy became pregnant yet again and his family's hopes finally started to diminish. In a way, they were forced to consider that maybe he really did in fact love her. They reluctantly accepted the fact that he was never going back, but they also vowed to never accept his new family.

In September of 1957, María Imelda was born. She was a quiet little baby with dark skin, big cheeks, and not much hair. She looked more like Juan Manuel than their sister Rosa María, who had a lighter complexion and almond shaped eyes. Those children brought so much joy to Chuy. She didn't understand how her heart had not yet burst from the abundance of love she felt, a love so immense she never thought she'd feel again after the loss of Daría.

Chuy had changed since the birth of her children; she had a new purpose in life. Each of her children had made her emotionally stronger. She now spoke her mind and set her foot down at home with Manuel. She was no longer the submissive and ignorant girl he had met only a few years before.

Manuel loved his children dearly and his children loved him. His happiness could not be complete, however; he had not been able to make Chuy love him the way he wanted. He wanted her to want to be with him. His desire for her to love him was not normal. He knew deep down in his heart that she was with him only because she had been forced to stay with him, but he had hope that one day she would feel the same way he felt about her. She was always attentive towards him and regardless of what she felt for him, he was never neglected. He always had clean clothes and warm food on the table ready for him. Every day she would wake up early to make tortillas from scratch and prepare his lunch for work. She would interact with him when he spoke, but he could see her indifference and lack of enthusiasm towards him. She did not love him, and he knew it.

Because he was still supporting his children with his wife plus the three more with Chuy, he had to find a way to make more money to keep both families afloat. He tried to work overtime in the police force but there was only so much he could do. He had been a corporal for almost three years and thought it was time to seek a promotion. Becoming a sergeant would guarantee more pay and he wouldn't have to work so much. After talking to his superior, he found out that he would not be up for promotion for another six months so he knew he would have to do something else until the time came for him to be a sergeant.

One day after work he went to a bar to catch up with some of his friends. He had not been able to see them as often anymore because of his work hours. Furthermore, he was always too tired. He had been working various jobs each weekend, but more often than not, he picked up shifts with a construction company. Manual labor was not his strongest suit, but he stuck with it because he needed the money.

He had decided to go home after he finished the beer he was drinking when he saw his friends, *La*

Perra and Juan Carlos. He got up to get their attention and once they saw him, he signaled for them to sit with him at his table. They had not seen each other for a couple of months, and he felt he needed to catch up so he stayed. Juan Carlos told him he had been working with a group of men on his time off to make some extra cash. He suddenly had everyone's attention.

"The money is good *compadre*, now that you're a man with a big family, you should come with me and earn some extra dough. It's an easy job," Juan Carlos told him in an eager tone.

"I really need to do something, man, having all these children is going to suck me dry," Manuel confessed.

"Ha! But you wanted to be a Don Juan at all costs, didn't you? Now you must pay the price. How is Chuy anyway?"

"She's fine, tell me about this job," pressed Manuel, not amused by Juan Carlos's commentary.

La Perra simply listened and drank. He was not much of a talker and only spoke when he was asked a direct question.

"Look, you know how there are these people, mostly from Central or South America, some are from here, they're *paisanos*, Mexicans like us. Well, some people want to give the American Dream a shot, so they come to us. We're the professionals, you know? And they pay us to take them to Gringolandia and make sure they don't get caught by *la migra*. The guys I work for are the brains of the operation, I'm more of the muscle," he said as he flexed his bicep and then kissed it.

"They have plans to move people, sometimes ten or fifteen at a time. The goal is to get more people per trip if you can, but not too many because that increases the risk of getting caught. You want just the right amount. It also depends on if there are more men. Women and children are a liability and slow everything down, older people too. You can't rely on them to do exactly what you say, plus they get scared easily. So, these people pay us to cross them over and they don't have to worry about a thing, just follow our lead. We've taken some entire families. Men that come here alone would rather risk it on their own to save some money, but if they have their whole family with them then they want someone to help them and kind of give them some promise that they will all be safe," Juan Carlos finished.

"But how can you make those promises to them? How can you tell them that they will be safe for sure? What if someone drowns crossing the river? Or what happens if *la migra* catches them and they send them back to where they came from? Or worse, what if they get injured, or beat up? I've heard of women getting raped by their own *coyotes* or even by *la migra* and then left for dead."

Manuel concluded his questioning with a look of genuine concern. He had never given this situation any kind of thought, for good or for bad.

"Ay, compadre! Obviously, we can't make those guarantees, we never know what's going to happen, but they don't know that. They trust us because they want to, because they have no other option but to trust us. Yes, it's risky but that risk is worth it. You know how it is, sometimes the more you risk, the better the reward is. That's what they're hoping for. You more than anyone knows there is risk involved in everything, anything could go wrong, but we can't tell them that. If we do, then they're all nervous and they might be the reason why something does go wrong. We need them to trust us completely for the operation to go smoothly."

"So you lie to them?" Manuel asked.

"I wouldn't call it lying; I would just say we are avoiding telling them all the details for their own good. Besides, like I told you, we change the plan every single trip so *la migra* can't really track us down. We are *chingones, compadre!* Besides, since when did you grow a conscience?" probed Juan Carlos, laughing.

"Never a conscience, but this is different, private. It sounds risky and kind of fun, I guess; something like that would definitely put me out of my monotonous routine. Anyway, how much does each trip pay?"

"Of course, it's risky, that's why we charge these people *un ojo de la cara,* or like the gringos say, an arm and a leg. And they pay for it too! They come from really shitty places, so packing up their shit and taking this big step may bring more benefits than staying at home to probably starve or something. Who knows? And who cares? As long as they pay, we cross them safely. After that, they're on their own and responsible for their own decisions, actions, and their own lives."

"But how much do you make by doing this? And what happens if you get caught by *la migra*?" Manuel seemed to be growing even more interested in the details, as if suddenly considering all his new options.

"Let me just tell you this: I've only gone on three trips, one each month, and so far, I have already made what I make at work in almost an entire year. I'm telling you, it's something you don't want to miss out on. And you're helping people, man. Think about that for a second, you're helping your *paisanos,* your own people, have a better life. If you wanted to take that step for yourself, wouldn't you feel better to know that one of your own has got your back?"

"Alright, let me think about it for a day or two and then I'll look for you and let you know what I decided."

"*¡A los paisanos, y que viva México señores!*" Yelled Juan Carlos raising his glass.

Manuel finished the drink he'd been holding in his hand for a while, it was already warm, but he drank it anyway.

"Don't think about it for too long, the offer from the bosses might not be there for a long time. Another guy might jump in to do business and I would much rather have you with us. I think we work very well together, if you know what I mean," Juan Carlos nudged him with his elbow and winked a couple of times with a sinister smile on his face.

"Yeah, I'll let you know soon." Manuel answered pensively.

Manuel thought about the offer Juan Carlos had made him. He didn't know if he'd join but there was nothing to lose by requesting a meeting with the boss. He could get information about what would be asked of him and assess the risk. After a couple of days, he asked Juan Carlos to set up a meeting.

The boss told him almost the same thing that Juan Carlos had already covered at the bar. Talking to the head of the operation made Manuel feel better. By the end of the meeting, he didn't hesitate to join them. He saw himself not as a future *coyote* but a *pollero*, smuggling undocumented immigrants into another country. He knew both terms were interchangeable but metaphorically thought of coyotes as untrustworthy and betrayers. *Polleros*, on the other hand, he saw as someone who would gather a group of *pollos* and transported them together and safely to another location. He knew he had done many illegal things in the past, but never in another country. He had felt comfortable before because he was in a position of power and knew the system. The United States and *la migra,* however, were both uncharted territories.

They met every week to plan new routes, assign roles and responsibilities, and discuss the size of the group they would be smuggling into the United States. Manuel felt confident with the way things would go down as described by the boss's plan. It seemed foolproof. He was not ready to go on the next run, which was only two weeks away, he needed to prepare; so his first run would be in six weeks. He was excited and impatient to start working and make money on the side. Being a *pollero* was obviously illegal and he didn't want to jeopardize his job at the police department, so he kept everything a secret from everyone.

Three weeks after the first meeting, he and his patrol partner at the time, Felix, had been called on the radio about a disturbance. They took down the information, turned on their siren and went directly to the site. It was a bar fight between two drunken men. When they got to the site, they saw another patrol at the scene and the officers had already broken up the fight. Both men were being arrested for public intoxication and disturbing the peace. The other patrol took one of the men in their car while Manuel and his partner took the other. They put him in the back seat and took off. On their way to the station, they stopped to pick up something to eat. It had been a long day and neither of them had eaten.

Manuel, who was driving, had stayed in the car while Felix picked up the food. Once back on the road, both officers started chatting about their weekend plans with their families. Due to shortages in the force, they hadn't had a day off in over ten days and both were ready for some down time.

They turned the corner a few blocks from the station when Felix grunted and gripped Manuel's arm. When he turned to look at Felix, his face was panic stricken, and his eyes looked like they were about to pop out of their sockets. Blood was coming out of Felix's mouth and nose. He was trying to say something but could only cough. His partner was violently spitting blood on the dashboard and windshield. There was blood everywhere. Felix kept looking at Manuel with desperation as if pleading for his life, for help, for him to save him somehow. In the midst of the terror Manuel felt, he lost control of the patrol car and crashed into a corner light pole.

It took Manuel a few moments to realize what had happened. The drunkard had taken out an ice pick from inside his boot. It had not been detected at the time of his arrest while being patted down. His hands had been handcuffed in the front which had given him the freedom to pull out his weapon and attack Felix.

He waited until the officers had let their guard down. He placed the ice pick in the back of Felix's neck through the barrier that separates the front seat from the back. Without wasting time, he immediately drove it through the back of his neck, coming out in the front by his Adam's apple. A few seconds after the impact, Manuel stumbled out of the vehicle. He ran around the car to the passenger's side to tend to Felix after calling for help. The criminal was locked in the back seat and with no way for him to escape, Manuel ignored him.

Manuel looked into Felix's eyes with grief. Grabbing Manuel's arms with as much force as he could muster, Felix tried to say something. Everything was in vain; no words came out, only blood and a terrible gurgling sound as he gasped for air. Manuel grabbed him and with care took him out of the car and held him in his arms trying to calm him down. He placed pressure on both sides of the wound trying to stop the blood flow as much as he could with the ice pick still inserted.

"Stay put partner, everything is gonna be fine. The ambulance is already coming and they're gonna fix you up real nice. Shhhh, don't try to say anything, just sit back and relax for me alright? Look at what that bastard just did to you, it's gonna leave a mark, but it'll make you look manlier. Hey, we'll have lots of stories to tell after this one, won't we partner?" Manuel joked, trying to fool Felix into thinking the situation was not as bad as it was.

"Hey, maybe they can leave the hole in the front so you can smoke two cigarettes at once; one through your mouth and one through your throat, you son of a bitch." He chuckled nervously and Felix relaxed, there was a labored smirk on his face.

Manuel's attempt at humor didn't mask the anxiety churning in his stomach. The situation was dire, and he could feel the weight of it pressing down on him. His partner, Felix, was in bad shape, and no amount of jokes would change that. He kept his hands steady, pressing against Felix's neck, but blood continued to pour from the wound, making his efforts feel futile.

Felix's eyes met his, desperate and pained, but there was still a flicker of understanding in them—he knew Manuel was trying to keep him calm. The blood on Manuel's hands seemed to multiply, each drop a reminder of how quickly things had spiraled out of control.

"Just hang in there, man. The medics are coming, they're coming..." Manuel repeated, but the words felt empty even as he said them. The sirens in the distance were too slow, too far off. The reality of their situation was closing in with each passing second.

Felix's hand weakly gripped his arm. He tried to speak, but all that came out was a rasping cough, followed by a wet, gurgling sound. Manuel's stomach churned, unable to process the horror of it all.

But Felix still tried to smile, even through the pain. That smirk, though faint, told Manuel that he wasn't alone at that moment. His partner—his friend—was still fighting to stay with him, trying to cling to whatever hope remained.

Manuel took a deep breath, forcing himself to steady his hands, and whispered, "You're not getting rid of me that easy, Felix. We're not done yet."

But deep down, Manuel knew. They both knew. It was only a matter of time.

Manuel kept his hand on his partner's throat, but it wasn't helping much. The blood kept dripping from the sides of his hand. He was bleeding badly from the back of his neck as well, but if he took the weapon out Felix would bleed out instantly.

In a moment, three patrols arrived followed by an ambulance. They took the suspect in another car and the ambulance took Felix to the hospital. Manuel was taken to the hospital to be evaluated and then to the police station to record his statement. At the end of the day, he had minor scratches and a concussion but nothing too serious. He went to see how Felix was doing as soon as he could and was then informed Felix had died during surgery. He had lost too much blood and even with the transfusions, he was too weak.

Manuel went home, his uniform was heavy with his partner's blood. It was past midnight when he got home. He took all of his clothes off in the kitchen, washed his hands and his arms up to his elbows and sat on the floor next to the table. With shaky hands, he took out a bottle of tequila from the pantry and drank sobbing in silence until he passed out. When Chuy woke up in the morning, she found him asleep on the floor and a pile of bloody clothes next to him. He had a patch on his forehead where he had hit himself with the steering wheel, and a black eye. She made coffee and prepared a hot bath for him and without asking a single question, she led him to the bathtub and gently washed the blood off of him.

Manuel had two weeks of paid time off due to the trauma. He didn't leave the house the entire time and even refused to attend Felix's funeral. He was suffering from depression and all he wanted to do was sleep and drink. He could not stop thinking that this tragedy could've happened to him. He had always known that being a police officer was a dangerous job, but he rarely gave it much thought. He had never really encountered much danger, maybe he had been lucky. He liked what he had experienced in the ten years as an officer. People respected him, or feared him, and to him it was the same thing. He could get away with many things that he wouldn't otherwise be able to do. He enjoyed the taste of that power.

Many times, he would accept *mordidas*, from people trying to get out of a traffic violation. He loved to see how people always tried to be on their best behavior around him when he was in uniform. He had felt invincible for so long, and it had gone straight to his head and intoxicated him with naivety. He had never thought anything could go wrong. He had seen other officers hurt or even killed in the line of duty, but somehow that seemed infinitely far from him.

Having witnessed Felix's death in such a gory manner brought him back down to Earth and he was forced to acknowledge his own mortality. He felt vulnerable, weak, and at times paranoid.

When he finally decided to leave the house, he went to the office and asked to talk to his superior. He went in to turn in his badge, his uniform, and his weapon. He could not stay and continue to do a job where he could potentially lose his life the way that poor Felix had lost his. He was not cut out to be in a constant state of stress, now that he was fully aware of the danger. Nothing would be the same after that experience; he would not be able to do his job in the right frame of mind. So, he quit and decided that from that time forward, he would put all his eggs in another basket. He would be an efficient and professional *pollero*. Less risk and more money, there was nothing else to think about; or so he assumed.

He performed his first two runs flawlessly and without incident. He felt a great change in himself and was even convinced that what he was doing was a good thing even if it was illegal. And why should it be illegal? He was simply helping people realize their dream by aiding them as they went to a safer place than where they came from.

He was one of the reasons why these people would have a brighter future. He was giving them a real shot at the American Dream. It only took him two months to become comfortable with his new career choice. He had been a police officer for a while, so he had skills that other *polleros* did not have. Even with all that confidence in himself, lack of experience in the trade would eventually bring his career as a human smuggler to an end.

On his third run, he was captured along with half of the people he was supposed to cross over to the United States. As soon as *la migra* realized he was not one of the smuggled but one of the smugglers, he was arrested and taken into custody in El Paso where he would be charged, convicted, and sentenced to five years in prison.

Chapter XIII

From the end of 1957 to July of 1959 during Manuel's incarceration, Chuy thrived. She started off with very little because money and food were scarce, but she was a very hard worker and always found ways to manage.

At first, she had difficulty making a living, but later learned to find plenty of work. Although it seemed that Chuy did not have much time for her children, she never neglected them. She always let them know they were loved and, at night when they went to bed, she would religiously sing sweet lullabies to them. They all slept on the same bed taking advantage of the fact that their father was not home. They felt lucky to have her all to themselves and they loved it. She was alone with her three beautiful children, and she couldn't be happier, it was like a dream come true.

Since she did not have the best childhood herself, Chuy vowed to give her children what she lacked. She was very protective yet allowed them to be independent and learn things on their own. They all loved to play outside; making mud cakes was their favorite. They would make dozens and let them out to dry on the front porch and later sold them in a pretend bakery. Although the three of them had their own individual character traits, which sometimes clashed, they were very close. Juan Manuel always looked after his two little sisters and made sure they wouldn't get hurt or try to eat the mud cakes.

While Manuel was imprisoned, Chuy had to create a new career around her family. She could not go back to work at Doña Licha's with three small children. She had to find a way and the best thing she knew how to do was to create through her sewing. During her time as a single parent, Chuy officially became a seamstress and people all over her neighborhood got to know her and her craft.

Her clientele had grown very slowly during the previous four years since she wasn't doing it full time, but now word had spread and people came almost as far as downtown just to see her. She would use one foot to operate her sewing machine and the other to rock the bassinet when the babies would get fussy. Everyone loved her work; she was so meticulous with every detail and did every job with such professionalism that it was difficult to distinguish between a store-bought dress and her own creations. Sometimes her work was better than that behind a store counter.

People not only loved Chuy's work, but her as well. She had the most amazing personality and people adored her. She had come a long way since the day she set foot in Ciudad Juárez. She had become a strong woman in her own right but was able to stay gentle, not allowing her bad experiences to reign over her. She radiated with charisma and understanding. Furthermore, she did not like to get in people's business but was trusted with the most private of personal circumstances. Chuy was an amazing listener and people respected her opinion and sometimes asked her for advice. She seemed so wise beyond her years. In fact, she was respected and admired by everyone that met her, except for Manuel's family.

Her son, Juanito, became Chuy's most valuable helper. He would perform simple tasks that gave him a great sense of responsibility and pride. He felt like the man of the house even though his mother never placed that burden on his shoulders. She wanted him to have a happy childhood while at the same time learn a lesson or two about hard work.

Some of his responsibilities included helping stretch out cloth on the cutting table and hold it down at the corners. Chuy would then draw a pattern on it with white chalk before cutting it and sewing the pieces together. He would hold the pin cushion and give her two to three pins at a time. He liked to place checkmarks next to the items that had already been accomplished in the notebook. He was always careful not to mess with the measurements that had been recorded.

His overall favorite thing to do was to deliver the finished products to his mother's clients and collect payments from them. He was young so he was only allowed to go as far as a few blocks from their house, but, as he got older, his territory grew. Juanito would eventually ride a bicycle to fulfill his duties as a delivery boy. Very charismatic himself, it didn't take long for him to become very popular with the neighborhood mothers and Chuy's clients. At times, he would get paid to deliver handwritten messages to other people that lived close by. This made him proud, feeling like his contributions made a difference; plus, he was earning a few pesos a week to buy whatever he wanted.

Rosa María and Imelda were not only close in age, but they were also best friends. The two girls would have their own chores around the house while Chuy worked. From a very young age they would make their own bed, set the table, wash dishes, and clean the house. They also learned to cook as they got older. They wished they could go outside and run errands like their brother did, but they were too young, and it wasn't permissible for girls to do boys' work.

While in prison, Manuel grew desperate with every passing day. He was not necessarily upset at being deprived of his freedom in the confines of a small cell, but he did resent Chuy's freedom. He knew she could survive anything, and she would be just fine on her own even with three small children. She always knew how to come out of the ashes even stronger and he despised the idea of not being needed by her.

He was convinced that she would never love him the way he wanted her to, and he was fine with that, but the thought of her not needing him made him miserable. With him away, she could pick up and leave. She could take the children and never look back if she wanted to. There was nothing he could do about it but obsess over his situation. He envisioned another man replacing him in his own house and in his bedroom. He regretted not divorcing his wife when he first left her and marrying Chuy.

If they were married, she would not be able to leave him, not legally at least. Married to her, he could always find her and demand her to come back to him and she would not be able to deny his wishes. He could use his influences in the force and make her do what he wanted, just like he had before. Imagining Chuy in the arms of another man maddened him and the walls in his cell would end up bloody and his fists swollen. At night he would cry in silence with fear that he would lose her forever. He wasn't so concerned about another man raising his kids as his own, but that this woman whom he loved with such fervor would no longer be his. He could not allow that to happen, but he knew he couldn't prevent it.

Manuel's father and most of his immediate family had disowned him for the way he chose to live his life. They were outraged that he had abandoned his wife and children for a woman much younger than him. He could not be blamed though, they thought. It was all her fault; she must have tempted him and seduced him. The embarrassment he had caused them was unforgivable. Manuel was a very proud man but his passionate craze over Chuy trumped everything, so he swallowed his pride and wrote his father a letter asking him to help support his family until he was free. He promised to pay back every peso he spent on them.

One day when the children were outside playing, Don Celso appeared at the house looking for Chuy. As he approached the front door, Juan Manuel got up and stretched out his muddy hand to the stranger.

"Good afternoon, sir, my name is Juan Manuel and my sisters and I are making mud cakes. Would you like to buy one?" Juan offered, innocently.

"They look delicious, but I just had lunch, thank you very much. I'm sorry I don't shake your hand young man, but it's all muddy. Is your mother home?" Celso appeased him.

"Yes sir, she is. She is working on a big order. You know she could make a suit for you if you wanted, cheaper than anywhere else, I promise. Would you like for me to call her?" asked Juan trying to turn the conversation into a business transaction.

Chuy had already seen him through the front window. She always made sure she could see her children while she worked, so her sewing machine was strategically placed to allow just that. The children also knew that if they wanted to play outside, they would have to do it wherever they could be seen from that vantage point.

"Don Celso, what do we owe the honor of your presence in this house? Your son, as you probably already know, is not here," she said in a cynical tone through the window without interrupting her work. "Last time I saw you, I made it very clear to not come to my house again."

Juan opened the door and Don Celso took the opportunity to enter their house. He went inside and stood right next to Chuy, who kept working diligently without removing her eyes from her work.

"Good afternoon, María. I promise I won't take much of your time," stated Don Celso.

"I prefer the name Chuy but thank you for not taking my time. You know, my time is valuable and I'm very busy today; every day, actually. I see you met your grandchildren," she said with a hint of sarcasm.

"Listen, I'm here because I want to help. I know my son has been away for a while and I don't know how much longer he will be away. I want to offer a truce and help you with some money or whatever you need."

"I don't need your money, Señor Celso. As you can see, I am very capable of taking care of my own family. You and your family probably thought that I was with Manuel because of money, that I was a gold digger. Well, I have never been that person. And as you already know Manuel doesn't have money, he never has. Especially with all the children he has had to support and now more than ever, he has absolutely nothing to offer."

"Please María, leave your pride aside and allow me to help you. Do it for your children. I know times are hard."

"What do you know about hard times? I know more about hard times than you can ever imagine in a lifetime, and we are doing just fine. The children are fine, they're well fed, and I tell them to not get close to your daughters' house, so they don't get rocks thrown at them. Because let me tell you that they have done just that although Manuel promised me, they never would do such a criminal thing. These children are their own blood for Christ's sake!"

"I will talk to them, but you have to understand that they only see Manuel's other children as their own blood."

"I don't care! That's no excuse. They don't have to treat anyone that way, what have these poor innocent children done to them? Nothing! And whether they want to accept it or recognize it or not, they are their own blood, and no one can take that away from them. I would have hoped they had at least the most common decency to live and let live in peace."

"Yes María, you are right. I promise I will talk to them. They will not hurt your children; you have my word."

"I don't care, and you'd already given your word on the same matter. Now, tell me what you really want. I don't believe you came out here to offer your help out of the goodness of your heart. I am certain you and your family don't know what having a heart feels like. The sooner you tell me what you came here for, the sooner I can get back to work without interruptions."

"They are my grandchildren, María. I want what's best for them. Also, I received a letter from Manuel. He sent it from prison, and he is worried about you. You have not answered any of his letters and he is concerned. He asked me to come and offer you help, he promised he would pay me every single cent back once he got out. I don't need him to pay me back, I want to help. I also want you to know that he cares about you."

"Get out of my house! You are not welcome here and you have no right to come talk to me about money, about Manuel, or about anything else. I have nothing to say to Manuel and that is the reason I have not written back to him. Also, I don't care or have the time for those sorts of things. As you can see, I have a lot of work to do, and I need to feed my family. We are doing perfectly fine, and if what he really is afraid of is that I will leave, I have no intention of going anywhere. This is my house, and I will stay here. When he gets out, if he wants to come here, fine, if he decides he wants to go somewhere else, I don't care. We would probably be better off if he never came back."

Celso got up and walked out the door in silence. Once out on the porch, he noticed Juan Manuel had been watching them through the screen door. He got on one knee and asked Rosa María for one mud cake, "the one with the little flower," he said. She gave him the mud cake and he gave her a kiss on the cheek and then hugged Juan Manuel and put an envelope in his hand. As he was leaving, he ruffled Imelda's hair as she was still playing in the mud.

Juan Manuel opened the envelope and gasped when he saw what was in it. He had never seen so much money and felt overwhelmed simply by holding it. He ran inside to show his mother while yelling "We're rich!! We are rich!"

Chuy snatched the envelope from Juan's hands and told him what was in the envelope was not theirs and they had to return it. With a sad look on his face, he nodded. Even with his immature mind, he understood why they couldn't take it. After all, he had listened to the adult conversation through the screen door.

His mother quickly tried to explain in a way he could understand why they could not accept the money, but before she was done, he grabbed the envelope from her hands and ran towards his aunties' house. In the distance he could see his grandfather talking to them on the porch. He ran faster and stopped short of the house. They had not noticed him. Standing a few feet from them, while trying to catch his breath, he yelled "we are not for sale!" He threw the envelope at them before running back home as fast as he could.

Once back in the house, he went up to his mother, proud to have defended the family's honor. He didn't know what he had defended them from, but he was certain he had done the right thing. He told her exactly what he had done only to be scolded.

"He is your grandfather Juan Manuel; he is your father's father, and you must respect him."

"But did he disrespect us with that money? I could see your face and you didn't look happy."

"Yes, I believe that he did; but that doesn't matter. If that is the way he is, how his family is, that's their business. We are not that way. Do you understand me? We always must be respectful, especially to our elders."

"Is my grandfather my elder?" asked Manuel, trying to understand.

"Yes, he is your elder; but more importantly, he is your grandfather. You must never talk to your grandfather that way, do you understand that?"

"What about his daughters? Do I have to respect them too? Even if they throw rocks at us?" Juan Manuel kept getting more and more confused as the conversation progressed.

"Yes, we must respect them. We can do things, like walk around the other block and not walk in front of their houses. We can make our own choices and be better, treat others better. We don't hurt people, and we are not rude. We are not that way; do you understand?"

"Yes ma'am," answered Juan Manuel, lowering his head and making fists with his little brown hands.

She wanted her children to be respectful to others above all. They would be sensitive to other people's feelings, educated, and productive citizens of society. She wanted them to be nothing like Manuel's family.

Chapter XIV

Manuel was released from prison in 1959, having served less than two of the five-year sentence due to his good conduct. He had been convinced he would spend the entire time in prison, so when he went in for review and was told he could go home he was ecstatic. He didn't tell anyone about his release. He took a cab to the bridge and once he was on the Mexican side, he called Juan Carlos to pick him up and take him home.

When he got to his house, he saw his children playing outside but they did not recognize him. He approached them slowly. The girls saw him approach without much interest in him and then went back to tending the little store they had built with empty cans and bottles. One pretended to be the store owner and the other to be the client. Juan Manuel got up and went towards him, extended his hand to greet the stranger.

"Good afternoon, sir, my name is Juan Manuel." Just like he had done with his grandfather, Don Celso.

"Hello Juan Manuel, my name is also Manuel, like yours," answered Manuel

Juan Manuel giggled with amazement.

"You're my *tocayo*! We have the same name. Well, only half a *tocayo* since we only share one name. Unless you're also a Juan, then we can be full *tocayos*." wondered the boy.

"No, unfortunately, I am not a Juan. I am just a Manuel. Would you like to know a secret?" Manuel asked his son as he knelt next to him to be at eye level.

"Oh, a secret? I can keep it a secret. I promise I can be trusted. Tell me, what's the secret?" shrieked Juan Manuel with excitement.

"I'm your dad, Juanito," Manuel confessed.

"My dad? Does mom know? Quick, we have to tell her!" answered Juan Manuel, surprised.

"Of course, she knows, silly boy. But you promised not to tell. It was a secret!"

Juan Manuel ignored the last statement his father had said. He turned around to look at his sisters and yelled at them "Rosa, Imelda, come quick... This is your father!

The girls got up and left their make-believe store unattended and ran towards him. He picked all three of them up, squeezed them, and kissed them all over.

"*Papi, papi!* Is it true you are our *papi*?" asked Rosa María with excitement and jumping into his arms.

"Yes, it is true, I am your *papi*" answered Manuel, happy to see his children.

"Then how come we don't see you before?" replied Rosa María, confused.

"I didn't have a *papi* before," replied Imelda, unimpressed and not wanting to leave her store.

Chuy had heard some commotion and went to see what was going on outside. She stopped at the door and saw Manuel with their children. She wasn't expecting him for quite some time and was as surprised as the children. She opened the door for Manuel to go inside, he put Rosa María down and let go of Juan Manuel's hand and met Chuy in a warm embrace. Chuy ordered him to wash his hands so she could feed him and told the kids to leave their father alone so he could rest. The children started laughing sheepishly at the idea of having a dad in their lives.

"See? He really is our *papi!*" Rosa María said to Imelda with sweetness, while holding her hand.

Manuel continued to be fearful that Chuy would leave him. He knew deep in his heart how she felt about him, but also what she didn't feel for him. As the strong woman that he knew she was, the only way now to make her stay was if she had many children; he thought. Life for her would be much easier by his side, even if she didn't want to be there.

His entire life he had been used to getting everything he wanted. It started in his childhood. He had gotten everything he wanted, whether he needed it or not, even if he hadn't asked for it. With time, none of his tantrums went unanswered in a way that always benefited him, and never heard "no" to any of his whims. He grew up to be the same person he was as a child, demanding, and entitled. The result of his actions and how they affected others were of no consequence to him, he wanted what he wanted, and he always got it.

Josefina was born in 1960 and exactly two years later, María Alicia joined the family.

****

Years passed and when Juan Manuel was 12 years old, he started venturing out of his immediate neighborhood on his bicycle. He would ride as far as he could before his legs would give out. He would then stop to rest, look around, investigate the new territory, and then ride back home. He would ride farther and farther with time as his physical strength improved. During one of his adventures, he came to an old *ruedo*. He felt a strong pull of curiosity and pedaled closer to it. He wanted to see it and find out what kinds of things happened in that place.

He had never been that far and felt some fear, but his curiosity was stronger. When he got to the entrance of the arena, he left his bicycle outside and went in. He took a seat on the concrete bleachers with his mouth opened in awe. The scene of the *charros* riding their horses around the sandy ring was something magical he had never witnessed before and could not look away.

The traditional colorful clothing these men wore while participating in what he later found out to be *coleaderos* and *charreadas*, completely fascinated him. The way the *charros* maneuvered their horses and they in turn complied with strict obedience to what their riders demanded of them, was to Juan Manuel the same as being in heaven. He would ride as far as the *lienzo,* which was now being used for *charreadas* and not for bullfights anymore, every single day and marvel at the beautiful horses. It didn't take long for him to become completely obsessed with Mexico's national sport. He felt in his heart that had been born to be one of them. He *needed* to be a *charro*.

That same year, his sister Magdalena was born. The family was doing everything they could to save money and build a home of their own. With the family growing quickly, the rented house was beginning to feel increasingly cramped. Juan Manuel had an idea that was completely supported by both of his parents. He would help his mother make a number of burritos early in the morning, before the sun came up. A few of the burritos would go in Manuel's lunch box to the construction company where he now worked. Juan Manuel would take the rest of the burritos with him to the *lienzo* where he would sell them to the *charros*.

It was a foolproof plan as far as he was concerned: this would allow him to help the family earn some money to put towards the house and give him the opportunity to get close to these men and their horses. He didn't know much about being a *charro,* but he knew there was a very special and tight bond between the men and their horses. As if they were nothing without them. He saw the horse as an extension to the *charro's* own being and that was what fascinated him the most.

Unfortunately, Juan Manuel had grown up with an inferiority complex. He was a highly sensitive boy, and he had a difficult time with the absence of his father during his formative years. He also could not understand why his aunts and his own grandfather did not love him like their other relatives. He knew they were not fans of his mother, but that had nothing to do with him.

Whatever their issues were with her, they also transferred to him. He felt that he was an innocent bystander. Chuy had tried to explain to him that his father's family had a different way of loving and that they didn't hate him. He could not reconcile that explanation in his head when he had experienced their scorn in the flesh. He rode his bicycle through the main street and many times his aunts would yell hurtful things and the rock throwing never ceased.

"How can someone with their own blood treat me this way?" he thought. His own father rarely paid attention to him. He was always working or he would dismiss his questions and ideas as childish and not worth talking about. His mother loved him dearly and he knew it. He understood that she would do anything for him. But she also had five daughters that she had to look after. He understood, but that made him feel even smaller than everyone else in the world.

After a few months of selling burritos to the *charros,* he got the courage to ask how to become one himself. He expected these men to laugh at him, to dismiss him and send him straight home. His father had made him believe that children were to be seen and not heard, but that was not what he found with this group of men. Although he feared being told the *charro* life was for men and not boys, he was embraced instead.

Juan Manuel's curiosity for this sport full of cultural heritage romanticized the history and legend of the *charro* and he wanted to know everything about it. The *charros* told him stories of their equestrian feats and the glory that came with them, and he was warned about the dangers of being one of them. The hazards weren't only about the physical danger of the skills he would learn and master, but of the social pressures and responsibility as well.

There were privileges to being a real *charro de corazón*. He was taught charros don't cry, because men don't cry. Physical pain was a price to pay and he had to be able to stand it. The only exception to the crying rule was reserved for matters of the heart.

If his heart had been broken by a girl, his friends and *charro* family would always be there to help him get through it. Alcohol and other women obviously would be the answer to getting past it.

He also learned that women would want to be *with* him, and men would want to *be* him. Wearing that unique dress and having the skills of a *charro* would give him a certain level of masculinity that could not be matched by anything else. People would see his image when they heard the word macho, and it would be a badge of honor and pride for these men. He would have to put all his passion into the sport, and when he was able to afford his own horse, that would be his number one priority. Horses would come before all women, except his mother, of course. The mother of a *charro* was sacred and highly respected, fathers came second. His responsibility as a man was to embrace and cultivate his relationship with his father. This was a very important aspect of what his life was lacking, a father who was also a role model.

That day he rode his bicycle on a road made of puffy clouds. All these new ideas kept his mind running and he could not stop fantasizing. He saw himself handsome and brave while jealous people watched him ride a beautiful horse. He imagined fighting for his honor, surviving multiple heartbreaks, and building camaraderie with his new friends. A true *charro* was the epitome of passion. He had finally found his tribe, a group of men young and old, working together in unison to make beautiful and synchronized movements on their horses. There would be a support system, role models that he had been so hungry for, acceptance and love from strong men that would teach him how to grow up, how to be a man. He wanted to start training immediately but refused to learn to even ride a horse in his regular, ragged clothes. He knew that *charro* outfits were expensive. He had to have the hat, the boots, the elaborate fashioned pants and shirts, the tie, and even the jacket.

When Juan Manuel got home, he told his mother of the most amazing experience he had just had and his intentions of becoming a *charro*.

"*Amá, quiero ser charro*" he blurted out as soon as he went inside the house.

"Oh, a *charro* eh? Well, then I guess we'll have to take your measurements for a nice outfit. You can't be a charro in those rags! You know, being a charro is an honor. You must always look presentable while you're in the arena and representing your country in the sport," Chuy answered without missing a beat in her work or even looking at him.

Juan Manuel had initially thought he would be shut down. But if one thing was certain about Chuy, she had always been supportive of her children, especially when it came to them being their own person. If Juan Manuel envisioned his life as a *charro*, then his mother was going to help him reach his goal. She told him to keep the money from the burritos for the next month to purchase his boots and hat and she would take care of his suit.

Becoming a *charro* proved to be a socially safer yet physically riskier lifestyle for Juan Manuel. Not only did he place himself in great danger while learning the ropes, but he also started to smoke and drink heavily. By the time he reached the peak of his career, most bones in his body had been fractured. He had mastered *el paso de la muerte,* but there was always a natural margin of error.

The first time he fractured bones in his body, he had mounted from his own horse to the bare back of an unbroken one during *el paso de la muerte*. Three horsemen riding directly behind him. The *charro* is supposed to ride until the horse stops bucking but he fell off the second horse and was trampled. It took him four months to perform again. He then had another accident one day while performing the *jineteo de yegua,,* as well as in the *jineteo de toro*. He lost track of his injuries after a couple of years. If he wasn't limping, he was walking on crutches, or completely bedridden.

At the beginning of 1968, Chuy and Manuel built a house with their savings in *La Colonia Satélite*, a few miles away from where they lived. The house was big enough for the growing family and was finished just in time to welcome their seventh child, José Lorenzo. He was born in August of that year shortly after they moved in.

Juan Manuel and his sister Imelda were very close growing up. She was a spitfire and loved to follow her big brother around everywhere. Sometimes she would go with him to neighbors' houses to deliver dresses or outfits that their mother had just finished and other times they only went out to collect payment. There was only one bicycle in the family and Juan Manuel would use it all the time as it was his favorite mode of transportation.

Imelda loved to ride on the handlebars or on the seat while he would ride standing up. No matter how uncomfortable it was for her, Imelda always wanted to follow her brother and have memorable afternoons. Although she had a very adventurous spirit and would much rather be outside playing, she was terrified of horses. So, whenever Juan Manuel got annoyed by his sister, he would simply tell her the horses were coming and she would leave him alone. One time on a payment collection run she went with him even though he did not want to take her. He thought that maybe if he was fast enough and collected all the payments for that day early enough, he would have time to go see his *charro* friends and see them practice. Imelda would not listen to him.

"Mom, Imelda doesn't listen! I don't want to take her with me, and she won't get off the bike. Tell her to get off and leave me alone," Juan Manuel complained.

"Just take her, you know she gets bored here and she loves going with you. It doesn't hurt you to take her." Chuy decided.

"But mom, I want to go to the *lienzo* once I'm done and see the charros practice." Juan Manuel was practically whining.

"Take her with you Juan Manuel and stop arguing!" Chuy raised her voice at him.

Her voice was as strong as her will, and no one contradicted her once she gave an order.

Imelda was waiting on the bike sticking out her tongue at her brother, something that their mother had forbidden. It was rude and everyone was to be respected, including siblings. He decided to take her without any additional complaint and since all the payments had been collected, he went in the opposite direction from their house and towards the arena. Imelda was scared and started crying and complaining. She had never been that far from the house without adults, and she knew the horses would be there.

"You didn't have permission to come all the way out here, mom said." Imelda claimed, hitting Juan Manuel on his arm.

"She told me to take you with me and I did, she didn't tell me I couldn't bring you to see the horses" Juan answered sarcastically.

"But I don't like horses, you know that. They scare me a lot!" Imelda yelled, as she was starting to panic.

"Well, that's just too bad. I just happen to love horses. If you want, you can go home from here."

"You're supposed to take me home." she cried.

"That was not part of the deal, you wanted to come, now deal with it." he answered maliciously.

"Juan Manuel!" Imelda screamed.

"Look! Here come the horses!!" Juan Manuel said laughing.

Imelda jumped from the bicycle without looking to see if her brother was telling the truth. She turned around and ran the long way home. That day, Juan Manuel rode a horse for the first time. One of the *charros* let him borrow his the entire day and taught him how to maneuver and communicate with the horse. It had been the best day of his life.

He had been so excited that he totally forgot the incident with his sister from earlier. When he got home and was ready to boast about his experience, he got punished like never before. Chuy was usually understanding and supportive but could also be very strict with her discipline of her children. Their behavior and respect of the rules of the house was very important and she could be very stern. Chuy was waiting for Juan Manuel outside on the porch.

When he reached for the door, she stood up and grabbed him by the ear with her big strong hands and pulled it, dragging him inside the house. He tried to defend himself by giving his version of the story but there was nothing he could say. He was punished by not being allowed to go to the *lienzo* for two weeks.

"But I'm already learning how to ride horses and they told me I have to be very consistent, so the horse gets to know me and I get to know him. He is beautiful, his name is Palomino. Please ma, I'll do whatever you want, but not this please," Juan Manuel pleaded.

"I don't care what these men told you. You were responsible for your sister, and you left her out there by herself, she had to walk here alone. She's only eleven years old for Christ's sake. What if something had happened to her? You could've very easily brought her home and gone back on your bicycle, why didn't you think of that?" Chuy asked punishingly.

"I don't know, but I'm sorry. Please let me go back to practice. They'll be disappointed if I don't show up." A knot started forming in his throat, but he remembered *charros* don't cry.

"I already told you "No" and I don't really care what they have to say or if you break their heart, they're not your parents, I am! You listen to *me*, is that understood?"

Juan Manuel knew that no matter what he said or how much he tried to explain, nothing would change. He knew better than to keep arguing and he accepted the consequences of his actions.

During the following two weeks, he waited patiently for time to go by and tried to be overly respectful and obedient. He held out hope that he could get a shorter sentence in his punishment, but he was unsuccessful. After the allotted time had passed, he was allowed to go back to practice. When he told the *charros* what had happened and how upset he was, he expected sympathy but was scolded by them as well.

"Being a *charro* is a great responsibility." The charro leader told him "But the responsibility you have with your family, especially to your *madrecita,* comes first. Your mother and the family always come first, *mijo*. Before anything else, you understand? Now if you can't be respectful to your mother and your sisters, then there is no room for you in this group of fine men."

These experiences and lectures from both his mother and the *charro* leaders had him thinking long and hard. He really loved his family and he wanted to take care of his sisters, but he was also still a child. He vowed to always put family first, the sport second, and he promised to always be the best man he could be. He was learning lessons that would shape his character and personality for years to come. He gave his *charro* family two years of hard work, dedication, and daily practice. He got thrown off broncos, he'd fallen off mares, he'd ridden bareback, he'd been stepped on by a calf, and he had learned how to do amazing and entertaining tricks with his rope. After all his learning, practicing, and numerous broken bones, he mastered the sport and in February 1970, he was officially initiated as a *charro*. In March of the same year, his new sister Adriana was born.

Juan Manuel finally started performing in *charreadas* on weekends. He was the youngest official *charro* in the group and was growing to be a very handsome young man. With his amazing skills in the *ruedo,* and his good looks, it didn't take long for him to become popular with the young ladies. He remembered that he had been told once that being a ladies' man was part of being macho, and a good *charro*. So, he dated as many girls as he could handle, and he wore it as a badge of honor.

Charrería had become Juan Manuel's passion in life. He could not imagine himself not riding a horse or being a part of the weekend show. The danger of the sport made him feel superhuman. Dancing with death every time he got on a horse and running at full speed in a small space to perform dangerous tasks gave him a sense of belonging. Knowing that anything could go wrong exhilarated him to no end, and things did go wrong.

It was not unusual to see a couple of the *charros* with a cast on a leg or an arm; sometimes on both, depending on how dangerous the exercise had been. Juan Manuel knew that he could lose his life while he worked, but he didn't care. He would welcome a sweet death in the *ruedo* if that's the way God intended him to go. In fact, that's the way he wanted to go, performing, trampled by the strong legs of the horses, or mangled by a bull; he saw it as a death worthy of glory. Some of the more seasoned *charros* warned him against being so reckless, they asked him to be careful, but he would just scoff and dismissed their advice calling them "chicken."

He would ask the men if they didn't love the sport and in turn, they would answer that they loved their life more. He not only didn't see it that way, but he also genuinely loved the sport more than his own life. Week after week, he would only get more and more reckless. He was especially reckless when he would drink heavily not only after the practice or the shows, but also before. This added another level of danger to his routines and felt that even with his intoxication, he could perform with no trouble at all. He kept adding to the challenge and pushing the limits of his human abilities. He became addicted to taking risks and pushing boundaries.

In 1971, Juan Manuel started dating a young woman named María de Jesús. He had never met another woman with his mother's name, and he liked being around her. Her friends called her Chuya. She was a very good-looking girl, and she was fun. He had seen her and her friends hang out at the *lienzo* in the afternoons for a while when he practiced. She was not like other girls he'd seen. Chuya was not shy; she was confident in her own skin, and she knew what she wanted. She waited for him outside the arena one afternoon. They had been seeing each other from far away for months. That day, she officially introduced herself and he walked her home while they talked.

They liked each other from the beginning so it was no surprise to anyone when they started dating exclusively. He made it clear to her from day one, however, that his priorities in life were his mother, his family, his *charrería*... specifically in that order. He initially thought she would not appreciate being at the bottom of his priority list, but she agreed with him. She respected him even more after that. She told him family should always be first, especially his mother. She was more than happy to be his top priority in other categories and was very supportive in every decision he made. In his perspective, that was how he knew she was the one special girl for him. She was proud of him for being the bravest in the group; he always seemed so enthusiastic and didn't care how dangerous his routines were. As she grew to love him more, she started dreading the danger of the sport, but she never interfered. Chuya would just tell him to be careful, although she knew he wouldn't listen.

In June of 1972, Chuy was pregnant again, she was 38 years old, and this would be her tenth child. Manuel was 51 and this new baby would be his 14th.

He was excited with the news, while Chuy was exhausted. She vowed that no matter what happened after this baby, she would not have another even if they had to sleep in separate beds until the *change* came to her. She could not risk having even one more. Chuy had finally drawn the line, which Manuel did not take seriously at the time.

The family had been prospering, they owned the house they lived in, and it had plenty of room for everyone including the new baby. They had recently purchased three conjoined apartments right behind their own house as an investment property. The previous owner was an elderly man who could no longer take care of the rooms. His children decided to sell the buildings and take him to live with them against his own wishes. It took them a while to get him to agree, but as soon as he did, they took the first offer Chuy and Manuel made. They were anxious to close the deal for fear the old man would change his mind. It was a fixer upper, but the renovations started immediately. The entire family helped fix the apartments. Even some of Juan Manuel's *charro* friends would stop by for a few hours a week and help with whatever they could.

In January of 1973, without any complications, José Ramón was born. Manuel picked the name. This new baby had come in a time of great grief for him. His 24-year-old son Ramón, from his first marriage, had died only a few months before. No one had suspected a thing, being so young and in such good health. The tragedy had left everyone in the family completely devastated and with many more questions than there were answers available. As a matter of fact, no answers were available. So, the first thing Manuel asked when this new baby was born was if it was a boy, he believed in his heart that the soul of his deceased son could be reincarnated in this new baby. And that is how José Ramón got his name.

That summer, when José Ramón was six months old, Juan Manuel was voted *King of the Charros*. In such a short time, he had been able to master his routines while adding a little spice to his exercises by incorporating a few of his own adaptations. This made them a little more dangerous and more entertaining to the public. By unanimous votes, he had become *The Charro of Charros*. He had also won the popular vote in the public surveys given to people at the show for an entire month. Juan had never taken his sisters to any of the shows, he didn't want them to see the danger he would put himself through on an everyday basis. He couldn't run the risk of his sisters telling their mother and worrying her to death, not realizing that everyone knew what kind of danger goes on in a *charreada*.

At that point in his life, he knew that not even his parents had the right to forbid him anything; and if it came to that, he would move out. Maybe he'd ask Chuya to move in with him. He wasn't sure how he felt about marriage. It would be like getting his wings clipped and he was not going to do that. He hoped his situation would not come to that.

There was a yearly ball at the end of every season to celebrate the members of the club and the bravery and success of the team. It would crown the *King and Queen of Charros* during the opening reception followed by the ball. Juan Manuel escorted his three oldest sisters himself. A few of his *charro* friends had asked him for permission to take his sisters to the ball so they each had their own escort, but he got defensive and borderline violent with them.

"A man has to protect his own women and I know how you all are, bunch of womanizers!" he had warned them.

"Oh, it takes one to know one, right?" they would joke.

"You know Juan, you don't own a monopoly on women" or "Protect them from what, exactly?" Comments that he would brush off and completely ignore.

That night Juan Manuel walked in the reception hall with three beautiful women by his side, Rosa María, María Imelda, and Chuya. Josefina, although she looked older than 11 years of age, was not allowed to go. She had cried all day and all afternoon, but Chuy would not change her mind, and Juan promised her he would personally escort her and her alone when she was older. That calmed Josefina down for a while, but she was crying as she ran outside to see them off and wave goodbye.

Imelda had hesitated to go to the event. She had never outgrown her fear of horses and felt uncomfortable thinking there would be some around somewhere. She was afraid of making a fool of herself in front of everyone. After all, *charros* and their horses were inseparable. Juan Manuel joked saying the horses had not been invited.

Once at the ball, Juan Manuel took turns dancing with the three women he escorted. He wanted to make sure they all had a great time while also being ridiculously protective of them. His sisters were not allowed to dance with anyone else other than himself; this was a rule that was imposed by him, not their parents. They did not care either way, if there was dancing, they didn't care who their dancing partner was. They were very shy and cautious throughout the night, especially making sure they did not make eye contact with any of the men. They wanted to make sure they were on their best behavior and maybe Juan would take them out again sometime and risk at all costs being scolded by their mother. Chuya had been quiet throughout the night and didn't care to dance although she had been known to dance for an entire night.

"I want your sisters to dance with you, they never go out and I do; dance with them" she had told Juan.

But after Rosa María and María Imelda were exhausted from dancing so much, Juan tried one more time with Chuya only to be rejected.

"I'm tired and I don't feel like dancing tonight, Juan." She said unenthusiastically.

"Are you sure you're ok? You've been acting differently all night. Did I do something wrong?" Juan asked, concerned.

"No, you're fine, I promise. But at some point, tonight I'd like to talk to you."

"Why don't you just let me know? You can't tell me you want to talk to me and then have me wait."

"Well then, you'll have to wait. I'll tell you when you drop me off at home."

"Fine, then let's go now." Juan ordered.

"Don't be so distasteful Juan Manuel! Your sisters are having a great time. Please don't do that to them. They never go out so try to be a little patient and let them have a little fun." Chuya scolded him.

He grabbed her arm forcefully and took her outside. She was never that considerate of others. Chuya had a tendency to do what she wanted, and no one could stop her so Juan had a suspicion that she was using his sisters to manipulate the situation.

"Tell me what's wrong! Are you leaving me?" Juan barked with anger in his eyes. He knew she wouldn't hesitate to leave him, and he wanted her to be direct with him. She wasn't the type of woman that stayed if she didn't want to. He wanted answers.

"You're hurting me! Get your hands off me... I'm pregnant!" she replied. She was surprised that he could get so upset at something so insignificant.

Juan interrupted his sisters' conversation with some friends they had found at the ball. They were going home.

Juan Manuel

Chapter XV

Juan Manuel and Chuya's baby, Juan Manuel, was born in April of 1974. Seven months after Juan Manuel and Chuya had moved in together. His firstborn being a male was named after him, as is customary.

Chuya and the baby were released from the hospital two days after the child had been born. It had been a rapid dilation process from the time the contractions had started, followed by an easy birth no more than a couple of hours later. Chuya didn't suffer with many labor pains. She later told visitors, in her usual blunt fashion, that the baby "slid straight out, like nothing."

He was a beautiful and healthy baby, with dark skin and eyes like his father and curly hair like his mother. She felt almost fully recovered by the time they got home, but still rested for about a week before resuming her normal life. One day when the baby was two weeks old, Chuya got up and got dressed to go out with her friends.

"Wait! You're not taking the baby?" asked Juan in disbelief.

"Hell no, why would I take him? He's a baby and babies are supposed to stay at home until they're older. He's a newborn, for Christ's sake!" Chuya retorted.

"Well, where are you going without him that can't wait until he's older?" Juan questioned her.

"I'm going to lunch with my friends. Since when do I have to tell you of my whereabouts? I've been a prisoner of this house for long enough, I'm leaving." Chuya answered decidedly.

"What about your son?" he asked.

"Well, you stay and watch him. Last time I checked, he had two parents. I'm not the only one responsible for him."

"You can't do this!" he exclaimed with panic.

"Watch me! And good luck with your son, he likes to eat every two hours and shit his diaper every two hours with an hour difference in between both feats," she said as she walked out.

"Get back in here and take care of your son, he needs you!" yelled Juan, running after her.

"As a matter of fact, I never even wanted to have a child, you did. So, congratulations! He's all yours!" Chuya answered as she was leaving.

Chuya had told him from the beginning that she wasn't the domestic type, but he assumed it was only an expression since every woman in fact was the domestic type. He thought, then what kind of woman could she be if she wasn't what all women naturally are?

When Juan Manuel walked back into the house, the baby was crying. He had woken up due to his parents' commotion. Juan Manuel didn't know what to do with his new son, so he picked him up and rocked him in his arms trying to soothe him. After several minutes, he still had not stopped crying. Juan Manuel then sang to the baby in a sweet and low voice as he held him tight on his chest. He walked all around the apartment until the baby fell back asleep. Even though Juan Manuel had grown up with many siblings and there were always babies at his house, he had never learned how to change a diaper or even feed them. That was usually done by his mother and then later his sisters. He had always been taken care of by the women in his family and now realized he never had to do much growing up. Everything was done by women. Most of his childhood was spent outdoors either helping his mother collect weekly payments from her work or just being a child. Later, his entire time was dedicated to learning everything about being a *charro*. None of this was a man's work, this was to be done by women and he was no woman, no sir!

Feeling desolate, Juan Manuel picked up the sleeping baby and headed to his mother's house which was only a few blocks away. With tears in his eyes, he told his mother everything that had happened earlier with Chuya and how she refused to take care of her own child. He called her a heartless mother and a bad woman, but his mother only shook her head in response. What good was a woman for if she couldn't take care of her own child? That was unnatural and definitely not what God intended for women!

"Stop talking like that Juan Manuel! You don't know anything about being a woman or birthing a child, so I would appreciate it if you stopped judging and bad mouthing your wife," Chuy scolded him.

"But what type of woman abandons her child like that?" he whined.

"She went to lunch with friends, is that really abandoning? Does she not deserve time to herself? Or do you think that because she had your child, now she must be a slave to you and the baby? She is still a person, Juan Manuel. If you're going to come to my house, I need you to change your attitude." She did not hesitate to lecture him about common decency while he was in her house.

"I don't know what to do, Ma!"

"Don't you worry about it mi'jo, she'll go back to being herself in a bit. Just give her some time and don't be too harsh with her. Meanwhile, bring the baby to me and I'll watch him until she comes around. I'll even show you how to change his diaper," Chuy said to him in a kind manner.

"Don't be too harsh with her? You must be kidding me; this is her son. She can't just abandon him like this. She must be responsible for him."

Juan Manuel was beginning to get furious again.

"Son, have you considered that you may not fully understand women, especially how they may feel after giving birth?" she questioned.

Having been a victim of postpartum depression herself, Chuy completely understood where her daughter-in-law was coming from and was certain Chuya would feel better soon, she just needed help, kindness, and some space.

"Sometimes the hormones in a woman's body go crazy after having a child and it does funny things to the mind," Chuy continued. "Sometimes it forces a woman to completely reject her baby. It's natural and although it doesn't happen to everyone, or with every birth, it does happen. And it also happens more than we talk about it. You have to be kind and caring to her, do you understand? She'll soon come to her senses , you'll see."

"Why are you telling me this? She can't just run away from her child, from her responsibilities!" answered Juan with frustration.

"Ya basta! Go home, take a nap or something and stop talking that way. You are not listening to what I'm telling you. I'm trying to help you understand your woman. What is wrong with you? Stop worrying about it, I promise you she's not abandoning him. I'll take care of Juanito for now. Go get some rest. Go before I get more upset with you!" Chuy scolded her son.

Juan Manuel went home and sat at the kitchen table smoking and drinking. He did not go pick up the baby at night or ask his mother if the baby could stay the night there with her. He waited and waited to see what time Chuya came home, but he passed out drunk on the kitchen floor. Chuya didn't come home that night.

The next morning, Chuya returned home and found Juan Manuel still on the floor. She woke him up and asked him to move to the bed while she made some coffee. She gave him an aspirin with a glass of cold water to help him feel better. She had spent the night at her mother's house who had passed away before the baby had been born. She was still mourning the loss of her mother. She always begged Chuya to give her a grandchild, and now that Juanito was here, her mother wasn't and she didn't even have time to meet him.

All night she thought that maybe her place was with her man and her baby, but she ignored the thoughts as they came. She needed the night away, on her own, to think things through and to rest. Her entire life had been turned upside down with the birth of her baby and she wasn't sure if she could handle it. Chuya's mother had assured her that sometimes women felt very sad and out of it after giving birth and that it sometimes takes a little bit of time to learn to love one's baby. Chuya knew she was not sad and as a matter of fact, she felt like her mind had never been clearer.

When Juan Manuel woke up later that afternoon, she called him to the kitchen. She needed to talk to him and hopefully have a productive discussion. She spoke in a very calm and resolute manner. At first, Juan Manuel thought he was imagining things, that his mind was playing tricks on him.

"This must be this wicked hangover," he thought.

Chuya was very serious and very clear with her message; she did not want to be a mother.

"Don't you think it's a little too late? You can't say you don't want a child when the child is already here. Now you have to suck it up and take care of your responsibilities."

Juan Manuel lost his temper but kept his voice down because his headache was so intense.

"I don't have to do anything I don't want, Juan. That's what you don't understand. I don't want to have a child, I'm not ready and I am not going to do it." Chuya's mind was made up.

"Well then, now what? What do we do with Juanito?" he asked with confusion.

"You figure it out! He still has one parent, doesn't he? Why do men always think taking care of a child is only the woman's responsibility? He still has you, a fucking drunk, but he still has you. So, figure it out." she retorted.

"But I don't know how to take care of a baby!" Juan Manuel cried.

"Well, neither do I! Or do you think I do? You think women are born with that skill implanted in their brains? The truth is, we're not! It's as difficult for women as it is for men, maybe it's time you start learning." she scolded him.

"Listen, my mom told me that sometimes when a woman gives birth..." Juan Manuel wasn't finished when she cut him off.

"I am not sad, I am not confused, nor am I depressed!! Goddamn it, Juan! My mother told me the same thing a while back before she died and depression is not what I have. I am scared! I never wanted a kid. At least not at this time in my life anyway, but maybe never. I just can't do it." she said furiously.

"What does this mean for us?" he asked desperately.

"I said I didn't want to be a mother, I never said I didn't want to be with you."

Just when he thought he couldn't possibly be more confused about women, he learned that some women don't want to be mothers. How could that be? He always thought that was what all women wanted and fantasized about, more than anything in life, to be a mother. Isn't that all they sing and play about when they're little? Life didn't make sense to him anymore.

Chuy kept the baby for months. She was convinced that Chuya was suffering from postpartum depression and one day she would get better. Then she would pick up her child and take him with her and become the great mother Chuy knew Chuya could be. Meanwhile, Juanito was being taken care of by his aunt, Josefina, for the most part. He would sleep with her at night and she would tend to him as if he was her own.

"Motherhood is an instinct for us women, it just takes a little longer for some to get to that point." Chuy kept telling Juan Manuel, trying to not lose hope.

Chuya never came around or got better from her supposed baby blues. One day, when Juanito was five months old, Chuy asked both what they decided to do about the baby. Juan Manuel wasn't sure what to say. He had been hoping for a miracle, but Chuya had been perfectly clear from the beginning: she was not meant to be a mother.

"You know what? I'll take him. It doesn't matter, *donde comen ocho, comen nueve.* We can take care of him, I have Rosa María and Imelda to help me, Josefina is old enough too and she's the one who takes care of him anyway. I have help, and I will not allow this innocent child to grow up without a family or be forced to live where he is not wanted."

Chuy made the decision to keep Juanito, and his parents did not object.

Chuy had come to this conclusion without consulting Manuel. She didn't care about his opinion or if he agreed or was against it. His opinion did not matter, and she finally registered her grandson as her own natural son. María de Jesús and Manuel were the official parental names on Juanito's birth certificate. Josefina, who had just turned fourteen a month before the baby was born, was ecstatic with the new baby. She was even more excited than when her baby brother José Ramón had been born. Since Juanito wasn't really her brother, but her nephew, she wanted to try to raise him by herself as much as she could. Whenever there was something she didn't know how to do, she wasn't too shy to ask for help. She was always delighted to learn all the new skills necessary. Caring for the baby gave her such a sense of accomplishment. So, Juanillo, as he was known in the household, grew up much more attached to Josefina than to any of his other relatives.

Once everything had been settled with the newest member of the family, it was time to concentrate on the new business. The fact that the apartments they had just purchased were directly next to their house was such a convenience. Manuel had been working in a construction company for a few years by this time and what he had learned in that job helped with the many necessary renovations. The apartments were in a good location but needed a lot of work. Chuy refused to rent to anyone until the apartments were suitable for new tenants; the place had to be perfect for a family to live *como Dios manda*- like God intended.

The entire family helped with the new project. When Manuel was at work, the children helped by cleaning newly installed windows, tightening bolts and screws in fixtures, washing walls, and picking up trash. The older ones installed the roof with Chuy and helped her replace shingles after mopping hot tar on the roof. Everyone worked diligently every day, and, in a matter of a few months, the apartments were ready for new residents.

In the winter of 1974, all three apartments were rented out. Two of the apartments were occupied by young families. The third, and largest apartment, was rented to a family of six. The family consisted of three sons and a young daughter. Narciso was 18, Pedro 15, Lorenzo 14, and Belém 12. The father, Nicolas, had made the decision to move to Ciudad Juárez, his wife Elena had followed him against her will. She had been warned that if she did not move to Juárez where there were better opportunities for work, he would go to the United States alone to make a better living. He had gone before, leaving the family behind in their hometown of Santa María del Oro, Durango. The family had suffered greatly during his absences while he had the time of his life in *el otro lado*.

All three of the sons worked multiple jobs to help support the family, something they had been doing from a very young age. They had only finished sixth grade back home, but once they moved to Juárez and were older, they had the opportunity to attend a technical school. They attended class in the evenings after work and sometimes on Saturday. They always strived to better themselves no matter how much they worked. Education was always very important to them. Belém, their youngest, and a girl, had started middle school against their father's wishes. He had never appreciated the value of a traditional education.

"We need money now and school can't provide that, it only takes away the little money that we have," he asserted.

"I have to pay for books and materials, then you need to buy a uniform, and then the teachers always ask for more things they don't really need. We can't afford it! What we do need and can afford is another income."

Nicolas seemed to gripe constantly.

Since all three of the sons were working full time, they argued that they could pay for Belém's school materials and Nicolas would never see a single cent of his money go towards the education of her daughter. Very reluctantly, he gave his permission. They all wanted an education for themselves, which unfortunately, had been denied to them by their father. They decided they would fight tooth and nail to make sure their little sister would stay in school as long as possible. Meanwhile, they worked wherever they could make extra cash. Sometimes, they sold pastries or fruit out of a cart pushed with a bicycle attached to it. Even Elena made teddy bears by hand and sold them at the square outside the church to help the cause.

Because they were almost never home, it took the hard-working brothers a while to meet their neighbors. Early evenings and weekends were the best for visiting with friends in the neighborhood. Soon the talk and gossip between the neighborhood girls about the new boys in town started. Imelda had grown to be a very shy and quiet girl, but curious nonetheless, like any other young woman her age. She had noticed Narciso, the oldest of the three brothers, walk from his house to the bus stop and back home. In her opinion, he was the best looking of the three. He had shiny straight black hair, a little long and parted on the side. He had a miniscule mustache that looked like it took a very long time to grow, and a gracious way of walking that radiated confidence.

It didn't take her long to figure out his schedule. She knew that once he got home for the day and possibly after dinner, he'd sit outside with his brother Pedro and his guitar. Pedro played the guitar beautifully and the three of them sang, but Narciso was the one with the best voice of the three. She was fascinated by him. Without saying a word to anyone, so as not to raise suspicions, she made sure she was outside on the porch every day at the time he would walk by her house. He had noticed her alone most of the time and liked her immediately. He thought she was beautiful. He liked the way her dark curls formed into coils and rested freely on her shoulders. Her skin was a beautiful caramel tone, and the look in her eyes was alluring. He knew she was looking at him, but when he turned to meet Imelda's gaze, she would avert her eyes. The thing that he liked most about her was the lighthearted smile she always wore on her face; it made her look joyous and carefree. That smile of hers was captivating; he was charmed by her at first glance.

Narciso tried to introduce himself and talk to Imelda one free afternoon, only to find out there were eight young women on the porch, socializing. In a "sea of women" he couldn't distinguish who was the one who had caught his eye earlier during the week, so he continued walking around the block and went back home. Later that afternoon he saw someone leave the porch and head to the neighborhood store by herself. He got up and followed her, rushing to catch up. Thinking he was about to talk to Imelda, he spoke too soon and asked if he could walk with her and if maybe they could go out sometime.

"No thank you, we are not allowed to date, and also I'm only fourteen." Josefina answered with a curt undertone to her voice.

"Fourteen? Oh, I'm sorry; I must have confused you for someone else. You do look much older than fourteen though. Do you live in that house in the corner?" Narciso asked, embarrassed.

"Oh, why thank you! I like that. Yes, I do live there. With my parents, three brothers, and five sisters. Why?"

"You have five sisters?" he asked in disbelief.

"How the hell will I know which one it was?" he mumbled to himself.

"Yes, two are older than me and three are younger," Josefina continued. "Do you have any sisters? Wait, how old do I look again?" she happily questioned.

"As a matter of fact, I do. She's twelve years old; maybe you can be friends and visit each other. Her name is Belém. What's your name?"

Narciso hoped this conversation could be a clever way to meet Imelda.

"I'm Josefina. Tell me how old I look. What did you think when you saw me?" she asked again.

"Oh, I don't know; fifteen maybe. What are your older sisters' names and how old are they?"

"Rosa María is eighteen and goes to school to be an accountant and María Imelda is seventeen and goes to school to be a beautician. I also have an older brother who doesn't live with us anymore, he's very brave and isn't afraid of anyone or anything. He's the king of the charros," Josefina added proudly.

"Oh, that's very nice. Hey, do you know which one of your sisters likes to sit outside on the porch alone in the afternoons?"

He was getting closer to getting the answers he needed.

"That's María Imelda; she's very shy and quiet and likes to be alone sometimes. My mom says she's very dreamy and is possibly planning things in secret and will never tell anyone, but I don't think so. She wouldn't even kill a fly without feeling bad for it. Then my mom says that's how the quiet ones are, they look like they'll never do anything and when you least expect it: BOOM!"

"I agree, she does sound like a dreamer. What does she look like?" Narciso had to make sure they were talking about the right sister.

"She doesn't look like a Chinese girl like Rosa María does, her eyes are slanted and small. Imelda has bigger eyes, curly hair, and darker skin."

"Ok, can you do me a favor? But it has to be a secret. While you go to the store, I'll go home and write a note. Do you think you can give it to Imelda?" He winked as he asked Josefina for her secrecy.

"Why is it a secret? Do you like her like for a girlfriend? My mom doesn't let any of us have boyfriends and she'll get in trouble if she finds out and then I'll get in trouble for giving her the note," Josefina paused. "So, no thanks." She answered with finality.

"Come on, it'll be fun. You can be the messenger, when she writes back, you bring it to me. I'll give you five pesos for every note you take and bring back," Narciso offered.

"Fine, I'll do it. But I'll take the payment upfront please. I'm going to the store and would like to maximize the use of my time."

Josefina extended her hand waiting for her five pesos.

Narciso laughed, reached into his pocket, and paid her. When she came back from the store and turned the corner in her street, he was already waiting for her with his note ready. He handed it to her and reminded her to not let anyone else know about their secret.

"It's very nice doing business with you. Oh, before I forget. I feel like you know my entire family's history and I don't even know your name."

"My name is Narciso and it's very nice to meet you and do business with you as well. Don't worry, hopefully it won't be a secret for long."

"What do you mean? If it's not a secret anymore, I'll lose the business side of it."

"Well, maybe soon I can be your *cuñado*, unofficially. But don't worry though, if that happens, I'll still do you favors. I can still buy you a little something occasionally or give you five pesos or something. But also, if she doesn't want anything to do with me, there goes your business side of it too so if I were you, I'd convince her to like me. What do you think of that?"

"You're a little sneaky don't you think? But I see your point, and I'm on board. I only have a few words left for you; I have to get back before I get in trouble myself... over five miserable pesos." Josefina started rolling her eyes.

"Okay, what is it?"

"YOU.BETTER.PAY.UP."

They both laughed and each went their own way. Narciso kept going outside looking towards his landlord's house right in front of him and for a sign from Josefina. An hour after their business exchange had taken place, she went outside and saw him. Before she returned inside, she gave him a secretive thumbs-up.

There was no need for Josefina to try to convince Imelda to write a note in response. She had already liked Narciso from afar and had been thinking of ways to talk to him but couldn't come up with any. She knew her mother, being as clever as she was, would find out immediately. She could not tell a lie; she would've gotten so nervous that Chuy would've immediately suspected something was going on. So, the note exchange had made things much easier for her.

Imelda and Narciso sent each other notes for two weeks before they were able to meet and talk in-person. They were so close to each other in distance, yet so far away with all the obstacles between them. He gave her his schedule for the week and told her when he was off, and she sent a note back telling him when she could potentially see him. Chuy was a very strict woman when it came to her daughters. They were only allowed to go outside to socialize with the neighborhood girls. Boys were completely out of the question under any circumstance. It was a small neighborhood and all of Imelda's and Rosa María's friends were well known at the house. The first three planned meetings did not work out because she did not have the chance to leave the house, or he had missed his very small window of opportunity. Narciso knew that trying to date Imelda would be difficult but meeting her in-person proved to be even harder. Fortunately, he was a patient man, and he would wait if he had to.

The day Imelda and Narciso finally met, Chuy had asked Imelda to finish washing the dishes from lunch and get a few things she needed from the store to make dinner. She washed the dishes and noticed there was only enough detergent for one more day but said nothing. She hoped she'd be asked to go get more the next day, giving her an opportunity to see Narciso again. She finished the dishes and took off to the store. She walked by the apartment where Narciso lived, and he noticed her from his bedroom window. As soon as she turned the corner, he went outside to catch up to her. She was waiting for him behind his house.

The store was only three blocks away and they both knew they didn't have much time. Imelda didn't want to raise any kind of suspicions at home and jeopardize her limited freedom. Narciso went up to her and smiled, then grabbed her hand in his. She trembled and her hand was clammy.

"Are you nervous?" Narciso asked in a whisper.

"No, I'm not nervous. It's just hot outside" she replied, taking her hand back and wiping the sweat on her jeans before giving it back to him.

"Your hand was trembling," he insisted.

"It's just that if my mom finds out..." Imelda got quiet at the thought of her mother.

"She won't find out, I've already made a few of your younger sisters my allies; In case they see us, they won't say a word. I promise." Narciso told her with a gentle voice to make her feel safe.

She felt a little at ease after hearing that. He noticed the change in her and smiled at her, winking an eye.

"I got this," he assured her.

Once at the store, she asked him to stay outside and wait for her. The store owner was friends with her mother, and she couldn't take any risks. She made a quick purchase and they both started walking back home slowly while he carried her bags.

In the limited time they had, he had told her he thought she was the most beautiful girl he'd seen in all of Ciudad Juárez. She blushed and looked down avoiding his eyes.

"Oh yeah? Do you say that to all the girls? Didn't you ask my little sister out a couple of weeks ago?" she asked, laughing.

"No, I only say that to the pretty ones. And you must cut me some slack. As you already know, my schedule is full every day and I'm almost never home. I have seen you alone on your porch several times. I didn't know there were five others."

"I wouldn't even know what to do with myself if I had no siblings. I would probably be bored all day!" Imelda observed, smiling.

"Ah, but I would recognize that big and beautiful smile anywhere."

"So, back to you asking my sister out..." she teased.

"Well, I'd only seen you from that side of the street and when Josefina went to the store that time, I thought she was you. I didn't want to waste any more time. I'm glad we got everything straightened out though because I can't date a fourteen-year-old... that's a little too young for my taste and I'm sure it's illegal," Narciso joked.

"Well, I was sitting on the porch alone because I already knew the time you came home and I wanted to see you," she admitted shyly.

Narciso smiled to himself.

They stopped at the corner behind his house. He put the bags on the ground and held both of her hands in his. She was very nervous and blushed while looking down to avoid his gaze. He took her chin and slightly lifted it towards him and gave her a soft and tender kiss on her full lips.

"So, do you want to be my girlfriend then?" he whispered.

She nodded slowly.

He kissed her again then gave her the bags and waited for her to get home. He went back towards the store and around the block, just in case anyone was outside the house.

The following day they had an opportunity to see each other again. It was a Sunday, so Narciso didn't have any responsibilities that day. Keeping an eye on his window, he noticed her walking alone, possibly towards the store. He waited for her to turn the corner, looked towards her house to make sure no one was watching, and went to catch up to her. As Imelda had predicted, the dish washing soap had been used up the night before after dinner. That morning she volunteered to wash the breakfast dishes and pretended to be surprised the detergent was all gone. She then asked her mother for money to go to the store. Chuy yelled at her as she left the house "*No te tardes!*"

Imelda nervously wondered if her mother suspected something since she had never made this demand before when running errands.

Chapter XVI

Imelda walked on clouds knowing that Narciso was her boyfriend. He was the only man who had interested her so much since she laid eyes on him. Her friend Isela, from across the street, had told her that maybe she liked him so much just because he was "fresh meat" in the neighborhood. She considered this for only a moment before reasoning that Narciso's brothers Pedro and Lorenzo were also new, but she wasn't interested in them. In fact, she had not felt so intrigued by anyone before. Being noticed by a person of the opposite sex, who had the same intentions she had towards him, felt like a great victory to her own personal insecurities.

Imelda had the most radiant smile to match her personality. When she smiled, she lit up the room and that just made everyone around her smile in return. She always thought of herself as the least pretty of her sisters, the least interesting of her group of friends, and the least likely to have something to offer. For all of these reasons, she always kept quiet. She believed in her heart that if she came up with an idea, it would be ridiculously laughable, and she would only make herself look like a fool; so she barely spoke. She was ashamed of her darker skin and her black curls, and she found her mouth too big to be ladylike. She didn't think of herself as intelligent and since she made the decision not to go to school after sixth grade, she didn't consider herself very educated.

Imelda and her two older siblings, Juan Manuel and Rosa María, had been born in El Paso, Texas. Chuy had saved enough money during her pregnancy to hire a midwife in the United States. She set everything up towards the end of her second trimester, and when the time was close, she'd cross the border to the midwife's home and stay there until the baby was born.

The opportunity to give birth across the border meant those children would have dual citizenship in Mexico and the USA. She made the effort to do this for their future as well as the future of the next generation. She knew they would have access to opportunities that simply did not exist in Mexico. After the first three children were born, it became more difficult to support the household and pay a midwife every time she became pregnant. So, the rest of her children were born in Ciudad Juárez.

Because she was a U.S. citizen and nothing impeded her to work, Imelda decided to look for a job across the border. When her friend Isela heard of her plan, she wanted to join the American job hunt as well. She owned a car, so if they got the job, they planned on carpooling. They thought it would be fun to finally do something grownup and maybe save some money. Both were given a job at a factory, making denim jeans, not far from the border.

Imelda worked while Narciso worked, she commuted home while he was in class, and in the early evening, they would see each other for a short time. They met any chance they had. Going to the neighborhood store gave them another opportunity to see each other, but with a time limit. Sometimes Imelda would lie to her mother by saying she would be visiting Isela or another one of her neighborhood friends and would enjoy more time with Narciso. When she would take longer, or Chuy had a gut feeling that she was lying, she would go out on the porch and yell her name at the top of her lungs for her to come home.

That would embarrass her, but she obeyed her mother's calls immediately. She knew her mother was a force to be reckoned with. She would stay on the porch until Imelda came back home and would always tell her *"muchacha jacalera, que andas haciendo en la calle? ¿No tienes casa? ¡Andale ponte a lavar la ropa!"*

Imelda was certain that Chuy knew about her relationship with Narciso but couldn't figure out how. She never knew how her mother always found out about things that happened in the neighborhood. She wasn't one who would give into gossip or even visit the neighbors because she was always working, but she did have visitors all the time. Her seamstress business had been continually growing and she never had time off. But Imelda felt that her mother knew everything, she was sure of it. She started suspecting her mother might be a psychic when she was no longer allowed to visit her friends at their houses. Instead, Chuy told her to ask her friends to visit her at their house as there was no need for *her* to be out in the street where anything could happen. And when she offered to run the necessary errands, she was told one of her siblings could run the errands and she needed to stay home and help her in the house with other chores.

Seeing Narciso became more and more complicated. She never thought of talking to her parents about the young man she was seeing. She was terrified of that idea. Instead, she was always thinking of ways to be able to leave the house and see him. He had already complained to her that they hardly ever saw each other and when they did, they only had a few minutes before she had to go.

Imelda was very good at keeping her relationship with Narciso secret. She did not tell anyone about it, not even her best friends. The only ones that were aware of the relationship were Narciso's brothers and Josefina, who had been the initial messenger. Her girlfriends couldn't believe that Narciso had not yet found a girlfriend after so many months of living on the block. They remarked that they had never seen him even try to talk to anyone. Even Pedro and Lorenzo had already been dating some girls from a few blocks away, and they had the same rigid schedule as their older brother. He became the topic of discussion due to his "mysterious" personality, and they all wanted to know more about him. Imelda still kept her secret; she couldn't risk turning her mother's suspicions into certainty. Girls started talking among themselves and the rumors and gossip around Narciso's romantic life began.

Imelda had not been able to see Narciso for at least a month because of her mother's protective nature. She would still sit on the porch like she did before, when she knew the bus that was taking Narciso home was about to arrive. She didn't see him come home for two weeks and she hadn't heard from him or even received a note. Imelda started to get uneasy but did not have the freedom to go looking for him and she did not feel comfortable asking about him. She felt that she would raise suspicions and her main goal was to keep everything about their relationship secret. Chuy had started to be lenient with her again. She even gave Imelda permission to go to a friend's birthday party if she was home before 8:00 pm.

At the birthday party, after all the major festivities were completed, she reluctantly asked if anyone knew what the deal with that new guy Narciso was. She was devastated when everyone started gossiping about things they had heard. One of her friends claimed to have seen him with a girl downtown.

"That explains why I haven't seen him, and he hasn't even tried looking for me," she thought. She started feeling nauseous and immediately excused herself from the party and went home early.

"*Y ahora, ¿a ti qué te picó?*" Chuy asked surprised.

271

"Nothing, why?" Imelda answered without making eye contact.

"You practically begged me to go to this party and you're home early. What happened? I thought you really wanted to go."

"I did want to go, but then I started feeling ill, my stomach hurts. It must've been something I ate. I'm just going to lay down for a bit and see if I feel better."

"Take some warm 7-Up with salt. That should make your stomach settle a bit. When you do feel better, come help me with this wedding dress. I'm almost done with it but I still have to do a lot of work by hand." Chuy ordered without looking at her broken-hearted daughter.

In her room, which she shared with two of her sisters, Imelda couldn't stop thinking about what she had heard.

"Of course, he looked for someone else. I can't give him more than fifteen minutes per week." she thought to herself. "And why wouldn't he go look for someone else? It's like he only wanted me only until he found someone better." Imelda tortured herself imagining the worst scenarios when Chuy went into the room and asked how she was feeling.

"I'm still in pain," Imelda answered.

"You drank the 7-Up with salt like I told you to? Maybe take some aspirin too." Chuy added, feeling her face for fever.

"Yes ma'am, I did" she replied in a low voice not wanting her to know she'd been crying.

"Your pain is so strong it made you cry? Maybe they're cramps."

"It's not my time yet for another two weeks."

"Well then there's nothing wrong with you. Come help me now and you'll see once you stop thinking and start working, the pain will go away." Chuy ordered. For mothers somehow always know everything when it comes to their children, even if they don't let their children know. Somehow, she knew Imelda needed a distraction.

Imelda went back to work and to her daily routine for a few more weeks without knowing anything about Narciso. She had already lost hope and was certain he had abandoned her for someone else in the most brutal manner, without an explanation. It was as if the earth had swallowed him. It also didn't occur to her to ask anyone, not even Pedro or Lorenzo, his brothers who she had seen several times.

One day, Chuy asked Imelda to go to the store and buy a few things she needed from the store. She was baffled since she hadn't been allowed to go in a few months and her other sisters would take turns running errands. It was a Sunday afternoon, the only day Narciso had off, from what she remembered at the beginning of their relationship. Since she hadn't seen him in over two months, she never expected she could run into him.

Imelda left the store after her purchase and was surprised to see Narciso waiting for her outside with a big smile on his face, appearing to be happy to see her. She didn't understand why he smiled, and immediately felt hurt by him, feeling laughed at. She ignored him and started walking back home. He caught up to her confused and softly tried to hold her hand.

"Hello there, beautiful. It's been a long time since we saw each other. I have so much to tell you. Here, let me help you with that bag." Narciso offered.

"No, thank you. Don't bother." Imelda answered coldly, avoiding looking at him.

"Come on, I always carry your bags to the corner," He insisted.

"I said I was fine, and you don't need to carry my bags anymore. I can do it myself." She responded defensively.

"Whoa! Ok fine, but I can still walk with you, right? Want to talk for a few minutes before you go back home?"

"I can't. My mother is waiting for me, and I told her I wouldn't be long," she said, picking up her pace.

"Oh, come on, we never take more than ten minutes. Stay a little, please. Otherwise, when will I see you again?"

"You don't get to see me again. As far as I'm concerned, you have plenty of people to see and plenty of people to talk to so if you would please excuse me, I have to go."

"Wait! I don't understand. What's happening? Don't you want to be with me anymore?" Narciso asked, perplexed.

"No, I don't," She shot back.

"Why not? Don't you love me anymore?"

"No, as a matter of fact, I don't. Either I stopped or I never loved you, but that was a long time ago."

"Listen, I'll let you go. But you have to tell me what's wrong. Is it because of something I did, or because it's true that you don't love me anymore?" He stood in front of her, holding her elbows in his hands, blocking her way.

"I don't love you." she repeated with a straight face and her heart pounding.

"Okay. That is all I needed to know. I give you my word; I will never bother you again. Have a good day, Imelda." He moved out of the way and let her go.

He watched her turn the corner, devastated. He wanted to run after her but didn't. After a few minutes, he walked back home with an empty look in his eyes.

When she got home, Imelda felt strong and brave. She would not allow him to play her for a fool, she thought. Now that she had told him how she felt and had some closure, she could move on with her life. She hadn't told him how she felt or why she didn't want to see him again. It didn't matter to her, he should know. She didn't have to think about him anymore or wonder why he'd stopped loving her. She knew the truth, he had someone else.

For almost a year she didn't talk to him. She kept telling herself that she had done the right thing and felt proud of it. She went back to sitting on the porch knowing he wouldn't walk by her house, and she wouldn't have to see him. She spent most of her time at work and, during the evening, she would go to beauty school. All other hours were spent helping her mother wherever she could during the weekend. Keeping herself busy would almost always help her to not think about Narciso and the way their almost one-year relationship had ended.

After the anger, pride, and feeling of betrayal had subsided, she found herself not being able to stop thinking about Narciso. She started doubting the way she had handled the situation. What if it all had been gossip? What if nothing had been true? He looked genuinely surprised when she told him she didn't want to be with him. He looked devastated.

For the first time, she felt as if she could've made a mistake. She had to find out the truth and ease her mind. The entire time they had seen each other, no one had known about it. She had made sure of that. She reminded herself that only Josefina and Narciso's brothers, Pedro and Lorenzo, knew of their relationship. She had to make sure she'd done the right thing. If she had been wrong, how would he ever forgive her? She felt anxious and nervous, she hadn't felt that way since she first heard he was seeing someone else almost a year before.

Imelda sat on the porch waiting for Pedro to get off the bus that afternoon. When she finally saw him coming, she let him walk past the house and then yelled "Mom, I'll be right back, I'm going to Isela's for a few minutes" and took off without waiting for a response. She heard Chuy yell out the window to not take too long because she needed her to help her make dinner and bathe the little ones. She ran until she caught up with Pedro and asked if they could talk.

"Hola, Imelda. How's it going? I haven't seen you in a while," Pedro said when he saw her approach, then gave her a hug.

"I'm doing well. I've been very busy with work and school. I joined a beauty school and I'm almost done with the course; I graduate next week. How are you?"

"That's great, I'm very happy for you. Congratulations! I'm doing well too. Tired, but can't complain too much," replied Pedro with a smile on his face.

"Thank you, I'm also glad you're doing well. Listen, I want to ask you something. Do you have a few minutes to spare and talk to me?" Imelda said abruptly.

"Of course, what's on your mind?"

"It has to do with Narciso." She lowered her eyes as she said his name.

"I figured as much," Pedro said, not surprised.

"I assume you know we stopped seeing each other quite a while ago," Imelda added.

"Yeah, I know. I never found out why. He said you told him you didn't love him, but I know that's not true. I mean, you can see those kinds of things, and I know you love him. What happened?"

"You really don't know why I broke up with him?" she asked in surprise.

"No, I really don't; and neither does he, but he is very proud and will not ever talk to you or ask you back. He said that he maybe should have insisted a bit longer if it was for anything else, but once you told him you didn't love him, he wasn't going to pressure you into being with him without feelings. So, he let it go. But believe me, he was devastated. He still is. I've never seen him like this. He tries to deny it, but I know him," Pedro explained.

"Oh my god, what have I done?" Imelda asked in panic. If Narciso had been seeing someone else, her brother would know about it and he didn't.

"If you don't mind me asking, Imelda, why did you break up with him? He really liked you. Trust me, I know. I've lived with him all my life and I'd never seen him so excited about anyone. Even if he could only see you or talk to you for a few minutes every week."

"Well, as you probably already know, I made sure to keep our relationship secret from everyone. I have very strict parents and we are not allowed to date and so I was afraid of them finding out somehow."

"Yes, I can tell your parents are on you all the time. Short leash, eh?" Pedro joked.

"Yes, very short. It was fine because I never really wanted to do anything outside or with anyone. I hang out with my friends for a bit and that's it. I'm not into socializing like most girls are, until I met your brother."

"I see," he nodded, encouraging her to continue.

"So, I hadn't seen him in a long time, I forget how long it was but it was a very long time. I didn't hear from him; he didn't send me a note. He didn't even try to communicate with me to tell me what was happening. At first, I thought you all had gone back to your hometown because I didn't see you or Lorenzo either. I asked my parents, and they said you had not given them a notice to vacate the apartment, so I was very confused," Imelda explained.

"Ok, go on."

"One day I was at a friend's house and there were other friends there too. They all started talking about you guys; you know, the fresh meat conversation. They knew things about you and Lorenzo, but they had no idea about Narciso. They all said he was very reserved, maybe an undercover cop or something. I laughed. Then someone said he had been spending a lot of time downtown because he had a girlfriend out there, that she had seen him with her."

"So, you heard that, and you thought it was true?" Pedro asked.

"Of course, I did. Someone saw him with her own eyes. Besides, I couldn't ask or say anything because I would have revealed my secret."

"Well, this is just hilarious." Pedro snickered.

"Why are you laughing? I went through so much pain for a long time with more questions than answers."

"So, you break up with him at the first opportunity you have without telling him any of this? You're so silly," he replied, shaking his head in disbelief.

"What was I supposed to do? He came to me as if nothing had happened. I hadn't seen him in months, and he just showed up one day without any explanation? No. I couldn't."

"Well, did you ask him where he'd been? Did you give him time to explain?" Pedro asked.

"I don't know. I think I did maybe, what my friend said made so much sense" Imelda stuttered, unsure if she'd asked for an explanation.

"No, you didn't, Imelda. You cut him off immediately. He told you he had so many things to tell you and you didn't give him a chance to recount his experiences from the previous two months. Look, we had the opportunity to enroll in English classes. We didn't have much time. The day we found out was the last day to sign up for free classes for the first two months. So, we signed up immediately and we started classes that same night," Pedro explained.

"So, he didn't have someone else downtown?"

"No, I was with him the entire time. All he wants in his life is to be better, to learn as much as he can. Now that we live closer to the border, we both thought it would do us good to learn some English. Just in case we might need it in the future, you know?"

"I don't understand. I've seen you get off the bus and come home, but not him. If you say you're always together, then where does he go?"

"Since you broke up with him, he gets off at the stop before this one and walks almost an extra mile around the back of the neighborhood. He then comes into the house through the back door. He's hurt and it pains him to see you, so he avoids it at all cost. I've told him what he's doing is crazy, but he won't listen. He still loves you but he's very proud. I'm sorry."

Pedro put his hand on Imelda's shoulder to show his support.

"Oh no! I feel like an idiot now. What have I done? Why didn't I let him just talk to me? What should I do? Tell me, you know him better than anyone," she begged.

"First of all, don't be so hard on yourself. Look, you probably felt jealous when you heard the rumor and not seeing him for a while probably didn't help. He didn't talk to you, and you just thought the worst," Pedro said empathetically.

"Something like that. Do you think he'll want to talk to me? I need to explain what happened."

"To tell you the truth, I don't think he will want to. I know him, he is very stubborn, and his pride gets in the way. I've told him that being so proud will destroy him one day, but he somehow just can't let it go. Besides, you told him you don't love him and to him, that's the end of it."

"Thank you, Pedro, for answering my questions. I have to think, I can't just let this go. I need to do something to get him back," Imelda explained.

"Good luck with that. Please, let me know if I can help you with anything. I like you and it's too bad that things happened this way," he gave her a hug and went home.

When she got home, Chuy did not question her whereabouts. While she was gone, Juan Manuel had dropped by for a few minutes to let them know the annual *charro* dance was coming up. This time he would take Josefina and María Alicia too since they were already seventeen and fifteen. Imelda was ecstatic with the news. Rosa María and she would be able to spend time with their friends and Juan Manuel would watch the two younger ones. Then Imelda thought of a brilliant idea.

Rosa María had started dating a young man named Agustín and only a few people knew about it, including Imelda. Their relationship had not been secretive, necessarily, but it had been kept quiet.

"Rosa, when are you seeing Agustín again?" Imelda asked, barging in Rosa's bedroom.

"This afternoon, he's driving to Isela's house. You know how her mom doesn't care if boys visit her or us there, why?" she answered with a puzzled look on her face.

"I'm coming with you. Mom won't ask questions if you and I leave together. I have something to talk to Agustín about."

"I don't understand what's gotten into you. You're acting all weird." Rosa said, confused.

Imelda confided in her older sister and told her everything that had happened with Narciso. She told her about the secret notes being delivered by Josefina at first. She talked about how Narciso had been her official boyfriend for almost a year and no one knew about it. She recounted how she believed the rumors and gossip and broke up with him without giving him a chance to explain. And now, a year later, she had to do something to get him back.

That afternoon, Imelda tagged along with Rosa María. They had told Chuy that they would be at Isela's for a while talking about what they would all wear to the *charro* dance. Maybe they would even design the dresses themselves and then Chuy could make them.

Agustín showed up at Isela's house in his new car. He had saved his wages for three years and finally, he had bought the car of his dreams. It was a green, two-door, 1971 Chevy Chevelle with big fat tires in the rear.

"Woohoo! Man, that's a sexy ride!" yelled Isela from her front porch.

"Thank you, ladies. Thank you very much!" replied Agustín walking directly to Rosa María. He always had a joking air to him no matter what. That was his charm.

"I need to talk to you right now!" Imelda declared, jumping in front of him. Without even letting Rosa get a hug, Imelda grabbed his hand and dragged him away so they could talk with a little bit of privacy.

"Okay, fine. What's going on?" answered Agustín blowing a kiss to Rosa as a last resort.

"Do you know Narciso?" Imelda asked.

"The guy that lives behind your house? The one whose parents are renting that apartment from your parents?"

"That's the one," Imelda answered excitedly.

"I've seen him around and I've been around once or twice when he's hung out with some mutual friends, but I can't say that I know him. I know of him, he probably knows of me too, but that's it. Why?"

"I need you to make friends with him, like immediately. Whatever you have to do, I promise I will help you and Rosa be together in whatever way I can. This could benefit you, Agustín; I just need your help with something, please. I don't have anyone else to ask," she pleaded desperately.

"Did he do something to you? Do you need me to take care of him?" Agustín asked, raising his fist in the air.

"I do need you to take care of something, but it's not what you're thinking," She told him what happened in detail.

"Look, I will ask his brother Pedro to help us out too. I think we'll need him, but you will play a larger role in this plan. It's foolproof, it cannot fail." she ordered.

"Yeah, I'll do it. But remember you said you'd help me be able to see Rosa María more. This deal of only seeing her once a week for a few minutes totally blows, man. Why are your parents so strict?"

"It's mostly our mother. I'm sure she has her reasons for being the way she is. I try not to judge her. I'm not a mother, so I don't know what her motivations are, and I don't think I'll have the guts to ever ask her. Sometimes she scares me, you know? She is the most loving and respectful woman in our town. We know she is appreciated by everyone, and people genuinely love her. And why not? She does what she can for everyone and the doors to our house are always open to people that need it, but when it comes to us girls... she is like a completely different person. I don't get it, but oh well; what can we do about it, right?" she shrugged.

"I guess so," Agustín answered while scratching his head.

Step one of the plan was for Agustín to go over to Narciso's house and ask for Pedro. Once he came out, he would introduce himself to him and tell him about the plan and recruit him as an accomplice on Imelda's behalf. Pedro had offered her his help in whatever he could, and she was keeping him on his promise.

Rosa María and Imelda were at Isela's house for days talking about the dresses they'd wear to the dance. They imagined the hairstyles they would create and how much fun they would have, all while making the final preparations. This dance had to go just as planned.

The day of the dance, Rosa María, Imelda, and Isela went to the reception early with the pretext of volunteering to help set up the place. Juan Manuel was very happy to hear that his sisters were interested in his passion; maybe they would even join one of the *charro* committees, maybe they could be escaramusas. Not Imelda though, with her fear of horses.

Back at their house, Agustín had shown up to pick up Pedro to go to the dance. They were both dressed appropriately, looking under the hood and admiring the car when Narciso showed up. He was walking from the bus stop looking exhausted.

"Hey, what's up *carnal*! Look, this is Agustín; you know him, right?" Pedro asked him.

"Hey, what's going on? That's a pretty nice car you got there," Narciso answered, attempting small talk. He was so tired it was almost impossible for him to feel excited about anything.

"Hey! We're going to the annual *charro* dance, wanna come with us?" Agustín asked as casually as possible.

"Oh no! I am tired and just want to shower and go to bed. Besides, it looks like you guys are all ready to go. I would have to make you both wait for me to get ready," replied Narciso.

"We have plenty of time; we can get there late and make an entrance. I'll rev my engine as we are parking, and we'll have all eyes on us. Three handsome single guys in an awesome car."

"Single guys? I thought you were dating Rosa María. Is that over?" asked Narciso, astonished.

No, it's not over. It hasn't officially started yet. So, I guess I'm still officially single, no? And Pedrito, here; well, he was just telling me that he hasn't had time to make the moves on the girl he likes. So, we can all just go out and have some fun. We'll have some drinks, dance with a few girls," Agustín continued trying to lure him in.

"Oh no! I'm telling you, I'm dead tired. I would just be a bump on a log and ruin your plans for a good night," Narciso insisted, as he started to walk towards the house.

Agustín and Pedro looked at each other and they followed him in.

"*Vamos carnal*! Come with us. It will be good for you. You're always working and studying, and you don't have fun. It will be good for you to go out and relax and have some drinks. Who knows, maybe you'll be able to find a girl you like. You know what they say, *un clavo saca otro clavo*." Pedro noted, patting him on the back.

"Oh, problems of the heart Narciso?" asked Agustín, pretending ignorance.

"Don't listen to him; he doesn't know what he's saying. I don't need to look for another girl to forget the one I love... uhm, loved. I'm perfectly fine the way I am." Narciso's tone started to sound a little defensive.

"Oh, now that I know this much. We, in good faith, can't go to the dance by ourselves and leave you here alone with your misery. You look like shit!

Go, take a shower and then off we go!" said Agustín enthusiastically.

"Really, I don't want to make you late to the party. Just go without me."

"Never! Come on. Go, get ready. We'll wait for you here, take your time," declared Pedro.

Doña Elena, Narciso and Pedro's mother went into the living room and scolded them for the loud noise they were making.

"For Christ's sake Narciso, get in the shower and go away with your brother and his friend or they will stay here all night begging you and I don't have the patience to listen to this entire ruckus. Just go! They're right too, you know? I'm also tired of seeing you this way, dragging your feet as if you'll never be happy again. Go, drink, dance, laugh, meet people and have a good time. I don't care what you do, just go and leave me in peace! Your brother Lorenzo is already sleeping, poor thing, he was so tired. Now, go shower and get out of here!"

"Alright *jefa*, I'll go. Jeez, you don't have to get so angry about it!" Narciso told his mother giving her a kiss on the forehead "And you two... you're paying for my drinks for dragging me out there when I really didn't want to," he teased, pointing to his brother and then to Agustín.

As soon as Narciso was gone and they could hear the shower running, Agustín and Pedro high-fived each other and laughed loudly. Then, with their tails between their legs, they turned to Doña Elena and apologized for the noise.

"Go wait for him outside, I'm going to try to watch my telenovela and I don't want any distractions," Doña Elena ordered, shooing them out onto the patio.

The three friends arrived at the dance an hour late. Imelda had been worried the entire time since she hadn't seen them when they were supposed to, according to her schedule. She imagined her accomplices not being able to convince Narciso to join them.

"Stop worrying. Agustín and Pedro would already be here without him if they weren't able to convince him. Just relax, okay? Go dance with someone to take the edge off, you're making me nervous," advised Rosa María.

Imelda was on the verge of a nervous breakdown when she saw the young men come in through the main entrance.

"Look! They're here... quick, take your spots!" she told her sister and Isela.

The three women went to the back of the dance hall and faced the wall, pretending to be deep in conversation.

"I'm going to go get us some drinks, are you guys okay with beer? Pedro, the next round is yours." Agustín remarked as he walked towards the bar.

"Yeah, beers are fine. And yes, I'll pay for half of the tab, you stingy bastard!" answered Pedro laughing.

"Yeah, beer is fine," said Narciso, distracted. He kept looking around as if searching for someone. He knew perfectly well that Juan Manuel was a famous *charro* in the community and his sisters would probably be there, but he didn't find who he was looking for.

Agustín went to tell Rosa María and Imelda that they had arrived and that they had the most difficult time getting Narciso to agree to go with them. He swore that he would've stayed there all night until he got annoyed enough to just agree to show up.

"You guys owe me one, big time!" he told the sisters.

"I'll give you some smooches later, darling." replied Rosa María with a smile and a wink.

"YES!" said Agustín with excitement "Okay, I'm gonna go get drinks for us, I don't want Narciso to suspect a thing. Give me about thirty minutes and we'll execute the plan. I'll wait for the signal, give me one song's length in time and I'll deliver the package," he told them both as he was leaving, winking at them and pointing at Rosa María.

"You think this is going to work? What if it doesn't work? Oh my god, I'm so nervous," said Imelda.

"Relax! You look beautiful. Once you talk to him and tell him everything, if he doesn't want to see you again, then he's just a prick and you shouldn't even be all crazy about him. Just try, tell him what you want to tell him. If it doesn't work, at least you won't be thinking all the time what could have been or that you should've done something else," Rosa told Imelda, rubbing her arms to comfort her.

"Yes, you're right. Let's get this show on the road and if he doesn't want to listen to me, the night is still young, and we'll dance it away."

"That's the spirit!" said Rosa, hugging her sister.

Agustín and the two brothers had already had four beers and almost an hour had passed since they first got there. The place was full of people, young and old alike. They could see who the *charros* were since they were all wearing their traditional dress and hat. The dance floor was packed, and everyone was enjoying themselves. Then suddenly the upbeat music stopped, and the band started playing slow songs.

"Yeah, this is our chance! Come on boys, let's walk around and look for some pretty señoritas to dance with," suggested Agustín.

"You guys go. I'll just sit here by the bar and keep drinking. Don't worry, I'll put all my drinks on your tab," answered Narciso with the first hint of a joke. He had started to loosen up already.

"Don't be such a punk *carnal*. Come on, we never do this together. You're my older brother and should always set an example, go on... this is your chance," answered Pedro winking at his brother.

"Oh, what the heck, let's go!" agreed Narciso.

"Maybe we'll be lucky and find some dates. We can go on a triple date! Your broke asses better buy a car soon because I can't fit three couples in my car." joked Agustín.

Agustín led them around the building looking at girls and deciding himself if those were the ones they should ask out to dance. He seemed to be disenchanted by them no matter how pretty they were, even if the girls showed interest in them.

"How about those girls over there, Agus? Looks like they're here alone and they keep looking our way," suggested Narciso.

"No, no, no, no. You leave everything to me, the new kid on the block. I know one of them; she's dating this guy you don't want to mess with. We better leave that pack alone," Agustín replied, lying "Look, there's a group of girls out there. I saw them earlier when I went to get the first round. One of them smiled at me. Okay, let's plan. I'll take the one with the long hair and blue dress. Pedro, you take the one in the white dress and Narciso, you take the one in the peach dress and long straight hair. Got it?"

They all nodded in agreement.

Agustín took the lead. He walked around and faced Rosa María and said, "he's coming, get ready." She stood stone-still so Narciso wouldn't recognize who she was. Pedro was behind Narciso, slowing his pace and without anyone noticing, he turned around and went back to the bar, he needed a fresh drink. When Narciso approached the girl he had been assigned to, he slightly touched her shoulder and in a low voice said "Excuse me ma'am, would you please do me the honor of this dance?" Imelda turned around and grabbed his arm "yes! I would love to dance."

Narciso could not believe his eyes. How was this coincidence such a possibility? It seemed completely improbable. He looked around and did not see Pedro. He turned to look for Agustín and he was dancing with the girl in the blue dress and long hair. He recognized her. It was Rosa María, the girlfriend he had pretended earlier he didn't have! Imelda smiled sweetly at him while he hadn't been able to utter a single word. The band kept playing slow songs. He could feel his face hot and drops of sweat running on his scalp and down the back of his neck. What had just happened?

The band stopped playing to take a short break but reminded all the *enamorados* to get ready for another round of romantic melodies.

Narciso and Imelda stopped dancing and before he could say a word, she asked him "So, do you want to be my boyfriend, or what?"

He answered her with a long and sweet kiss on the lips. He could hear Agustín and Pedro yelling in excitement from the bar and cheering them on. They were all relieved the plan had worked and felt proud to have been a part of their sweet reunion, even if it had to be done by tricking Narciso.

"I never thought you'd be capable of anything, especially at conning someone this way," whispered Narciso in Imelda's ear.

"That's because you don't really know me," she replied with a flirty smile.

"Josefina told me once that the quiet ones are the deadly ones! But seriously, how can I know you, when I only got to see you fifteen minutes a week? Come on, you gotta give our relationship more than that if we are to get to know each other better and hopefully take it a step further," he answered.

"I will, I promise. But you must give me some time. I have to figure out how to talk to my parents, well, to my mom," she replied nervously.

"Why are you so scared of your mother?" he asked incredulously at the same time the band started playing again. Without answering the question, Imelda pulled him to the dance floor.

At the end of the dance, while people had started leaving, everyone gathered by the bar. Imelda and Narciso were holding hands when Juan Manuel approached them; she nervously took her hand out of his. Juan Manuel grabbed her hand and put it back in Narciso's and said to her and Rosa María: "You girls be ready in fifteen minutes. If I'm not the one that brings you home tonight, our mother will kill me."

He then turned around towards Narciso and said "Juan Manuel, at your service." shaking his hand "I've heard many good things about you, I hope they're all true. I've been asking around. Don't worry sis, no one told me, I have my own ways of finding out. I'm glad you two made up, you make a great couple. I'm going to go get Josefina and Alicia and then we'll go."

"Well, your brother knows, and he approves," said Narciso.

"He's my brother, not my parents," answered Imelda, hitting him lightly on the arm.

******

Three months had passed after the *charro* dance and Imelda had still not had a conversation with her parents asking for permission to date Narciso. Even though they had been spending a little more time together with the help of Juan Manuel and Rosa María, it was still not enough in Narciso's eyes.

In one of their short weekly visits, he decided to put his foot down and voice his grievances.

"When will you talk to your parents?" he asked impatiently.

"I don't know, please stop pressuring me. There hasn't been a right time yet," she answered, trying to smile.

"There will never be a right time, you need to tell them or I will. I swear..."

"Shhhh, please don't say that" she answered knowing he was serious.

"Ok, here's the deal. Tell them before the end of the week or I will come and talk to your father, unannounced," he declared.

"Oh, no you won't. Please, you don't know them."

"Do they beat you? Why are you so scared of them? Tell me," asked Narciso, confused "I don't understand why you act so terrified of them."

"No, they don't. It's just respect, that's all."

"Respect? Please, I don't see respect in your eyes, only fear. You can't live like this; you need to talk to them."

"I can't." Her eyes started to get moist.

"Okay fine. It seems like you'll never want to talk to them, and I don't know why. But if you can't talk to them and won't let me talk to them, then I don't know what to do. This relationship can't go any further. You gotta meet me halfway, it's only fair. If I can't talk to your father by the end of the week, this relationship is over. Do you understand? I mean it," he said with a stern voice.

"No, please, don't do that. That year that we spent apart was terrible. I don't want to have to go through that again."

"I'm going home now. Think about it, you have four days. Let me know what you decide," he said to her.

Narciso kissed her cheek softly and walked away.

That evening Chuy could tell Imelda was acting odd and she demanded to know what was going on with her. Imelda thought that if she was going to talk to her parents about Narciso, that would be as good a time as any other.

"Narciso wants to come talk to you and dad over the weekend," Imelda blurted out.

"And why are you crying? Is something wrong?" Chuy answered.

"No, there's nothing wrong. I just didn't know how to say it," she replied.

"Well, you just did, and you did a good job. Do you know what he wants to talk to your father about?" Chuy asked, already knowing the answer.

"No, I don't," Imelda lied, drying her tears with her hand.

"I'm sure you do, otherwise you wouldn't be crying all over Mrs. Silva's daughter's wedding dress. Stop crying child; you'll ruin the dress I've been working on for two weeks. Go dry your face and start dinner. I'll tell your father about it tonight. When did you say he was coming?"

"Well, he only has Sundays off because he works, goes to school in the afternoons and at night he studies English, also on Saturday sometimes," she answered from the kitchen, feeling a little more confident.

"I'll make sure we have something decent to eat. I'm sure after that conversation his parents might come for dinner. I really like that family; they seem like they're all hard workers. I don't know about the father though, we'll see," mumbled Chuy, already making plans and hearing wedding bells in her mind.

The following Sunday Narciso showed up at the exact time he was expected. He went inside the house and met Doña María de Jesús. Don Manuel immediately asked him to follow him outside on the patio. They talked for over two hours, while Imelda inside was sitting nervously next to her mother. The two women were in the studio as they worked on the wedding dresses Chuy was finishing.

"For Christ's sake, Negra, stop biting your nails, it's not becoming. Why are you so nervous? It's not like you're the one outside talking to your father asking for your hand. He's the one that should be worried, not you. Although I didn't see him worried at all, he looked as fresh as a head of lettuce. Good for him. He looks confident and I hear he's a very hard worker." said Chuy without taking her eyes off her sewing work.

Imelda looked up at her mother in disbelief.

Outside on the patio, Don Manuel and Narciso talked about life, their own background, and what they thought of the current political position of the country. Don Manuel asked what Narciso's own personal plans were for the future and lastly, what his intentions were with his beloved and sensitive daughter.

They discussed the terms of the relationship in which she had official permission to date him. He was allowed to take her out on the weekends as he saw fit, if she was back home by eight in the evening. No exceptions were to be made. Those were the conditions, and they were to be obeyed without exceptions.

Imelda and Narciso agreed to the conditions imposed by Imelda's father. After three months, however, they grew tired of only watching the first half of the films they paid for at the theater. The early curfew made it hard for them to ever complete an activity on their date. Defiant, one night, Narciso took Imelda home late. He decided he wanted to watch the entire film and so they stayed, to Imelda's dismay and obvious anxious disapproval. Imelda got home almost in a state of panic. Narciso walked her to the porch where Don Manuel was waiting for them, smoking a cigarette. He let her in the house and then walked back to Narciso to have a serious conversation with the young man who dared disobey his instructions.

"Don Manuel, *buenas noches*. I sincerely and deeply apologize for bringing your daughter after the curfew. We were having a conversation at the end of the film and lost track of time. I also would like to humbly ask for your daughter's hand in marriage." Narciso started without giving Don Manuel time to get a single word in.

"Oh, and does my daughter know this is what you want?" answered Don Manuel in surprise.

"Yes sir, she does."

"And does she agree with you? I mean, does she also want to marry you?"

"Yes sir, I asked her, and she said she does."

"Very well then," replied Don Manuel. He half entered through the door and called for his wife and daughter to join them on the porch. Some of the sisters were peeking through a window to see what was happening, they knew Imelda would be in trouble but they never imagined what was about to happen.

Both went wondering what was going on. Imelda thought she would be refused to see him again since she had gotten home almost two hours late.

"This brave young man has asked for your hand in marriage. Before I give my permission, I have to ask you: do you want to marry him?" asked Don Manuel.

"Yes, father, I do," Imelda answered nervously.

"I was going to come back and ask next week and bring my parents with me," confessed Narciso.

"Very well," said Don Manuel "please tell your parents that they are invited to have dinner with us on Sunday of next week. We would love to get to know them and welcome them into our family."

Then, with a subtle smile on his face, he shook Narciso's hand, "Congratulations, young man. You are marrying a very good girl, I mean, woman. A very good woman, indeed, and I don't say that simply because she is my daughter." he said sternly.

"I will see you on Sunday. Thank you, sir and good night to the both of you." Narciso said, looking at Imelda and smiling.

Imelda and Narciso were married on September 30th, 1977. Almost exactly one year later, on October 3rd, they had their first child.

Imelda and Narciso

Part II

Beginnings:

The Paternal Side

Chapter XVII

"You are the man of the house now," Nicolas snapped at his son.

He had crouched down to be at his eye level and shook his shoulders with both hands at the first sight of tears.

"Listen, you are a man now... no more crying!"

He noticed the boy didn't understand what was happening. He realized it would be difficult to get through to him so with a softer voice he said, "You are the oldest of your siblings, and without me around, you will be the man of the house. Now, because you are a man, you have to protect the family. You can't protect them if you cry, men don't cry, you understand? You are in charge of everything. The family, they are your responsibility. Don't disappoint me. Are you listening to me? Stop crying! Here, take this... if you need it for anything, use it!" Narciso's seven-year-old hands took the loaded revolver from his father. "Look after them, and mind your mother... and for God's sake, stop crying already! You're a man and you're crying like a little girl. Men don't cry, ever!"

Those were the last words Narciso heard from his father. Nicolas turned to go without any sign of worry or hesitation. He was relieved and with a proud sense of satisfaction. He was going north, to the United States to make money and see the world.

His main objective was to make a name for himself, then one day return to Santa María del Oro and everyone in town would finally respect him.

He would show them his accomplishments and the entire town would treat him like he deserved to be treated. They would maybe even admire him. Nicolas believed in the idea that money couldn't buy him everything, but it could buy him a whole lot of things he wanted. The thing he wanted most was respect and admiration. *"Con dinero baila el perro"* he would think *"y todos me van a bailar como perros"*. If not rich, he would at least have a lot more money in his wallet than most people make in a year.

Narciso was the oldest of four and the one to look after the family. He didn't quite know what "being the man of the house" really meant or what was required of him other than not crying. He hadn't learned any leadership qualities from his neglectful and abusive father. On the contrary, he had seen nothing but disrespect towards his mother and his siblings from the man that was supposed to love and protect them from everything. He had a difficult time debating whether he should feel glad that his father trusted him and made him feel grown-up or if he should continue crying because of his feelings of helplessness and despair and he was still a child.

He decided to be proud. He stuck his chest out and put his head up for the world to see him and recognize him. At his age, he was going to be the man his father couldn't be. There was a sudden feeling of anxiety rushing through his body. His heart pounded faster and harder in his puffed out chest as if it had fists trying to break free, about to explode.

He sat on the ground taking deep breaths to calm down; something his mother had taught him to do when his father got violent. Everything was spinning out of control around him and he had started to hyperventilate.

"There is no time for childish behavior, get up!" He imagined his father demanding him.

"I have a gun now," he mumbled repeatedly as if trying to convince his mind that the gun would do all the work for him and that he was safe. But the gun could not prevent worries or calm his anxiety and fears. The gun did not make him feel better, in fact, it made him feel worse. "What good is a gun for?" he thought, a gun could not help him feed his family.

Narciso got up when he could finally breathe without feeling sick to his stomach. He touched the gun with care, noticing the cold metal on his miniscule hands. Then mustered all his strength and with sheer bravery put it inside his pants' waistline. He felt chills and goosebumps on his skin, his belly sucked in, sending shivers to his spine. He was afraid of it, his mother had incessantly repeated to him guns were the devil. He remembered his father yelling at him when he was younger that boys don't cry, and he had never seen a grown man cry.

Now that he was a man, he knew he was never to cry a single tear in his life again. His eyes got watery. He knew he had to hold it in, swallowing several times while forcing the knot in his throat to slowly go away while he breathed long and deep. The last tears he'd ever shed ran down his dehydrated and cracked brown cheeks. He felt as if the weight of the world had been laid on his shoulders.

If he wasn't allowed to cry again, he would give himself the satisfaction of letting those few tears that escaped without his permission run down and dry on their own. That was his statement of rebellion against his father's harsh wishes. After savoring the rawness of his emotions and the salty tears on his face, he took a deep breath and looked around.

No one was out that afternoon, no one had seen him, and he didn't have to explain anything to anyone. He felt relieved. The sunset was beautiful. He recognized this as possibly the last sunset he'd enjoy for weeks, months maybe. He stood there silently, looking at the marvelous and almost magical blend of colors in the sky. In what seemed like an instant, the sunset was gone. Narciso started walking slowly back home, ready to start his new life.

Narciso had seen his father leave many times and then return drunk a few days later, but this time he knew it was different. Following the path his father had taken, he ran in the same direction with the gun in his pants to see him one last time, if possible.

His father was nowhere to be found. He had stood in the spot where he had become a man longer than he realized. His father was gone and he couldn't stop asking himself if he would ever see him again. That had been his farewell: no advice, no hug, no words of wisdom and encouragement or a sign of love. Not even instructions of how to shoot the gun he had just given him, especially after having forbidden him to touch it before.

He didn't feel better having a gun in his hands and he didn't feel like a man. He was scared. How exactly was he going to protect his family as head of household? How would he feed himself, his siblings, and his mother? He was at a loss. With his head hung low, dragging his spirit through the empty and dusty streets of Santa María del Oro, he walked home.

That time, no more tears escaped. Narciso had never held a gun before, much less loaded one. He had seen it in the house when his father was home, but his mother did not allow him to touch it. She reprimanded Nicolas for leaving it out loaded at the children's reach. Narciso had tried to touch it once, when his father first took it home. Before he was close enough to place his hand on it, he ended up on the floor in the corner of the room with a loud ring in his ear and half of his face on fire. He had blood dripping from his nose and his lower lip, and he didn't know exactly what had happened.

"That slap doesn't hurt as much as shooting yourself with that thing would hurt, now get up from there and don't you ever try to touch it again!" his mother had warned him "that thing belongs to the devil."

Elena then tried to put the gun away in a place where the children would not be able to reach it, but Nicolas came at her with rage and a leather belt in his hand. She didn't know what she had done wrong, but felt the belt strike her arm then her back a couple times. She crouched down covering her face and head with her hands. Between sobs and cries, she asked him what she had done from where she laid on the floor. He looked at her with disgust.

"Don't ever touch my things, Elena. I don't feel I should have to tell you this. Just don't do it."

That was the only thing he said to her before putting his belt back on.

"The children can have an accident with it if you leave it around where they can reach it," replied Elena, with blood and spittle dangling from her trembling lower lip.

"Look, just teach them to not touch it, the way I just taught you. Because I bet you'll never touch that thing again, not because it's dangerous, but because it's mine! They must learn to respect me and my things, you all do! It's ridiculous I still have to tell you like if you were a child yourself!" he started to walk away, then turned back and took a few steps towards his wife and kicked her while she was still on the floor, "You got blood on my favorite belt, you bitch!"

Elena did not want to hurt her children. She loved them and wanted to protect them from everything, especially from their father, who was their greatest threat. She started to believe that if she made her children afraid of certain things just enough, then maybe Nicolas wouldn't feel compelled to teach them the lesson himself. So she taught them in the only way she knew how. She would much rather hit them herself than let that monster touch them and hurt them worse. At least she knew how far she could go. She didn't hate them the way Nicolas seemed to. She loved them.

Nicolas had slept with the gun under his pillow since he had first gotten it, even though he'd been afraid of guns most of his life. He was always paranoid. He was afraid that someone would break into the house while he was most vulnerable. He had made so many enemies in the most trivial manner. The night he won the gun in a poker game had gone like no other, he usually lost and that time he felt very lucky right from the beginning.

He had beaten his opponents fair and square and to try to win their losses back, the two men had also lost their boots, a gold watch, and even a hat. He had never owned a gun before, much less shot one but he started carrying it with him everywhere. It gave him a sense of superiority. He imagined people talking about him, admiring him as he walked by, feeding his vanity and enlarging his ego. He also imagined the gun would come in handy if he was ever insulted at the bar again. Nicolas relished the idea of punishing those who he thought disrespected him. His wife and kids were his only victims at that time. He had been quite the coward most of his adult life, so he took it out on the most vulnerable people he could find in order to make himself feel powerful.

He would spend countless hours at the bar, sometimes days, causing trouble for no other reason than obnoxious drunkenness. As the big bully he had always been, he was always antagonizing others and causing fights. He would then slip away at the first sign of serious trouble and never claim any responsibility for his actions. No one in town ever took him seriously enough though, even with the gun. He was a young vile man with no scruples. He did not care for anything but himself and getting his way.

Nicolas had always dressed very well with a suit and tie even if his children had to go to school barefoot. His wife only had two dresses that had been hemmed and mended several times.

"Why would a woman who is in charge of taking care of her husband, the house, and the children, need new clothes anyway?" He would ask her. "Now, that would be a ridiculous sight! Just imagine a new dress and shiny shoes all full of dirt, food, and children snot. What a waste of money!" He would scoff.

Besides all the household chores, Elena was also responsible for making sure her husband looked more than presentable when he stepped foot outside. So besides hand washing and carefully ironing his clothes, making sure the creases were perfectly straight and crisp, she would also shine his leather shoes every night. Nicolas loved to wear a hat, slightly tilted to the side. He thought it made him look classy.

"I need people to know I mean business and I will not be taken advantage of by anyone." As far as he was concerned, appearances were worth a lot more than the truth. And he succeeded at keeping them up. People who didn't know him well enough always thought of him as a kind man, a gentleman who would give a hand to people who needed it without asking for anything in return.

Candil de la calle, oscuridad de su casa is what Nicolas was. He had smooth baby skin and a dark black mustache very well trimmed. He always left a trail of the scent of excessive strong aftershave. He was a womanizer. He was a very good looking man, but his soul was rotten. Nicolas was unable to love anything or anyone other than himself and his own personal interests but he was charismatic and that fooled people. The United States was the perfect way to start something new, he'd have opportunities to do whatever he pleased.

Nicolas had left for the United States once before, when Narciso was only a few months old. It was the first time he had left anywhere and he was scared, but his dream for greatness was larger than life. He had traveled as far north as Chicago to find work.

He had gotten a temporary work visa and moved in with two of his cousins. They had left a few years earlier and promised him he would find work immediately and make money hand over fist. Nicolas spent an entire year in Illinois looking for work but could not find anything that met his standards.

He returned to Durango with only a few hundred dollars in his pocket. His cousins accepted any jobs they were offered in the United States, making money without complaining. They would work two jobs six days a week. They had construction jobs during the day and worked in restaurants during the night, taking naps during their breaks. Sundays were their days to rest and recharge for another brutal week.

They knew it was hard work, but they could provide for their families back home. To save money on rent, the three of them shared a one bedroom apartment with two other men, also from Mexico.

Nicolas felt indignant; he thought he was better than that. Working in a construction site and always being dirty, smelly, and full of cement was not what he had been born for. His skin would get tanned and dry with the elements. He had avoided working the fields back home for the same reason, he was not going to do it in the United States too where he was supposed to be living like a king. He did not worry for his family. His mother lived right around the corner so he knew she would keep an eye on them.

Doña Belém did keep an eye on them, but not in the sense she promised Nicolas she would. She had always thought Nicolas deserved a better woman and treated Elena with disdain.

While Nicolas was in Chicago that first time, Elena was left alone to fend for herself. He had taken her from her hometown so she had no family support. She was alone with her child and this man in a strange town without any allies or someone who could sympathize with her.

Their relationship had not begun with a romantic courtship. In fact, Elena had been in love with a young man from her village before she met Nicolas. They both felt the same for each other and had planned to someday get married, but Elena's family did not approve of him.

When Nicolas showed up with his flashy personality, her mother was deceived. *Se la robó, ahora se tienen que casar*, is what people in her village had rumored after they found out how he had taken her.

Elena had to marry him even if she was not in love with him. She had no choice but to leave with him. When it was time to do the right thing, Nicolas

318

decided to not marry her after all. Doña Belém started to hate her son's woman for "dragging her son to live in sin" and decided that Elena was a bad woman, when she was completely isolated and without hope for the future.

"How can she walk around the town like that, without any shame for what she has done? If she had some dignity, she would go back to where she came from," Doña Belém would gossip with the neighbors.

As much as Elena wanted, she couldn't go back home. Taking a woman from a neighboring village was something some men did. They did not waste time courting women. They were machos and took what they wanted, when they wanted it.

Sometimes, they would roam around for days looking for a woman they liked. They'd go to the river and watch them bathe, wash dishes or clothes, looking for the younger ones to see which ones they liked. Once they decided who they liked, they would take her and most of the time it was against her will. After being taken, the only option they had was to marry the man or risk being shunned by the community and shame their families. They would end up completely alone for the rest of their lives. No parent wanted a spinster in the house especially if the reason for never marrying was the loss of their purity even if by force.

So without much choice left, Elena went to live with Nicolas only to realize that he felt that living together was enough.

Shortly, Elena became pregnant with Narciso, their first son. Nicolas was never romantic, sweet, or even kind to Elena. He mostly treated her like a servant. He spent most of his time out of the house, which were the best times for Elena. She had the house all to herself and she was happy with the baby. It wouldn't take her long to do her daily household chores and try to always have food ready in case Nicolas showed up.

If she stayed quiet and did what he wanted, her time with him around wouldn't be so terrifying. However, it was difficult to please him. He was a very emotionally volatile man and his temper was most unpredictable. He would snap at her with the most un-provoking acts. Sometimes he would get irate because his dinner was too hot, or his soup was too cold, or his boots hurt his feet, or someone at the bar looked at him funny, or if he simply felt disrespected because of the way her voice sounded.

Elena's first year with Nicolas had been a difficult one, especially after he left for Chicago. Not having to put up with his daily abuse was a relief. And she reveled at the sight of her beloved little boy, without a care in the world. But Nicolas had left without leaving any money for rent, food, or any of the necessities. He never mentioned any intentions of leaving to her or even said goodbye the day he left. She had to find out from one of his drinking friends.

Nicolas's messenger showed up at the house that evening. At first, Elena thought it was Nicolas because he had entered the house without knocking. She was startled when she saw the stranger standing in her living room with his hat in his hands.

"*Buenas noches* Elena, Nicolas asked me as a favor to come give you a message for him." the man told her.

"*Buenas noches, pásele*. Would you like a cup of coffee?" Elena answered, trying to calm her nerves.

"No, thank you. I'm not going to stay long. I just came to tell you that Nicolas left for the United States." The stranger shifted his weight awkwardly while folding his hat in his hands.

"Oh! *Se fue al otro lado?* When? Why? He didn't say anything to me about this. What about us, is he sending for us?" Elena asked, visibly upset.

"I don't know Elena. He went to his mother's house before coming home and she gave him a letter from a cousin that went there two years ago. He said he was going to join them because they have good paying jobs there and he can help Nicolas find one as soon as he got there. He went to the bar and told everyone there to fuck off and that he was off to get rich. Right before he left, he asked me if I could tell you he wasn't coming home for a while."

The man was clearly concerned to see her so disturbed.

"Did he tell you anything else? He didn't come here at all, he didn't even come to say goodbye to his own son," Elena answered sobbing "I don't have any money. Did he tell you how I can contact him?"

"I don't know anything. I wish I did. I'm sorry, that's all he said to me. Here, take this. It's not much but I hope it helps you while you wait to hear from him. If anything, you can always ask Doña Belém for help, maybe she'll have more information. If anyone would know, it would be her, I'm sure." He gave her all the money he had in his pocket and a couple of sympathetic pats on the shoulder, and then he was gone.

The first week without him was not bad, she had plenty of food to last her a couple of weeks, at least. Elena was certain she would hear from Nicolas soon. She had been optimistic, thinking maybe he would send for them and in no time they would all be in the United States together. She had never gone anywhere and wondered what kind of life they would have in a different country. Would her son grow up speaking English? She would catch herself giggling at the oddest things she would come up with while daydreaming.

After a week had gone by, Elena decided to only eat two small meals a day to conserve food. In the third week, she was eating only one meal a day and she needed to know what was going to happen, she couldn't let herself starve and leave Narciso alone. Three weeks after Nicolas's departure, Elena still had not heard from him and she started to worry. She thought maybe something had happened to him and she didn't know how to find out. She had never wanted to set foot in Doña Belém's house. She had sworn she never would, but she considered her situation an emergency. She was almost out of food and didn't know what to do.

She wrapped the baby up in one of her shawls and walked the three blocks to her mother-in-law's house. When she reached the front door, she knocked a few times and waited. She could hear noise coming from inside the house. The windows were open to let the cool air of the afternoon in. She thought maybe no one had heard the knocks, so she knocked again and again. Doña Belém appeared at one of the windows, looked at Elena with the baby in her arms and walked away without saying a word.

Surely, she went to open the door, Elena thought. After a few minutes of no response, she knocked again and called Doña Belém's name.

"Doña Belém, it's me, Elena, your daughter-in-law. I have your grandson with me, can we please come in?"

The doña went to the door and opened it just enough for her to be able to see Elena standing outside.

"Oh, I heard you, and I saw you. But you are not welcome in this house so I don't feel the need to acknowledge you. I also don't feel like being interrupted from my knitting, so come, tell me what you want," Doña Belém answered while looking at Elena from head to toe.

"I'm here to know if you've heard anything from Nicolas," Elena asked, swallowing her pride.

"Yes, of course I have. I am his mother. He has sent me a few telegrams from Chicago. Anything else?"

"You have? Has he said anything to you about us? He didn't even tell me he was leaving. I don't know what's going on and I'm almost out of food." She was now pleading for any information.

"Look Elena, you seem... like a nice girl, I guess. But I have no concern for you, you are not my daughter, you are not my daughter-in-law, and I really don't care what you do. And as far as that brat being my grandchild, how do I really know he's my blood? I can't, can I?" Doña Belém answered as she tried to close the door in Elena's face.

Elena blocked the door with her foot. She could not believe what she was hearing. Just when she thought maybe this woman would take pity on her and her child, she proved to be a cold woman with no room for love in her heart. What happened to her to make her as bitter and hateful as she was? She wondered.

"I am begging you, please! I need to know what is happening. Why hasn't he communicated with me? Doesn't he care about his own son, even if he doesn't care about me?" Elena yelled at the crack in the door.

"I don't know and to be quite honest, I also don't care. He is communicating with me and I am content with that. Now, I need to get back to my chores," she spat back in reply.

Then, with a final look of disgust, she pushed the door the rest of the way closed. She walked to the front window and said "Good luck with your life," before closing it as well.

Elena walked back to her house broken hearted, panic rising in her mind. What was she to do now? How will they survive? She couldn't believe Nicolas had abandoned them the way he had. She was even more surprised he did not care for their well being or even their survival. He cared more about his mother who didn't need him at all to survive. She felt sorrow, disappointment, and great pain in her heart. She cried the entire walk back. That night, she went to bed without dinner. When the baby cried, she wrapped her arms around him and they both cried in unison until they fell asleep with exhaustion.

The following day, Elena sent a telegram to her mother asking her to visit her. Doña Josefita immediately arranged a way to see her daughter as soon as possible. She arrived at Elena's doorstep the following morning. One of her neighbors had driven her to the town for the day. He had business to take care of and would pick her up in the late afternoon to take her back home.

As soon as Doña Josefita walked in the house, she knew something was terribly wrong. Her daughter had lost so much weight, the soft skin on her face was sagging and she saw some wrinkles in the corner of her eyes. She was much too young to look like an old lady, she thought. The house was cold, the baby was crying, and her daughter's face was pale with an ashy tone.

"Elena! Mija, what's happened to you? Where is Nicolas?" Doña Josefita asked her as she warmly embraced her.

She touched her face gently and gave her a kiss on the cheek.

"The baby is crying, poor thing. Oh god, when was the last time this poor child had some comfort? It looks like he needs a diaper change. Quick, let me change him and get him comfortable and then you and I will talk. This is no way to live, you just wait until your husband comes home and he will hear what I have to say," then in a murmur, she said to herself "this is no way to treat my child and grandchild. What a beast he is!"

Elena sat at the edge of the bed watching her mother change the baby's diaper and wrap him tightly with a clean blanket.

"This boy is teething, that's why he's so fussy. Also, it looks like his temperature is a little high. We'll just keep him cool for a while and he'll be as good as new as soon as those little pearls break skin." She stood up and grabbed her daughter's hand leading her to the kitchen table where they would talk.

"Let's start from the beginning. First, you look terrible, Elena. Where is your husband?"

"Oh mother! I haven't seen him in weeks. One day he just didn't come home, instead, he sent one of the men he hangs out with at the bar to tell me he had left for the United States. That he had left to find work and that was it. I haven't had word from him, he hasn't sent me any money, and the food I had in the pantry is gone... Look, I have nothing left!" Elena cried pointing at the pantry.

"When was the last time you ate something, child?" her mother asked with concern.

"Yesterday morning. I ate the last two tortillas with a little bit of beans I had left. I don't have any more milk left for the baby." Elena cried inconsolably.

"What about your mother-in-law? She lives around the corner, have you tried to reach out? I know you're not that proud. This is her blood!" she said pointing at the baby who was now peacefully asleep with a clean and dry diaper.

"I went to her house a week ago. She was cold towards me and wouldn't even look at Narciso. She said that there's no way for her to be sure that he's her blood. I have not been with any other man, what kind of woman does she think I am? I never even wanted to come here in the first place, I had no choice. He took that away from me and then he abandoned us!" replied Elena sobbing, speaking only as she could catch her breath in between desperate cries.

"She said he's been writing to her weekly and that he hasn't sent any money for us. I don't know what I'm going to do, ma. I have nothing."

"You lie down next to your boy, get some rest. You can't feed that baby this way. You will pass on all that suffering through the little milk you have left. You don't want your milk to go bad do you?" asked her mother kindly.

"I already told you. I hardly have any milk to give him. We're both going to starve and Nicolas doesn't even care!" Elena could not stop crying.

"No, you won't. As long as I live, you'll have someone on your side. Now get some rest, I'll be back soon."

Elena fell right asleep holding her baby in her arms while Doña Josefita walked to the town store to get some groceries for her daughter.

Elena woke up with a grumble in her stomach and her mouth salivating. The baby was still fast asleep and she could smell something coming from the kitchen. She got up clumsily and walked towards the smell. There, she found her mother over the wood stove making lunch for them. She sat on a chair at the table and immediately, a bowl with hot *caldo de res,* appeared in front of her with a pile of fresh hot corn tortillas.

"Eat up while it's still hot. We can't talk about what's going on with an empty stomach. *Ya sabes, las penas con pan son menos.*"

It was true, all grieves with bread were less. Not having anything to eat was enough grief to drive someone mad. Doña Josefita, thinking the worst when she first received Elena's telegram, had taken part of her life savings with her. She didn't know what was happening, but she was ready to tackle whatever was in front of her. If she had to move her daughter back home with her, at least she had money to hire someone to take her back. If it was a medical issue, she could pay a doctor to make her or the baby better. She, however, never thought that all she needed was love and comfort, food, and advice and to know that everything would be just fine.

After lunch, they talked about what had been going on. Elena confided in her mother about Nicolas's coldness towards her. She told her how she felt like nothing more than a warm body in his bed at night and a maid to his every wish every other minute of the day. She shared her fears about her life and her future now that she felt abandoned by the man that refused to be her husband without any type of support in the town. Doña Josefita listened intently and held her daughter's hand in sympathy, rubbing her arm in solidarity.

"Listen Elena, you must be strong. You have a child to take care of and you must figure out a way to survive, a way to live, with or without Nicolas. You have options, child. I have never met a woman who starved because her husband left. On the contrary, when men leave, we are usually better off. We don't have to put up with their crap, we don't have to hear them, we don't have to smell them, and we don't have to do anything for them. We just live for ourselves and our children."

"I'm listening, Ma." Answered Elena attentively.

"Some of the women back home have left. They have gone up north to find jobs. They went to a city where they find work real soon after they get there. They leave their children behind with the grandmothers to look after them and then they work their butts off to save up money. They send money back home for their kids and save the rest, and then they come back and take their kids with them when they can afford to do that." Doña Josefita was giving her options.

"No Ma, I am not leaving my baby behind," Elena answered abruptly.

"Think about it *mija*, in the long run it would be better for both of you. You can leave now and not look back. You're not even married to Nicolas, you don't owe him anything, and you don't even have to divorce him. This would be the easiest thing to do. I know it would be a little sacrifice and some time away from the baby, but I would take care of him, he would be safe. This is the best chance for you and for him."

"I said no! I am not leaving him behind even for a day, I cannot do that to him or to myself and I don't want to hear another word about it. What type of mother leaves their children, ma?"

"Don't be silly, it's not leaving him. It's making sure he will have a better future. It would be temporary," her mother assured her.

"The best future he can have is with his mother, where he belongs!" Elena snapped back.

"Fine, I won't bring it up again. But you'll have to figure something out, a way for you to support yourself and that poor innocent child of yours. You can't live like this and now you know you can't count on that good-for-nothing man of yours who won't even marry you. And his mother... aye, don't even get me started with her. What kind of woman is she anyway? You know I would help you in any way I can, but I don't have money to help you every two weeks when you've run out of food."

"I'll figure it out ma, I promise. Thank you for coming to see me. Thank you for the food. Thank you for everything you do for us." She said, speaking in a low voice.

Elena kissed her mother's hand with tears in her eyes.

"Hush now, you're my child... everything you'd do for yours, I'll do for mine. That's what being a mother is all about," Doña Josefita assured her.

Doña Josefita had bought her daughter enough food to last a couple of weeks. She had two of the boys that worked at the store help her carry the bags to the house. She had bought potatoes, corn, rice, beans, lentils, tortillas, and even some beef and chicken. She knew that to keep the baby healthy, the mother had to be nourished and healthy or she could lose her milk for good.

That afternoon, after her mother had been picked up and taken back to her house, Elena felt a surge of energy and confidence. She had been awakened by her loving mother's presence. She understood now that she had to find a way to make money to feed herself and her child. She didn't know how long Nicolas would be gone. She was also aware she could not ask Doña Belém for help, so she decided to take matters into her own hands.

Chapter XVIII

The following morning, Elena woke up early and bathed the baby. She made herself a large breakfast and drank some cinnamon tea. She then wrapped her baby around her body with a large shawl and went out. She walked the streets of Rosa María del Oro knocking on her neighbors' doors looking for work. She introduced herself and without giving too much information, she asked if there was anything she could do for a few pesos. She explained that her husband had gone to the U.S.and that she hadn't heard from him since he left and she needed to support herself and her child.

Most of the people she talked to were either in a similar situation or just could not afford to pay someone to help with chores. "That's what the children are for chulita, they help out and we don't have to pay them. Good luck to you." Some would close the door with a sympathetic look in their eye.

Elena came up to a house with a short brick wall and a wrought iron fence on the top part. The house looked different from all the others she had been to. The front entrance had two doors; the outer door was a wooden frame with a screen on it. She knocked on the fence a couple of times and waited a few minutes, but no one answered. It was the last house on the street and since she had not had much luck, that house was her last hope. She decided to not give up until she spoke to someone. She yelled "Hello! Is anybody home?"

A little girl with disheveled hair showed up at the screen door that allowed for the cool morning breeze to flow through the house without allowing insects in. "Maaaa! There's someone here asking for you!"

A short woman with brown wrinkled skin walked out of the house and to the gate. She tossed her long mostly black braid back and wiped her brow with the back of her wrist. She looked old but couldn't have been older than thirty-five. She had strands of silver on the side of her head, right above the ears, and a sprinkle on top of her forehead. She looked tired.

"Good morning ma'am. My name is Elena. I live a few blocks from here and I am looking for work, any kind of work. I can do anything, and if I don't know how to do it yet, I can learn. See, my husband left to *el otro lado,* weeks ago and I haven't heard from him. I have this baby to feed and he left me without a single peso." Elena said, repeating word for word like a mantra what she had said in all the previous houses she visited.

"Come in, Elena. It's starting to get hot outside. You look like you could use a cold glass of water. Let's get that child of yours out of the sun."

The woman opened the gate and stepped to the side to allow Elena to walk in then opened the screen door.

"Please come in, let's go to the kitchen." She closed the screen door behind them and wiped her wet soapy hands with her apron.

"Come, take a seat. Would you like to lay your baby down in one of the bedrooms so he can rest?" She asked as she poured some cold water in a glass for Elena and another for herself.

Elena shook her head no as she drank almost the entire tall glass of iced water at once. She was hot and parched from walking all morning.

"Thank you," Elena answered gracefully.

"My name is María," the woman said as she sat down. "My husband left too, two years ago. He had a hard time finding a job when he first got to California, it must've been the season. People could not find work to save their lives. He left me with six kids. We just couldn't feed them little bastards, they sure can eat and they're never satisfied. They just keep asking for more and more and more. Not sure if it's the worms in their bellies that steal all the food they eat, but some eat like grown men. Anyway, he religiously sends me money every week and that's how we survive. He never misses, first thing Monday morning, the money is there. On top of that, he was able to save some money for a few months and came back to build this house. He's such a hard worker and a great provider. I feel so lucky!"

Elena listened intently as she finished the last sips of her water. She hadn't realized how hot the day had gotten until she stepped inside the cool house. She had been walking under the sun for hours.

"Oh, God! How inconsiderate and stupid I am. I am so sorry." María exclaimed realizing she was gloating about her perfect man as Elena was there to find a job to relieve her life of hunger and financial insecurity. She had to find a job, because of her own man's inability to provide.

She placed her hand on Elena's shoulder, then took her empty glass and poured some more water.

"Anyway, as I was saying. We are finally out of the hole here and I have my *guardadito*, just in case he runs out of work or gets sick or something and can't send anything. We women gotta be prepared, you know. We're the ones that make the household run. We always make do no matter what. Even though I don't work as much or as hard as he does over there with the gringos, I am tired. Six kids is no joke."

"Yes ma'am," Elena answered as she took the first sip of her second glass of water.

"You look so young. How old are you, Elena?" María asked curiously after seeing the young face in detail.

"I just turned 22, ma'am."

"Please Elena, call me María. You're making me feel old. I'm not that much older than you, you know? But having so many children sucks the life out of you. Not just because you have them, but because once they're born you'll never rest another day in your life. That's why I feel like you knocking on my door came to me as a miracle from heaven." María confessed.

"Why is that ma'am? I mean, Doña María." Elena asked shyly.

"Just María, Doña makes me feel like sixty and I still have a long way to go."

"I'll try my best, I promise," answered Elena in a low voice.

"God knows I don't have money to waste, but I've just been so tired lately I think I need a break. If not a break, at least some help. Look, I can't pay you a lot of money, but we can help each other. I need help and the lord knows it. You think you can come in the mornings during the week for three days? We'll have breakfast and coffee together in the mornings and then we'll get to work. On Thursday, you can wash clothes and hang them to dry, on Friday you can iron them, and on Monday you can help me with the cleaning. I'll pay you on Mondays before you go home." María offered feeling relieved.

"Oh, yes ma'am! I can do that. Thank you so much. Oh, god bless you, god bless you!" Elena answered elated as she grabbed María's hand and kissed it.

"Oh child, no! You don't have to do that." María cried out, taking her hand from Elena's and signaling her to take a seat. "Now, now, we are put on this earth to collaborate with each other. We were never meant to do things alone, we all need help. I'm helping you and you're helping me, in my eyes it's nothing short of perfect harmony. That's why we have survived for so long in this cruel world, because we collaborate. Do you understand? I need you as much as you need me. This is not charity but collaboration."

"Yes ma'am. Thank you for collaborating with me then," Elena replied with a bashful smile.

"Thank you, Elena. Now I'll be able to rest some and regain some of the energy these kids drain out of me, and we can keep each other company. It's perfect! Right now you'll stay for lunch and after that you go home and get some rest. I'll see you Thursday for breakfast and we'll get to work." María said as she took Narciso from his mother's arms and walked to the nearest bedroom to lay him down. She wanted Elena to be her own person in that precise moment, not a mother, not a neglected wife, just a woman having lunch with another woman.

****

Elena was able to make ends meet with the help of María. Occasionally, she would help a few other ladies in the neighborhood with their chores thanks to María's recommendations to her friends. None of the other women could hire her more than for a few hours a day once in a while, but they all benefited from this arrangement. Elena, besides washing and ironing clothes, would also cook and clean, watch kids while their mother was busy tending to other business, help mend and patch children's clothes, and whatever else became necessary when she was around. She never said no to any opportunity for work and the women were glad to have some help and catch a break when they could afford it.

Six months went by before Elena heard from Nicolas. She received a short message in a telegram. It was sent from Chicago letting her know that he had arrived safe and had been doing different types of jobs. He hoped the fifty dollars he had sent her the previous month helped her with whatever she needed at home for herself and the baby. She didn't know what he was talking about, but she knew exactly who would.

Elena's face flushed, she could feel heat rushing to her face and ears as her anger rose. If she could be angrier, she would probably light up on fire. She walked to Doña Belém's house and knocked on her door violently. When her mother-in-law finally opened to the door, she asked her what she wanted with an indignant and cold tone in her voice

"Where is the money that Nicolas has been sending me? You took it and kept it for yourself without any regard for at least the life of your grandson, your own blood!" Elena screamed through the small crack in the door.

"Calm yourself! I have no idea what you're talking about." Replied Doña Belém callously.

Elena waved the telegram on her face.

"You know exactly what I'm talking about. I knew Nicolas could not be so heartless as to not care. Now I know for sure. You knew I had nothing and yet you didn't lift a finger to help. Where's the money? He says right here he sent me the equivalent of fifty dollars!"

"Let me see that!" Doña Belém replied, snatching the paper from Elena's hand. "Oh! That must have been what he sent last month. I swear I thought that was for me." She answered with a smirk on her face.

"Why would he send you money? I am his wife, I have his child here with me, and we are his responsibility, not you," Elena answered, trying to stay as calm as possible.

"Oh, you poor ignorant child. I am his mother. I will always come first, even before you and that bastard child of yours. God only knows if my blood really runs through his veins. It's not his fault, I get it. But that's just how life is." She then put her hand inside one of her apron pockets and took out a few bills and straightening them up along with the telegram, she handed them to Elena. "Now leave and don't come back here again!" Doña Belém barked and slammed the door behind her.

Elena walked back home, her hands trembling, her heart racing, and her teeth clenched at the jaw. She had never experienced such anger in her life.

She couldn't understand how anyone could be so cruel. When she got home, she opened her hand where the money and the telegram had been crumbled up to a ball with her rage. It was only thirty dollars! Doña Belém had kept almost half of the money. In her eyes, it was the same thing as taking food from the mouth of her baby. At that point, she realized she had to learn how to pick her battles so she decided to let it go. There was no point in going back there and convince her mother-in-law to give her the rest. The fact that she had given her anything at all was already a win. Besides, she had been able to stay afloat with her own money and those thirty dollars would be saved for a rainy day.

Two months after the altercation at Doña Belém's house, a boy knocked at her door with a message for her. It was a blank envelope, inside was a handwritten note that read "from Nicolas" and twenty dollars. The boy stood there looking at her until she grabbed a peso from her purse and gave it to him. Without a word having been exchanged, he took off running with his bare feet into the streets. Elena went inside and took a small tin can from under the mattress and stuffed the money in there with the thirty dollars she had gotten before.

"Why is he writing to his mother and not to me? Why did he think it was acceptable for him to send the money to that woman expecting her to give it to me? He clearly doesn't know the type of person he has for a mother," she murmured to herself as she vented to the walls of her home.

In May of 1958, almost two years later, Nicolas went back to his hometown in the same way in which he had left. He showed up without notice and without his pocket full of money as he had predicted. His first stop back in town was the bar where he spent countless hours telling tales of his travels to anyone who would listen. He then boasted about how much money he had made, and to prove that he had made so much money, he paid for everyone's drink that night. It didn't make people respect him or look up to him; they all knew him. But they did take advantage of the free drinks. It wasn't every day, or any day at all, that they got to drink for free.

That same evening, María showed up at Elena's doorstep. "Amiga, I just came to tell you how happy I am for you and that you don't have to come tomorrow. Just come on Thursday, I'll manage tomorrow by myself. Enjoy your husband. Gotta run though, I left the beans cooking on the stove," María said to Elena in a rush, then hugged her before turning to go.

"Wait! I don't understand. What do you mean by enjoy your husband? Why would I not come tomorrow? I always come on Mondays, María. I haven't missed a single day." Elena asked, baffled.

"Oh!" María gasped with incredulity and then hugged again, only tighter. She looked down and saw little Narciso running towards the door, grabbing her mother's skirt to prevent a fall. "You don't know."

"What is it, María? Just spit it out for God's sake, please! What's happening?"

"Carlitos saw Nicolas walk into the bar earlier today, this morning actually, when he was on his way to school. I figured I'd give you two enough time to spend some time alone before coming over to tell you to just stay home tomorrow. You probably have a lot to talk about, and you know, you've been apart for so long now. I know how that goes."

"No, María. I don't know how it goes. As far as I'm concerned, Nicolas is still in the United States. Or maybe he's somewhere more important for him in town. He has not been here all day at all. I have no doubts about his priorities anymore. What a fool I have been! Thank you, María, for letting me know." María could hear the pain in Elena's voice.

"Look, you know how kids are. Maybe it wasn't Nicolas. I'm sure he would've come straight home to you and his child. He might have been confused when he saw him, it's probably someone else that looks like him," offered María nervously.

"No María, I'm sure it was him. In the past couple of years, he's proved to me that he doesn't care. We are not his priority. It's ok, don't worry. I'll still come tomorrow unless something happens, is that fine? I wouldn't want to miss breakfast and coffee, like always."

María hugged her one more time.

"Breakfast and coffee, amiga. Good luck tonight." María answered as she walked away. Elena bathed the young toddler early that night and put him to bed against his wishes. He was so tired he wasn't able to put up much of a fight. She made dinner and sat at the table waiting for her husband to come home. She was hungry and the food was getting cold but she decided she would wait for him just a little bit longer.

After a couple of hours she ate her dinner while contemplating two possibilities. Maybe Carlitos had really confused someone else with Nicolas and he wasn't coming home that night. Or, maybe it really was Nicolas at the bar and he didn't care about her and the baby and he would show up whenever he felt like it. Nicolas was the type of person who didn't answer to anyone but himself, and maybe his mother. Whatever it was, there was nothing she could do. Everything was out of her hands so she didn't feel guilty having had her dinner without him. She washed the dishes and left his plate on the table just in case and went to bed.

Around three in the morning, a loud noise outside the house woke Elena. She got up in a panic and went to the door in a hurry to find out what was happening. She approached apprehensively, but couldn't see anything. She was wearing a thin long white sleeping gown and a loose braid was holding her long hair. She looked out the window and still didn't see anything. Thinking it may have been one of the neighborhood dogs, she headed back to bed.

Suddenly there was a loud thump outside her house, she ran back towards the door and opened it slowly. There was a drunken man violently knocking at the neighbor's house across the street.

"Elena! Open this door right this second. I.... I have the right... to see my son... My uhm, only child. You'll open this door at once if you know what's good for you." Nicolas was yelling so loudly that she could hear him and clearly recognize his voice.

Apparently he was so drunk he hadn't realized he was knocking at the wrong door. She ran across the street to grab him and before she reached him, all the lights went on and a man in underwear came outside with a rifle in hand. Nicolas was on the floor when she got to him, passed out cold. The man's wife went to join them as soon as she found out it was relatively safe. The man gave his shotgun to his wife and helped Elena pick the drunkard up and drag him across the street to put him to bed.

"And here I thought all this time that you were either divorced or widowed. Now I know I was wrong. I'm sorry seño, for assuming."

"Oh, please don't worry about it. I'm deeply sorry he woke you up like this and so early in the morning. I didn't know he was coming today, he must've confused your house with ours."

"I'm sorry you had to practically see me in my birthday suit, but I get too hot at night, I can't sleep

345

otherwise. I didn't have too much time to put clothes on, I thought there was a burglar trying to break in," the neighbor apologized.

"Don't apologize, please. I'm so very sorry he woke you up that way. Thank you for helping me bring him inside. Please, apologize to your wife on my behalf, I feel so embarrassed."

"Good night Missus, you get some rest." They dropped him on the couch and the almost-naked neighbor went back home.

Nicolas looked as good as dead, the only thing Elena could do was take his boots off. He was too heavy for her to move to the bed and he was unresponsive. So he left them right where he lay.

The following morning, Elena woke up early and got ready to head to María's house like every Monday morning. She made sure she didn't make much noise so as to not wake her husband up, not because she cared for his rest but because she didn't want to miss work and have to put up with him during the day. She had not been able to sleep that night. She had tossed and turned trying to keep one eye open in case he got up and tried to climb in bed with her.

She knew he would get violent and there was nothing she could do but comply with his wishes if she didn't want to be hurt. When she did fall asleep, she was repeatedly startled awake by loud and violent snores coming from the living room. She didn't feel safe until she reached María's house. She relaxed some while she vented to her friend during coffee.

Both women thought it comical the way he showed up at the wrong door and an almost naked neighbor had to carry him to his own house. He could've been shot if she hadn't shown up.

Elena felt nervous and uneasy on her way home. She talked to Narciso, and tried to warn him as best she could that his father was home. She knew he probably wouldn't recognize him and wanted things to go smoothly. She prayed to the Virgin that Nicolas would be in a good mood and that there be peace at home. When they entered the house, the whole place smelled like alcohol. Nicolas was sitting at the table half naked, holding his head with his hands. He looked terrible.

"Where have you been all day? I needed you here and you were nowhere to be found," he said in a low and monotonous voice, without looking at her.

"I went to work." Answered Elena calmly.

"Work?" snarled Nicolas, laughing. "What do you know about work?"

"Yes. I work. How else did you think I was going to survive in this hell hole of a town you brought me to? How else did you think I was going to feed my child... your child, when you abandoned us?"

"Fine. But now that I'm here, there will be no more of that. You're not going anywhere."

"Oh, so now you're back to your responsibilities? You left two years ago without telling me where you were going or why. Took off like a thief in the night without a single word to the mother of your child or even worrying about how we would make ends meet or if we would even have something to eat. How dare you?"

"What are you talking about? I sent someone to tell you where I was going and I wrote every week and sent money for you and Narciso. What kind of monster do you think I am?" Nicolas answered displeased.

"The type of monster that is raised by a vile and heartless woman. She gave me a total of fifty dollars in two years, Nicolas. What kind of misery is that? She kicked me out of her house three weeks after you left, when I went to ask if she knew anything about you. She said she didn't know anything and you never sent me any money."

He got up from his chair, towering over her.

"That is a lie!!" he yelled. Then immediately sat back down in pain, holding his head "that is a lie," he murmured, "my mother would never do such a thing."

It was clear he was offended, but couldn't do much in his drunken state.

348

"She would, and she did. That is why I had to look for work. I wash and iron people's clothes to make some money to feed myself and your child. By the way, your mother denies him as her blood. And then you come home and I don't see you until almost 24 hours later? What kind of a man are you?"

"The type of man that does not tolerate this kind of behavior from a fucking woman!"

This time, he didn't care that he was in pain. His rage was stronger than the hangover he was experiencing. He beat her until his knuckles bled, Narciso crying hysterically in a corner of the kitchen behind the ice box, yelling for his mother.

"Now make me a proper and decent meal. What kind of welcome is an old and cold plate of food after working my ass off for two years? Stop being so ungrateful. Some strong coffee too and some aspirin, my head is going to explode." Nicolas demanded as he sat back down at the table and she bled and grunted on the floor. He had never hit her before. She always wondered, not if he would ever hit her, but when. She never thought, however, that he would start the day he saw her for the first time after two years.

Elena got up and went to the stove, limping and holding her side with her hand. She extended her hand to Narciso and he ran towards her frantically, still crying but this time in silence and panic. He sobbed quietly in her arms. She made a sound like a wounded animal and gently held him close to her with her arm, stroking his hair and assuring him everything was ok.

"Be gentle with your mother, she's hurting." Nicolas said to his son, as if the toddler understood what had just happened. As if Elena could be hurt because Narciso wasn't gentle to her after having been beaten by Nicolas.

When his dinner was ready, Elena put it in front of him with a cup of coffee and some warm tortillas. When she turned to go, he grabbed her arm and pulled the chair next to him out. He then yanked her arm hard to force her to sit next to him.

"You sit here until I'm done with you. What the hell has gotten into you? I haven't seen you in two years and this is how you welcome me?" He was fuming.

She sat there without saying a single word. Narciso stood on her other side, frightened, crying and holding his mother's hand close to him.

When Nicolas was done, he got up and went to the living room to read the newspaper. He told her he didn't want to be interrupted and to make sure she kept her son quiet and away from him. He wasn't in the mood.

After being left alone in the kitchen, Elena cleaned everything up. When she was done, she washed her face with warm water, removing the dried blood from her nose and lips. She could feel her face hot and swelling up, everything hurt to the touch but she knew she had to get the wounds cleaned to prevent an infection.

After she cleaned herself, she broke off a piece of ice from the icebox and wrapped it in a towel, placing it gently on her face. The cold ice on her skin gave her great relief. She wished she could leave it on all night, but after a while her skin started to burn. She took a couple of aspirin for the pain and took Narciso to bed. He had fallen asleep crying on the floor holding on to her leg. She put on her gown, braided her hair, and with a heavy heart, laid down next to her son and fell asleep.

It hadn't been long before she had gone to bed that she was woken up by Narciso's screams. She got up immediately, despite her pain, and saw Nicolas grab the small child's arm with one hand and drag him to the living room. She quickly followed behind begging him to not hurt him.

"I'm not going to hurt him, he's my son. But his parent's bed is no place for him to be. I don't care if he naps there during the day, but that spot is mine. He is not a baby anymore and has to understand that from now on. He will sleep on his own on the couch, or on the floor anywhere, but not in my bed or in my room!" and looking at Narciso defiantly, he yelled "understood?"

Narciso sat on the couch crying desperately, but too afraid to move. There was a strange man in his house hurting his mother, and now preventing him from being close to her. Elena went to comfort him, only to be stopped in her tracks and dragged violently back to the bedroom by the hair. She knew that if she screamed, she would scare her son even more and she didn't want that. So she bit her swollen lip as hard as she could. She tasted the blood as she bit down.

Elena tried to comfort her child trying to fake a sweet smile towards him to assure him everything would be just fine. "Go to sleep like a big boy okay? I love you so much. I'll see you in the morning. Sweet dreams *mi nene hermoso.*"

That night was violent. She felt impotent and helpless. Everything in her body hurt, but nothing hurt more than her heart. She had just been shown the type of life she was to have with this man. While he took what he wanted, she closed her eyes thinking of the offer her mother had made two years ago and she flew herself in spirit to that alternate reality. Her child would be safe and happy with her mother while she worked in a city to provide for him and give him a future he could be proud of.

Instead, she felt her stubbornness and naivety had led her to this. She had thought she knew better, she thought her son needed a father and that Nicolas would provide for them because that's what fathers and husbands do. She had been wrong. She had made a choice and she couldn't change that now. She stopped resisting and her body went limp. It hurt a lot less if she didn't fight it.

Chapter XIX

In February of 1959, a month before Narciso turned three, Pedro was born. Nicolas had wanted his wife to stop working. Having his woman work to support the family made him feel like a *mandilón*. He was not okay with being emasculated. Elena argued that she had to work if they wanted to eat, since the money Nicolas had brought back from the United States was almost all gone. He had spent half of it at the bar the day he got back and lost the other half. He didn't know what happened to it and blamed it on people taking advantage of his vulnerable state to pickpocket him and left him without a single penny.

"Everyone is laughing at me right now, Elena. I came back rich and the next day I'm back to being poor. Then I can't find work and the embarrassment of my wife supporting me, I just can't show my face out there to anyone."

"You wouldn't be in this predicament if you would've come straight home. You could still have all the money you had when you first arrived. You left your family starving while you drank madly, spending money with people that don't even care about you. You bought them all drinks but couldn't even buy your family a sack of beans!"

"I will not have you speak to me in that manner, do you understand me? You have no idea what I had

354

to put up with out there, gringos talking to me like I'm shit and not being able to defend myself. I had to swallow my pride many times." barked Nicolas.

"We have another baby now and I can't support us all by myself. You need to find something to do to make money, we can't live like this!" Elena tried to reason.

By that time, Elena was working every day. She kept the same schedule at María's and had started doing people's laundry at her own house on the other days, even Saturday and Sunday. People would drop off their dirty clothes wrapped in a sheet at her house and she would deliver it to them in exchange for payment. Narciso was a good boy and didn't make much fuss, but now she had another baby to look after and as all babies do, he required a lot of attention.

As soon as little Pedro was sleeping throughout the night without much crying of hunger, Nicolas sent him to sleep with his big brother in the living room. The house was small, but he had made clear what his domain was and he was not going to allow being thrown off his throne even by his own baby boy needing his mother.

"You'll turn them into pussies at best and maricones at worst. I will not have faggots living under my roof!" he would tell Elena "You don't think I'm right, but I'm doing you and them a favor."

Lorenzo was born in August of 1960, when Pedro was a year and a half old and Narciso four and a half. By that time, Nicolas had a steady job working the fields and had forced Elena to quit her job. He hated his job, but hated feeling emasculated even more. So he sucked up his pride and went to work at a job he felt was completely beneath him.

He was gone most of the day and sometimes he would spend the evenings at the bar. She was used to it and never worried. *Hierba mala nunca muere*, her friend María would tell her.

"They sure don't, amiga. Don't I know it!" Elena would answer back.

And because she knew her husband was a bad weed, Elena stayed out of his way as much as possible. For a while, there had been rumors that he had a mistress, but Elena didn't care. All she knew was that when he wasn't around, she and her boys had a much better day without having to put up with his temper or his unpredictable bursts of rage. Although he had forbidden her to work, he was hardly ever home to realize that all that laundry she was washing and ironing did not belong to them. She had to continue working if she wanted to feel safe. Sometimes Nicolas would drink his entire paycheck and she wouldn't see a single peso for weeks, so she did what she had to do to survive, even if that would put her in physical danger with him. The risk was worth it.

In July of 1961, Elena found out that she was pregnant once again. The home remedies to prevent pregnancy she had asked her friends for had only worked for so long and in April of 1962, a tiny little girl was born.

Nicolas had never been too excited about his children before. Contrary to the worldview of first born children being male and the overall preference of boys over girls, he had hardly expressed any satisfaction or love for his three sons. But when his fourth child was born, he was in the best of moods. He never needed an excuse to spend his entire weekend and weekly paycheck drowning in alcohol at the bar, but that day was different. He bought one single drink for everyone present and he announced he was the father of a beautiful baby girl. He warned everyone at the bar with boys, to watch out because she was off limits to all of them. After only one drink, he went to his mother's house to give her the good news.

"I just don't understand why you're so obsessed with keeping that woman by your side. I thought for sure by now she'd be gone, but she's either stupid or extremely stubborn. I know you don't love her, why are you still with her? Release her and tell her to go back to her hometown and let her own mother deal with her and those little brats of hers." Doña Belém declared apathetically.

"Those little brats, as you call them, mother, are your grandchildren," Nicolas answered curtly.

"If you were my daughter, I would believe that they were my blood because how could I deny it? But I didn't see them come out from your loins, so how can I be sure?" sneered his mother.

"I know they are mine and that's all that matters. Of course they're mine!" he barked back.

When he got to his house, he was angry and mad with jealousy. The only thing that saved Elena from a beating that day was the fact that she had just given birth and was fast asleep resting with her baby girl in her arms. They both looked so peaceful.

"Of course they're my children," he thought, giving his daughter a kiss on the forehead before going back to the bar to continue the celebration. He did not get stupidly drunk as he was used to, on the contrary. He drank moderately and went home earlier than usual. He slept on the couch with Lorenzo on his stomach while Pedro and Narciso slept on the floor. He wanted to let Elena and the new baby rest.

Nicolas woke up early in the morning trying to make as little noise as possible so as to not wake anyone up. He made breakfast and had the boys follow him quietly to the kitchen to eat. He told them that they had to be quiet and let their mother and their new little sister rest and that they had to be good to them. They were big brothers now and had to take care of each other, especially the baby. He told them to mind their mother with everything she needed them to do.

Narciso was in first grade and had to go to school that morning, but before leaving, he stopped to ask his father if he was feeling ill. He had never seen him in a good mood and speaking with a calm and collected voice.

"I'm feeling better than ever son, here's some money. Go buy yourself something in school during lunch time. See you later. I'm gonna stick around for a while until your mother wakes up. I know she's tired and the baby was fussy all night long. Now, go before you're late."

Elena woke up and was surprised to see her husband had breakfast ready for her. She didn't know what to think and asked "*Y a ti, que bicho te picó ahora?*"

"I wasn't bitten by no bug, woman. What? A man can't cook breakfast for his family?" he answered with a smile on his face.

"Any man can cook for his wife, but you? I want to know what you're doing, what you're up to, and why you're acting like a decent human being for once."

"I'm just happy, that's all."

He waited until she had finished her breakfast to tell her that he had decided to name the baby Belém, after his mother.

"The hell we are! That woman doesn't even think these children are yours and you want to name our daughter after her? After she has called them bastards and wouldn't lift a finger for them?"

"Well, I have made up my mind and that is it, woman. Tomorrow morning I will go to the court and register her as Belém, whether you like it or not."

That day marked a turning point in the household. Nicolas, in a rare gesture of tenderness, had cooked a meal, offered softness, and spoken gently—but none of it felt real. For Elena, it was a mask she had seen him wear before, one that always came off too soon, learning never to trust what seemed too good to be true. For Narciso, the damage had already been done. Whatever illusion of normalcy his father attempted to create that morning had shattered by all the times he was neglectful, and violent to everyone in the house. A storm had settled inside him, quiet and patient, taking root in the space where his childhood used to live.

Elena didn't press him—she knew better than to ask a child to put pain into words he didn't yet have. But from that afternoon on, something inside him hardened. He watched his father with wary eyes and listened more than he spoke. Each word Nicolas said, each time he raised his voice or slammed a door, Narciso filed it away, learning what kind of man *not* to become.

Even with a sister at home, tenderness had always been fleeting in that house—if it had ever truly existed at all. The moments passed quickly, the memories faded, in a cycle of gaslighting and violence for years to come.

****

Those other days had been nothing like this one. It had started with violence—his father crouched down, shaking him by the shoulders, forcing him to swallow his tears. Then came the words that changed everything: *"You're the man of the house now."* The weight of those words had been heavier on his soul than the revolver was in his waistband.

Now he stood alone on a dirt road, dust on his cheeks, a gun tucked in his waistband, and the weight of a man's burden too heavy for his small frame. The boy who had once cried openly was gone.

That afternoon when Narciso got back home, Elena knew something had happened. Her son had changed. The look in his eyes was different, vacant. His shoulders were slouched; she knew he had been crying. She could see the traces of caked tears on his dusty, dry cheeks. They looked like the dead and empty creek in town that had once flowed with a strong current.

Elena with Lorenzo, Pedro, Belém, and Narciso

Chapter XX

Narciso sat at the end of the table where his father always sat. Elena saw him, but didn't say anything. She simply gave him a plate of beans and a corn tortilla, the usual dinner. No one sat at that spot other than Nicolas. He had a way he liked things to be done at all times, and like a territorial animal, he didn't like to share anything.

Pedro and Lorenzo were in the living room playing with their sister, who had recently turned one. Elena sat next to Narciso and watched him eat carefully, studying his facial expressions and his behavior. He took a small piece of tortilla and moved the beans from one place on the plate to another with a fixed stare into it, yet not looking at anything. She saw his eyes water a few times but said nothing. After a couple of bites, he told his mother he wasn't hungry and was terribly tired and would like to go to bed. Elena knew her son and she knew he was lying.

"Not until we have a conversation first," Elena said softly to him while placing her hand on his bony shoulder.

With his stare fixed into nothingness, he quietly said, "He left us, ma." Narciso took the gun out of his pants' waistline and placed it on the table in front of them. She gasped and put her hands over her mouth.

"What do you mean, he left us?" Elena asked at once with a look of desperation.

He turned to look at her and took one of her hands, looked at her, and then held both of her hands with his.

"He left. I bumped into him on the street. I was on my way home from swimming in the river with my friends when I saw him. He had a suitcase as if he was going somewhere. I had a strange feeling, so I ran up to him and asked if he was going somewhere. He said he had some business opportunity in el otro lado, in Nuevo Mexico, and that he was leaving to make some money."

"Oh god, please! Not again... NOT AGAIN!!" She let out a wail and started sobbing, covering her face with both her hands.

The boys went running from the next room when they heard the commotion but didn't dare to go into the kitchen. They stood at the door with puzzled looks on their faces. They looked at their older brother and then at their pleading mother. Pedro approached his brother and putting his hand on his shoulder asked him why their mother was crying. He saw the gun on the table and asked:

"Is dad okay? Why do you have his gun? You know we're not supposed to touch it, you're gonna get in trouble!" Pedro was visibly anxious.

"You are not supposed to touch it, this gun is now mine. He gave it to me when he left." Narciso answered him, moving the gun to the other side of the table out of his brother's reach.

"Dad left? Where did he go? Let's go get him; I know where he's at. We can talk to him and ask him to come home." Lorenzo added, not realizing what was happening. He knew where the bar was and was certain they would find him there.

"I'm old enough. I can touch it too if I want to, especially if dad is not here anymore. Ma, if he can touch it, then so can I, huh?" Pedro blurted out, reaching out with his hand.

"This is my gun now and I forbid you to touch it! It's mine, he gave it to me, and he left me in charge so you have to mind me." Answered Narciso raising his voice and defiantly looking at Pedro. He then looked at Lorenzo and asked "is that clear?"

Belém walked in stumbling, still laughing and tugging at her brothers for them to go back to having fun. Elena picked her up from the floor, held her tightly in her arms and kissed her face several times as she wiggled around trying to get free. All she wanted was to go back to playing with her brothers.

"We have to talk about this, boys. Sit down, all of you," Elena demanded with a calmer voice "and I don't want to hear another word about that goddamn gun anymore. Narciso gets to keep it because that's what your father wanted. He gave it to him, but he will not carry it around and he will not use it. Is it understood?"

She turned and looked at Narciso as she sat down in the same spot where she'd seen him lose his innocence as he communicated to his family that he was now the head of household. That the family was now in his hands, that he was now a man. He lowered his eyes with shame and yet, he understood perfectly.

"We understand." the three boys answered in unison.

"This is not the first time that your father has left us," she started in a calm voice. Then she began to tell them about the first time their father had left when Narciso was just a baby.

The three boys gave their mother their full undivided attention. The baby was too young to understand. She nestled in her mother's arms and started yawning, she was tired and the boredom was putting her to sleep. Elena rocked her gently. The boys wanted to know everything about the man who never gave them any explanation, never a word of advice, and who would teach them to do as he said not as he did.

Nicolas was a man who fixed everything with a good beating while expecting his children to understand why they were being beaten. Nothing was ever talked about because he believed they should know better, simply by existing.

Pedro and Lorenzo cried when they realized what was happening. They had been used to their father's beatings and not seeing him for days at a time. Especially during the weekend after payday, when he would spend days at the cantina and then went home only after being thrown out when he ran out of money. They remembered waiting for him so they could go to the market and buy food for them to eat, sometimes in vain. They were used to their empty stomachs growling loudly in class and how they would laugh because they weren't the only ones who were hungry. The classroom was an entire symphony of growling bellies. They knew in their hearts that their father would, at some point, take care of his family, even if it was at a bare minimum level.

Now that he was gone, they feared there would be no bare minimum, no silver lining, nothing. They couldn't rely on their father sending money once every six months and even though Elena could start working again, Narciso felt responsible.

Elena knew for a fact, that if she was able to survive before, she could do it again. She had acquired a thicker skin and learned new skills. There was no way her children would go without, even if it was just scraping by. They would make it, if it was the last thing she did.

She didn't want Narciso to bear the burden of being the man of the house, he was just a child. Narciso would help her of course, she couldn't do it alone. Not with five mouths to feed, including her own. But she would make sure to minimize that burden Nicolas had placed on him.

That weekend, Narciso went around town looking for work. He would run errands, help men in the fields, help women carry their heavy bags from the market, or laundry baskets to and from the river. He would carry water in buckets for different households, among other things, all in exchange for a few pesos. It didn't take him long to realize this was not enough. He could not earn enough money to buy enough food for his entire family. Sometimes he would go to bed on an empty stomach.

When Elena would ask him, he would lie about having eaten with the people he had worked for that day, but he couldn't lie all the time. He was hungry like he had never been before. He'd needed new shoes and clothes, everyone at home did, but he knew that food had to be his priority. What good were newer shoes on his feet if his stomach was always empty? He could feel himself getting weaker with every passing day.

With winter approaching soon, he knew they would all need warmer clothes. Narciso decided he had to stop going to school so he could work more or they would all starve. In 1963, he was forced to drop out of school without finishing third grade and started working almost a full time job.

Elena was concerned with her son working all day in the fields or hauling firewood for certain families. Her concern was not only the straining physical work, but the dangerous exposure to scorpions. The Mexican state of Durango had been famously known as the scorpion capital of Mexico. Although only about eight out of over two hundred species had deadly stings, no one wanted to risk being stung.

Elena was terrified that Narciso would succumb to a sting, especially being so far away from a hospital. Even the nearest city was inaccessible to her since she did not drive. There were daily prayers to Jesús, the Virgin, and all the angels in heaven so that her son would stay safe.

The previous year, one thousand people had died of scorpion stings. She knew it could happen in a blink of an eye. The neighbor's son had been stung before and was fortunate enough to have made it to the hospital just in time for treatment. However, he was left with a bad limp on the foot he had been stung on. After she heard of that story, she would spray every single corner of the house with insecticide.

Once school was no longer an obstacle, Narciso started working in the alfalfa fields. Depending on the season and the pay, he would also pick cotton, beans, vegetables, or grains such as wheat and corn. One of the men he worked with in the fields gave him a lead on another job he could do on the weekends. There was a high demand for firewood, most houses still had firewood stoves in their kitchen and the demand was even higher during the winter.

He started gathering firewood from the empty fields a little way from their house right outside of town. The man who employed him lent him a donkey to ride to and carry the load back from work. Because it was a weekend job, Pedro would go with him. He wasn't as strong but any help Narciso could get was greatly welcomed. Together they would get the job done in almost half the time which allowed him time to rest.

During the summer, without school responsibilities Pedro would help Narciso in the field for half a day. Most days he would go home crying of exhaustion and would sleep most of the afternoon after eating lunch. At night, they would both dip their hands in hot salt water to help with the cuts and scrapes, especially when picking cotton.

In the mornings, before going back to work they would dip them in ice water to reduce the swelling they would wake up with. They had the option of wearing gloves to protect their skin, but that slowed their work down. Narciso was very patient with Pedro and tried to assume the responsibility of a parental figure. He would teach him ways to work without hurting his hands so much. He would show him methods in which to work faster. The more they picked in a day, the more they would get paid. Sometimes, when they worked together, they had enough money to buy a little meat. Everyone they worked with was empathetic towards them. They knew who their father was and how he had abandoned them yet again.

The following year, Pedro started second grade and Lorenzo first grade. Narciso did not register for school and missed the entire school year. He had hoped their father would have returned from New Mexico, wherever that was. He fantasized seeing him walk up to him and resume his fatherly responsibility as meager as they were and relieve him of that burden. Only then could he go back to school and worry about things boys worry about: homework, girls, and sometimes house chores.

Durango has a hot desert climate. The temperature was always higher in the middle and end of summer, and typically scorpions would become more outwardly active. They would show up even during the rainy season. Elena always made sure to remind Narciso to be extremely careful and to look twice everywhere he stepped, everywhere he crouched, especially when he was collecting firewood.

"You know those bastards like to hide in every little tiny crevice and when you least expect it, you feel the sting. It's extremely painful and very dangerous. Please be careful, mijo!" Elena warned him every day he went out to work.

She would do the sign of the cross on him, giving him her *bendición*. He never left the house without his mother's prayers as a protection.

What his mother didn't know was that he had killed many scorpions while at work. He always wondered how long he would be able to go without getting stung. Every day, he wondered if that would be the day when it would happen. Inevitably, one late summer evening as he was returning the donkey with a large load of firewood attached to it, he got stung. He was waiting to get paid for his day's work when he felt a slight tickle on the back of his left hand. He slapped it with his right palm, but he was too late. He felt a sharp pain and burning sensation in the area where he had seen the scorpion.

It was tiny, light brown in color, and almost transparent. His hand immediately swelled up and became sensitive to the touch. Fear immediately overcame him, remembering what his mother always told him.

When his employer saw him, he noticed a look of anxiety and desperation in his eyes. He asked him to go inside the shop with him and sit down. Don Arturo's house was attached to the shop. There was access to go between both places through one single door towards the back of the building. He yelled for his wife to help, trying to not cause Narciso any more fear. She entered the shop rushing with a glass of milk and a piece of onion and a lime, home remedies believed to help with the sting of a scorpion and neutralize the venom. Narciso drank the milk while she rubbed his hand with the onion and then with the lime. The concoction made his hand burn even more, but Don Arturo assured him it was safe.

He was told that he would feel much better in the morning and the swelling would go down. Narciso tried to get up and experienced a blurry vision and nausea. His fear grew, but didn't say a word.

The couple noticed Narciso was not feeling well so they asked him to stay longer so they could keep an eye on him. They needed to make sure he would be fine before they'd let him go home. If he got worse, at least there was a vehicle in the house in which they could rush him to the hospital, if needed.

While they waited, they all had dinner. Eating a warm meal made him forget about his fears. It had been such a long time since he had eaten caldo de res. The broth had the perfect temperature, and he couldn't remember the last time he had meat. His bowl included a piece of bone with marrow which he sucked dry, a small piece of corn on the cob, squash, celery, cabbage, and some carrots with a side of warm freshly made corn tortillas.

His belly was full but he didn't reject the second helping when it was offered. There was no way he would say no to something so delicious! While he ate, his left hand rested in a bowl of ice water and the swelling started to subside. It seemed he would be just fine but right before he left, he was made to drink another glass of milk, just in case. He did not complain. He thought maybe he should be stung by a scorpion more often, if that was the way he would be treated.

He politely thanked the couple for their hospitality and the dinner and said goodbye. Once Don Arturo's wife went back inside, he called Narciso back to the shop.

"Hey *Chicho*, before you leave, let me talk to you about something really quick. I was going to tell you about this during dinner but I knew my wife would have something to say about it. I wanted to tell you alone, you know, man to man." Don Arturo said in a low voice.

"Yes, of course, Don Arturo, whatever you need. What can I help you with?" answered Narciso ready for anything else that he could make money in.

"No mi'jo, this is about me helping you. More like helping you help yourself. But you must promise me to be *bien abusado*. You have to be very, very careful, you hear?"

"Yes sir, anything you say, I promise." Narciso answered wondering what this conversation was about.

"Look. The city is paying a bounty on scorpions. I just heard about it this morning when I went to deliver the weekly load of firewood in my work truck. Cities are paying a few cents for every dead scorpion you bring them in. I guess more than a thousand-people died from scorpion stings last year and they're trying to use them in the hospital for research in developing antidotes. They pay more for

374

the really dangerous ones, the type that would kill you. Imagine this, if one thousand people died in one year from stings, how many more people were stung and didn't die? Most scorpions are harmless, other than the pain in the ass when they sting you. You know what I mean, right?" He said, chuckling as he pointed at Narciso's swollen hand.

"Yes sir. You want me to kill scorpions for you?" answered Narciso immediately.

"No *chamaco*, I don't. I'm telling you that, maybe if you don't tell your mother, you could be making more money by being an *alacranero*. You know, a scorpion hunter. Look, you work in the fields and you gather firewood. If you pay close attention, even more than now, everywhere you step, every place your hand touches. I guarantee you there's a scorpion hiding around somewhere. You've probably already killed many. Take a little bag with you and while you're working and making money, if you find a scorpion, kill it and put it in the bag. When I go to the city to take the firewood once a week, you can come with me and you can collect the money. It may not be much, but then again it could. I also believe that if you're actively looking for them, the chances of being stung again will be less."

"Oh! I get exactly what you're saying, Don Arturo. I'm going to start right away." Narciso replied, excited about the opportunity to make more money.

"Just please be extra careful, you hear? I don't want you to be another scorpion statistic." Don Arturo sounded somewhat concerned at this statement.

When Narciso got home, he apologized to his mother for being late. She was waiting for him with a small plate of beans and a tortilla that had turned cold and hard. He lied to her about his hand and told a story about a red fire ant stinging him while delivering the day's load at Don Arturo's.

"Oh, thank God it was just an ant. Please son, be very careful." Elena begged him.

"I will Ma, I promise," Narciso answered as he ate his dinner, feeling as if his belly would explode.

That night he went to bed looking in every single corner of his house, under the shoes, under tools, and in the crack crevices on the walls of the room he slept in. He was going to be more careful about scorpions, but he also couldn't wait to make his first kill as a scorpion hunter. The title alone excited him to no end.

****

Towards the middle of fall, Narciso had killed and collected thousands of scorpions. He had found a few good ones that had paid, not cents, but pesos! Those were the dangerous ones.

He was glad his senses had been heightened with all those weeks of looking everywhere and he was as careful as could be. He loved his weekly rides with Don Arturo to the city. On those days he got a week's pay for scorpion hunting, free breakfast and lunch courtesy of Don Arturo, and the experience of being outside of town.

He loved walking by the local markets seeing people buying and selling all kinds of knick knacks. The first time he went, he couldn't believe how many souvenirs he saw with scorpions on them. He saw them encased in everything from key chains, wall clocks, ashtrays, and pretty much every other little thing in the market. That day he learned he wasn't the only person profiting from killing these potentially deadly insects.

Chapter XXI

One cold afternoon in February of 1965, almost two years after Nicolas had left to go to the United States, Narciso was summoned by his paternal grandmother.

Doña Belém was waiting for him in front of her house as he was walking home from work. He knew very well that he and his siblings were not welcome at their grandmother's house unless their father was around. He was shocked his grandmother came out of the house just to talk to him and even more surprised when she said she had something for him.

"Ándale chamaco!" she barked "I don't have all day to be waiting out here for you. It's so cold!"

"What is it, abuelita? Do you need me to do anything for you?" Narciso asked politely.

"Here's something your father sent you. I got it last week but then I couldn't find it. I didn't know where I'd left it, but here it is. Now take it and leave, I'm freezing my fingers out here in this cold." Doña Belém said to Narciso. She handed him an envelope that had once been sealed.

He took the envelope from her and thanked her, kissing her hand before leaving, as a sign of respect.

It had started to get dark. Narciso wanted to wait until he got home to see what was in the envelope so he could share it with his family. He ran as fast as he could and curiosity was killing him. When he got home, he could barely catch his breath as he told his mother what had just happened. Everyone gathered at the kitchen table as Narciso opened the envelope.

It was a letter from Nicolas. In it, he informed his family that he had moved to Arizona and had been working in the fields after the work ran out in New Mexico. He was staying with some friends he made at his first job and apologized for not being able to send more money because life in el otro lado is very expensive. He mentioned he barely had money to pay his own rent and feed himself. Narciso mumbled that he was probably drinking the little money he did have.

"More money? He didn't send *any* money!" Narciso replied angrily looking twice inside the envelope and between the sheets of paper for something he already knew wasn't there.

"Your grandmother probably took it. Didn't you say the envelope was already open?" Elena asked, remembering perfectly well Doña Belém had a habit of swiping funds.

"Why would she take the money that Dad sent, if it's for us? She has a big house and eats meat and fish all the time!" Pedro asked, confused.

"Oh! I want to eat meat and fish, too. Why don't we ever eat at her house?"Lorenzo asked, naively.

"Because she hates us, *menso!*" Narciso answered, knocking Lorenzo on the head with his knuckle.

"Don't make your brother cry, he doesn't know and he's just asking questions! Just forget about all that, forget about your holy grandmother, and forget about your father. The sooner you do that, the better you'll be. Trust me. I know what I'm telling you! We will eat now, you hear me? No more of this talk, that is enough!" Elena ordered while she served dinner.

"Yes ma'am," The three boys replied in unison while the baby walked around with a rolled corn tortilla in her hand.

Early the next morning, before going to work, Narciso stopped at his grandmother's house, knocking on the gate loudly with a rock. He had taken the gun from the house without his mother's knowledge. Even though it was his, he was not allowed to touch it. Elena didn't want any accidents to happen and she knew Narciso had never learned how to use it. He did not stop knocking until his grandmother appeared at the door.

"*Que chamaco tan bribón*! What the hell are you doing here, and so early in the morning? You almost gave me a heart attack! Go on, get out of here and don't come back!" barked Doña Belém furiously.

"Open the door, right this second!" Narciso ordered with a stern tone in his voice.

"What is wrong with you? Where's the respect? I am your goddamn grandmother. Just you wait until I get my hands on you. I will beat you into a pulp for talking to me like this. If your father knew what a little shit you are he would be angry. Get your ass in here!" Doña Belém yelled at him and then grabbed him by the ear and pulled until his ear popped. She then slapped him hard on the back of the head as soon as they were inside.

"Don't you ever put a hand on me again!" Narciso said, pointing his father's gun straight at her face.

The look in her eyes completely changed from a controlling and demanding heartless woman, to that of a cornered mouse looking straight at its predator's eyes. She was so shocked she was unable to move or make a sound.

"You opened the letter my father sent me. It was addressed to me. In it, he mentions not being able to send us more money. But as far as I'm concerned, he's never sent us any. Unless..." he stopped for a second and took a step closer to her, "You have been taking it for yourself. How many letters has he sent? And how much money have you kept for yourself?" he asked his grandmother in a calm voice.

Doña Belém did not move.

"Answer me!" Narciso yelled at his grandmother.

"I don't know what you are talking about *Chicho*, you know how your father is..." she said, stuttering.

"I need you to sit down and think about it. After you've remembered what you did with those letters, I need you to go get them and I need you to tell me how much money he has sent. You will then give me that money," Narciso said without blinking and with a steady hand.

She looked at him, wondering for a second if he was bluffing. It was impossible for him to harm her, she thought. He was an eight-year-old boy. No matter how heartless she had been to them, there was no way he would harm her. No boy his age would be capable or hurting anyone, especially his own grandmother.

He had always been respectful to her, even when she treated them like lepers. That was the way Elena had raised her boys, to respect everyone. However, this was different. Doña Belém had been taking the only form of communication from their father for such a long time, yet she didn't care.

She knew they were practically starving, all of them, and she had kept the little money their father had sent them. And yet, even at that time, with a gun pointed at her face, she had no regrets. She had not been moved when she found out that her oldest grandson, at the age of seven, had been forced to leave school to work in the fields. If their own father had not cared about them, why should she?

Especially if there was really no way of knowing if they were really her blood.

Then something changed. She looked into Narciso's eyes and they were not the same eyes she had seen before. There was pain, hunger, desperation, and hate all together coming out of that stare. She felt chills thinking of what this child would be capable of when pushed to the limit. Then she thought, if he really was her grandchild, he probably would pull the trigger.

"Oh, wait! I think I know where everything is!" Doña Belém answered with a rush and asked him to follow her.

She took a box from under her bed, and when she opened it, she pulled out some opened letters tied together with a string. She handed them to him and said: "Here, these are all the letters your father has sent you. I'm sorry I kept them from you. I didn't want you to get false hope of him coming back. I really did it to save you boys some grief." she manipulated.

"Where is the money?" Narciso asked without looking away from her.

She put her hand inside the pocket of her dress and pulled out a wad and without batting an eye, she handed it to him. He put everything she gave him in his pants pocket and then went to the kitchen.

He took a bag that was on top of the table and started stuffing it with whatever he could find. He grabbed a few oranges and apples, a loaf of bread, and a box with eggs. He had not had eggs in almost two years. Breakfast had stopped including eggs after his mother had killed the only chicken they had left. That's what they had for dinner after not having anything to eat in almost two days. He walked backwards towards the door, the gun still pointed at her.

"I am proud of you, son. You are acting like a man. It makes your grandma really proud. Doing what you must do to survive, to feed your family. Your father would be so proud too." Doña Belém told Narciso as he was leaving her house.

She kept talking and he listened to every word until he couldn't hear her anymore. Every word she said felt like a stabbing knife right in the middle of his heart. How could his own grandmother be so evil? So vile that she kept the money his father had sent them without any remorse? Knowing they had nothing. What kind of woman does that to anyone, much less her own son's children? Did she say those things to him only because she had been found out and forced to return the money? Or was she a heartless psychopath?

Narciso walked back to his house and found his mother getting Lorenzo and Pedro ready for school. Belem was still asleep. Elena saw him walk into the kitchen with a bag. He handed her the wad of money

Doña Belém had surrendered to him and then she watched him put the gun away.

"No need to worry mother, I paid my grandmother a little visit. She sends her love to all." Narciso said with a slight tone of sarcasm as he turned to go.

His mother knew exactly what he was talking about and stared at her son in shock.

****

That weekend Narciso and Pedro picked up the donkey at Don Arturo's and went straight to the hills. The scorpion catching business, although lucrative for a while, came to a screeching halt shortly after being implemented. Some of the wealthier families in the cities had started to financially exploit the bounty given out by the city by having their own breeding programs. They would grow them, especially the dangerous ones, and then kill them and take them in for the reward money.

The local authorities had decided to end the program after finding out about the scams. The end of the payouts ended up hurting those who needed it most, the poorest families. Without this little extra income, more hard work had to be done.

The boys gathered as much firewood as possible. Every weekend they would go farther into the hills and the donkey was of great help for carrying large loads. That day had started out cold and cloudy. It did not appear it would rain, so the children didn't think about the possibility of getting wet. After gathering as much as the donkey could carry, and a few bundles extra that they would pull themselves, it started to sprinkle. Narciso looked up at the sky and noticed how large and heavy clouds were forming in the sky. They were approaching quicker than he thought they would.

"Let's hurry up, carnal, before we get caught in the rain. I don't want this bundle to get wet, and I'm already starving." Narciso warned his brother.

"I'm seriously tired, Chicho," Pedro answered, his eyes were watery. "I'm also very hungry!"

"I know, let's hurry up and maybe when we get there, Don Arturo will give us some soup or something. But we need to go soon," Narciso urged.

Narciso took the donkey's reign and gently pulled to make the donkey walk but he didn't respond. He clicked his tongue a couple of times and pulled again. Nothing.

"Come on *burro*, let's go for a walk. Come *burrito, burrito, burrito,* let's go home." Narciso said softly to the donkey to try to coax him as he softly petted him and rubbed his cheeks with both hands.

"Is that why they call them burros, because they don't listen?" Pedro asked.

"No, that's why they call you one in school, because you don't listen and you don't learn." Narciso joked trying not to panic.

"Come on burro! Start walking!!" Pedro screamed at the donkey. "*Chicho*, I'm hungry. Please, let's go."

"I'm trying, can't you see?" Narciso snapped "This stupid donkey won't listen. Motherfucker!"

"You said a bad word! I'm going to tell mom!" Pedro threatened.

"Oh spare me! Mom doesn't need to know what words we use. We're out here working hard, we should be able to say whatever we want!" Narciso snapped at his brother.

Pedro grabbed the reins and pulled hard while Narciso tried to push the donkey from behind, being careful to not get kicked. It was as if the donkey was a statue, he would not move an inch and the sun was fading in the horizon. The rain started to pour down and the boys felt desperate. The wood bundles were getting wet and they were so cold, they started shivering. Pedro was afraid of the impending night and the donkey would not walk.

The boys did everything they could think of but nothing worked. They didn't know what to do. Narciso started thinking about their options. They could go home and leave the donkey and the bundles there. If the donkey took off, he would have to answer to Don Arturo and probably pay him for the lost burro. All the effort they put in collecting the bundle would be an entire day of work completely lost. Leaving the burro and going home was not an option.

Narciso grabbed a long and thick mesquite branch from the bundle Pedro was going to carry and he asked his brother to move to the side. Then with all his strength, swung the branch as hard as he could onto the donkey's behind. The donkey brayed loudly but did not move. Pedro pulled on the rein and still no movement. Narciso hit him again, no movement. He hit him hard three more times. The donkey flinched on the first two blows and kicked violently on the third and yet, he still did not take a single step.

Pedro had started crying inconsolably. By the looks of the clouds, it would rain all night long. They were both desperate, and Narciso didn't know what to do. He knew they would have to abandon the donkey soon if the situation didn't improve. He dropped the branch and went to the front and pulled the rein and the donkey would pull back, not moving its feet one inch.

Narciso punched the donkey on the neck. Hyperventilating, he yelled at it "Walk you beast! You piece of shit! Walk!"

Pedro grabbed the bundle he was supposed to take himself and started walking towards the town, crying. Narciso didn't stop him. He pulled the donkey's hair and punched him one last time, to no avail. In a moment of hopelessness he grabbed the donkey's ear and bit as hard as he could.

The donkey let out a loud bray and started running in the direction Pedro was walking. Narciso picked up his own bundle and started running after the donkey. He soon passed Pedro who was standing there like he'd seen a ghost.

After a while Narciso stopped to catch his breath and waited for Pedro to catch up. They were both in shock and walked back to Don Arturo's to deliver at least the bundles they had with them. On their way, they picked up several of the pieces that had fallen off the donkey. When they reached Don Arturo's house, the donkey was standing in front of the gate, its bundle almost untouched.

The boys ran to him laughing, it was like a miracle. Don Arturo had them come in to get them dry and fed while he put his delivery away. He then went in to pay them.

"I thought you'd gotten lost, it's late and the rain is hard. What took you so long? I was starting to get worried about you two," their boss asked.

"Narciso decided to eat a donkey's ear sandwich and we got a bit delayed. Sorry Don Arturo," Pedro answered with a chuckle, winking at his older brother.

"What do you mean a donkey's ear sandwich?" Don Arturo asked, with a puzzled look on his face.

"Nothing sir, he's just being a jackass. We have to go. Our mother will probably be worried for us. Thank you so much for everything and see you next week," Narciso answered as they walked towards the door.

Chapter XXII

By 1965, Narciso had gone back to school two more times, and dropped out once. His brother Pedro was already two years ahead of him in school although he was three years younger. Narciso had always loved school and was a very bright boy. He was a fast learner and did not need to put too much effort in his studies like some of his friends, who, no matter how much they studied, sometimes couldn't understand certain concepts.

He finally finished third grade as a nine-year-old. He was so proud of himself and he realized he had missed school so much. He would day dream of becoming someone important in life. He thought of not having to work so hard every day for such long hours and to never have to eat beans and rice again. He was grateful for having something to eat, but he wished something else was available. Maybe a little fish or beef once in a while. He thought maybe he could be an engineer. He was really good at math and his logical mind could solve any complex problems without having to exert himself with pencil and paper. First, he would have to finish fourth grade, hopefully in one school year and without any interruptions.

Back in school, Narciso was only able to work half a day and attend school in the afternoons. He would work all day on weekends. His mother had been working again doing people's laundry and ironing. Sometimes she would crochet scarves and sell them during the cold weather. Elena did not want her boys to be out in the field risking getting sick so they came up with an alternative job.

Elena would make *empanadas* and donuts as well as tamales and the boys would go door to door selling them. Lorenzo was five years old at that time and could carry a small basket, so all three boys would leave together. Narciso would take one route while Pedro and Lorenzo would go the opposite way to cover more territory.

One day in February of 1966, the boys found themselves with their baskets still half-full with tamales towards the end of the afternoon. It had been a very slow day for business and they were getting tired. They liked selling food for work because whenever they got hungry they could just grab some lunch from their basket and continue working. It wasn't like working in the field or gathering wood, this job was easier.

Because it had been so slow, the boys ended up on the same route. Narciso took the lead and his brothers followed him. They tried every house they could think of and the shops in town. The only place they hadn't tried yet was the bar. Narciso knew that as a nine-year-old, he wasn't allowed to go inside the *cantina*. He understood that. But he also saw the cantina as the perfect place to sell.

The bar didn't have a kitchen so food was not served. He decided to sneak in and try to sell some tamales and make a few pesos. His plan consisted of stealth and speed. He planned on not getting found out by the bartender, but if he was, he hoped he could at least empty his basket. He told his brothers to wait for him outside. He couldn't risk being too visible.

Narciso walked in not knowing what to expect. The place looked like the restaurant on the other side of town, only dirtier. It was small and warm. There were tables around everywhere where men sat playing cards, domino, or just talking and laughing loudly. The stench of alcohol was so overwhelming he felt the need to cover his nose with his hand. There was a large cloud of smoke hovering over everyone's head. The smell reminded him of his father, only he hadn't smelled it on such a large scale. He remembered his father's breath being a combination of rancidness and stale alcohol.

When Nicolas went home right after the bar, he was usually angry and took all his frustrations out on his family. That's when he'd get up close, yelling right at their faces. He hated that about his father, his dire need to control everything and everyone around him. Narciso kept thinking of the smell; it triggered memories of neglect, violence, and abuse. He became uncomfortable but swallowed his fear and went to work.

"I'll just sell a few tamales and I'll get out of here," he told himself.

He went around the perimeter of the room asking every table if they were hungry and if they'd like to buy some delicious and fresh tamales his mother had made. Some people bought a few, one said no because eating killed his buzz, and most only had money for the booze. One man asked if he could buy them on credit and he'd pay him later. That's what they did at the bar sometimes. They'd show up in the middle of the week without money and on Friday, they would be served only after they'd paid their debts.

Narciso had been lucky to not be seen by the bartender, it had been a busy evening and he was not paying attention other than to those at the bar. Narciso had just one last table to visit. It was right towards one of the corners of the bar. He approached it slowly. There was a man with his head on his arms resting on the table. He couldn't quite tell if the man was asleep, crying, or dead. Narciso reached out to someone at the table closest to the unresponsive man.

"Excuse me sir, is this man okay? He looks like he's dead"

"He is not dead, although he ought to be. He's been here for the past three days. Hasn't left, I haven't seen him eat either. He only drinks and drinks and drinks. I've seen him before somewhere, I just can't recognize him. If you can wake him up, it would be good for him to eat something otherwise he's probably just as good as dead. He has money too, so don't let him lie to you about that. But I'll take some of whatever you got there, boy. After that, you need to go. This joint is no place for a young boy your age. I know I wouldn't want my son in here for shit. He's way older than you, too! No sir, you can lose your innocence just by being around things that happen here." The man told Narciso with a fatherly tone.

"Thank you, sir, but I'm sure it's a little too late for that." Narciso answered unenthusiastically.

"Look, he is not dead!" The man laughed loudly, nodding towards the unresponsive patron. "Dead men don't snore like that. Wait, he sounds more like a bear!"

The bartender approached the table where Narciso was and made a purchase. After paying for a half dozen of tamales, the bartender walked with Narciso to the table in the corner and shook the man to wake him up. Narciso put his basket on the table and helped with the shaking.

"Mister, please wake up. You need to eat something. Here, I have tamales for you. You don't even have to leave the bar to go home and eat. Please wake up!" Narciso spoke to the man loudly.

The man finally lifted his head. His eyes were bloodshot and empty. His breath reeked of something familiar, mostly alcohol and cigarettes. His skin was wrinkled and dry, as dry as his mouth. He tried to say something but no sound came out. He looked Narciso in the eyes and immediately faced the other way and puked.

When he was done, he cleaned his mouth with the back of his sleeve and grabbed the bartender by the arm. Without making eye contact, mostly because he couldn't lift his head up, he asked the bartender for more alcohol.

"Otra botella de tequila, camarada."

"Oh no! No more booze for you, and I'm not your camarada. It's time to go, come on... get up." The bartender demanded with annoyance.

"I have money to spend here, I said to give me another bottle!" ordered the drunk man.

"You know the rules. If you puke in my place you either clean or you are banned. You're too drunk to clean, so get out. I said, get out!" barked the bartender, grabbing his arm and pulling him violently so he could stand. He walked him towards the door and kicked him out.

"And stay out!! *Pinche borracho de mierda!*"

Narciso watched without saying a word. Who was that man? He looked familiar, but he couldn't put a name to his face.

"My money is as good as anyone else's. You don't kick me out, I leave on my own. This bar sucks!" The drunken man yelled at the closed door of the bar.

Narciso squinted his eyes to see him better.

"*Ay mamacita linda*!" The man said as he fell to the ground, unable to keep his balance.

Narciso kept his eyes on him, and then it hit him. He recognized him. He gasped and dropped his basket of tamales and ran away from the bar like a lightning bolt.

Pedro and Lorenzo had just crossed the street to meet their brother. They had not been able to sell anything and their baskets were still full.

"What's gotten into him?" asked Lorenzo.

"Who knows? Come on. Let's finish this," answered Pedro, opening the bar door yelling, "Tamales! Tamales!"

The bartender stopped them and asked if they were with the other boy. They nodded shyly and were immediately escorted outside. Pedro picked up Narciso's basket from the ground.

"This is no place for boys like you, you're too young. Go on, get out of here." Said the bartender.

"Hey! That's my dad!" exclaimed Pedro "That man right there is my dad!"

He gave his basket to the bartender and ran to hug the half-passed-out man on the floor. His shirt was covered in vomit.

"Get away from me, *chamaco igualado!*" answered the man with annoyance.

The bartender grabbed Pedro by the arm and dragged him inside the bar. Before going in, he motioned to Lorenzo to follow them. Lorenzo walked in to join his brother, his feet dragging, and his head down. Tears were rolling down his face.

"How many tamales do you boys still have?" asked the bartender without receiving an answer.

"Look! You guys are almost done. You're hard workers. I bought six from your brother earlier but it looks like he still has a few left. Why don't you put them all together in this bag, go ahead and empty out your baskets. I'm gonna leave them out on the bar and then whoever wants them can just grab them. Sounds like a deal?" the bartender asked Pedro.

Lorenzo cleaned his face and did as the man said and then forced a smile of gratitude at him.

"Thank you sir. Now we can go home," Pedro answered after clearing the knot in his throat. He looked defeated.

The man took the tamales and paid for them and gave them a little extra.

"You kids be safe, now go look for your brother and make sure he's okay, you hear? Stick together, be there for each other." The man rubbed his hands on their head then sent them out.

Inside the bar, he placed the tamales on a large plate with a sign that read: "FREE: take one," he then took money out from the cash register to reimburse himself for the purchase and placed it in his pocket. He took the book of credits and wrote the amount on it with Nicolas's name next to it. "*Hijo de puta!*" the bartender mumbled as he closed the book before returning to work.

Chapter XXIII

Since his return home, no one talked about the bar incident. Nicolas, in his drunken stupor, had not even remembered what had happened. If it had not been because his sons disrupted his sleep at the bar, he could've just stayed there and died of   alcoholic intoxication.

That day at the bar, the bartender had not felt the need to kick him out. He had not been obnoxious or started any fights. All he did was drink. He figured people made their own choices and whatever happened to them was their own fault. He changed his mind when Nicolas threw up all over the place and then saw the three brothers' hearts break right in front of his eyes.

After being kicked out of the bar, Nicolas slept outside on the street until he sobered up and woke up freezing in the middle of the night. He walked to his mother's house to eat and bathe. He changed his clothes before going home the next morning. Surprisingly, he didn't want his family to see him that way.

Nicolas had not saved much money during the time he was gone and what he had sent home to help his family was meager. His young sons had made more money in one month of work than what he had sent them during his entire stay in the US.

He promised to never leave again and although no one believed him, he kept his word. He had brought with him several cameras he had purchased while in New Mexico. It was expensive equipment he had been able to buy at a discount during a closeout sale. He also showed up with an extensive brand new wardrobe, and as was expected, nothing for the family. His excuses were the same as the first time he left: there was not much work and the work he could find paid very little.

He insisted life in America was much more expensive and sometimes his boss didn't pay him. Everyone knew, however, that there was always enough money for him to buy new clothes, eat good food, and drink until he could no longer remember who he was.

Proud of his new equipment, Nicolas became a street photographer in town and eventually a traveling photographer. He would take Narciso and Pedro with him on the weekends to attract clients. The photographs were instant and people would pay a few pesos for them at the fair or outside concerts in larger towns. In the city, they would roam the town square and photograph couples in love, women with their babies and little kids on their birthdays. Eventually, they would show up at weddings and quinceañeras and freelance there.

The more known Nicolas became, the more work he had. He worked every day and he enjoyed it. He even worked on the weekends. The life of a photographer was not difficult and he thought he'd finally found his calling. He was so busy that he needed help and his sons were the perfect assistants. He tried to take them out of school, but Elena pleaded with him to allow them to finish at least sixth grade. The conversation did not end well for Elena. She ended up with a few bruises and cuts on her face, but he reluctantly agreed to wait.

Narciso's six grade teacher had become very fond of him. He admired the boy's intelligence and ability to understand new concepts almost immediately. He was certain Narciso was destined for greatness and did whatever he could to obtain a full scholarship on his behalf. The scholarship paid complete tuition, room, and board to a military academy in Mexico City. If he accepted, he would finish middle school and high school free of charge. Uniforms and books were also included. The teacher kept it a secret from Narciso until he had received the acceptance letter and proper formal documentation in his hand. He did not want to get the boy's hopes up until it was official.

"Not everyone is lucky enough to get an opportunity like this, Narciso. You are a brilliant boy. I know you will do great things, you were born to excel. You've had a tough childhood, but this will open so many doors for you." Narciso's professor told him this while explaining to him what was going to happen if he agreed to go to school in Mexico City.

"No, *profe*, thank you. You can give it to someone else," replied Narciso with a tone of helplessness.

"I can't, *mijo*. This scholarship is for you, no one else can go in your place. If you don't go, then it goes to waste. It was given specifically for you. I applied for it on your behalf right after the beginning of the school year. I know you can't afford it but you must go to school."

"My dad won't let me go, I already know this. So, I won't even ask him. I don't want him to punish my mother for the inconvenience of having an undesired conversation with me," Narciso replied defeated.

In June of 1970, when Narciso and Pedro graduated 6th grade at the ages of fourteen and eleven, their education had come to an end.

The Sunday after the graduation, Narciso's teacher showed up at their house. He stood outside for a few moments, thinking of what to say and then purposefully knocked on the door. Elena answered the door and was surprised when she recognized who he was. The boys were out working in a nearby town church with their father, photographing a baptism ceremony. He decided to wait for them and took the opportunity to explain to Elena what the purpose for his visit was. He asked for her opinion and her help in trying to convince Nicolas to allow Narciso to attend school.

"You ask for my opinion but I will tell you that my opinion doesn't count. I have no voice in this house. Believe me, *profe*, I want to be on your side. I am on your side. But that means I am against my husband's side. I want nothing more than for my boys to have an education, and if only one of them can go at this time, that would be okay too. I don't want them to live this life of misery and hunger. No shoes or clothes, no good shelter in the winter. They're always working hard jobs outside as if they were grown men. No sir, that is not what God intended for children. They no longer have innocence; they have scars in their souls that will not heal even with all the time in the world. But I cannot be against my husband. It is easy to talk about it, yes. But once you leave, we are the ones that will pay hell. Come hell or high water, he will make sure he always gets what he wants." Elena confessed hopelessly.

"Even if it means sacrificing a bright future for his own son?" asked the teacher incredulously.

"Yes. Even at his son's expense. You don't know him the way I do." confessed Elena.

"If you allow me, Doña Elena, I would like to talk to him and see if maybe I can convince him. I will do it in the most respectful and non-threatening manner. I think maybe I can change his mind. Some men, especially the ones that don't believe women have a voice, with all due respect ma'am... they listen more to a man. Even if we are communicating the same message. I would like to try, if you allow me to." The teacher offered.

"Would you like another cup of coffee? I guarantee you, even though you are a man, you won't have a voice around here either."

They waited until early afternoon, chatting about the school and the opportunities that Narciso would have if he was allowed to attend. He would receive a great education in a military school. When he finished with high school, he would have a military career if he wanted it. If a military career is not what he wanted, he could apply for a scholarship for college as long as he worked part time with the government while he finished his studies. He could go very far.

Nicolas and the boys got home from work in the early evening and they went straight to the kitchen where their dinner was already served. He was surprised to see a strange man sitting in his spot at the table where no one was allowed to sit other than him. Elena had been worried about everything else that she didn't notice him sitting in that chair. The teacher stood up and introduced himself, extending his hand. Nicolas politely asked him to sit somewhere else because that was his spot and left the teacher with his hand stretched out.

"Elena, please serve a plate for our guest since he has taken the day to be here instead of with his own family," Nicolas said sarcastically.

Narciso was very anxious. He knew exactly what his teacher was doing in his house. He knew the conversation would not go well and his father would not budge. But he knew more than anything, that his mother was in danger.

"No thank you, I will have dinner with my family. I won't stay long. But thank you, *señor*, for your kind offer. *Señor* Nicolas, would you agree to go outside with me to talk about something very important?"

"More important than our daily bread? I doubt there is anything important we need to talk about now, *profe*. School is out, Lorenzo has been on vacation since last Friday, isn't that so? Belém will be going to third grade I think. So I don't know what this could be about," Nicolas answered as he started eating.

"It's not about Lorenzo or Belém, Señor Nicolas. I'm actually here to talk about Narciso."

"Narciso?" Nicolas laughed "He's done with school, both him and Pedro. They just graduated. That means they're grown up and they don't need to be wasting their time with ideas of school and books. They get to have a job now, and help the family."

"Narciso has had a job since he was seven years old, if I'm not mistaken, sir, with all due respect. He has a brilliant mind and I think it would be great for him to continue with his education." added the teacher.

Elena walked towards the door and motioned the children to follow her, leaving the men to talk alone. Lorenzo complained silently, he was hungry.

"I have a full scholarship in Narciso's name. All I need is your signature. This is a free ride to a great education. Narciso could get a free education, with free books, free clothes, and free stay at the school in Mexico City. It's a scholarship, which means you don't have to pay any of that money back. He'll even get free food. It's a gift from the government and the school wants your son to study there. He is a brilliant kid and I would hate for him to miss out on this great opportunity."

"Nothing in this world is free, *maistro*. What do you get from this?" Nicolas asked skeptically.

"The satisfaction of knowing a good student would obtain an excellent education and change his life. That's too great of an opportunity to pass up."

"Well, what do I get from this? I still haven't heard of any benefits." retorted Nicolas.

"Well, just to start, there would be one less mouth to feed. He could have a career in the future which in turn will help your entire family."

"Will you take Pedro as well?" Nicolas answered.

"I only have one scholarship, señor Nicolas. I wish I had more, but I don't. Look, it has taken me almost an entire year to get this approved. I can't give it to anyone else but him, it has his name on it, everything is ready I just need your signature."

"It also means one less person to help me work. This doesn't help me at all. Now if you don't mind, I would like to finish my dinner in peace with my family. Maybe you should do the same."

"Please, señor Nicolas, I beg of you. Think of your son, think of his future, he would love to be an engineer one day, did you know that? He is brilliant and this is his ticket out."

"Get out of my house! I say what goes on in this house because this is my house and my family. Go and take care of your own family and leave me to mine. Now leave or I will make you leave!" Nicolas yelled violently, getting up from the table.

The teacher got up to leave. As he was picking up his things from the table, he saw Narciso's face peeking in through the door. His face reflected all the sadness of the world. He left the scholarship's official certificate and the school's letter of approval on the table. As he left, he patted them while making eye contact with his star student. Narciso went out through the front door and ran towards his teacher and hugged him.

"I know what the final answer is. I know I won't be going although I really wish I could. Thank you *profe*, for believing in me so much. I will never forget what you tried to do for me." Without waiting for a response, Narciso ran back inside his house. He didn't want to be missing when his father looked for him.

Once everyone was back at the table and dinner resumed, Nicolas grabbed the documents the professor had left behind and tore them to pieces. Narciso felt a knot in his throat as he saw his dreams and fantasies of a great life disappear in a matter of seconds. That night, although hungry, he could not touch his food.

"Did you really think about abandoning your family like that? Is it possible that you can be so fucking selfish and leave us when we need you the most? Especially now that you will be handling one of the cameras?" Nicolas asked Narciso with disbelief.

"No sir. I didn't want to go. I would never want to leave my family. I told him so and I also told him not to come because I wouldn't go even if I had your permission." Narciso had learned how to handle his father.

"Good boy." Nicolas said, resuming his dinner.

All Narciso and his brothers ever did was work. Since they were already men, according to their father, they had to contribute to the household. It was as if they hadn't already been doing that exact thing since before they lost all their baby teeth. Nicolas stopped contributing to the household finances as soon as Narciso and Pedro had graduated 6th grade and dedicated their entire time to work. Nicolas told them he had to start putting money away for his old age. Since the boys were still young, they didn't need to worry about retirement just yet. Once Lorenzo finished school, he shared his brothers' fate.

In 1974, Nicolas decided that it was time to go back to the United States. He was bored of his home town once again. With his sons being of age, he claimed he didn't have to worry about his family struggling while he was away. When he realized that he would be away from his three cash cows, he changed his mind and decided he wanted the entire family to go with him.

"I'd miss them too much, we've bonded greatly in the past few years," he would claim.

In the United States, the boys would all have jobs and he could make more money by having them "help with the rent." The decision came at a time when Nicolas couldn't find a house to rent after they were kicked out of the house they had been staying in. Even though the incomes between the four men in the family had never been better, they had been evicted in the middle of the night for not paying rent several times.

The boys always complained amongst themselves but knew better than to say anything to their father. They never saw a single peso for their work. Nicolas always managed the family earnings, but they all knew he drank everyone's money. Several times they had been thrown out in the streets with only those things they could carry with them as they walked out the door. Their reputation as tenants became tarnished and their options were very limited.

Elena did not agree with the decision of moving. She loved the idea of the United States, but not the consequences that would come with that move. They would be undocumented, which meant that once safely in the states, she would not be able to visit her aging parents again. She had visited them regularly since she moved in with Nicolas, and sometimes they would visit her. But going to another country was asking too much of her. She stood her ground and told Nicolas she was not going. The boys all said they'd stay where their mother was.

Nicolas, like all his time with Elena, felt that he was the only one allowed to decide anything regarding the family. He felt disrespected and provoked by Elena for voicing her concerns and blamed her for his sons' apparent disobedience. He wanted their loyalty above everything, even above her. He took off his belt and folded it in half, then charged towards her.

She was already used to flinching with his sudden movements, even if he wasn't going to harm her. She put her head down and covered her face with one arm and extended the other to try to stop the leather from striking her. She could grab the belt, but she could not stop him. Nicolas punched her on the side and when she fell to the ground gasping for air, he whipped down the belt hard on her repeatedly. She couldn't even sob. She felt the stings of his weapon of choice striking her back, then a few times on her leg as she flinched and moved as she could. She could hear him breathing heavily, he was getting tired.

"Maybe he'll stop when he can't hit me anymore." Elena thought.

He dropped the belt and kicked her a few times, then grabbed her by the hair and dragged her to the bedroom where he took three large valises from under the bed. He opened the armoire without letting go of her hair, and then shoved her to the ground.

"I will give you a choice, Elena. You win. We go to Chicago together, or we go to the border together. Be happy you have some choice in the matter. Now start packing! We leave by the end of the week." Nicolas yelled.

"Why can't you just go alone? You never cared before!" Elena asked, struggling to get her words out.

Her mouth was full of blood and it hurt to talk. She had difficulty breathing.

"Because I don't want to abandon my family again, I suffered too much without you and the kids." He answered in a way that almost sounded sincere.

"Oh, you suffered?" asked Elena trying to laugh while holding the ribs he had smashed in. "Lies! You only care about yourself. You want to take us so you can have your sons do all the work and pay all the bills and you can live like a goddamn king. I know you!" Elena knew this would cost her another blow at least, but she didn't care.

She had to get it out and tell him exactly what she thought. She wanted him to know she knew what he was up to and what kind of a man he was.

Nicolas crouched down to the floor and grabbed her by the hair, pulling her already swelling face close to his and in a low and collected voice he said, "Start packing." Not a single sign of emotion appeared, he then shoved her head violently to the ground and left.

Nicolas didn't spend the night at home, as was expected. In the morning when he got back from the bar, everyone had already had breakfast and was packed and ready to go. He pulled his old truck to the front of the house and asked his sons to load it up. Narciso and Pedro were to ride with him in the truck while Elena and the younger children would go by bus.

After the truck was loaded, he took Elena and the two kids to the bus station and bought them tickets to Ciudad Juárez and then went back to the house to pick up his two oldest. That was the first time anyone else other than Nicolas knew what their final destination was.

****

Once settled in a two-bedroom apartment they rented from Doña María de Jesús in a neighborhood called *Satélite*. Everyone went to work immediately. Finding a job was a lot easier than everyone had anticipated. Narciso and Pedro found jobs in nearby factories during the week and helped with the photography during weekends and holidays. Nicolas' work as a photographer was making much more money than he ever did back in Durango.

Ciudad Juárez was booming, with the *maquiladora* industry, there were factories everywhere. Some made electronics like RCA, others made medical equipment, and some made clothes. Factory work, although dull and repetitive, was beneficial to the boys because they could choose any of the three shifts. The night shifts paid more because less people were willing to work the late hours, so there was a little bit of an incentive.

After getting comfortable enough with public transportation and with the job in the city, Narciso and Pedro felt a sense of freedom for the first time. There was also an ambition they'd never had before.

For once, they could think about things other than being evicted.

They had been so poor back in Durango that they were used to eating only beans and corn tortillas. The city brought progress to their lives and a curiosity and want for things other than their most basic needs. Pedro enrolled in classes in a technical school which allowed him to expand his skills at the factory he worked at. He was able to receive higher pay as a result. He joined a gym and started working out in order to compete in lower level bodybuilding competitions.

Narciso joined Pedro in English classes and he became interested in boxing, and also joined a local gym. On the weekends, they pursued their photography career at the fair or wherever there were public events. The churches always had some type of celebration in need of their services. The *charros* loved getting their pictures taken during their *charreada* routines, and there were always a few lovebirds walking around wanting to capture their time together. Work was never scarce.

Nicolas was against all the extracurricular activities his sons became interested in. There was not much he could do about it because they were no longer little boys he could manipulate or beat into submission as when they were younger. He had no choice but to accept what they wanted to do with their lives, up to a certain point.

When Belém graduated sixth grade, her brothers were prepared for what they knew was about to happen. She had hoped she would be able to attend middle school, and her brothers told her she would. They made it their own personal mission to make sure she did. They enrolled her and bought her the books, materials, and uniform with their own savings. When Nicolas found out, he was completely against it. She had to get a job just like everyone else, otherwise it wouldn't be fair to his sons.

Narciso, Pedro, and Lorenzo were old enough to come together and defend their sister. If they had not been able to go to school, at least they would make sure their sister had that opportunity. Elena had taken craft classes and learned how to make teddy bears by hand. She would sell them at the park outside the church on the weekends and used that money to help with the costs.

Finding himself outnumbered and not able to do much about it, Nicolas agreed to allow his daughter to go to school. The only conditions he had were that they never asked him for a single peso for the cost of his daughter's education and that their contributions didn't diminish.

Belém finished three more years of school but unfortunately, nothing could be done to convince Nicolas to let her finish high school. So after three years, school was over for her and it was time to get a job.

****

In Ciudad Juárez, Elena missed her parents tremendously and found it much more difficult to adjust to the city life than she thought. She felt very lonely and she couldn't visit her hometown for the first few years. Nicolas said it was too expensive and she would have to save for the bus fare on her own. So it was either visit her family in Durango or send her daughter to school. She, of course, chose the latter.

It took her another full year to take that first trip back home after Belém had transitioned to a full time job at a shoe store. After that, Elena was able to visit and stay with her parents for two weeks every summer. She would travel by bus, which would take almost twelve hours. There were many stops in little towns on the way that added more time to the trip. Sometimes the drivers would stop in random places and pick people up if the bus was not full, but Elena was patient.

Many people from their town in Durango had gone to Ciudad Juárez. Some went to other large border cities, and others tried their luck crossing the border. Nicolas was disappointed that they weren't in the US, but he could easily drive to El Paso from their new home.

One February day in 1982, Elena bumped into Jesús, her sister's husband, while she was shopping at the market in Ciudad Juárez.

"Elena! How are you? Did you just come back from Durango? That was fast. I thought you'd stay longer with what happened! How's your dad?" Jesús asked her, surprised.

"Oh no, I went a few months back. I try to go around the same time every year. They're both okay, but dad looks a little tired. They're getting old, you know? I worry about them." Elena confessed.

"Elena, I just came from Durango a few weeks ago. When I got back I went directly to look for you. Nicolas said you weren't home."

"Oh, and how was your trip? How's my sister and everyone back home? You know, when I go back I just want to stay. I get so sad when I leave," Elena admitted, oblivious to Jesús's anxious questioning.

"Did Nicolas not tell you anything about my visit?" Jesús asked in shock.

"No, that man never tells me anything unless it's something that will benefit him. We hardly even speak to each other. Actually, I've always wondered if he hates me. I'm sure he does."

"Goddamn it, Elena! We gotta go, please come with me." he said with urgency.

Jesús grabbed Elena's arm and pulled her towards him.

"What is going on Jesús? You're scaring me," Elena tried to pull her arm away but couldn't.

"Please Elena. Just trust me, let's go."

Elena followed him in a rush to his truck. As soon as she was in the cab, Jesús told her about the conversation he had with Nicolas the day he'd gone to look for her.

"Your dad was very sick when I went to visit, Elena. I found out the day I was leaving Durango. I came straight to your house to tell you but you weren't there. I told Nicolas about it and I asked him to tell you. He said he would as soon as you got back from the market. I had no reason to not believe him. I feel like a fool. I should've looked for you to make sure you knew about this. All this time I thought you were back home with them." Jesús talked to her in a sympathetic way, holding her hands in his.

Elena could not speak. She moved her mouth as if she was trying to say something, but no sound emerged. She then covered her face with her hands and immediately started to sob.

"Tell me what you want me to do Elena, I want to help you. I'm so sorry. They gave him only a few weeks to live. Maybe he's still alive. We might be able to make it if we leave now. I'll take you myself."

"Take me home, I need to get a few things and in ten minutes I'll be ready. Can you please take me to the bus station? I need to get home as soon as possible. I don't want to inconvenience you. You just came back from there."

"No Elena. I'll take you home to pick up your stuff and I'll drive you myself. I'll spend the night and drive back tomorrow. You can come back on the bus whenever you're ready to come home. Who knows what time the next bus leaves and we'll get there five hours faster. He was in bad condition, your dad was, and we need to get there fast. I hope we get there on time."

Elena thought about the gravity of her father's situation and agreed to allow Jesús to take her. She needed to see her father one last time before she lost him forever.

Durango had traditionally been a mining state. There is evidence of mining activity in that region of the country that dates back to pre-Columbian times. Eventually, after hundreds of years of mining, the industry would give birth to the state of Durango.

Elena's father had worked in the mines his entire life. His work days were long and the job was difficult and very physically draining. Very little protection was available to mining employees. His exposure to a hazardous environment throughout most of his life led to chronic bronchitis. Dust from the mines had accumulated in his lungs. He had trouble breathing at times during most of his time working.

Don Arnulfo, Elena's father, always thought all the bad air he breathed in would come out when he coughed up mucus. He never worried much about it though. Since the symptoms were minimal and there was no pain, he was never diagnosed with anything. By the time the symptoms started showing up, the pain was intolerable and his quality of life had diminished greatly. He was unable to breathe normally without pain or coughing. By the time he visited the clinic for help, it was too late. His lungs were failing.

Don Arnulfo knew that his daughter had been notified about his condition and he was waiting for her. The townspeople said he waited as long as he could and longer than any other dying man could. He died an hour before Elena got to him. She was devastated. Nicolas had robbed her of the opportunity to be with her father on his last days. She could've spent three weeks with him. She could've taken care of him and comforted him as well as her mother. Elena's parents had been married for almost fifty-six years and they had been inseparable during their entire marriage.

Elena would never forgive Nicolas for what he did. She stayed in Durango for two weeks after the burial to help her mother and to keep her company. She needed to make sure her mother would be fine. Her parents were each other's best friends, and they had loved each other like they had loved no one else in the world. When Elena went back home, her mother seemed sad, but she had high spirits and a will of her own to live.

Two months after Elena had gone back home, while still grieving the loss of her beloved father, she received word that her mother had died in her sleep due to heart failure. People that knew her swore she died of a broken heart. That was one of Elena's darkest moments in her life, to lose her parents and not being able to be there with them. She could've been there with them. Because of Nicolas, she had missed valuable time with both of them.

Part III
Endings:
Truths Revealed

Chapter XXIV

It took over thirty-five years for Chuy to find out the truth about Victor's mysterious disappearance. For decades she didn't know what happened to her fiancé that fateful day.

Juan Carlos, Manuel's friend from the force, sent Chuy a message with one of his children. They had remained close while their children were young. In the message, Juan Carlos informed Chuy that he was very ill and, on his deathbed, needed to talk to her urgently. He stressed the importance of the meeting and asked her to see him at once.

Chuy asked Rosa María to drive her to his house where he was resting after many exhausting months in the hospital. They were both warmly welcomed in his house by Juan Carlos's wife and children. Chuy could feel the somber mood as soon as she entered the bedroom where he lay. As soon as he saw her, he asked everyone to leave. He wanted to talk to her alone.

"I'll leave you both to it. I'll be right outside if you need me." Rosa María said, turning to go.

"My daughter stays with me. Whatever you must tell me, you can do it in front of her." Chuy said plainly.

"If that's what you want, Chuy." Juan Carlos replied slowly. It was evident he was struggling to speak. He was nervous. "Rosita, you can pull that chair and bring it next to your mother."

"Mom, are you sure you want me here?" Rosa asked supportively by placing her hand on her mother's shoulder.

"Yes, I want you here with me." Chuy knew that if Juan Carlos had called her on his deathbed, she was about to learn something she would need support with. She didn't want to be alone with him.

Juan Carlos coughed violently and couldn't speak for a few minutes. He was short of breath and exhausted. His wife knocked on the door slightly and peeked her head in to make sure he was fine. She had agreed to the visit with the condition that if at any point he got too excited, the visit would end immediately.

Juan Carlos closed his eyes and with a weak hand, motioned to her that he was fine. She looked at him for a few seconds, then shook her head and closed the door.

"Chuy, I am not going to beat around the bush here. I'm dying. My time here is running out and there's something that I need to tell you before I go. First of all, I want to thank you for coming to see me. I wasn't sure you'd agree to talk to me, but I am glad you did. I still remember how you looked when I first met you. You had just gotten here from Durango. You were so young, so innocent... "

426

"…and so naïve. Yes, of course I remember. I am sorry you are not well…" Chuy said with a soft voice, while holding his hand.

"Don't be. Sometimes I feel like I deserve all the misfortunes that come my way. God, I was such an asshole, Chuy." He squeezed Chuy's hand and got choked up.

"Shhh. Don't say that, please. Be kind to yourself. No one deserves something like this. We were young and we were doing the best we could. You can't blame yourself for that." Chuy said, trying to comfort him.

"I do. I deserve this. It's okay, I've made peace with it and I'm fine. I remember you back then. I remember how strong and dedicated you were in spite of being out of your comfort zone. Chuy, you moved to the city on your own without anyone to wait for you and help you. You did all that and you weren't afraid. You have no idea how much I respect you for that. Some of us just do what we're told, or what we feel we have to do, and never question the motives. You've always been so strong. You were beat down by life and yet you always picked yourself up. You always did. God, you were so young and all alone here, and you were so beautiful. Well, you've always been beautiful. You're still beautiful now. But beautiful in a unique way, you know? You've always been kind. Your heart is always open to everyone, whether they deserve you or not. Even during adversity, you've always helped others.You have helped so many people when you didn't even have enough for yourself and your family. That is being kind, Chuy. That's what everyone should aspire to be. I remember myself back then, when I met you, and I feel so pathetic. I used to think you were a fool. Now I realize that we were the fools. Manuel being the biggest one of all."

Juan Carlos stopped to rest and take a few deep breaths. Chuy listened to him without interrupting. She never stopped holding his hand. His pain could be felt in the air and seen in his eyes. Rosa María didn't know which of his pains were more difficult to witness, the physical or the spiritual.

"Manuel. What a fucking fool, that man. He was a fool then, he's always been a fool, I guarantee you he hasn't changed a bit and he is still the biggest fool. You know the best thing about being alive for a while is? That we can sit down and watch our children or grandchildren run around on any given day. We can watch them and realize that they are the purest and most innocent things we've ever made. That changes a man, Chuy. I have changed so much, I don't recognize myself anymore. And you know what? That's a great thing. Because the more I think about my old self, the more I thank life for second chances. Some of us get second chances, others don't."

Juan Carlos pulled Chuy's hand and motioned her to get closer.

"I am partly responsible for at least two people not getting a second chance, Chuy. It has been eating me alive for years. I kept thinking it was too late, that maybe I should just take it to my grave. That is until I learned that the grave was part of my very near future. This is weighing down on me and I dread it more than death. I need to release it, I can't carry it anymore. There is so much darkness in my soul. I need to be able to die in peace." confessed Juan Carlos with pain in his soul.

"You're tiring yourself, Juan Carlos. You don't have to do this, please rest. Know that whatever happened cannot be changed, it is already in the past. We can't change it." Chuy tried to convince him to stop talking, for the sake of his health. She had a soft voice and compassion in her heart.

"Please! I must do this. Goddamn it, Chuy. I thought about telling you long ago, but I was afraid you'd never forgive me so I didn't. I've been a coward. I've acted like a coward all my life. But not today, today I am going to be brave. I know I don't deserve your forgiveness, I just have to get this off of my chest," Juan Carlos pleaded.

"Listen to me!" he demanded, although Chuy had not interrupted him, "Do you remember that one day at the square, when I came to talk to you myself? Manuel had been a total asshole and you never wanted to see him again. You were sitting on a bench alone, I came and sat next to you and I apologized for his behavior." Juan Carlos stopped for a few minutes to catch his breath. He was visibly disturbed and his breathing had become shallow and rapid.

Chuy didn't want him to get agitated, so she appeased him. Rosa María got up from her chair and got closer, placing her hands on her mother's shoulders.

"I remember," Chuy answered, intrigued.

Her heart had started to race and the curiosity was killing her. What was so important that he had to tell her on his deathbed? What had this man done and then kept hidden for decades?

"Go on, Juan Carlos. I'm listening." Chuy said softly.

"He sent me, Chuy. Manuel sent me. He had told me he was crazy about you and you didn't give him the time of day. He told me how he got drunk one night and kissed you by force. He said you slapped him. He wasn't used to that, no one said no to him. You started out as a challenge to him. That was until you told him you were engaged and that made him crazy. You should've seen him. He was obsessed. That day at the square, he sent me to look for you. I went to your work and they told me it was your day off so I looked for you at the square and there you were. Manuel wanted me to find out who this man in your life was at all costs. He's never liked competition, he always had to win. He always had to have the last word. He always had to have the last

430

laugh. He wanted you and he had to have you, come hell or high water." Juan Carlos stopped to gasp for air.

He had been having a difficult time speaking, but he continued.

"He wasn't going to allow another man to come and take what he already saw as his. He was going to make you his if it was the last thing he did. And he did, Chuy, he did. And I helped him!" Juan Carlos squeezed Chuy's hand and sobbed.

"What did you do Juan Carlos?" Chuy asked, her heart pounding.

"Chuy, I am so sorry!" he couldn't stop crying. Rosa María gave him the box of tissues on the nightstand and they gave him time to catch his breath.

"The day you were waiting for him at the plaza. You were waiting for your man. I had manipulated you and you gave me all the information we needed. I snitched it to Manuel. That day, *La Perra* and I waited for your man by the bridge all morning. We finally found him. He was there punctually, just like you said he would be. We picked him up in the patrol car and took him to the city limits where no one could see us and we roughed him up. This happened while you were waiting for him." He stopped to collect himself.

Rosa María gave him a glass of water and helped him up so he could drink. His throat was dry and his voice was getting hoarse.

"Let him finish!" Chuy raised her voice while holding Rosa María's hand and telling her with her eyes to sit down.

"While you waited, Manuel was watching you. He sat a block away waiting for our signal on the radio. We roughed him up, Chuy. We beat him up so bad his clothes had blood everywhere. We laughed at him, we mocked him, we lied to him, and then we broke him. He fought back the entire time, but he was a gentleman. He was respectful as much as he could be. I told him that while he was away you had married our boss. We told him that you had gotten tired of waiting for him and that you left with the first man that offered you something. That you hadn't waited for him like you promised him you would. He believed us. Why wouldn't he when we had all the information only the two of you had shared and that you later shared with me? He dropped to his knees and sobbed. Then we beat him again, that time for being soft and a coward. I always thought that men who cried for a woman were pussies. Men who cried were not men, not really." Juan Carlos coughed.

Chuy's hands were trembling. She tried to take her hand back from his but he grabbed harder. Tears inundated her eyes and rolled down her plump cheeks. Rosa had never seen mother that way and was worried. She too was crying, imagining the pain her mother had suffered at the hands of this man and the whim of her own father.

"We dropped him off at the bridge and we saw him walk back to the other side. Manuel said we had to make sure he never came back later and ruin his plans. There was nothing else we could say to him to leave. When I told him things in detail about you and him, he knew in his heart we were telling him the truth. We saw him walk back with his head down, his shoulders were slumped, dragging his feet. That's why he never showed up to meet you, Chuy. I did that. I took what you confided in me and used it against you and against him. I used it to benefit Manuel. It's my fault you ended up with my *compadre*. He didn't deserve you then, he doesn't deserve you now, he never has. I am so sorry it took me so long to tell you this. I never imagined how it would eat at my soul. Back then I didn't see anything wrong with what we did." Juan Carlos coughed blood into the tissue.

Chuy got up from her chair and wiped her tears. She walked closer to Juan Carlos and placed her hand on his head and kissed his forehead.

"I forgive you Juan Carlos. Let this pain and darkness in your heart go. It's in the past. What's done is done and there is nothing to do about it anymore. Thank you for your honesty, at least now I have answers. I never knew what had happened and I've never been able to stop wondering. It still hurts

433

even after thirty-five years. God bless you Juan Carlos, for giving me answers and with them the peace I never thought would come." Chuy was whispering to him with her eyes closed, just as if she was praying. She then kissed his forehead one more time and got up.

Juan Carlos looked Chuy in the eye, his pupils were dilated. He let out a long sigh and slightly smiled. He grabbed Chuy's hand that he'd been holding and placed it on his chest then let go. Chuy cleared her throat and dried her tears and walked towards the door.

"Thank you so much for your brave confession to my mother. You may think it's too late, but you gave her answers to questions that she'd otherwise never had. Questions she's had for so long. It means the world to me. I know she will have peace now. Thank you!" Rosa María held Juan Carlos's hand and kissed it. She then followed her mother to the door.

Juan Carlos's wife was waiting by the door, making sure he was okay. She had been anxious to stop the visit if it became detrimental to him. Now that it was over, she extended her arms out to Chuy.

"Chuy, I don't know how to repay this most generous gesture of yours. He told me this story not long ago. I was very angry at him. I don't know what I would've done if I were you. You are a brave and strong woman, I wasn't expecting you to react in this manner. He wasn't lying when he said you were the most compassionate and strong person he'd ever met."

"I know he does. Thank you so much for your words and your hospitality. I'm sorry but I have to go. Rosa María, *vámonos!*" Chuy snapped.

On the way home, Chuy cried while Rosa María held her hand. It took almost the entire trip back for Chuy to finally break the silence.

"Thank you for being there with me *mija*, I didn't know what he was going to tell me. It was like a bucket of cold water was dropped on me. I thought I was going to faint, I didn't know if I was breathing or not. Your presence gave me strength."

"How can you forgive something like that, ma? That is terrible, what he did. He could've ruined that poor man's life and he altered yours in the most violent and tragic of ways. And Dad, my God!" Rosa uttered with disbelief at her mother's immediate forgiveness.

"*Escucha, hija:* We either forgive or we hold a grudge. Forgiveness comes from love, which is our humanity in the purest of forms. Grudges are like never-ending storms. If you hold one of those in your heart long enough, they grow big and destroy everything in its path including ourselves. When you forgive someone, you don't necessarily do it for their benefit, even if in turn it does benefit them; that's just an added bonus. You do it for yourself. Juan

Carlos is dying. No one should go to the grave with regrets of that magnitude, you understand? We should try to go meet our father in heaven with a clean conscience and a pure heart. I didn't want him to live his last days in torment. He answered the questions I had about Victor, even if it was not until now, he gave me the gift that I needed, the truth. In turn I gave him what he needed, my forgiveness. I feel better knowing what happened, this brings me peace. All I ever wanted was to live a happy life. If I had married Victor as we had planned, I wouldn't have you kids. Things would've been very different. You are the loves of my life and for better or for worse, I don't regret a single thing." Chuy answered in a soft voice, patting Rosa's leg with a sad melancholic smile on her face.

****

Chuy patiently waited until the following morning to confront her husband. During the previous 35 years, she had decided to have a happy and peaceful life or die trying. Those nights she spent in jail when her first child with Manuel was an infant had changed her perspective on life. Life could be simple and beautiful if she recognized that she couldn't have light without the dark. She never had everything she wanted to have, but she had everything she needed. Manuel was darkness in her life, she knew that. But that darkness had brought her the brightest of lights, her children and grandchildren. *Uno pone y Dios dispone,* she thought.

436

****

Chuy had been struggling with a knee injury for two years after a bad fall, and the pain was constant—her knee throbbed relentlessly. Her recovery had been long and painful; she never walked again without the aid of her walker. Despite a series of attempts to heal it—including surgery with large pins driven through her leg, hot wax treatments, a heavy cast, and months of physical therapy—nothing worked. Even traditional remedies like limpias and brujería failed, though she still had faith in such spiritual cleanses. A thick surgical scar, running from the middle of her shin to the top of her knee, remained clearly visible beneath the dresses she always wore.

Each day, Chuy cared for two of her five-year-old grandchildren, Alfredo and Karina, while their single mothers, Alicia and Josefina, worked. That morning, the children slept in late. As soon as the last of Chuy's own children stepped out the door to begin their day, she made her way from the kitchen to the living room—leaning heavily on her walker—and confronted Manuel, who was still on the couch where he had been sleeping for years.

She stood in front of him, gripping the walker between them. She knew she could control what she did, but not what she wanted to say.

"Rosa María took me to see your *compadre* Juan Carlos yesterday," she started. Her chest felt heavy and her breathing was difficult.

"Oh," Manuel answered without looking at her.

"He's dying, you know?" She took a step closer to him.

He looked up and met her eyes only after the walker touched his foot. There was fire in her gaze. He had never seen that look in her eyes. Her white face was flushed, her lower lip was quivering.

"That son of a bitch always made terrible choices. I wonder what the hell he did that is now killing him. Probably the liver or the lungs. He drank and smoked like there was no tomorrow. I don't feel sorry for him. " Manuel responded coldly.

"Have you ever made terrible choices, Manuel?" she asked with a sarcastic tone.

"Excuse me?" he shot back.

"Let me rephrase the question. Have you ever done terrible things? Things that you have regretted?" she asked again.

"No. I have never done anything that I regret. *Nothing*." He returned her gaze coldly.

"You know, he did. He did terrible things in his life that he regrets. And now that he is dying, he

438

wants to make amends. He wants forgiveness. He wants to die in peace without guilt," Chuy went on.

Manuel got up and pushed the walker away from him, making her lose her balance and almost falling. He was being blocked by her and couldn't physically get out of the situation.

"I don't know why you're telling me this. I haven't talked to him in ages and I really don't care to know about him." Manuel said, averting Chuy's eyes.

"Well, he asked me to go see him. He had a secret that was eating him up. You wouldn't know anything about that, would you?" she asked.

"No, why would I?" Manuel finally started to look uncomfortable.

"Stop lying! He told me everything Manuel. *Everything.* How could you? You knew I loved him, you knew he loved me. You could've ruined his life, you almost ruined mine! How could you be so cruel? Everything always comes to the surface, no matter how much time has passed!" Chuy yelled at him with tears in her eyes.

His eyes were big, all pupils. His face turned pale. His thin, almost non-existent lips completely disappeared and the edge of his mouth convulsed.

"I don't think there's any use talking about this now, do you? Don't you love your children? You wouldn't have them if things didn't go the way they did. I loved you." He answered.

"I don't care if you loved me, why must everything always be about you? You were fine with ruining two lives just so you got what you wanted? Are you even sorry about anything? Do you regret any of the pain you've caused? Why must everyone always suffer so that you can have what you want? So that Manuel can be happy? Have you ever been happy? And how could you be happy to have what you wanted, me, when you knew I didn't want you in return? How?" Her voice was loud and it echoed against the walls.

"Only the strong survive, my dear. I am that person, I survived. I was strong. I won. And to make sure that everything is clear, no, I am not sorry about anything. I do not regret anything. To tell you the truth, if I had to do everything all over again, I would not change a thing. Even after knowing everything I know now. I would not change a thing." The hint of a smirk curled in the corner of his mouth. He knew that would hurt her.

"You are vile! You are an evil man. No, you're not a man, you're a monster. You have never been a man. You can never be happy, so you want everyone around you to be as miserable as you!" she yelled, raising her walker at him.

He grabbed hold of the walker and started walking towards her slowly. He steadily held the walker with his hands, menacing, pushing it against her. She slowly walked backwards as best she could. His eyes locked on hers, satisfied with himself.

"I hate you!" Chuy blurted out.

She never thought she would say those words towards anyone but she couldn't help herself. The feelings produced were more that she could bear.

Manuel violently pulled the walker from her gripping hands and threw it across the living room. Chuy had a difficult time maintaining her balance, and then she saw him coming at her. He combatively put his hands on her chest and pushed her with as much force as he could. She fell back and landed on the couch sideways. Her knee was throbbing, her head was spinning. She thought he had sat on her chest making it hard to breathe. She felt pins and needles when she tried to take a deep breath. The feeling became a piercing sensation with pain rushing through her entire body. Everything turned blurry and her body went limp.

When Chuy woke up, she was in the hospital with tubes and cords attached to her.

Chuy had predicted Manuel would have admitted to his crimes even if he showed no remorse. He had not been a good man, but he had never laid a finger on her before. She knew that after the embolism he had seven years prior, he didn't have much strength. He had been permanently disabled after half of his body had been paralyzed, taking him several years to recover.

Even after recovery, he was never quite the same. He had been sleeping on the couch for a few years by that time. He would wake up before sunrise and go for a walk. His doctor had recommended walking to improve his motor skills and lengthen his life expectancy by being active.

Every week he would go farther and farther until eventually he was able to walk up to five miles per day. Even with this amount of physical activity, he was slow, his back was hunched and his shoulders slouched. He hardly ever smiled. The rest of the time at home, he would sit in a chair in the backyard swatting and killing flies under the pear tree. That was his favorite pastime.

He either couldn't hear or he would pretend to not hear people when they spoke to him. He had seemed defenseless, weak, and at times, not all there.

In the hospital room, Chuy's children surrounded her bed awaiting the doctor's diagnosis. She had suffered three micro heart attacks just minutes from each other. She was stable after the sedatives and anti-anxiety medication she was given. She would've been able to go home in a couple of days if it wasn't for the acute pneumonia that was also found during her chest x-rays.

During her stay in the hospital, Chuy received many visitors. People she had known her entire life, and even people she'd just met, came to see her. With all the free time she had during her stay, she talked to her visitors for hours until the nurses would kick them out. Some would overstay the visiting hours and got scolded.

Chuy talked to everyone about anything people wanted to know. She talked about her life for hours, telling her story to whoever wanted to hear it. She was a great story-teller and conversationalist, and easily held everyone's attention. Her children visited her daily and learned things they'd never known about her. She had started finalizing her legacy without knowing.

Chuy shared different anecdotes to different people. "Sometimes telling the story is the thing that saves your life," she would tell them.

The people that knew her well and spent time with her, remembered some of the things she'd lived through. She was fierce in the indiscriminate way she loved. And she loved hard. It was a special kind of sight to see her interact with people; it was like magic. She was a beacon of light, and more than loved by all, she was revered. Chuy was all wisdom. She was humble, strong, and kind and she passed those traits to her children and grandchildren.

Her stay in the hospital was extended to four weeks to treat and monitor her pneumonia. During that time of rest, her knee started feeling better. She was amazed at how much her knee had healed and during the last few days of her stay, she was able to go to the bathroom without her walker.

Early on the morning of June 5th, 1999, her doctor went into the room to let her know she would be going home the following day. He simply needed to get all the paperwork ready for her discharge and to send the bill to her health insurance company. She was happy that her knee seemed to have finally healed and there was no pain. She assumed that one month in bed without work had something to do with it.

"Oh, how the body and soul heal when you actually can do nothing but rest" she thought to herself.

The following day she spoke on the phone with some of her children, and she wished the woman she shared the room with a happy birthday. She went to wash her hands and wait for her breakfast. She was having a conversation with her roommate when she stopped talking mid-sentence. There was a loud noise in the bathroom. Chuy's roommate pressed the panic button after she received no response from Chuy.

Chuy lay unconscious on the bathroom floor when the nurses arrived. She had been prescribed blood thinners to manage a heart condition, but they came too late. A blood clot had silently formed in her leg, gone undetected during the intensive tests performed just the day before, and traveled to her lungs. The hospital staff did everything they could to save her. They performed CPR, performed a tracheotomy to insert a breathing tube through her throat, and shocked her heart with a defibrillator. Chuy had survived a life marked by pain and disappointment—the death of her husband, the loss of a baby daughter, years of cruelty from the man she married, three micro heart attacks, and a bout of acute pneumonia. But that morning, at just 56 years old, Chuy's strength finally gave out. A blood clot took what so many hardships could not.

By that afternoon, the house was bursting at the seams with people stopping to pay their respects. Mountains of Tupperware brimming with food, boxes full of fried chicken, casseroles with rice and beans, enchiladas, and different types of dessert appeared out of nowhere.

Handfuls of women took turns in the kitchen rotating in shifts. Chuy's body had not yet been released to the morgue and her house already looked like a funeral home. People wailed loudly. Pain could be heard in their voice, and disbelief was mirrored in the look of their eyes. Some people rocked themselves trying to soothe themselves, others hugged and cried, and the stronger ones rubbed the backs of the inconsolable. People fainted and some even threw up.

Her two younger boys looked comatose, not a word, not a tear, not a single cry. Everyone mourned the loss of the most excellent human being they had ever known, in any way they knew how to.

Once her body was released for viewing, the funeral home was full day and night for the three days of mourning. The church that held the Mass with her body wasn't large enough to hold everyone, so some people stood where they could while others listened to the service from outside.

Some people went to the cemetery early. Her life had touched and empowered so many. She helped when she could and gave what she had without expecting anything in return. *Haz el bien y no mires a quien*, that was her. She was loving, supportive, and loyal. That is how Chuy is remembered, strength, love, and compassion is her legacy.

****

Chuy's death forced many buried issues to the surface. Manuel became combative towards everyone. He felt he didn't have to live in the shadow of the great matriarch any longer. Now that Chuy was gone, people would start respecting him and loving him. He had been jealous of the unending love Chuy always received.

When he realized that he was not going to gain respect, he insulted the memory of his wife and of his children only hours after she had died. None of his children wanted to talk to him, they didn't want to see him, and they didn't want to be around him.

Manuel spent the last fifteen years of his life bouncing back from house to house, from child to child. He became even more cynical and bitter. He insulted people at will. He spewed hate and vitriol while demanding love and respect. His children would inevitably ship him out to live with someone else because they could no longer take his behavior.

He pushed everyone away and alienated himself. Even at the end of his life, he had not known how to love himself or others.

Rosa María and her husband Agustín were the last people Manuel lived with. They had turned their laundry room in the house she shared with Alicia into a bedroom for him to stay. He was already an 84-year-old frail, resentful man.

One morning, after not hearing him in the kitchen early in the morning as they always did, Rosa María went to check on him. She knocked on the door of his room and had no response. She knew he hadn't left because his shoes were outside his door. She knocked one more time and after not receiving a response, she opened the door. She found her father lying face down on the floor, his head in a small pool of blood.

Papá Manny, as everyone called him, had tripped and fallen after getting out of bed. During the fall, he hit his head on the sharp corner of Chuy's industrial sewing machine that was being stored in the room he was sleeping in. He lay unconscious for several hours until he was found. He had fractured his skull. He was taken to the hospital in an ambulance, alive but in a coma, and his internal organs were not responding.

On the evening of April 24th, 2005, Papá Manny, surrounded by all his children and grandchildren, was removed from life support. Within a few minutes, his body shut down forever.

****

That same year, nine days before his 77th birthday, Nicolas died in his sleep. He wasn't ill and he wasn't in pain. He simply went to bed and never woke up. His heart just stopped beating. His son Pedro found him in the morning and thought he was still asleep. His funeral was small and the church was almost empty. During his burial, only Elena, three of his four children and their spouses, and most of his grandkids were there. The entire process was short and fast.

Elena lived until April of 2024. She lived the rest of her years in peace and surrounded by her children, grandchildren, great grandchildren, and she even lived to see her first great great grandchild

Afterword

Life, like the intertwining paths of a family, is rarely simple, and rarely without hardship. The stories of Chuy, Manuel, Nicolas, and Elena are filled with moments of love, pain, loss, and resilience—each life a testament to the complex dance of human emotions and connections. As we reflect on the legacy they left behind, we see not just their triumphs and failures but the ways in which their actions rippled through generations.

Chuy's fierce love and wisdom, despite her painful past, taught those around her the true meaning of selfless devotion. Even in her final moments, she remained a symbol of strength and kindness. Manuel, in his bitterness, showed us the consequences of a life lived without self-reflection, without redemption. His final years served as a tragic reminder of how a life built on resentment and refusal to change can lead to isolation and pain, not only for oneself but for others.

Nicolas and Elena's quiet endings also reveal a lot about the quieter ways in which people live their lives, how sometimes the greatest legacies are those that are understated and go unnoticed by the world. Their deaths, though almost unnoticed by society, were deeply felt by those who loved them, showing that it is not the grandeur of one's life or death that matters, but the depth of the connections forged along the way.

In the end, each person—no matter how flawed or perfect, how strong or weak—leaves behind a legacy. What we leave is often not in the loud moments of our lives, but in the quiet, enduring love, lessons, and sometimes scars that we leave with those who continue after us. Families move forward, carrying both the light and the darkness from the past, learning from it, but never forgetting it. It is the heartache and the joy, the quiet sacrifices and the loud, passionate moments that shape them, that shape us all. And in the stories we share, we find not just our past but our future, intertwined with all those who came before us.

Author's Note

I grew up listening to *dichos* from my grandmother and my mother. Although I did not fully understand their meaning at times, I adopted them enthusiastically. I will admit that, despite my best efforts, I often used them in the wrong context. As an adult, I now understand the meaning of these *dichos* that I used to hear on a daily basis. I can attest that "*sabe más el diablo por viejo que por diablo*" is quite accurate.

Understanding not only the way people speak to each other in my culture, but the context in which it is spoken, has given me insight into the lives of my grandparents.

The story of our ancestors is rarely told, and we hardly ask questions. Family history as a whole, as well as individual anecdotes, is more than forgotten after a couple of generations. Some of these stories are important and may carry lessons worth recording and preserving. By learning our family's history, we can learn about ourselves. Family secrets, on the other hand, can change how we perceive ourselves and our affinity to others by discovering how interconnected we are to one another while discovering our roots.

When I started thinking more in depth about my family and its history, I decided to build a family tree through an online ancestry agency. Through my research, I learned many things about my grandparents and parents that I did not know. This has given me the opportunity to meet family members I didn't know existed and learn from them pieces of family history that I didn't have access to before.

I now am aware of certain details in the lives of my grandmothers that have forever changed me. I have learned about their sacrifices, lessons they learned, and decisions they made. I was very inspired by their strength to continue their lives as they pushed against injustices. It's amazing to see how their effort to make the world a better place for their own children, if not for themselves, actually came to fruition.

Even though I knew about the blatant abuse in my grandmothers' lives as I was writing their story, I didn't understand the full scope of their suffering. The more I wrote, the more I realized that they were also victims of abuse that is not so obvious. Different clues started to make their way to the surface. Men who had the potential to be great husbands and parents ended up ruining their lives and the lives of those they cared about because of their fragile and toxic masculinity.

Misogyny and sexism has been prevalent in Latin American cultures for generations, and my family has not been immune to it. Machismo and jealousy created controlling men who have ruined the lives of others through manipulation. Physical abuse is not the only form of violence, it can also find itself manifested in neglect and victim blaming. Both of my grandmothers were subjected to this treatment. They felt they had no way to escape their situation because they felt committed to keeping their families intact. These were the types of abuse that I found my grandmothers subjected to, and in which without a strong support system, they were unable to escape.

Writing this book has allowed me to appreciate the lives the women in my family, especially my grandmothers, have led. The more I learn about them, the more I admire and respect them and understand the decisions they made at that time when they were young and were fighting alone against the world. This new light helped me understand my mother's life and her silent courage that, from a different perspective, could've been seen as weakness.

Lastly, it has helped me understand things about myself and that I could not understand before. I now understand the way that I have lived my life in the past, the way I live now, and the way that I want my future self to live. I am proud of having such strong women in my family and their matriarchal blood running through my veins. Because even the most seemingly docile woman's survival is an actual act of resistance against her oppressor. Our grandmothers and mothers persisted, they survived, and that gave time the opportunity for us to exist.

About the Author

Maribel is a Chicana Mexican writer, visual artist, activist, and community organizer. Her work weaves together clinical psychology, intergenerational healing, and social justice, creating safe and transformative spaces for women, queer people, and racialized communities. She is currently pursuing a master's degree in clinical psychology, focusing her research and practice on trauma, patriarchy, and ancestral forms of resilience.

She is the author of The Woman Before Becoming a Mother, a journal that guides mothers and daughters through a process of deep reflection, cultural connection, and mutual healing. Her other work includes stories that honor women's resistance in the face of systemic machismo.

Maribel is also the founder of Wander Women Outdoors, a project that empowers women and girls to reconnect with the land and their ancestral wisdom through outdoor activities, approached from an anticolonial perspective.

From literature to community organizing, Maribel works toward a world where healing is a collective right, and where love and memory are tools of resistance.

www.ingramcontent.com/pod-product-compliance
Lightning Source LLC
Chambersburg PA
CBHW031027030726
47497CB00004B/1035